The Winter Tiger
&
The War Eagle

Also by Bret Kissinger

Forever Fleeting

Gone the Way of the Dodo Bird

The Final Edit

The Winter Tiger
&
The War Eagle

Bret Kissinger

ISBN-13: 978-1-7361071-5-7

Book Cover Design by Damonza

Edited by Mark Swift.

Dedicated to strong women and honorable men. And to my family.

Not a Bad Way to Go

It wasn't a bad way to go. The lean roe deer grazed on the lush grass, the sun shining on its back, unaware its life neared its end. Isn't that how we all want to go? Here one moment, gone the next. Completely unaware with blissful ignorance? It wasn't how her mother had gone. Her death had been cruel and slow. Even though Kira had only been nine, she had known it was so painful she had prayed to God to end her mother's suffering. For too long, God ignored those prayers. When she did finally pass, the silence that replaced the screaming was equally agonizing.

Kira wiped her mother's fate from her mind. She needed a clear head. She steadied her grip on her father's rifle. The Mosin–Nagant rifle was nicknamed the three-line because of the caliber being equivalent to three lines in the Imperial Russian system of measurement. It'd been in her family since her father's service in the Great War. Her breathing was melodic, meditative. Deep breath in, slow exhale out. Inhaling the earthy smell of grass. She'd been hunting since before her mother had died. The rifle was an extension of herself. The rules of the rifle had been engrained within her. She couldn't remember when she learned how to count, nor could she remember when she'd learned those cardinal rules: never point the gun at something you don't intend to destroy; always treat the gun as if it is loaded; and always keep your trigger finger straight and off the trigger until you're ready to shoot. Kira's father had also instilled a fourth, yet equally important rule: kill quickly.

"It's your responsibility to grant a quick, merciful death."

Kira never forgot the reverence with which he had spoken those words. She had thought they were about the animals they hunted. It wasn't until she woke to incoherent rambling that she remembered those words held both a deeper and darker meaning. She had crept out of her bedroom, peering around the hallway. Her father, squeezed into his Great War uniform, was standing in front of the fire, toasting his vodka to the flames. Drunken tears were dripping from his dark-circled eyes, rolling down his red cheeks and absorbed by his coarse beard. He slurred names, then only descriptions and ranks. Her mother massaged Kira's shoulders, then whispered for her to go back to bed. Kira retreated halfway to her bedroom and spied as her mother consoled her father. She pressed his head against her chest, his tears saturating the silk of her nightgown. She had never failed to pull him from his darkest depths. And since she'd been gone, there was no one to shed light on his darkness.

The Mosin–Nagant rifle held five 7.62x54mmR rimmed cartridges. But Kira would need only one. She pressed the stock against her shoulder, securing it in place. One final breath, then she squeezed the trigger. The shot rang out in the early morning air. The roe deer was here one second and gone the next. If it hadn't been for the blood, it could have passed for being asleep in a bed of dandelions. Kira crouched beside it and placed a hand on its side. She said a prayer of gratitude for its sacrifice.

"A damn fine shot!" her childhood friend, Gerasim, shouted, beaming a horse-like smile.

He was twenty-six, a year older than Kira, and as far as traditional looks went, he didn't have any—his nose was long and hooked, and after his brother had inadvertently broken it while wrestling, it looked like a misaligned S. His greasy, reddish-brown hair was disheveled, looking like he made a habit of touching live wires. But none of that prevented him from smiling. Kira loved that about him. He was eternally positive.

Together, they cleaned the animal and dragged it back to Gerasim's truck.

"Did you hear the story of the two hunters?" he asked.

Kira shook her head.

"Two hunters killed a stag. They dragged the deer to their truck, but the antlers kept getting stuck in the ground. Another hunter saw them and told them that if they dragged it the other way, the antlers wouldn't get stuck in the ground. They thanked the man for the advice and dragged the deer the other way. The first hunter said, 'He was right. This is easier.' The second hunter said, 'Yes, but now we're getting further away from the truck.'"

Gerasim's mouth spread into that horse-like grin once again. Kira stared at him, trying to not let her thin lips spread into a smile. But she failed.

"You're so stupid," she said, laughing.

Once the deer was loaded onto Gerasim's truck, he drove them back into town and to Kira's house. He tapped the side of the truck to the beat of the song he was humming. The truck had quite a cough, and the interior reeked of exhaust fumes. It groaned to a halt. Kira stepped out.

"I'll stop by later," she said, heading toward the front door.

"Kira!" Gerasim called. She turned. "Marry me?"

Kira smirked. "Maybe tomorrow."

He smiled that grand smile of his and tipped his gray newsboy cap to her. Kira stepped inside and climbed the stairs. Her father sat at the kitchen table reading the newspaper. But upon seeing Kira, he folded the paper and reached for the rifle. Kira handed it to him. He unloaded the remaining four rounds and disassembled the rifle. It was a task Kira could have done. But her father insisted. His eyes showed little life, like they were from a painting, but his hands always shook while performing the task. After having taught Kira to shoot, he never fired the rifle again. Igor could clean the crucifix that performed an exorcism, but he couldn't perform the act itself. While he disassembled and reassembled that rifle, the world made sense. And while he failed in the upkeep of his own body, neglecting his hygiene and relying too heavily on booze, he took extreme care of the rifle.

Kira washed her hands and face in the bathroom, then grabbed her copy of *A Hero of Our Time*. Reading gave Kira peace. And while her sisters had glitz and glamor to share with their mother, Kira had books. Saturday mornings were spent reading in silence, just the two of them, the others still asleep. Her mother challenged Kira to read classics not just from Russia, but from around the world. Kira's mother had spoken German and had many German books in her possession. Word by word, Kira's German grew. As she read, she'd be able to pick out certain words and tell her mother what she thought was happening in each book. Speaking German was something they had that was solely theirs. Kira didn't have to share it with Anousha or Alina, and certainly not her father. She and her mother never even whispered German when Igor was around.

Kira read for an hour, then had to go to Gerasim's family's butcher shop. She told her father, but he was deep in concentration. That rifle was a magical artifact containing a part of his soul. It had been with him during the bloody battles of the Great War and the Russian Civil War. Was the link between man and Mosin voluntary or involuntary? It brought him serenity and rage. Imperfect amounts resulting in perfect harmonious balance. Did the rifle remind him of the kills he had committed with it, or the man who had once wielded it?

The Petrovs lived above their butcher shop located roughly a kilometer away. Like so many small business owners, they had to choose which—home or business—to maintain, and if they didn't choose business, there'd be no house to maintain anyway. Kira stepped inside; the bell atop the door rang. Gerasim, slouching at the counter, stood tall when she stepped in. The air wreaked of blood, as if there were a billion pennies inside. No amount of cleaning could conquer that smell.

"You've reconsidered my proposal?" Gerasim said, flashing that horse-tooth smile.

"Not quite. Is the meat ready?" Kira asked.

"My father finishes cutting as we speak."

The sound of *thwacks* carried out as blade struck through bone and meat, and into the cutting board. Kira examined the offerings in the glass-enclosed meat case. Filets and flanks from pig, deer, cow, and goat.

"He was impressed with your shot. He thought I exaggerated the distance. 400 meters."

"You did. It was closer to 390."

Gerasim frowned at her humility. "You gave it a quick death. All that matters."

The first deer she'd ever shot hadn't been quick, hadn't been painless. She'd broken her father's most important rule. She and her father had tracked the deer for hours. When they found it, darkness had descended. Only its cries of pain, of suffering, broke the silence. Igor's eyes had filled with horror. He plunged his knife into the deer's throat to end its pain. It was the only time she thought her father might strike her. He didn't talk to anyone for days. Even at that young age, Kira knew those bellowing cries had broken free the cries of dying men on muddy battlefields.

"Kira!" a raspy voice called, freeing her from the memory.

Petyr Petrov lumbered through the door frame. His white apron was stained pink and red. He was a towering man who greatly resembled a bear.

"Good evening, Comrade Petrov," Kira said.

"My boy spent the better part of twenty minutes bragging about your shot." He set a package of meat, wrapped in brown packing paper and tied with string, down on the counter. "And your *roubles*," Petyr said, opening the register.

The amount he handed to her was too much in her opinion, so she set a *rouble* back on the counter. Petyr nodded his appreciation. He should have been intimidating given his size, the prominent bloodstains covering both his apron and his knuckles, and that he always had some sort of knife or cleaver in his hand, but to Kira he resembled Father Frost.

He waved goodbye and disappeared behind the clear plastic strips. Seconds later, the whacking and chomping resumed.

"Oh, Kira, you are beautiful and kind," Gerasim said.

"No, maybe just beautifully kind," Kira said.

She'd never given her looks a lot of thought. Nousha and Lina were far better-looking. They were experts with a makeup brush, knowing that makeup didn't make someone attractive but amplified a woman's natural beauty. While Nousha and Lina changed their hairstyles, Kira kept hers in two braids. She had ever since she was a small girl. Kira had her mother's raven-black hair and emerald-green eyes. Her father said Kira looked so much like her, but the few grainy black and white photographs of her mother proved otherwise in her opinion.

"I will walk you home," Gerasim said.

Kira refused, but Gerasim looked at her sternly. "Please, I am beautifully kind, too."

He hopped over the counter and lunged for the door before Kira could open it for herself.

Gerasim could relate to how she felt. His brother, Semyon, was strapping and tall. He had a glorious smile. The list of women who found him handsome was as long as an ancient scroll. He'd gotten the best features his parents had to offer—his father's height and powerful hands, and his mother's vibrant blue eyes—while Gerasim had inherited the scraps.

They filled the walk with small talk but were comfortable enough with each other to allow silence to fill spaces. Once at her home, he removed his cap, opened the door, and said goodnight.

"Marry me," he said.

Kira smirked and shook her head. "I said tomorrow."

"It is tomorrow … somewhere in this big world."

He'd never genuinely attempted to kiss her. He'd been proposing to Kira since they were thirteen. But she wouldn't lie that having somebody nearly worship you felt amazing. Not in a conceited way, but as a pillar of strength, a safety net that would always catch her. He was her best friend. He always had been.

She wished him goodnight and disappeared inside.

"Don't wake Papa," Nousha said, once Kira ascended the stairs.

He was asleep in his rocking chair beside the unlit fireplace. Nousha was in the kitchen chopping vegetables while Kira's younger sister, Lina, watched her with a bored expression. They both had blonde hair and dark brown eyes. Their beauty wasn't subtle, it was blunt. Strangers could easily identify them as sisters. Kira couldn't even pass for a distant cousin.

Kira opened the package and set the meat in a frying pan on the stove.

"Did Gerasim walk you home?" Lina asked.

"He did," Kira replied, keeping her gaze on the frying pan.

"That poor, tortured soul," Nousha said.

"He is not tortured."

"Sure …" Nousha said, delivered in a way she knew would enrage Kira.

Kira was the middle child. She had no trouble admitting that Anousha and Alina were far closer to each other than they were with her. There was very little common ground for them to stand on. Kira's hobbies were considered foreign, disgusting even. And for Kira, she couldn't think of anything she'd rather do less than futz around with makeup and styling her hair. Their lives revolved around men. *What made men worthy of such obsession?*

Lina went to the bathroom to wash up while Kira stirred the sizzling meat.

Nousha put a hand on Kira's shoulder. "He would take good care of you."

It was a well-meaning sentiment. But Kira hated that phrasing. She didn't want someone to take care of her. She didn't need someone to take care of her. Marrying for a protector or provider instead of a partner was something she'd never get behind. Nousha was widowed. Her husband Radomir Tryvosky had been killed in the Winter War—the Russo-Finnish War of 1939. It had devastated Nousha. There'd been no body to grieve for closure, only a letter. Lina had provided comfort to Nousha that Kira didn't know how to. Nousha wanted to be a mother. It was part of the reason she acted like one to Kira and why they weren't close. Kira was grown; she didn't need a surrogate mother.

Lina was in love with the idea of love, and having been only five when their mother passed, she welcomed Nousha's motherly care. Their mother's passing had come at unique points in their lives. Nousha had been thirteen. She was most able to comprehend the devastating loss, but she had the most memories to draw back on.

6

Lina had only a few profound memories, but she was too young to fully grasp the loss she had sustained. Kira fell in the middle. Fewer memories than Nousha but feeling the full suffocating loss that Lina hadn't. Nousha and Lina knew what they wanted out of life. Kira had no idea. Whatever it was, she doubted she'd find it in her small, quaint hometown. But she was too afraid to leave the familiar place behind.

Summer at Jade Bight

To say life had been difficult after the Great War would be a gross understatement. The Great War had crippled the economy, doomed an entire generation of young men to their grave, and wounded German pride. Germany had been victimized and vilified, held responsible both morally and financially. But, over the last few years, life had improved. Reinhardt hadn't voted in the 1933 election. To him, politicians were rich men posing as a voice of the people, promising substantial change who once elected only further padded the pockets of the rich. But Germany had regained its decadence under Adolf Hitler and the Nazi Party's adamant and frenzied resolve. Not only were they making improvements, they were rectifying the long list of grievances thrusted upon them by the Treaty of Versailles. They had restored the Sudetenland. Rightfully so. Reinhardt had family there. Proud Germans who had been told they were Czech. No child of Germany born shortly before or after the Great War didn't know how that war had started: the assassination of Archduke Franz Ferdinand and the entangling alliances that had dragged the whole world into war. Some radical fool had nearly ended the world.

The city of Rastede was located in Northwest Germany. And it was home. Reinhardt and his best friend, Mathias, had memories on every block. It was summer; Reinhardt's favorite season. He and Mathias spent weekends west in a city shaped like a spade called Jade Bight. Sometimes they'd go with other friends; sometimes it was just the two of them. Reinhardt was tall, confident, and outgoing. Everything Mathias was not. They often got mistaken for brothers, not because they looked alike— Reinhardt had wavy black hair, Mathias straight blond—but because people assumed Mathias was years younger. For Mathias, it was one thing for older women and mothers to assume that, but something else entirely for women their age to think.

Reinhardt and Mathias strolled the beach, their bare feet kicking up hot sand, the sun beating down on their necks. Their eyes fixed on the women sunbathing or strolling along the shore. Reinhardt's body had all the desirable angles, broad shoulders, and a tapered waist. Mathias had a short torso and rounded shoulders.

"See anyone?" Mathias asked.

"Had you worn your glasses, you'd see the same world I do," Reinhardt said.

Mathias nodded like a child being reprimanded by a parent. Reinhardt put his hand on Mathias's wrist to stop him.

"What is it?" Mathias asked.

"Not what. Who."

Mathias sighed. "*Who* is it?"

"Ingrid."

Mathias squinted to see better. "Ilse, too?"

"Ilse, too."

"Shit, I should have brought my glasses."

"There's only one of each," Reinhardt jested.

Ingrid and Ilse wore blue-striped one-piece bikinis. Both had their hair tied back. Ilse had hair the color of leather and dark, almost black eyes, whereas Ingrid had hair the color of sand and pale blue eyes.

Reinhardt and Mathias waded after them like fish to bait.

"Reinhardt Friedel. Have you come to fish?" Ingrid asked.

Reinhardt smiled, his blue eyes gleaming. "Something like that."

"You can't catch the same fish twice."

Reinhardt shortened the distance between them, fearlessly taking her soft hands in his and swaying them playfully.

"Catch and release," he said.

Ingrid scoffed, pushing his hands away. "Is that what you call it?"

Mathias could only guess what sort of emotion was on Ilse's face. He squinted and smiled.

"Why do you keep hanging around him, Mathias?" Ingrid asked.

"Well, he drives me. I can't see over the steering wheel."

The girls laughed. The water was lukewarm, but the sun shone fiercely. Reinhardt's vivid blue eyes took in Ingrid's curves. Her pale blue eyes focused on his lean stomach and sinewy arms. Reinhardt had her. He knew it. She knew it. He smiled at her; she returned a brief one of her own.

Jade Bight was a tourist destination, and Ingrid and Ilse spent their summers there. Ingrid was from Schönfeld, too far for Reinhardt to consider visiting. They'd met last summer. Reinhardt had promised to write.

He had not.

They swam, playfully splashing each other. Mathias and Reinhardt lifted Ilse and Ingrid on their shoulders, then fell backward with them into the water. When the scorching afternoon surrendered to the cool winds blowing in from the North Sea, they toweled themselves dry. Ingrid and Ilse strutted away without a word.

"Where are you going?" Reinhardt called after Ingrid.

"To eat," she called back.

"Us, too. Where?"

"*Der Wasserand.*"

"Us, too!"

Ingrid shook her head and wouldn't give him the satisfaction of turning to look back at him, but Reinhardt took satisfaction in watching her leave.

Mathias and Reinhardt changed into their clothes and used the side windows of Mathias's car, a 1932 Opel, to fix their hair. Mathias slipped on his glasses, and then the two hurried to the restaurant. Reinhardt told the hostess that they were with the two gorgeous women in the booth nearest the bathroom, pointing at Ingrid and Ilse, to which Ingrid ignored.

"I'm sorry, *Herr*, but the ladies were quite adamant that they were alone. No other guests," the hostess said.

Reinhardt flashed a smile and stroked her shoulder. It was like a non-lethal venom that even the grandmotherly hostess found herself inflicted with.

"Oh, nonsense. We'll seat ourselves," Reinhardt said.

Ingrid shook her head. Her eyes flashed disapproval, but her lips curved into a smirk. She didn't make room for him.

"No need to scooch in. I enjoy a good squeeze," Reinhardt said, which made Ingrid slide over.

Reinhardt couldn't get the smirk to leave his lips. Dinner was delicious, the drinks more so. After dinner, Ingrid and Ilse went on their way; Reinhardt and Mathias followed like shadows.

"Has anyone ever told you you're like an annoying insect?" Ingrid asked over her shoulder.

"My mother. My sisters. A few of my teachers … most of my teachers, actually. But I always thought of myself as a dog," Reinhardt shot back.

"Because of the smell?"

Reinhardt laughed and jogged to catch up to her. The four returned to the beach for a bonfire. Most of the twenty-somethings staying in Jade Bight were there. The soothing smell of the smoke offset the unpleasant stench of seaweed and the reek of rotting fish. Laughter echoed and combined with the waves lapping onto the beach and the crackle of fire.

"So, Reinhardt," Ingrid said.

"Well, I don't like the sound of that," he replied.

"Why?"

"Because you're going to complete that sentence with some sort of passive-aggressive insult."

"Am not." A pause, then she laughed. "Oh, whatever. It seems improbable that I can offend the great Reinhardt Friedel." She paused and met his gaze. "What will you do? Germany needs men, not boys."

"Well, I was wrong. No passive aggression, only unchecked bluntness."

Ingrid arched her eyebrows in a good-natured jest but looked for an answer. "Will you answer Germany's call?"

"Oh, dear Ingrid, I didn't know you were a patriot," Reinhardt said.

"And you're not?" Her eyes locked onto his. She wasn't going to let him get off the hook with a cheap, deflective joke.

"I love Germany. But I don't want to go to war. I don't want Germany to go to war."

"It's necessary."

"War is never necessary, dear Ingrid."

"Our hand is forced."

Reinhardt nodded exaggeratingly. "Perhaps Chamberlain and Hitler can duke it out themselves then."

Ingrid put her hand on his chest. "Don't speak that way."

"I'd rather two men fight than the whole word."

"We have to take back what is ours, Reinhardt."

"We have. The British and French have allowed Hitler his desired victories. Let it be."

Ingrid hesitated. They could debate about diplomacy all night, but they weren't strolling the shore to debate diplomacy.

"Well, if you ever change your mind, Germany can always use idealistic fools," Ingrid said.

"Are you calling me an idealistic fool?"

"Not idealistic, but a fool, yes."

"I'll consider that a compliment." He turned to face her, gently clutching her fingertips with his.

Ingrid broke his touch and stepped back. "Consider it however you'd like."

Reinhardt stepped toward her, reaching for her hands again. "Your consideration is considerate."

She rolled her eyes. "By definition, you fool."

Reinhardt traced the lines of her palm with his finger.

"For fools rush in where angels fear to tread," Reinhardt recited.

"Oh, how that defines you. Rushing in, thinking I'd make the same mistake as last summer," Ingrid said.

"You say mistake, I say memory. A rather blissful memory." He entwined his fingers in hers.

"A rather brief memory."

"The greatest things in life are fleeting."

Ingrid shook her head, an annoyed yet impressed smirk curling on her lips. "Only Reinhardt Friedel could come back with such a line."

Reinhardt locked his piercing blue eyes on her pale blue ones. He smiled. It was all over for Ingrid. They'd strolled further away from prying eyes for privacy to surrender to their desires. She balled the front of his shirt with a fist, arched her toes, and planted her soft lips on his.

The fire crackled, shooting flaming embers at those closest to it. Even the flames seemed to know Mathias was the weakest and sent both its embers and smoke his way. Mathias sat beside Ilse, an uncomfortable silence between them that not even fire could penetrate.

Mathias glanced at Ilse, trying to think of something natural to say. "Are you warm enough?"

She nodded. "I'm fine."

He squeezed his eyes for his stupid question. Was she warm enough? They were next to a gigantic fire. Half the hair on his legs had singed off. Mathias had waited for this moment since last summer. He'd spent all year constructing scenarios of being alone with Ilse. Rehearsed a hundred conversations. But now that the moment had arrived, the words escaped him. He stared at the fire, transfixed, as if the flames held the answers. But Mathias wasn't like Reinhardt. He didn't have that caliber of confidence, didn't have a silver tongue. Reinhardt could go from reviled to reveled. Women were indifferent toward Mathias, and he stayed indifferent. He could think of no way to change that now. No way to break free from that invisible prison women kept him in.

Reinhardt and Ingrid stood barefoot on the shore, letting the waves wash over their feet.

"And Mathias … does he share your sentiment about the war?" Ingrid asked.

Reinhardt skipped a stone, then patted the sand from his hands. "He is going to enlist."

Ingrid looked nervously at him. She wouldn't say it aloud, but Reinhardt knew what she must be thinking. Mathias was not the ideal soldier. He was short, skinny, and borderline blind. But Reinhardt knew Mathias possessed attributes you couldn't put on a chart.

It was Ingrid's last night at Jade Bight. She'd avoided Reinhardt's web all summer until now. Tomorrow, she'd return to Schönfeld and her normal world.

"Well, Reinhardt Friedel, you stay safe hiding from the world," Ingrid said.

"Promise to write to me?"

He caught her playful punch before it connected with his chest.

"Jerk," she said.

Reinhardt caught her follow-up blow and pulled her close.

The fire granted Mathias the cruelty to see his best friend effortlessly go from being borderline hated to Ingrid cozied against him. If he didn't do something, he'd stay in this unbearable zone of indifference. Fortune favors the bold.

"Ilse." His voice cracked. He cleared his throat, hoping to go from sounding like a twelve-year-old boy to a twenty-four-year-old man. "I enjoy spending time with you. I think you're pretty beautiful. I mean pretty and beautiful—separate adjectives … And I, umm, I've wanted to give … rather, I wanted to … in a gentlemanly way … deliver a kiss you … to you … kiss you …"

Oh, God. What a natural disaster. He should just walk out into the water and let the waves take him.

Ilse's face contorted with many emotions, none of them good. He'd traumatized the poor girl. She bit her lip, calculating on not what to say—the answer was no; her face confirmed that—but how to say it. She was bailed out when Reinhardt and Ingrid returned.

"We should head back," Ilse said.

Reinhardt and Mathias escorted the girls back to Ingrid's car.

Reinhardt leaned into the open window. "Take care, Ingrid."

"You, too. I'd tell you to write, but we both know you won't."

Reinhardt sobered. "You're not hurt, are you?"

"You have *Wanderlust*, Reinhardt. You come and go like the wind. I pity the woman who thinks she can catch you."

14

Reinhardt and Mathias watched them drive away, taking summer itself with them.

"Well, don't take a vow of silence," Reinhardt said, driving his shoulder into Mathias.

"Well, there was engine failure, a burst of flame, and then a mighty crash. No survivors."

Reinhardt searched for words. "Don't get discouraged."

"Oh, I won't *get* discouraged. That implies a future emotion. I've *been* discouraged."

"Well, be encouraged."

They headed to Mathias's Opel, one with a victorious gait, the other with a defeated lumber. Mathias was silent for most of the drive.

"You ignore Ingrid all year and she falls back into your arms. I'll go to war a born-again virgin."

"We could go to that brothel again."

Mathias laughed; his mood instantly lifted. "Stealing our wallets, I can understand. But our pants?"

They laughed at the memory the entire way home, one recollection leading to another. A young lifetime's worth of memories. But as the world crept toward war, for many, there would be no more memories to make.

Questioning Quality

On 23 August 1939, mere days before the Second World War broke out, Germany and the Soviet Union signed a non-aggression pact, called the Molotov–Ribbentrop Pact. Each side vowed to take no military action against each other for the next ten years. On 1 September, Germany invaded Poland from the west, and the Soviet Union invaded from the east. It had not taken long for the war to not be just some newspaper headline in a far-off place. And in June 1941, Germany betrayed the Soviet Union, launching Operation Barbarossa—the invasion of the Soviet Union.

Anousha and Alina volunteered as nurses, while Kira and her father worked at a munitions factory. The war demanded munitions and weaponry on a scale never before seen. Factories dotted across the Soviet Union produced rifles, ammunition, artillery, bombs, tanks, and planes. Kira assembled rifles, more precisely, the Mosin–Nagant. Kira knew, her father more so, how imperative it was to trust the weapon in your hands. For Kira, a poorly constructed rifle meant a missed shot during a hunt or, worse, a cruel death. But for men fighting, like Igor had, an errant shot or a jammed rifle costed you your life. The thirty-four-piece assembly required precision. She'd assembled thousands of three-line rifles with the same awareness she did her father's rifle. Before Kira placed a completed rifle in a large wooden crate, she worked the bolt, verifying it moved smoothly.

Her father made the 7.62x54mmR rimmed full metal jacket ammunition the rifle used. He was precise, methodical. As with any work, quality and quantity were demanded. But so often, to reach goals set by superiors, quality was sacrificed for quantity. Seldom could quality and quantity coexist. To the men deciding the war while surveying it on maps laid out on mahogany tables, 950 bullets out of 1,000 to spec was an acceptable percentage. But Igor would not forsake his countrymen with a faulty bullet.

The days were long and uneventful. There were three types of people working in the factory. The first were those driven mad by the molasses speed at which time moved, painfully aware of every tormenting moment. The second, those who could disappear into their imagination, mindlessly completing tasks on autopilot. And the third were the rare people like Igor who were aware of every minute that passed, but fully engaged in their tasks. Kira delved into all three. At times, minutes felt like hours. Other times, she was fully aware of how imperative her task was. Her eyes were glued to the rifles. But the task became so mundane, so known, she could assemble one with her eyes closed. And at times, a lot of times, she thought of the greater world she'd never seen. Wishing she could be on a hike, reading at the bluff, or stargazing.

On a summer-like Thursday in early September, the monotony of the factory broke. A captain of the Red Army stopped by to inspect the quality of the weapons and ammunitions produced at the factory. He introduced himself as Vali Zarkovsky, delivered in a way as if everyone should have already known that. His hair was dark blond and kept short. He had an air of arrogance as thick as a musky cologne. He strutted about the factory, scowling. Kira finished assembling a rifle, but before she could place it in the crate, Captain Zarkovsky pried it from her hands. His eyes went from Kira to the rifle. It was hard to know which he was more skeptical of.

"Do you know what you are doing?" he asked, turning over the rifle in his hands.

Kira glared, unwilling to hide her dislike. Her supervisor, Nikita, a balding man with pince-nez glasses, knowing Kira was as volatile as a Molotov cocktail, intervened.

"Comrade Captain, she does a very fine job. Her knowledge of the weapon is mastery."

Captain Zarkovsky took in Nikita's troll-like figure. "What would a woman know about the weapons of war?"

Kira recognized men who had served in combat. Some bore physical scars or deformity caused by battle. And there were men like her father who had that distant look in their eye. A matte gleam where most had gloss. Zarkovsky hadn't seen battle. To him, the uniform was a power trip. A way to be heard when he otherwise wouldn't have been.

"I know this weapon better than you do," Kira said.

A hush fell inside the factory. Zarkovsky studied her, then deciding she wasn't worthy of getting upset over, smirked. "We shall see."

He handed the rifle to a lower-ranking soldier and ordered him to load it. Behind the factory was a long field of dead grass and dry dirt. Straw target dummies were spaced at various distances—ten, fifty, one hundred, and the last, at four hundred meters. The captain puffed his cigarette then exchanged it for the rifle. The private covered the cigarette with a cupped hand to ensure it wouldn't go out.

Beside a black GAZ-M1 automobile, a higher-ranking officer studied files laid out on the hood of the car. He was uninterested in the shooting exhibition. Captain Zarkovsky readied the rifle, securing the stock to his shoulder and massaging it into his chest. He aimed at the straw-filled dummy ten meters away and fired. The bullet ripped through straw and burlap. It had neither been a headshot, nor a kill shot to the heart or lungs. Instead, it had struck a superficial wound to the stomach, one that would have missed all vital organs. Had the dummy been able to return fire, Captain Zarkovsky would have a wound of his own. And probably one better placed. But Zarkovsky didn't know that. Judging by his grin, he thought he had delivered a kill shot. Of course, that was because of his skill, not that he used a competently crafted rifle.

Zarkovsky aimed at the second dummy fifty meters away. The shot struck a piece of protruding straw where an arm would have been. He thrusted the rifle out for the private to take and then reclaimed his cigarette, pacifying himself with it like a baby would a nook.

"I have seen enough. The craftsmanship of this rifle is appalling. I trust that any rifle this *woman*," he nodded at Kira, "assembled to be of the same horrendous quality. Destroy them all and fire her."

Nikita slouched. The others in the factory looked dejected. Some scowled at Kira. The soldiers reached into the crates to retrieve the rifles.

Kira stepped forward. "Bullshit! The rifles are fine. Your aim is shit."

Nikita bent his head, squeezing his eyes shut. Now, instead of looking defeated, the other workers looked appalled. Igor looked on without much emotion. He was not ashamed or worried about her brazen action. He'd taught her to stand up for herself. Never let someone question your honor. And she wouldn't. Least of all from a pathetic man such as this.

Kira had never had an anger gradient. There was no build-up. It was brash and brisk and brutal.

Captain Zarkovsky turned toward Kira, his eyes glaring, then laughed derisively at her. "Is that so?"

It was her chance to back down, apologize. It would be the wise decision. Instead, Kira stepped closer in defiance. "That is so."

She stood by the quality of the rifles she assembled. His errant shots were easy to predict before he even fired. His stance was too narrow, his hold on the rifle too tight. He held it like he was trying to restrain a tiger's leash.

"Perhaps you would like to demonstrate then?" Zarkovsky said, gesturing toward the field.

He snapped his fingers, a non-verbal command for the rifle. Kira had entered a point of no return. She would have to shoot the rifle whether she wanted to or not. And my God, did she want to.

The young private handed the rifle to Zarkovsky. He'd fired two of the five rounds. He shoved the weapon into Kira's chest. Any experienced shooter knew to test fire an unknown weapon. Zarkovsky should have known that, but Kira knew even if he had, he wouldn't grant her a test fire.

"Shoot the head," he ordered.

Kira raised the rifle, securing the stock against her body. She had always considered a rifle to be a living, breathing creature. A wild animal that could never be fully domesticated, but it could be harnessed. She took a few breaths to gauge how the rifle responded, much like a cowboy advancing on a wild colt.

"Sometime today," Zarkovsky taunted.

She drowned out his voice, her eyes zeroing in on the dummy's head like an eagle glimpsing a fish. The world slowed down. She squeezed the trigger. Straw exploded into the air. Smoke filled her nostrils. The straw head snapped back then drooped.

Zarkovsky laughed. "I did not mean the first dummy. The second dummy."

Kira exhaled her anger. She wouldn't let passion alter her shot. She drowned out Zarkovsky, taking aim at the second target fifty meters away.

"The heart," Zarkovsky added at the last second.

Kira's trigger finger had nearly applied enough pressure to fire. She exhaled and refocused, visualizing the shot then executing it.

A perfect shot.

Unfazed, Zarkovsky commanded, "Third target, heart."

Kira focused, studying the way the air moved and at what speed. The target was one hundred meters away. Her vision locked in. She fired the fifth and final round. It was too far away for Zarkovsky or the others to know if she had struck the target. But Kira knew she had. The private jogged to the target and gave a thumbs up. Kira dragged the bolt; the bullet casing ejected out. She held the rifle for Zarkovsky to take. He ignored her.

"Get her ammo!" he ordered.

A fresh-faced private held five rounds in his palm for Kira to take. She loaded them into the rifle.

"Four hundred meters. Head," Zarkovsky ordered.

His smirk and arrogance were gone, replaced with a scowl. And dare Kira say, worry. His pride was on the line. Kira had been shooting moving targets from this distance for years. Animals that ran faster than any man. A stationary dummy offered little challenge, especially now that she had fired three rounds with the weapon. She aimed, securing her footing, digging her boot into the dirt. She fired. The dummy jerked backward. Zarkovsky watched through binoculars.

Enraged at her success, he shouted, "Again!"

Kira fired. Zarkovsky yelled a second, third, and fourth time. The successive shots knocked the dummy's head off. Kira dragged the bolt, releasing the remaining round. She caught it and tossed it to Zarkovsky. She handed the rifle to the young private, who did his best to conceal his smirk. Applause broke out from the high-ranking Soviet by the black car. He approached them, clapping.

"I would say the rifles are just fine, Comrade Captain Zarkovsky. Wouldn't you?" he said.

The last thing Zarkovsky wanted to do was admit that out loud. But a higher rank had asked him a question, and he had to answer. Zarkovsky had aimed to embarrass Kira, and the higher-ranking officer was giving him a taste of his own medicine.

"Yes, Comrade Colonel. The rifles are fine."

He saluted, then stormed to the car and sulked in the driver's seat, waiting for the higher-ranking officer.

The highly decorated officer stopped in front of Kira. He appeared to be in his early fifties. His peaked cap hid his graying, chestnut brown hair. His cheeks were square-shaped, sharply slanting at the chin. He introduced himself as Colonel Kirill Volkov.

"Impressive shooting," he said, a cigarette dangling from his lips.

There was no sarcasm (how could there be?) or contempt in his voice. His praise was genuine. And most importantly, there were no questions about how a woman had come to possess such skill. He viewed her as an excellent marksman regardless of gender.

"You have a gift, a true mastery of the rifle. Have you given any thought to joining the fight?" he asked.

Kira hadn't. War had always been decided by rich men and waged by poor boys. As a woman, she hadn't even truly considered the possibility.

"It is hard to understand what is at stake when the war has not come to your doorstep," Colonel Volkov said. "I pray we can keep it far from you, but should you decide to fight, I would be honored to have you."

He handed a card with his information on it to her. He bowed his head respectfully, then returned to the black GAZ-M1 automobile. Though Kira's demonstration had been a success, most viewed it as a temporary victory. Captain Zarkovsky would now keep an annoyingly close eye on the factory to exact his revenge. *Let him.* Kira had proved him a liar once. She'd gladly do so again.

By the time she and her father returned home, the story had spread through the small town, iteration by iteration morphing fact into fiction. It even arrived in their living room before Igor and Kira did.

Lina met Kira at the top of the steps. "You challenged a general?"

Kira laughed at her younger sister and then went into the bathroom without uttering a word. Of course, her hobby-less sisters had heard the rumor already.

"Papa?" Alina looked to her father for clarification.

He offered a concise, far-from-colorful recap. "What have I told you about honor?"

Nousha, who had been at the stove, unenthusiastically answered. "It's our only currency, and we can never allow someone to steal it."

"So, will either of you be telling us what happened?" Lina asked.

Kira filled a glass with water and took a swig. "Why? You seem to have gotten all the answers. When did Stalin make me a Hero of the Soviet Union, though?" she mockingly added, tapping her finger on her chin.

"Fine. Don't tell us. Maybe the rumors were false. Maybe you really missed every shot," Lina said.

Kira wouldn't give in. Her sisters could poke her with jests all they wanted.

"Did you miss, Kira?" Nousha asked, elbowing Kira.

"If I missed, we'd be eating flowers you two plucked, not venison stew," Kira said.

Igor held his hands out at the table, instantly ending the conversation. They locked hands. Igor never prayed aloud, but this holding-of-hands was mandatory before any meal. Spiritual was the best word Kira could use to describe her family's faith. Kira and her father prayed after a hunt. Her mother had always taken the time to appreciate a beautiful horizon, a star-filled sky, and fresh rain. They didn't put a label as to who they were thanking. After the moment of reflection, they ate their venison stew.

"Papa, Lina and I have news," Nousha said.

Ever the one with words, their father waved his piece of bread, bidding Nousha to continue.

"We leave for Leningrad tomorrow," Nousha said.

Igor sighed softly. He knew his daughters wouldn't be checking a person's reflexes or staring into their ears. It was war where they were headed. They'd be aiding in amputations, sticking their hands inside somebody to clamp off a severed artery, and squeezing somebody's hand as they died. Anousha and Alina may know that on the simplest level, but they couldn't *understand* that. You can't fathom what that is like. You can think you are prepared, but there is no way to prepare for the visceral violence that is war.

The Germans had *blitzkrieged* into Soviet territory, advancing toward Vladimir Lenin's namesake city. Her sisters were going to where the war was. A surge of guilt curdled in Kira's stomach. They'd always been there, asleep in the other room, except for the month Nousha had moved in with Radomir. The guilt came from the acknowledgment of missed opportunity. They spent time in the same room doing different things. Close but far away. Now, it would be just distance between them. They hadn't asked Kira to join them. They both knew she'd say no. But Kira couldn't lie and say it didn't hurt that she hadn't been asked. But it hurt more to understand why they hadn't.

The following morning was difficult. There was an eerie silence as they ate breakfast. Change had come, and even when change is planned, it is never gradual. It is always glaringly abrupt. Saying goodbye was hard. Kira had always protected her feelings, kept them concealed.

She kept silent, but she tried to show how much Nousha and Lina meant to her when she hugged them. They argued more than they got along, but in that moment, Kira couldn't recall a single argument worth remembering. Igor treated his hug the same way, rubbing his cracked hands across their backs. Nousha and Lina thought they'd be gone a month, but that date was malleable depending on how the defense of the city went. If the Germans continued their lightning assault, they would leave sooner. If the Soviets delivered a ferocious counterpunch, it could be longer. Kira wanted a set date. The unknown was poison.

Nousha and Lina smiled and waved, and then boarded the bus. Kira couldn't help but look on feeling as if she was adopted. Nousha and Lina weren't just sisters. They were best friends. Kira had always been the odd woman out. But as she watched the bus drive away, leaving a cloud of gray smoke and a tinge of exhaust in the air, it affected Kira more than her sisters knew. More than Kira could ever tell them. More than she could ever put into words.

A Promise

Mathias couldn't be swayed, and neither could Reinhardt. They'd had conversations, and they'd had arguments. And now, in silence, Reinhardt drove Mathias to the recruitment center.

"I don't understand. You love flying," Mathias said.

True. Reinhardt had loved it since Mathias's father had taught them when they were fourteen.

"I like it when no one is shooting at me," Reinhardt said.

"Germany needs us."

"So will its women."

Mathias shook his head. His last attempt at talking Reinhardt into enlisting had failed. Reinhardt waited outside, not wanting to listen to recruiters spew propaganda. He pulled a cigarette from his green pack of *Ecksteins*. Mathias was visible through the glass window. He appeared even shorter than he was because his shoulders were always slumped. It was an overcast day, the kind that threatened rain but hadn't delivered it so far. The recruiter led Mathias to a back room. Several minutes later, the entrance door burst open, the bell atop jingling. Mathias lumbered out.

"What happened?" Reinhardt asked. Though he knew what had happened. Mathias had been deemed unfit to serve. What was the reason? A single thing or a collection of maladies?

"I'm fine. Just take me home, please," Mathias said, as he stormed to Reinhardt's black BMW 327.

Reinhardt drove, trying to find something worth saying. Mathias chewed on his fingernails. His eyes focused on the disappointing world outside. When Reinhardt pulled into Mathias's driveway, he opened his mouth to speak, but Mathias dashed out before Reinhardt could get a word out.

Mathias didn't respond to phone calls over the next few days. Time that should have provided Reinhardt with the words to say. But he didn't have any. Only that he was sorry. Reinhardt had often been told by people how hard it must have been for Mathias to be his friend. Mathias was insecure. Insecure about his height, his weight, his looks, his relationship with women. Reinhardt had never suffered that infliction. Not that he thought of himself as some immaculate being. But of all their physical differences, it was health Reinhardt had been most aware of. Growing up, he and Mathias climbed a hundred trees. One of them was in the yard of an ornery wench named *Frau* Stückerfeld. She had spotted them in her tree and shouted at them. Frightened, they lost their footing. Reinhardt was two branches above Mathias. He landed gracefully on his feet; Mathias awkwardly collapsed, rolling both of his ankles.

But Reinhardt wouldn't lie and say he wasn't relieved his best friend wasn't going to war. It wasn't just because his friend was short and frail. Being big and strong had stopped being an advantage in war with the invention of the bullet. Now, it was only more area to shoot at. It was because war changes people. His father's generation were wounded men. Some bottled up their pain and cast themselves away from the outside world. Some men hated everyone and everything.

The following week, Reinhardt got off to a late start. Even after splashing cold water on his face and neck, Reinhardt's tiredness lingered. Someone knocked at his door. It wasn't the polite *knock knock*; it was a relentless fist-against-door pounding. *Frau* Holdenbrücke was at his door. She was an attractive woman, something all of Mathias's friends—apart from Reinhardt, who knew how much it annoyed him—teased him about. And apart from the blond hair, Mathias hadn't gotten any of her looks.

Her normally kind eyes had gone manic. Worry lined her face. "It's Mathias!"

"What happened?"

The uneasy feeling in his stomach exploded.

Her words came out in a frenzied stutter. "He has been so depressed! Hasn't left the house! I-I-I spoke—"

Reinhardt brought her inside and guided her to his couch, telling her to take a deep breath and speak slowly.

"I tried to brighten his mood, you know? I thought it had worked. He seemed better. I went to get ready and when I returned, he was gone!"

Reinhardt struggled to hide his confusion yet felt relieved. The gurgling in his stomach subsided. He had feared something horrible. Yet the relief was short-lived because *Frau* Holdenbrücke did not reciprocate it.

Reinhardt turned his head, still confused. "What is it?"

"He to-took his father's rifle!"

The volatility in his stomach was no longer a gurgle, it was an erupting volcano. It was in moments like this where most people froze. *This can't be happening.* But for Reinhardt, these moments always slowed down to grant him clarity. A clear sight of what needed to be done. Reinhardt sprung from his seat. Every thought disappeared except that Mathias was somewhere with a rifle. Reinhardt dashed to his BMW, telling *Frau* Holdenbrücke over his shoulder to call the police. Her face was ghastly white, her hands trembled, and thick tears contoured down her cheeks.

Reinhardt sped down the street. He stopped his thoughts from running rampant by focusing only on what he could control. Worrying would do him no good. *Rational thoughts only.* Mathias may do something—'something' a placeholder for a phrase he wouldn't dare use. Mathias didn't have a car. Public transportation was a slim possibility. Stepping aboard with a rifle would surely go noticed. So, that meant wherever he planned on doing it had to be within walking distance of his house. And if you planned on *doing something,* you would do it in a secluded spot. There were woods less than three blocks from his house. Reinhardt pressed on the gas pedal. He flew past Mathias's house toward the woods. He smashed the palm of his hand into the horn as he drove onto the grass. He sped toward the tree line, the car bouncing. Once he could drive no further, he jerked the shifter into park and jumped out. He sprinted into the woods, leaves and twigs crunching underfoot, screaming Mathias's name. The thick trees and foliage blocked his view. His ears tuned to his surroundings, waiting for that fatal shot to ring out.

He bounded over above-ground roots and overturned trees, and crouched below branches. He could run as fast as possible, faster than any person in history, but it didn't matter if he didn't know where he needed to run to. He emerged into a clearing. Mathias sat on the grass, the gunstock sandwiched into the ground and the barrel pressed into his chin.

"Mathias!" Reinhardt called.

Mathias didn't jump or turn around. He didn't react at all.

Reinhardt paused, his hand extended out, pleading for him not to do anything.

"I'm not even worthy to die, Reinhardt," he said.

It was said with a level of desperation Reinhardt had never heard a person have. Emotion swirled in Reinhardt. If Mathias felt that way, then Reinhardt had failed as a friend. It meant that he hadn't told Mathias how smart he was, how funny he was, and how honorable. Mathias was a positive soul, the kind of person everybody needs in their life. That was Mathias's greatest quality. So many people in life feed off our own energy, never giving, only taking. Mathias never did that. He only ever enhanced and gave away his seemingly unlimited supply.

"Don't say that," Reinhardt said.

"I want—wanted to fight, Reinhardt. For Germany, for my family, our friends." He fell silent for a moment. "Do you know why they turned me down?"

Reinhardt wouldn't guess. It could only offend.

"My heart. Apparently, it's weak. All the girls thought you had no heart, and I had a big one." The laugh that followed was filled with a deep pain. "How's that for irony?"

"I know you wanted to serve—"

"No, you don't," Mathias cut him off. "This meant more to me. My father served. My grandfathers served. My uncles served. The Iron Cross … having it around my neck … it would have proven that I'm not a mistake. A collection of maladies. You know, people would have seen that and instantly known I'm worth something."

They'd been best friends their whole lives, but Mathias had now exposed a vulnerability neither had ever addressed. The crippling self-doubt he had kept to himself his whole life. Reinhardt took a breath, breathing in the herbal and earthy aromas from the forest's fauna and flora.

Reinhardt cautiously sat beside Mathias. "You don't need to fire a gun or fly a plane to fight for Germany."

"Yeah? And what is it I'm supposed to do? Grab some pompoms?"

"What do soldiers fight with?"

For the first time, Mathias turned his head, looking at Reinhardt confused. "What?"

Reinhardt repeated the question.

"Guns," Mathias answered with a shrug.

"What do guns fire?"

"Bullets."

"And where do you think bullets come from? Do you think they magically appear on battlefields? What do soldiers eat? Do you think the food they eat just shows up? Or do you think men and women harvest and hunt that food?"

Mathias was silent.

"You want to do your part?" Reinhardt asked. "Then do your part however you can."

Mathias sighed, his eyes down. "I just feel like I'm running out of time."

"Time for what?"

"Life. A wife. Children. A job I like. A home I want to grow old in," Mathias said.

"I have none of those things, either."

"You could marry any number of women."

"Doesn't mean I have a connection with them. I want that, too. I know I don't always act like that. But I do."

Mathias looked from Reinhardt to the rifle in his hands. "You're not going to wrestle it away from me?"

Reinhardt shook his head. "No. You're going to decide you want to live." He put his hand on Mathias's shoulder. "Besides, you know it'd destroy me."

Mathias sighed. "Just sick of being a mistake."

"You are not a mistake. You've made mistakes. Most of them because of me."

A brief laugh escaped Mathias's lips. "Most? How about all of them?"

Reinhardt smirked, then held his hand out for the rifle. Mathias handed it to him. Reinhardt stood and offered his hand to his best friend and hoisted him to his feet.

Reinhardt looked from Mathias to the surrounding area. They'd played in these woods thousands of times. He enjoyed listening to the wildlife, the feeling of the early-

Autumn breeze brushing past. This was home. A home worth fighting for. A home worth dying for if necessary. He took a deep breath. A quote came back to him. One he had read many years ago. *The true soldier fights not because he hates what is in front of him, but because he loves what is behind him.*

"I will fight on your behalf," Reinhardt said.

"What do you mean?" Mathias asked.

"I will fight in Poland or France or wherever the war brings me. I'll fight for you. For our families. Our friends. But you promise me you'll fight here. Look after my family. That is your mission."

Mathias locked eyes with his best friend. "I will."

They spat into their hands and shook. An oath they'd made since they were kids. Blood oaths at seven were hard to fathom. But they liked the idea of them, so spit oaths were a fair compromise. Though now that they were older, that seemed even grosser than blood oaths.

"I hope you know your way out of here," Reinhardt said. "Because I sure as hell don't."

Greek Tragedy

Neither knew how to fill the palpable emptiness that had filled their home. Kira tried to remind herself that the emptiness was temporary. Not like the absence felt from her mother. That emptiness, that void, would always be there. Neither she nor her father would confront these feelings. Instead, Igor surrendered to sleep quicker than usual or was particularly enthralled by a newspaper article. If he kept to his routines, he could pretend nothing had changed. It was something he had mastered since returning home from the Great War: Bury your feelings and keep applying a fresh layer of dirt. Kira stuck to her own hobbies, too. During daytime, it was easy to forget that Nousha and Lina were gone. Nighttime was impossible. Dinners were quiet and empty. No fighting about who got to wash and who had to dry and who had to fold clothes. After dinner, no gossip was shared between Nousha and Lina. It was just quiet.

One night, Kira wrapped a blanket around her shoulders like it was a shawl and went for a nighttime stroll. The temperature was cool, the bugs and pesky insects seemingly a summer memory. She breathed in the smell of nature, each breath soothing her. She left the city behind and came to a grassy field. The shin-high grass blew in the night breeze, brushing against the cotton of her pants, carrying with it its sweet aroma. Kira removed her shoes, feeling her bare feet and the earth become one. Something her sisters never understood. They only noticed the permanent dirt stains on the bottom of her feet. Too worried about the possibility Kira may have stepped on a worm to consider the overwhelming relaxation walking barefoot provided. Nature calmed her. Revitalized her.

She fanned out her blanket onto the grass and laid down to gaze at the stars. Her solitude lasted less than five minutes before a figure approached. Even with her eyes still adjusting to the dark, she recognized Gerasim's outline.

"I figured you'd be out here," he said.

"I figured you would be, too," Kira said.

A mutual love of the stars had always linked them. Gerasim aways followed Kira's new interests, but his love of the stars was organic. It was a love they had discovered together. They first had gazed at them from one another's rooftops, but it didn't take long for them to realize how much more spectacular the stars were out here, far from the few city lights of Lyokhta.

"Wouldn't dare miss them on a night like this," Gerasim said.

It was a moonless night with low humidity—perfect conditions for stargazing.

Gerasim laid down beside her, then pointed. "Look at Vega tonight. Such clarity."

This was her favorite Gerasim. Out here, stargazing, Kira wasn't the most beautiful thing in his world—the stars were. He was knowledgeable in a way that would surprise everyone else, including his parents, but not her. She knew the depths of his intellect. He knew the stars and their many names. For instance, Polaris. Throughout history, it had been called other names, such as Alruccabah, Angel Stern, Cynosura, and the Star of Arcady, among others. It didn't take much effort to imagine Gerasim crossing the Atlantic only with the stars to guide him. As children, they camped out in shelters they built. Only nine or ten years old spending a weekend in isolation. Their parents only worried once they became teenagers. Boy+girl+isolation, multiplied by hormones, is a scary equation for parents.

"Have you heard from Nousha and Lina today?" he asked.

"No, but I know they are busy," Kira replied.

Gerasim listened to her answer, but he didn't divert his eyes from the stars. Leningrad was under immense attack. The Germans had circled the city and laid siege to it. In the few months since their invasion began, the Germans had *blitzkrieged* through Belarus, Estonia, Ukraine, and into Mother Russia. Every day, the war became less of a foreign war and more of a war in her own backyard. What had once seemed impossible now seemed inevitable. That this overgrown field they lay on to gaze upon the celestial constellations would soon be torn apart by Tiger tanks, half-tracks, and *Wehrmacht* boots.

"Do you know the story of Orion?" Gerasim asked.

Kira shook her head. She knew what was coming. Gerasim was about to narrate a myth, and he had a storyteller's flair. She focused her eyes on the Orion constellation as if it would enact Gerasim's words.

"Orion was a mortal hunter, loved living as a hermit. Like you."

Kira chuckled at his playful jest.

"He was a fabled hunter, boasting he could slay any creature on Earth. Any beast on land, any fish in the sea, any bird in the sky."

"Wouldn't that make him a fisherman or a fowler?"

"Kira, please! I'm telling a story! A story is like a river, it must flow! Interrupting is diverting flow!"

Kira chuckled. "Apologies. I did not mean to redirect your river."

"May I continue?"

"You may."

"Are you sure?" Gerasim played up an annoyed sigh before continuing. "Artemis was the Goddess of the Hunt, but she was also responsible for carrying the moon across the night sky. On a night, clear like this one, as she carried the illuminating moon, she saw the boastful mortal. Instantly, she became infatuated. Every night, she looked for him. Orion's boasting made its way from town to town until even the gods heard it. Gaea, Mother of all life, did not care for his hubris, so she sent a giant scorpion to kill Orion. The scorpion scampered forward in the darkness as Orion slept. But fortunately for him, Artemis saw. She descended toward Earth and fought the scorpion. Orion woke from his sleep and joined the fight. Here's where the story becomes uncertain."

His story transfixed Kira. She visualized the competent hunter, the immortal goddess, and the terrifying beast.

"Whether by a fatal sting or an errant arrow launched by Artemis, Orion was killed. Fueled by her rage, Artemis flung the scorpion into the night sky."

He leaned close to Kira, so that when he pointed to the eighteen-star constellation, it aligned with her eyeline.

"And as tribute, Artemis cast Orion into the night sky, and every night as she carried the moon, she gazed upon him."

"Beautiful and tragic."

"Tragically beautiful."

Kira smirked. Greek myths were thousands of years old, yet so many of their stories had never been bested. Love stories so grand in scale. Nousha had fallen for

Radomir. Lina claimed to be in love every other week. Kira had never experienced love. Had never even mistaken infatuation for it. Would she ever? At times, she thought she was abnormal. Why wasn't she crazy for men the way her sisters were? The way every woman her age appeared to be. She'd heard stories of women forsaking reason, embracing madness, and she couldn't grasp it.

"But there is another story of the death of Orion. Do you wish to hear it?" Gerasim asked.

"I wouldn't dare divert a river's flow."

Gerasim comically glared at Kira.

"I want to hear it."

"The other story is that Artemis' twin brother, Apollo, grew jealous of his sister's infatuation with the mortal. So, while Orion bathed and swam, Apollo challenged his sister to an archery competition. He claimed she could not hit the target in the water. The object was far, far away, too far for even her divine eyes to see. Her brother taunted, enticed, and ridiculed until, out of frustration, she drew back her bow and launched an arrow. It soared like a shooting star across the night sky." Gerasim whistled for effect. "The arrow found its mark. Apollo cheered. Artemis found it odd that he cheered his own defeat. 'Go gaze upon your trophy,' he said. They mounted their stallions and rode to her trophy. Once there, they dismounted their loyal steeds. To her horror, a body floated face down. Artemis slowly approached it. She turned it over and gasped in heartbreaking horror, seeing she had killed her true love."

"That's even more tragic than the first story," Kira said.

Gerasim turned onto his side, so that he could look at Kira as he spoke.

"I believe their story is our story. I am no expert hunter, fisherman, or fowler. But you are a goddess with a great shot. No matter what tale, fable, or story, the ending is the same. You and I will never be together. I would do anything to change that."

Kira diverted her eyes from the constellation of Orion to him. Guilt gleamed in her eyes. "Gerasim, I—"

"You do not have to explain. I just need you to know. I love you, Kira. With every fiber of my being. Since I was a boy."

She stared into his kind brown eyes. She wished she felt the same. Often, she thought about saying yes to his daily proposals. If she did, she would be marrying her best friend. All the older people she knew advised her to marry for love, not passion.

Passion fades, they warned. Kira loved him. But that love was platonic. Was it too much to ask for love and passion? When Nousha had first met Radomir, she described tumultuous butterflies taking flight in her stomach. Flu-like symptoms debilitating her. Kira didn't have those with Gerasim. She hadn't had them with anybody. And as her mid-twenties ticked away, she wasn't sure if she'd ever get them. In the novels she read, love was a grand adventure. A plane ride away, over a mountain, across a high sea, and through storms. Love was earned, fought for. Never given. And Kira wasn't ready to stop looking, wasn't ready to stop fighting for it.

Not yet.

Kira took his hands in hers. They were dry and cracked. "I can't be what you want me to be. Be what's fair to you. I love you, Gerasim. You're my best friend. But the love I have for you isn't the same as you have for me. I wish it was."

She hated the pain she caused him. If she had been selfish, she'd give him false hope. Keep him tethered to her like a dog on a leash. But she loved him too much. Selfish people kept love shackled. If she truly loved him, and she did—she was closer to him than her own sisters—she had to let him go.

Gerasim squeezed his eyes shut and nodded. The pain in his face was unbearable to witness.

"Marry me?" He smiled, exposing his crooked, horse-like teeth. His eyes twinkled.

Kira laughed. Even when he was hurting immensely, his instinct had been to make her feel better, to make her laugh. Clichéd as it was to say, every woman should yearn to find a man that defaulted to protecting her, bettering her even at his own expense. Curse any woman who couldn't see men like Gerasim for what they were. She cursed herself more than anyone else, because she saw him for it but still couldn't find the feelings he deserved.

"There is something else I must tell you," Gerasim said.

His demeanor shifted again. Drastically. Dramatically. Whatever he was about to say wasn't a lighthearted joke. It would be another life-altering sentence.

"I have been drafted, Kira. I leave tomorrow."

Kira wasn't shocked. It was impossible to be shocked. It was only a matter of time until every able Soviet man was in uniform. She knew the day would come, but it was still a gut punch. Her life was changing fast. Too fast. First, Nousha and Lina. Now, Gerasim. For the first time, the war affected her personally. She thought of the colonel who had spoken to her at the factory. His words were no longer a warning, but a fulfilled premonition. And Kira was powerless to do anything but hope. Hope that their absence was temporary.

Kira stared into Gerasim's big brown eyes. There was so much kindness in them, a dog-like level of love reflecting at her. "You come back, you hear me? Stay alive. No hero stuff."

"Look at me. Do I look like a hero?" He said it in a joking fashion, but it was something he believed.

"You're a good man, Gerasim. A brave man. Promise me."

She offered her hand, not her right as is customary, but her left. Any secret they had ever told or oath they had ever made had been sealed with a left-handed handshake. Why? Because everyone shook hands with their right hands. Left-handed shakes were something they could uniquely share. Gerasim smirked and shook her hand. They were silent the rest of the night, turning their attention to the stars. Fireflies buzzed around overhead, looking like shooting stars. Kira tried to think tonight was like any other night. That tomorrow she and Gerasim would hunt. Her sisters would tease her. But not even the infinite cosmos could ease her anxiety.

That night, as she struggled to sleep, she couldn't help but think that the war had issued a warning. Displaying its power, its boundless reach. A dictator demanding tribute. But what was the war demanding of her? How could she appease it, so that it wouldn't fully display its destructive power and crush everything she loved?

The following morning, Kira joined Gerasim's family at the bus station to see him off. His brother, Semyon, also drafted, had left weeks earlier. Petyr beamed proudly through damp eyes. Gerasim's mother, Varvara, was beside him. A tiny woman who barely reached her husband's navel. However inappropriate it was, and it certainly was, Kira couldn't help but gaze upon physiological opposites and wonder how they could have sex. The act must take a great deal of creative planning and awkward angles. Whatever that plan, and whatever those angles, it worked, for lined among them were five children ages five through twenty. Ekaterina was the oldest girl, and the sibling Kira knew best. Ekaterina always conveyed dislike toward Kira, something Kira attributed to a sister protecting her lovesick brother. While some women would match hate with hate, Kira recognized her animosity came from the love of her brother. How could she fault her for that?

Gerasim hugged his little siblings, then embraced Ekaterina. "No marriage until I can approve. Yes?"

His parents were next. His mother struggled to release her hold. Kira had been with Gerasim when Semyon had left. His mother had been less anxious. As if Semyon was destined for greatness. And even though a good mother would never admit it, her hug with Gerasim was quite different. His success wasn't preordained. It was dubious. But Kira knew war didn't care about somebody's destiny. It cared only about fodder.

Kira didn't want her goodbye to be last. It shouldn't have been. The whole family studied it, critiquing if platonic had morphed to passion, friend to lover. Kira hugged him, ultimately deciding she didn't care how his family perceived her hug. She rubbed his back, and then, when the hug broke, she held out a book for him. He took it and examined it. It was a book of Greek myths. She whispered into his ear, so that only he could hear.

"Read this and when you come home, regale me with their tales."

He nodded and smiled appreciatively, then placed the book in his rucksack. Gerasim took one last look at Kira and his family, then boarded the beaten-down bus. The mechanical door closed with a hiss. The bus groaned and shuttered ahead, taking her best friend and delivering him to the war's doorstep.

Flight Training

Reinhardt didn't say goodbye to Mathias. He had kept his date of departure to himself, knowing that watching him board a bus would only cause Mathias pain. To help ensure Mathias wouldn't be there, Reinhardt had gotten him properly drunk the night before. At this early hour, Mathias was either asleep or still on his knees in front of the toilet. Reinhardt's own family thought his date of departure was a day later. Goodbyes were hard and something he'd rather avoid. So, Reinhardt had no fanfare to see him leave. The streets were mostly barren, save for the few people heading to work. He stepped onto the bus, the gray exhaust coating his mouth and clinging to his clothes. He had a book to read, but he wouldn't open it until he savored every view of his hometown. The familiar houses and businesses flashing past unwrapped memories. People, places from days past. They unlocked emotion, and if he continued the trip down memory lane, he'd jump off the bus and sprint home. He opened his book and disappeared into the fictional sanctuary it provided.

He would come back home.

Reinhardt had signed up to be a pilot, but first, he had six months at a *Fliegersatzabteilung* (recruit training depot). Here the emphasis would be on drill and physical training. Everyone thinks they're in decent shape until they have to run a couple of kilometers. Reinhardt learned quickly to keep his mouth shut. The military didn't share his appreciation for witty comments. Swallowing sarcasm was certainly an adjustment. The effects of physical training were evident. His shoulders thickened, his waist slimmed, dormant muscles were chiseled away at, and veins tunneled under his forearms. He wrote letters home to his mother (to be shared with his father and sisters) and to Mathias. He kept the military aspect brief in those letters to his friend. But if there was a particularly horrible experience, he was sure to include it. Anything to help dull that longing ache Mathias felt. He asked how the home front was. Equally as interested in Mathias's work at the factory and what that entailed as Mathias was with *Fliegersatzabteilung*.

After completing basic training, Reinhardt advanced to a *Fluganwärterkompanie*, where they taught him aeronautical studies. Mathias's father had flown a crop duster for years, and Reinhardt had been up in the plane hundreds of times. He knew the basics he was taught. After general studies of aeronautical subjects, Reinhardt went to an A/B school. The training aircraft was the Klemm 35, similar in style to the plane Mathias's father flew. Achieving his A2 license tested his love of learning. Courses in aerodynamics, aeronautical engineering, elementary navigation, meteorology, and flying procedures. He learned to read and send Morse code. School had come effortlessly to Reinhardt, but this was much different. It was one thing to get a math problem wrong, resulting in poor Friedrich being short on the lemons his grandmother had sent him to the store for. But when even the slightest miscalculation could lead to not only your death but your crew's as well, you needed to be able to recall information instantly.

Reinhardt learned how to work. His God-given abilities had given him an advantage he wouldn't squander by resting on his laurels. He clocked 150 hours of flying time and received his pilot's license (*Luftwaffen-flugzeugfuehrerschein*) and his pilot's wings (*Flugzeugführerabzeichen*). He learned formations. The *Geschwader* comprised three or four *Gruppe*. Each *Gruppe* was three or four *Staffel*, which was a squadron of ten to twelve planes. Reinhardt would fly the Messerschmitt Bf 109. He learned all its specs and limitations. Equipped with 1,100 horsepower and a max speed of 640 km/hr, it was equipped with two 7.9mm Cowling machine guns located above the engine that were synchronized to fire through the propeller arch with a 20mm cannon that fired straight through the center of the propeller's hub.

Reinhardt was sure to test the plane's limits. Not out of recklessness, but because up in the sky, he needed to know what his true limitations were, not those printed in a manual. He flew at night and during the day. He asked for extra lessons, not that he felt he needed them, but because flying at night was the greatest sensation a person could experience. It was soaring through stars and space. He could enjoy gazing at them now, and he took full advantage of it. When real missions came, a pilot who diverted his gaze but for a moment to look at Venus or Sirius would pay for it with his life.

He enjoyed the company of his fellow pilots, but Reinhardt didn't fit the mold. They were cocky, competitive. Reinhardt had been accused of arrogance, mostly by the opposite sex, but while other pilots ran their mouths—either fully believing the crap they said or trying to jest the others and gain a psychological advantage—Reinhardt didn't feel the need. He knew he was the best pilot. And the others seemed to know it, too. None of them jested him, bragged to him, or challenged him. They recognized that in this pride, Reinhardt Friedel was the full-maned king. Reinhardt kept to himself, reading or scribbling math equations on a small handheld chalkboard. He calculated how much fuel he'd have left if he traveled at x for a duration of y. He studied the night sky the way sailors did hundreds of years ago. The modern instrumentation was great, but if it went, he wanted a backup plan. He studied the wind and how it affected his flight if he flew into it, had it at his back, or if it struck from the side. He wanted variables to become constants, the unexpected to be expected, and the unknown to be known.

And then, training was over. The Battle for Britain was about to begin. Before departing for the northwest coast of France, the *Luftwaffe* granted Reinhardt and the graduates leave, allowing them to return home.

He stepped off the bus and straightened his gray *Luftwaffe* uniform. The national emblem, the Nazi Eagle with its outstretched wings and the swastika in its talons, gleamed on his cap and on the right breast of his uniform. Home appeared to be as it always had, which was exactly how Reinhardt wanted it to be. And a big part of home was waiting for him at the bus stop. Mathias stood when Reinhardt approached. Reinhardt knew the pain seeing the uniform caused him and tried to hide it with his bag. But Mathias was too selfless to let his own issues diminish Reinhardt's return.

"Thought you'd like to walk," Mathias said. "See home."

Reinhardt did. He overloaded his senses. His eyes darted everywhere. He breathed in the smell of home, a blend of restaurants and industry; listened to the faint traffic, and the birds flying overhead; ran his fingers along the brick shops and businesses. Each one home to a halcyon memory. This is what he would fight for.

"How have you been?" Reinhardt asked.

Mathias shrugged. "Sure wish I could have gotten off that bus with you."

"You did."

Mathias appreciated the sentiment. Reinhardt always used inclusive words like we and us. Nothing that would separate the pilot and the civilian. Mathias asked questions the whole walk to his house. When Reinhardt answered he would fly the Messerschmitt Bf 109, Mathias knew most of its specs, and of those he didn't, his guesses were impressively close.

At Mathias's house, Reinhardt dropped his bag off beside the couch and plopped onto it. His body begged to lie down and stay put. The couch was far more comfortable than the cot at training. But Mathias had other plans. Reinhardt reluctantly changed clothes. He ran cold water onto his face and neck, hoping the jolt would wake him. He was three quarters of his way through a damn good book, hoping he had enough energy to finish it before surrendering to sleep. But it would have to wait.

Together, they walked to Reinhardt's parents' house, where his family surprised him. His father was half-a-foot shorter than Reinhardt. He shared his son's large hands and wavy dark hair. His mother had given him his striking blue eyes. His sisters Evonne, Griselde, and Lonita were all older and shared his pleasant looks and those cerulean-colored eyes. Mathias had always been like a member of the family, but at dinner, as Reinhardt listened to the banter between his chosen brother and inherited family, it was clear that Reinhardt had missed much over the last few months. He was outside on inside jokes. Missed memories and milestones. He experienced his first casualty during his service: the loss of time.

His mother tried to hold back her tears, the relief of having him home at her table too much to bear. His sisters had wrapped him in tight hugs but had no trouble falling back into jesting him. He ate too much sausage, potatoes, and cabbage, and then ate too much cake for dessert, and craved the comfort of a couch. After his offer to wash and dry dishes was declined, Reinhardt and Mathias said goodbye. Reinhardt prepared his own goodbye for Mathias, but one look at his friend's boyish face made it clear that Mathias had more plans. This night wasn't ending anytime soon.

Mathias skipped ahead; Reinhardt lumbered behind. The fresh air and exercise helped fight the food coma. He'd eaten more calories in a single serving than he sometimes ate in a day. Germans had a word for it: *Kaloriebombe*. And the bomb had gone off. As they passed houses, Mathias provided updates on the people who lived in them. Their kindergarten teacher *Herr* Franklich had finally retired. He was one of those people who had looked seventy since they were thirty. Michael Murkel had married Gwen Klein. *Frau* Fischer had a steamy affair with a traveling salesman from Hamburg. But apart from that, home hadn't changed. The war was still away from Germany.

The walk was never-ending. Reinhardt finally asked where they were going. Mathias shrugged, a guilty smirk on his youthful face. He dashed across the street, gambling that the driver of the car approaching was paying enough attention to not hit him. Reinhardt waited for the car to pass, nodding at the honking horn. Mathias opened the door to a dance club called The Limber Limb. Music blared so loudly it raised the hair on their arms. Cigarette smoke lingered. The stench of beer was ripe. Men and women of varying skill packed the dance floor. Overwhelmed bartenders poured drinks, and patrons didn't care what they poured as long as it made them feel good. And it all made them feel good.

"When did this place open?" Reinhardt asked, having to shout to be heard.

Mathias gave a quizzical look. He couldn't hear anything but the drum solo. They squeezed and shimmied their way to the bar. Reinhardt flicked a match and lit an *Eckstein*, observing the dance floor while Mathias tried to get a couple of beers. Reinhardt knew Mathias would have a hell of a time getting a drink. Beautiful women got their drinks first, then ornery, drunk men. Mathias was neither. It was a full ten minutes later when Mathias handed Reinhardt a *Hefeweizen* beer. It tasted like sweet nectar. Reinhardt was tired, but he couldn't pretend he didn't see the attractive women dancing. The way their bodies moved, twisting to the music. It was caffeine. As he scanned, he found a familiar face. One that was both friend and foe. Ingrid. She danced with a man a good foot taller than her. Her hands hung around his long neck. Her eyes caught Reinhardt's. Emotion drained from her face. She whispered into her dance partner's ear and then approached Reinhardt. Her footing was clumsy. She could dance drunk but not walk.

"Reinhardt Friedel," she said.

Reinhardt's lips curled back into a smile. "Ingrid Hauser."

Her hair was longer than it had been the last time he'd seen her, but other than that, she hadn't changed. She studied his physique. He had changed. He was manlier now than he had been. He'd lost some of that boyish charm in exchange for muscles. They were both doing the math on how long it had been since they'd last seen each other. On that beach … It'd been close to a year, which explained why Ingrid was so close to Jade Bight. It was summer. Neither spoke; both laughed because of that.

"You look different …" Ingrid said.

"Is that a good thing or a bad thing?" Reinhardt asked.

"I prefer not to answer."

Reinhardt smirked, then explained that he had joined the *Luftwaffe*.

"You're the same Reinhardt from the beach last summer?"

"I had a change of heart."

Reinhardt wouldn't explain his promise to Mathias. Ingrid studied him. While sober, she could suavely check him out, but her deft touch was absent in her drunken state. She stared into his eyes and then shook her head, like how you look at a magician after you've accepted you'll never know how the trick is done.

41

Silence crept over them.

"So, how have you been?" Reinhardt asked.

"I'm here with my fiancé …" she said at the same time.

She nodded toward her partner, who now stood on the borders of the dance floor, looking lost and alone like an abandoned puppy. Reinhardt glanced at him before bringing his eyes back to Ingrid.

"Congratulations, Ingrid. I'm happy for you. Truly."

She smiled, biting her lip. "Are you upset?"

Reinhardt shook his head. "No. You deserved someone great, Ingrid. You know that, don't you?"

Ingrid couldn't help but smile. Reinhardt's charm would always afflict her. "I know."

Reinhardt waved to the bartender and ordered two shots of whiskey. While Mathias struggled to get another drink, Reinhardt's shots were at the bar in less than thirty seconds. Reinhardt was tall, chiseled from marble now. People took note. He had never asked for it, but he had the ability to walk into a room and have everyone turn to look at him. Reinhart and Ingrid raised their glasses to each other and downed them. She grimaced at the burn. Reinhardt leaned sideways against the bar; his hands folded together.

"So, you are home for a bit?" she asked.

"A few days. I leave for France on Wednesday."

Her eyes filled with horrified sorrow. "Be careful, won't you?"

Reinhardt nodded. "Don't worry about me, dear Ingrid. You should return to your fiancé before he gets jealous."

She rolled her eyes, but in a way that showed she had missed it. Missed him. She leaned in and hugged Reinhardt with one arm. The simple smell of a woman sent an urge throughout his body. He'd been without a woman's touch for months. As she walked away, he couldn't help but think how nothing changes yet everything does. The last time he had seen her, she had been wrapped around him. Now, she was engaged. Once more, he was aware of the time he'd lost. People had gotten married, moved away, returned home, got new jobs. Reinhardt had done nothing but train.

Reinhardt called Ingrid's name. "You are an extraordinary woman, Ingrid. Never settle for ordinary."

She smiled and returned to the man that could have been Reinhardt had he so desired it. He liked Ingrid. She was pretty and witty. But to no fault of her own, there was something missing there. A deeper connection. His mother and father had married at twenty-two and nineteen. His sisters had married young. But Reinhardt hadn't found that someone that changed everything. Changed his world.

Mathias slithered back to him. He'd kept his distance to let Reinhardt and Ingrid speak.

"How'd that go?" he asked.

Reinhardt downed his beer and nodded for the bartender to refill his glass. There was a strong desire to try to win Ingrid back. She was sexy with all the right curves. There was the desire to compete for her. He'd win. He knew he would. If he wanted to, he would leave with Ingrid and the puppy-dog fiancé would whimper back home. But he wouldn't do that to her for one night of pleasure. He truly believed she deserved to be happy, and he wouldn't screw that up because of untamed lust.

"Time to dance," Reinhardt said.

Mathias shook his head. "No, no, no. No way!"

"Let's save time. You've wanted to come to this dance club since it opened, but you needed me to drag you out onto the dance floor."

Mathias uttered a retort, one that not even he believed. Reinhardt paid no attention to it. He had scouted the dance floor, finding those women he believed to be eligible and those who would be eligible should he ask. He confidently merged into a group of five women. They were all brunettes except for one who had dark red hair. Her eyes were a soft brown. Her dress hugged her body like a pair of nylons. Reinhardt locked his eyes with hers.

To Mathias, he was a seal swimming out to a school of sharks. He nervously treaded water close by. Reinhardt, shoulders pressed back, offered his hand to the redhead without a word. She eyed Reinhardt, then accepted his offer. Mathias offered his hand to the brunette a few inches shorter than him.

"Care to da-dance?" he asked.

She took his hand.

Reinhardt loved to dance. He loved the music, the way his body knew how to move to it. Dancing was something that made people feel alive. Silly or stupid, it didn't matter. It was also a great gauge of a woman's interest. If she kept her distance during a song, the message was obvious. You were strictly a dance partner for the next couple of minutes. If she allowed your hands to travel further south, if her fingers caressed the back of your neck, or if she arched back, laughing, she was willing to be more than a dance partner. The best bands could read a room. They were the ultimate wingmen, continually advancing the style of music. Faster and faster, the music destroying any inhibitions. But then they slowed it down, so that a man and woman could dance, gaze into each other's eyes to see if this moment should continue into a bedroom.

The beer had diminished Mathias's self-confidence issues. Women seem to be born with rhythm, knowing how to move to the music. That is not how it is for most men. But the key is to simply be unafraid to look like a fool. Smile. Laugh. Bonus points for any dance floor that dimmed the lights like The Limber Limb had. Darkness was best when it came to dancing. Sweat beaded on their foreheads, and their shirts clung to their skin. Beer and sweat overpowered any cologne or perfume they had worn. After three songs, the redhead leaned toward Reinhardt and told him she had to use the restroom. Reinhardt nodded, then made eye contact with Mathias and nodded at the door. Mathias translated and followed Reinhardt outside. The fresh air was most welcome, but what it gave in refreshment, it took by making them realize how intoxicated they were. They had completely missed the buzzed stage. Instead, they had boarded a runaway train from sobriety to shitfaced.

Reinhardt leaned against the brick and lit a cigarette. He squeezed his eyes, trying to calibrate his vision. The front door opened and his red-headed dance partner stumbled out, laughing. If she had felt drunk inside, heaven help her once the fresh air hit her. Mathias smirked at Reinhardt, nodded politely at the redhead, then went back inside.

"Sneaking out on me?" she asked.

"Maybe. Convince me otherwise?"

She smirked, then arched onto her tippy toes and pressed her lips against his. She balled the front of his shirt in her hands and steered him into the alley. She smashed her lips into his, more aggressively than she would have sober. She drew away as a realization dawned on her.

"You don't even know my name."

Reinhardt dismissed its insignificance. "I never asked."

Her eyes widened in shock at his audacity, but a smile curled on her lips because of it. "It's Maureen."

Their kissing escalated, hands first intertwining, now exploring, caressing, and squeezing. Reinhardt stopped her, holding her at bay as she tried to eliminate the distance between them.

"This won't be anything more than tonight," he said.

Her eyes widened, offended. "Brutally honest."

"I need to be upfront."

She nodded, the embarrassment not fading. Unsure of her next move.

"I leave for France in a few days' time."

Her eyes that had showed shock and embarrassment now filled with understanding and worry. They'd never met before tonight. And the war may see to it that they never meet again. But that was the thing about war. Everyone knew not everyone came home. There was that macabre thought that you could be talking with someone who had but days left to live. And that knowledge brought on a level of brazen action.

"Then let's enjoy tonight," she said.

After their embrace, she returned inside. Reinhardt stayed behind. To no fault of her own, there had been something missing. It had been purely physical. No lasting connection. A great distraction from what lay ahead. But after that post-coital clarity evaporated, those worries returned. Reinhardt smoked a cigarette before heading back inside. It was after midnight. It seemed Mathias was only standing because his body was in constant motion. If he should stop, he would collapse—a clear sign it was time to go. Mathias tried to argue with Reinhardt that he was fine, but he dry heaved in the middle of his pitch. He smiled at his dance partner, then went in for a kiss, looking like a woodpecker pecking at a tree. Reinhardt grabbed him before he could headbutt her and draped his arm over Mathias's shoulder. Reinhardt walked. Mathias shuffled. Reinhardt was buzzed, but alcohol didn't go down as smoothly as it had before. The war loomed over every moment. A cloud always threatening rain. Potential impending death was quite sobering.

Reinhardt's days home went by at a blistering speed. It was time for him to leave. When he had left for basic training, he thought he would return home at the end of hostilities. But now, he wasn't sure. There were no guarantees. It could be the last time he gazed upon his home. The last time he saw his family. It was a barbell on his shoulders he couldn't toss off. His parents had planned a going-away breakfast with his sisters and Mathias. He had agreed to it, but he knew he would leave before it. Goodbyes were too unbearable, too emotional. He snuck out of his parents' house early in the morning, leaving them a concise note that simply said: "With all my love, Reinhardt."

He climbed aboard the train. It whistled a warning for the final boarding. The wheels powered forward with their rhythmic chant of *chug chug chug chug*. His home city passed by through the window, and knowing it could be the last time he saw it, Reinhardt focused his gaze upon it with unblinking eyes, trying to ignore the train's mournful wailing.

The War Arrives

The days that followed Gerasim's departure were the loneliest Kira had ever experienced. Her sisters were gone. Her best friend was gone. Her hobbies had always been solitary, but there was a tremendous difference between reading a book alone versus reading a book with others in the room. So often she had found the background noise of conversation annoying. It snapped her from the realm of fiction. Kira hadn't cared for any of the drama Nousha and Lina felt compelled to share. Now, she found she couldn't disappear into the fictional world without it.

News came that the fighting in Leningrad had swayed in favor of the Germans. Local field hospitals were set up in towns and cities east of Leningrad. While that news was unfavorable to the Soviet Union and anybody opposed to fascist dictators, to Kira, it was welcome news. It meant Nousha and Lina would be coming home. News affirmed later that day when a letter stated they'd be home Saturday evening. Kira woke early that morning, feeling like it was Christmas. She vowed she would attempt to find common ground with them, to not let the first minor argument turn into an all-out shouting match. Let them fix her hair or do whatever it was they wanted to do. She wouldn't add her own condescending commentary and wouldn't get worked up when they critiqued how ratty her hair looked or why she spent so much time reading, or why she walked barefoot, or spent all day outside.

She washed their bedsheets and hung them out to dry. Hoping the smell of freshly laundered sheets and the comfort of their own beds would help them sleep better than they had since they left. Kira knew she would sleep better. She wouldn't spend the first ten minutes falling asleep thinking about them and what they were doing or if they were safe.

Before noon, Kira stuffed a rucksack with snacks, a water canteen, books, and a blanket. Hiking was one of her favorite activities. It was peaceful, yet active. Meditative. The path she took was one her mother had taken her and her sisters on. The dirt was soft enough that she could feel it spread beneath her shoes. The trees surrounding it were on the cusp of losing their leaves, and their colors were never more vibrant. Was it cruel or kind to be at your most beautiful before death? Kira thought of her mother. She had died at her most beautiful. Until the cancer ravished her, at least. The changing of the leaves had always reminded Kira of her mother in that way. Slowly dying, falling leaf by leaf until the tree was bare. Utterly powerless to stop it.

The ground topography ebbed and flowed, an increase here, a steep decline there. The path took her along an uprooted tree. Its tentacle-like roots branching off like the tributaries of a mighty river. It was a sight that always saddened her. How much history had that tree seen? Well over a hundred years. Nousha and Lina loved big cities, raved about big-city skylines. They never gazed at trees with the same marvel she did. There are trees that are over 10,000 years old! That unbelievable statistic had little effect on them. They were always enamored by what man had created; Kira was enraged at what they had destroyed.

The foliage-filled forest floor disappeared, replaced with limestone. A bluff stretched out before her. A precipice overlooking the forest canopy awning hundreds of feet below. Birds of prey swooped over it. It was Kira's favorite spot in the world. Here on this bluff, it was Earth. Majestic, beautiful Earth. If time travel existed like the device of an H. G. Wells novel, the time traveler would find this place identical for hundreds of years, if not thousands. Each breath she took was an antidote to all life's woes. It was the perfect place for perspective. Your problems were miniscule. They would pass. Our collective novel of life was but a single line in the history of this place. It rejuvenated her soul.

Kira removed the blanket from her rucksack and spread it over the stone. She took a swig of water from her canteen, then grabbed her book. She read page after page, chapter after chapter, stopping only to eat her packed lunch. Every turn of the page she would glance up to appreciate the view another time. The book detailed romantic Paris, the exotic Serengeti, and glitzy-and-glamorous Hollywood. Places that may as well have been planets in a distant solar system. To Kira, the world was a collection of contradictory adjectives—terrifying and titillating, dangerous and docile, alarming and alluring. She could never decide. Yet, the irony of indecision is that it is a decision. Reading granted her the ability to travel to Paris, Berlin, New York, or Rome. Allowed her to be someone else. Nousha and Lina never understood that. They didn't need the asylum of being someone else, somewhere else, and sometime else. And good for those who didn't. But Kira needed that reprieve. As she struggled to decide what to do with her life, life continued to speed past. But in the pages of fiction, the world made sense. And here at the bluff, book in hand, it stood still.

She read until the sun, appearing ten times its normal size, hung low. There was no better reminder of time than the sun on the horizon. Time to go. She had supper to prepare. Nousha's favorite dish was *pirozhki*—baked puff pastries filled with potatoes, meat, cabbage, and cheese. Lina's was beef *stroganoff*. But neither cared for the other; however, they both loved *pelmeni*—a dumpling filled with minced meat and served with sour cream. Nousha was the cook of the house, but Kira had watched her make it enough times to feel confident she could manage it. Besides, she was banking on the adage, *It's the thought that counts.*

It was always best to get out of the woods before dark. She'd traversed them hundreds of times but navigating them at night was different. No more birds singing, just owls hooting and crickets chirping. You couldn't see the animals, but they could see you. Trees looked indistinguishable, nothing but giant silhouettes. She knew she could make it out, but why risk it?

Kira emerged from the tree line. The smell of smoke wafted toward her. Not the smell of campfire smoke—one of her favorite smells—this smoke was different. As she came closer to the city, a muffled, amplified voice rang out. She could only make out three words.

Bürger. Häuser. Verlassen.

German.

The hair on her neck rose like blades of grass in a strong breeze. Her stomach plummeted, the crater impact sending a geyser of bile into her mouth. Her legs weakened, but her hands stayed stoically still, incongruous with the trembling fear surging through her.

How long had she been gone? Days? Weeks? Had the bluff felt timeless because it was? Had it ceased to move? The German Army couldn't have invaded in the hours that she had been gone … could they?

A gunshot rang out, startling Kira. She crouched. It sounded as if the Earth's crust was breaking and the skies were exploding. It had to be artillery. Her city, her *home*, was under attack. The fear was paralyzing. Her body rejected her desire to move ahead; its only offer was backward. But her body didn't control her mind. She had to move forward. She had to get home. Kira crept closer, swallowing the instinct to scream when the next gunshot crackled or artillery barrage blasted. Along a main street, German tanks and jeeps sped past. Black smoke billowed toward the sky, so thick she could taste it. A megaphoned voice commanded all citizens to step outside. Shops and businesses were ablaze. Flames roared. Children cried. Women screamed.

Men gawked in abject horror as their homes burned to ash. Kira continued. She had to get home to her father.

Two blocks away.

A block.

Shots rang out. She recognized the sound. She'd heard it hundreds of times before. It came from a Mosin–Nagant. On her street, she stopped. A black leather-clad Nazi, in his early forties, took cover behind a jeep. Three German soldiers lay motionless around him. The *SS* soldier shouted, cursing the man in the house, telling him to lay down his weapon. Kira's father knew less than ten words of German, and he had made sure those words counted.

"Indulge in piss and shit, you fascist pigs!" he shouted.

It had been over twenty years since Igor Kovalyov had fought in the Great War, but the war had never truly left him. Warriors were always prepared for war. It was engraved in their DNA. He fought fiercely from the second-floor window, sniping from behind the overturned kitchen table. His shots shattered the jeep window, showering the Nazi officer in glass. The Nazi officer shouted an order at the tank. The tank's long gun barrel lifted and turned. Kira's eyes widened. She was powerless. Powerless to run. Powerless to scream. Powerless to make any difference. She had nothing but a book. The tank's gun barrel blasted backward as the shell fired. The entire southern wall of Kira's house caved inward. Rubble rained down.

No more shots were fired from the second floor. The Nazi officer stood, straightening his uniform. He spat in the house's direction, then opened the passenger door of the jeep. He used his peaked cap to dust the glass off the seat. His head was shaved on the sides, the graying hair on top slicked back. He had fierce, menacing gray eyes. Kira stared at him, unable to break the hold.

The jeep sped off. Fear flowed freely through Kira's body, pulsating, but it didn't impede her like she thought it would. Her legs, which had been brittle, now felt like those of a Clydesdale. The world around her wasn't blurry, it was clear. She was propelled forward because that was what was needed. Her thoughts weren't a jumbled mess. There was only a singular, concise objective: get to papa.

Debris covered her backyard. Black smoke swarmed her, filling her mouth, staining her face. She coughed violently as she stepped inside. The staircase was half-destroyed. She climbed onto a heap of rubble to reach the still-connected stairs. The black smoke filled her lungs, feeling like two tar-stained hands were squeezing them and wringing them like a wet towel. In between her fits of coughing, she called out to her father.

She struggled forward, brass shell casings skidding along the floor when she inadvertently kicked them. Fire crackled then roared. Her eyes burned and filled with tears to lubricate and protect them. She pulled her shirt over her mouth to help combat the smoke. Searching and calling out for her father.

She found him pinned beneath the destroyed fireplace. Broken bricks scattered around him. His face was sweat-covered and stained black from the grime and smoke. The three-line was beside him, the box of ammo scattered about.

"Kira ..." he gasped. Blood trickled from the corners of his mouth. Even with his face stained, she could tell his normal coloring had faded.

Kira fell to her knees beside him and brushed the rubble off his chest. She wished she hadn't. A piece of broken copper pipe impaled the center of his stomach. No question, it had cut into major organs. Blood seeped out, circling the wound and expanding. His fingers curled from the pain, looking like dead spiders.

"Oh, Papa ..."

He reached for Kira's hand, calming his gasping breath to stockpile strength. Every word mattered, and he had no time to waste. He didn't know how many he had available to him. It was the moment all children dread. But her father wasn't old and on a hospital deathbed. He was in the middle of the kitchen where they had shared hundreds of meals. She'd lost her mother and now, she had mere moments left with her father. There was a strong desire to disappear into memories. Her heart begged her to take that reprieve. She was being stabbed from the inside out. Her breath vanished, her chest constricting further and further. Tears had filled her eyes before, but those had been to protect her from the smoke. These tears were from immense pain.

Her father stared into her eyes. As a young girl, he would lock his dark eyes on Kira's emerald green. No words were needed. One look, and Kira would stop whatever she was doing, fall silent in the middle of whatever argument she and her sisters had been having. His eyes had been how he communicated. How he showed he was angry, and how he showed just how much he loved her. He took Kira's hand and pressed it to his chest. Her fingertips felt his faint heartbeat.

"Your sisters ... you must ... find them ..."

Kira's eyes burned and reddened, feeling as if she was crying out battery acid, but she wouldn't break her gaze with her father. She squeezed his hand.

"I will, Papa. I swear it."

Moments before her mother had died, the room had taken on a different feeling. The air had changed; the temperature seemed to drop, an unexplainable faint breeze. Death hovered over her father, patiently waiting to claim another soul. There was no fear in her father's eyes. Death was neither a friend nor a foe to him. It was a long-lost acquaintance. One he saw nearly every day during his service in the Great War. One that had returned years later to claim his wife. Now, it had come to claim him. Seconds away now. Igor knew it. Kira knew it, too. His eyes showed only love. His hand reached for the rifle. Kira grabbed it for him. He secured her hands on it.

"Save … them …"

Igor Kovalyov had fought to deliver his last words, and now that he had finished them, his head sagged. What little life his eyes had ever shown was now gone.

Kira had been forced to ponder the profound pain of losing a parent at a young age, and that same pensive pondering came to her now. Her life would never be the same. She would never be the same. A parent is many things at several points in your life. Her father had always been like a warm blanket. He made her feel safe, supported, and protected. She glanced around at her home. Destroyed. Demolished. Dying. The few photographs they had were buried under hundreds of pounds of rubble. All save for the lone photo on the wall of Kira's family taken while her mother was still alive. The photograph was in flames. The fire consumed her beautiful mother first, and then her father. Her sisters were next. A pyro omen she couldn't let come to fruition. Grief had to wait. She summoned her courage and kissed her father's forehead, and then collected the spilled box of ammo. Mosin–Nagant rifle in hand, she descended the stairwell. Bits of small rubble cascaded down. The tears in her eyes were no longer from sadness, they were the byproduct of rage.

The integrity of the home was fatally compromised. Collapse was imminent. She looped the rifle's strap around her shoulder and grabbed a boning knife from the knife block in the kitchen. Under the cover of darkness, she crept through backyards and alleyways. She didn't know where Nousha and Lina were. Her only guess was the field hospital three kilometers outside the city. Her quickest, safest route was through the woods. German tanks, jeeps, and transport trucks congested the main streets. She stayed close to the tree line, hiding behind the thick tree trunks when headlights lit the caliginous forest. She ran, ignoring the tearing sensation in her side. The woods betrayed her, siding with the invading Germans as it thrusted its branches at her like spears, whipping her with flagrum-like pine boughs.

The field hospital consisted of dozens of white tents. A flagpole rose thirty feet; the red Soviet flag flapping in the wind smoldered. Patches of burning fabric eerily floated to the ground. Kira scouted the area, looking for German troops, but the smoldering rubble was evidence they had already come through. She stepped out, the rifle stock pressed to her shoulder. Aiming while moving, keeping the rifle in tune with her breathing, was second nature. But this was different. Though she had hunted bear and wolf, most of her hunts were on animals who retreated rather than fought. And she had never fired on a human being. That had always been the most paramount rule: never point the gun at another person.

She rounded the side of a long tent toward its entrance. She gasped. A literal mound of Soviet soldiers, tossed on top of each other, loomed ahead. The fire intended to burn their bodies had only charred them. The smell was putrid. Inside the tent, the white tarp walls were splattered red, as if Dracula had feasted. The soldiers, too injured to leave their beds, had been stabbed or beaten to death with rifles. The Germans had wasted no bullets for merciful deaths. The soldiers had been beaten so horrifically that their eyes dangled from their sockets from mucus-covered tendons. Bones broke through skin, heads were caved in, faces nothing but swollen sacks of meat. The Soviet doctors hadn't been spared. Their bodies were littered about, some lying dead in front of defenseless patients. They died as they lived—protecting.

She checked tent after tent. Each displayed the same horror. But there were no women amongst the dead. Even with it being so macabre, there was a desire to look around and take in the death around her, as if she needed to do so to believe it had happened.

Kira approached the pile of human bodies that stretched well over her head, staring into the burned, open, unseeing eyes of the dead. She forced herself to take slow, deep breaths to fight the onsetting panic. Her eyes would never have the same gleam they'd had. They would have some of that distant, matte dullness to them. Like her father's had had.

A hand reached out from the pile of dead, grabbing her ankle. Startling her too much for her to even scream. Only the arm was visible. The rest of the body was buried in the heap of corpses. After the initial shock subsided, Kira reacted and seized the hand and tugged. The mound collapsed, knocking Kira over. Legs and arms of the dead bludgeoned her.

The man who had grabbed her gasped for breath. How he was alive, she did not know. It defied logic. His body was completely burned. All his hair had singed off. The cartilage on his ears and nose had burned away. His uniform had fused into his flesh. Yellow puss bubbled across his body. Was he in immense pain or had his mind granted him mercy and cut off all pain receptors?

"Help … help …" he gasped, keeping his lips spread, not risking them touching. Even breathing caused him excruciating pain.

There was nothing she could do for him. To do anything to prolong his suffering would have been cruel. But there was something he could do for her. And though each word he spoke would cause him anguish, she had to ask.

"The nurses. Where did the Germans take them?"

The man gasped, his skin literally boiling. The tears falling from his eyes seared against his burning flesh.

"Please, they have my sisters."

The man hyperventilated, but she knew he was summoning what strength he had left to speak.

"Ba-ba-ba … ba-ball … roo … roo … room …"

He'd exhausted his ability to speak, but while no more words could leave his lips, his eyes continued to speak. Fear. Pain. Worry. Despair. The whites of his eyes were bloodshot. He was a monster brought to life from the pages of fiction. But he was aware of his monstrosity. He was a werewolf seeking the silver bullet. Kira could do nothing to help him but end it. End the tremendous pain and suffering.

"Close your eyes. Think of a happy moment. Picture what it looked like. Sounded like. Smelled like. Who is there? What are they doing?"

The man listened; his eyes closed. He didn't have the power to speak anymore. Kira stood and aimed the rifle at the man's heart. It was the first time she had ever pointed the gun at another human being. Not even by accident with an unloaded gun had she done so. Kira steadied her breathing by looking at the man's wounds. It would be far crueler to let him suffer another second than it would be to end it. There wasn't a single person in the existence of humankind who would have wanted to continue to suffer in such a hellacious way. And if God asked her why, she would tell Him she did what He did not. The shot rang out, ending the excruciating pain.

Unlike the Americans, the Soviet Union did not use dog tags. Instead, each soldier carried a small black Bakelite cylinder containing a rolled-up piece of paper listing the soldier's details. Kira found his in his left pocket. She opened it and read. His name was Barys Lukashevich. He was only twenty-two years old. She brought the name to memory and placed it in the cylinder and inside his pocket.

Kira stared at the pile of bodies, the horrible question playing on her mind. *Are any more of them alive?* She couldn't help them; she didn't have time. She had to find Anousha and Alina. How long would those still alive in the pile of semi-burned bodies have to wait to die? Wait for help? How long would their suffering last?

Ballroom. Kira knew the building. Weddings, birthdays, dances, concerts, and pageants occupied the ballroom nearly every weekend of the year. Kira clung to the shadows in her advance to it. The building was tan brick, four stories high. In the center of the building was a massive picture window stretching to the second and third stories. The large curtains covered the window, blocking any view of the inside. Music carried out whenever the entrance doors opened. Two German soldiers guarded the entrance. Across from the ballroom was a bell tower, and it offered Kira a better vantage point.

She crept toward its service door, her footsteps light. The deer she hunted were far more in tune with sounds than man could ever be. If animals didn't hear her approach, the German soldiers wouldn't, either. The door was locked. She pried the boning knife into the lock and wiggled it until the knob freed. She stepped inside and closed the door. Inside, it reeked of mildew and mold. Cobwebs hung everywhere. The old wooden floorboards creaked with each step. Would they hold? Kira ascended with caution. Once on the top, she crouched toward the ledge and peered down. The two German troops at the front entrance puffed on cigarettes. To the right of the building, a more diligent guard paced alongside, marching like he was in a parade. A half-track was parked alongside the jeeps, the lethal MG-42 mounted on it. A weapon capable of peppering out 1,200 rounds a minute. If the operator unloaded the weapon at Kira and the bell tower, it would require divine intervention to not get hit. The soldier on the western wall leaned against it, the sole of his foot resting on the brick. After ensuring none of the soldiers gazed up in her direction, she studied the windows. The white curtains revealed the veiled silhouettes of its occupants. She scanned the windows. There was no rhyme nor reason to those lit and those dark.

Then, the Nazi who'd ordered the tank to fire upon her father came into frame in one of the lit windows. His hat was off. His hair was disheveled, sweat dripping off his red face. He was the man responsible for her father's death.

She had no reservations about if she could make the shot. She could hit him a hundred times in a row. Nor was she hesitant about taking his life. He deserved to die. The hesitation came from if she should. Her sisters were inside. Shooting now would cause a panic. Would the Nazis kill the women before fleeing or fighting?

The Nazi in the window snapped a belt and bent forward, disappearing from view. The arched back of a woman filled the frame. The taut belt was wrapped around the woman's neck. Her face was out of frame. The horrible realization hit her. She was witnessing a rape. She couldn't fathom the terror the woman felt. As the Nazi raped her, he yanked the belt tighter and tighter. His face was a psychotic blend of pleasure and pain. Kira debated on shooting. But ultimately, she couldn't risk her sisters' lives. Kira was the only one who could save them. She wouldn't jeopardize them for a stranger. God could judge her for it.

Kira checked the five guards. No, make it six. A German barreled out through the entrance in a drunken stumble. His hand traced the brickwork like it was braille. He stopped and faced the wall to take a piss. The bell gears shifted, warning Kira it would ring. It would be the perfect way to drown out her gunshots. The first ring clanged painfully loud, the sound pulsating through her body, rattling her bones. She aimed at the soldier behind the MG-42 on the halftrack. He was the greatest threat. The shield in front of the gun covered his torso. His helmet protected his head. Her only shot was his forehead. If she missed large, there would be too little time to adjust. If she missed small, he would become aware and either take cover or fire the 1,200 rounds at his disposal. She closed her eyes for a moment to give them temporary rest. She snapped them open, steadying her sights on him. Taking in the stubble of his facial hair, the faint wrinkling on his forehead. The time was now. It had to be. She squeezed the trigger. The man's head snapped back, a mist of blood filling the air. She put the sights on the soldier lazily leaning against the western wall. He gazed at the halftrack. Had he seen something? But just as the realization struck that the soldier at the helm of the MG was dead, a bullet struck him in his forehead, wiping that thought and any future thoughts away. She scanned past the two guards at the entrance, past the soldier peeing on the wall. The pacing guard along the eastern wall was out of view, but if he kept the same pace he'd had, he'd come into view in three, two, one. His legs buckled when the bullet entered his head. The ringing bell approached its finale. The three kills would have to be quick. Whichever guard she shot first, the other would notice. It would take only a second for one to open the door and yell. Time and circumstance offered no mercy for a missed shot.

The guard to the left of the door leaned over to toss his cigarette. Kira took advantage of the milliseconds of reduced reaction time and shot the other guard. The smoke in his mouth escaped in a puff. The guard bending over turned to see what had happened. Another mist of blood sprayed into the air. The bell reached its outro. The drunken soldier's alcohol-induced marathon piss dribbled to its conclusion. He struggled to secure his belt, stumbling into the wall.

Kira reloaded the Mosin. The drunken soldier saw the bodies on the ground, shock trumping drunkenness. Kira chambered the round, aiming where he would be, not where he was. She fired. Had the soldier been sober, his brains would have decorated the brickwork. Instead, he had tripped, and the bullet missed, ricocheting off the brick wall. He used his hands to get to his feet, then fell again. The second shot hit the ground ahead of him, blasting bits of dirt and grass into his face.

The bell fell silent.

He lunged for the door, inhaling to power his scream. Before a single note made it out, a bullet eviscerated the back of his head. But where he had failed to scream, the Soviet women inside did not. The music stopped. Kira reloaded her rifle. She shot down the first two Germans who rushed outside to investigate. But more soldiers followed. Too many. They shouted, and to her horror, pointed up at the bell tower. Half of them fired up at her; the other half charged at the tower.

The tower door blasted open, clanging against the wall. The sound echoed up. The stairwell was dark. Shadows played tricks on where and how large her targets actually were. She narrowed her eyes, focusing until the shape of the soldier bounding up the steps cleared. She fired. The bullet thrusted him backward, knocking two soldiers over the edge of the stairwell. It wasn't a far enough fall to kill them, but was enough to break bones and knock them out.

From the height of the bell, it was over nine meters to the ground. If she jumped from here, her legs would shatter.

Think. Think!

Footsteps thundered up the stairs; blind shots cracked around her. One struck the bell with a *ping*. She had the advantage of elevation only. Even if she worked the bolt flawlessly, she had five shots. The soldiers storming up the stairs could unleash three or four times that amount in a fraction of the time. If she stayed here to fight, she would die. There had to be an alternative. Thinking, she eyed the ropes connected to the bell. She drew her knife and cut anything fashioned to the bell. The wooden support beams groaned, then collapsed. The bell fell, blasting through the floorboards. Rope coiled up like a snake. The bell crashed into the German soldiers, then let out a final ring on impact, drowning out the screams of the men it had crushed.

Kira grabbed the coiled pile of rope and secured an end to the belfry, then repelled down the red brickwork. At four meters, the knot gave way. Her ankle rolled on impact. She groaned, then got to her feet and limped forward, biting her lip from the pulsating pain. The Nazi officers inside fled to the jeeps, unaware they were under attack by a single entity. Instead, believing the Red Army had struck back. The Nazi officer responsible for killing her father gazed menacingly into the distance, steam rising from his sweat-covered forehead. Kira raised her rifle, but without the support of two feet, the weight was uneven. It made the weapon in her hand feel like an

57

untamed animal. She dropped to a kneeling position, putting her weight on her uninjured ankle. But by then, he was inside his jeep and speeding away.

The exodus ended. Kira limped ahead. She embraced the pain of putting weight on her right ankle, so she could move faster. She entered the ballroom and sidestepped the drunken soldier she had killed. Inside it reeked of sweat, smoke, and vodka. Boot marks scuffed the marble floor. Frenzied footsteps came from the mezzanine. Kira took aim. A gray-uniformed Nazi passed into view. The shot hit him in the throat. He smacked into the wall, then fell over the railing, crashing onto a table. Kira struggled up the steps, leaning against the railing for support. Her hands stayed poised and ready on her rifle.

Women in varying stages of undress dashed out of rooms. In their frenzy to escape, they nearly knocked Kira down the stairs. She steadied herself against the banister and waited until the rush ended. Kira stepped into the closest room. A blonde woman, nude, lay on the floor, knees curled into her stomach. Her hair covered her face. She'd been beaten and raped. She couldn't have been more than fourteen. Kira helped her to her feet. The girl stood hunched over, arms covering her beaten breasts, trembling. Kira yanked the drapes from the wall and covered the girl with them.

"You are safe now," Kira told her.

The girl lumbered out of the room and limped down the steps. Each room Kira entered told the same story, only the girl was different. Some were in shock. Others bawled.

Some were dead.

She made her way to the third floor. Her ankle had doubled in size, and had it not been for her boot, there may have been no limit to the swelling. She limped into a room. Two nude women sat against the wall, their heads drooped, blonde hair concealing their faces. Bite marks covered their breasts. Hickeys adorned their necks, along with markings of a belt. Their hands were intertwined. Each had a single gunshot to the heart.

Kira knew who they were. Her body knew. All its strength vanished. Her heart wanted to rip from her chest and leap out the window. She collapsed to her knees and crawled to them. She hugged them both. Their skin had turned cold—rigor mortis had set in. Kira's pain was visceral. They had embraced death and what follows it together. It had always been Nousha and Lina. Together. In life, and now in death. The initial shock prevented her from crying, but as it dulled, the tears fell like a monsoon.

"I'm so sorry! Forgive me! I'm so sorry!" she pleaded over and over, running her hands through their gnarled hair. There had been so many chances for Kira to run her fingers through it when it had been soft and brushed. She thought of their smiles, their laughs. She would never see or hear them again because she had been too late. Too overcome with trepidation to act. She'd pitied her ankle too much. That pain would last for days. This pain would never cease. Regret consumed her. She should have told them how much she loved them. She should have realized it before it was too late. The grief was suffocating. She couldn't breathe, only gasp.

As her reservoir of tears dried, she stared blankly out the window. A chilling realization dawned on her. This was the same room the Nazi officer who'd killed her father had been in. The woman she'd seen being raped had either been Nousha or Lina. Kira had witnessed their rape and hadn't acted. The cruel irony was that she thought if she had acted, she would have forsaken them to death. Instead, the inaction was what had killed them. She had promised her dying father she would save her sisters. How disappointed was he in her, gazing down from heaven, hugging his eldest and youngest daughters?

Kira didn't know how long she sat there holding them. Maybe she thought there was some invisible tug of war going on. She held them here on Earth while an angelic deity gently and effortlessly pulled them to heaven. Death is a concept impossible to grasp. Hours ago, Kira had been planning what to make for supper. Now, her whole family was gone. Why, instead of a sprained ankle, couldn't it have been a fatal wound? She'd have accepted the hellacious pain Barys Lukashevic had been in if she could only sit here and die with her sisters. But she couldn't. She was alive. Cursed with life.

She kissed their foreheads, whispering how much she loved them. When she rose to her feet, their lifeless bodies slid toward each other. Their hands were still entwined. She stepped out into the hall and searched the German dead for a lighter. She found one, silver with an engraving of a Nazi eagle holding a circular-enclosed swastika with the Armenian runes □□ beneath it. Kira limped back into the room, using her hand along the wall to steady herself. At the window, she grabbed a handful of the drawn curtains. She flicked the lighter and ran it along the curtains until they blazed.

The ballroom had been a place of halcyon memories. Joy. Laughter. Happiness. Emotions that should never take place on such hallowed grounds ever again. She didn't want anyone to see her sisters like this. Nude and beaten. She took one last look at them, declared her love for them and begged for forgiveness, then struggled down the steps. Outside, the ballroom burned behind her. Flames erupted through the windows, sounding like a dragon. The trek back into town took hours. The forest floor was unkind to injured travelers. The sun was rising when she made it back to her home. Home. The word no longer fit. It had been home because of the people in it. Now, they were gone. Now, it was just a house. If even that. The house was burned. The roof collapsed and an entire section of wall, gone. Homes would always be an untallied casualty of war. Some never understand that home is more than a physical entity. It is a psychological oasis.

Kira found her rucksack charred but intact. Her father lay where she had left him. Water from busted pipes pelted his face. Kira stashed her bag with crackers, cheese, and jerky. Meaningless items. All the photographs were destroyed or buried beneath the rubble. Without machinery, she could never lift and sift through it. The only family memento she could take with her was her father's rifle. She stashed the remaining ammo into her bag.

Kira set fire to the building that had once been her home. She wouldn't let her father lie there for God knew how long. Igor had often drunkenly demanded to Kira's mother that when he died, he should be burned. He had seen decomposition on the battlefields, the way rats feasted upon the flesh until it was too rancid for even them. At which point, the worms took over. She had failed her final promise to him, but she would see that her mother's promise to him was fulfilled.

Watching the house burn, memories of Kira's life in it played in the flames. Where should she go? What should she do? But as she adjusted the contents of her bag, fate provided an answer. A small piece of cardstock with a name and address. Kira reviewed it, then pocketed it. She slung the rifle over her shoulder and then left the place that had once been her home forever.

The Battle of Britain

Hitler delivered a directive to his air forces: prevent all air attacks against Germany; destroy British coastal defenses; engage the British Navy's ships; break the resistance of their land forces; and destroy British reserves away from the front. A herculean task. But one Germans believed achievable after their swift victory in France. Now, Hitler had set his gaze on the British isle. Reinhardt waited for the call to take to the skies. Nervous anticipation rooted in his stomach.

Reinhardt sat on the ladder resting against his plane, reading a novel. A group of pilots nearby played poker on a crate, wagering cigarettes, gum, and food rations.

"That is not worth a *Reichsmark!*" the one with a long-pointed nose and droopy ears said. His name was Walter.

"The hell it isn't!" a green-eyed blond named Günter said.

The other two, Klaus and Uwe, agreed with Walter.

"Of course you do," Günter accused, "you don't want me to win. Your opinion is biased."

"Majority rules, Günter."

"Bullshit, Walter." Günter looked around for another vote. His eyes found Reinhardt. "Friedel, come here, will you?"

Reinhardt, a page away from finishing a chapter, refrained from sighing. He slipped a Joker playing card into the book as a placeholder. He joined the others and gazed at the pot of loot.

"Friedel, here's what we have. I am adding to the pot this prestigious photograph of Avril Cartier for a price of one *Reichsmark*. Therefore, calling Walter's bet and raising it fifty *Reichspfenning.*"

"Who is Avril Cartier?" Reinhardt asked.

The other three laughed; Günter looked betrayed. "You uncultured barbarians! Avril Cartier is an upcoming actress. Soon to be seen in American cinema."

He pointed at the black and white photo. Reinhardt picked it up. A woman with porcelain skin puckered her lips at the camera. She was naked except for an open cardigan unbuttoned to her cleavage and so thin her nipples were visible through the sweater's snug fit. The woman was gorgeous, though the picture looked to be twenty years old. If she was going to make it as an actress in America, she'd better hurry. He turned the picture over. The name of a brothel was stamped onto it. Reinhardt bit his lip to hide his smirk. Günter studied him to see if he would out him, trying to fight his own smirk. Reinhardt handed the photo back to Günter, concealing the stamp with his fingers.

"She is a stunning woman. One who will only grow in beauty the longer I have to stare at only men. It's a bargain," Reinhardt said.

"You see?" Günter said. "Friedel is wise. He knows in a month's time you'll be craving this photo more than a ration of canned herring."

Walter wasn't sold on it as much as he was impatient to get on with it. Klaus and Uwe folded. Walter matched the bet then turned his cards over. Full house. Günter tossed his five cards down one at a time, concluding in four of a kind.

"Bullshit!" Walter shouted. He shot up from his box and stormed away.

Günter called his name. "Keep your canned herring. I'm sure it will look quite attractive in a couple of weeks."

He tossed the can. Walter caught it and pitched it back at him, smacking the wooden crate and leaving a dent. They laughed. Klaus and Uwe returned to their field camp while Günter gathered his winnings. Reinhardt gathered the playing cards.

"Thanks for the help," Günter said.

"Got the picture from a brothel in Berlin, huh?" Reinhardt asked, handing the deck to him.

Günter laughed. "No, my oldest brother took it from a bathroom at a brothel in Berlin. I took it from him."

Günter Mueller hailed from Wolfsburg. He had arrived a week earlier than Reinhardt, enough time that he knew the ins and outs and the order of things. He loved to shuffle cards. Never dealing, just shuffling. Some of the other pilots found his habit annoying, but it didn't bother Reinhardt. The sound was its own music.

"You have a girl back home waiting for you?" Günter asked.

Reinhardt shook his head, then nodded to ask the same. Günter smiled and dug into his pocket for a wallet-sized photo. In it, Günter stood behind a blonde woman, his hands wrapped around her waist. She had an immaculate smile, and she gazed at Günter in a way Reinhardt longed to be looked at. That complete and utter devotion. Günter reciprocated the look. There were no other men in the world for her and no other women in the world for him. They had found each other. A tinge of jealousy spread in Reinhardt.

"She loves you," Reinhardt said, handing the photo back.

Günter told Reinhardt that they had started dating when they were fourteen. Klara was the only woman he had ever been with and the only one he wanted to be with. He'd married her a month before he left for basic training.

"No photo like the upcoming actress Avril Cartier?"

Günter laughed. "No, if I get killed and some *Froschfresser* searches my body and finds a naked photo of Klara, she'll kill me again."

Günter's picture stayed on Reinhardt's mind as he tried to sleep that night. Not Klara herself, but the idea of Klara. Ingrid, Maureen, and the others had been good company. But their relationship to him was akin to two passing ships. A temporary stop before they both had to continue on their own way.

Günter looked at his picture every night before he fell asleep. War had a way of reducing time. He had yet to fight in a battle, but time no longer seemed endless. War offers perspective. Should Reinhardt have tried to love Ingrid? He liked her. She was good-looking, sassy at times. But love isn't something to be forced. And was it arrogant for him to assume she loved him? Yes, it was. Reinhardt didn't even have a fake photo that he could come up with some elaborate backstory for like Günter had with his photograph of a prostitute from twenty years ago. His someone was still out there somewhere. The who and when and where were all unknown entities, but the biggest question was would he have *time* to find her? The introspection led to a shit night's sleep. So much so, Reinhardt rose to watch the sun rise off the coast of France. The date was 10 July. The German High Command had issued the order to attack British supply convoys in the English Channel. Reinhardt Friedel was going to war. That anxiousness vanished, replaced by a lethal mixture of worry, excitement, and fear, and it fueled his body like gasoline.

Günter and Reinhardt paused at their planes and shook hands.

"Are you sure you don't want me to hold onto that picture of your wife?" Reinhardt asked.

Günter smirked. "If you see me shot down, come save the picture."

Their joking manner went serious, and they wished each other good luck. It seemed an odd phrase. Something said before a football match, not something with life-or-death consequences. They climbed into their cockpits and closed the canopies. Reinhardt brought his plane to life. The 1,100-horsepower engine grumbled in response. The three propellers clicked then spun. Reinhardt—along with 120 bombers and fighters—took to the sky, the group looking like a murder of crows fleeing a field. The earth faded below, replaced by a carpet of blue. The sky shook as if thunder crackled. The British were not defenseless. 1,500 barrage balloons—large, unscrewed, tethered balloons that looked like the famed *Hindenburg*—presented crash risks. 2,000 anti-aircraft guns dotted the shore, peppering the sky in black flak. British Hurricanes and Spitfires rose to meet them. The Spitfire was faster than its German Messerschmitt counterpart at altitudes above 15,000 feet, so while the slower Hurricanes went for the German bombers, the Spitfires engaged the fighters. Reinhardt's responsibility was to protect his bombers, and how he did that was by preoccupying Britain's air defenses.

In other words, by being a sacrificial lamb.

His heart raced and his breathing was shallow, but his hands stayed steady. The plane dipped left, then right, and back left. Spinning, twirling to avoid the Spitfires.

Even though the Battle of Britain had just begun, there was a feeling of finality in the air. The military of France, which had staved off defeat in the Great War for four years, had been defeated earlier in mere weeks. The Soviet Union had agreed to a pact of non-aggression. The United States had no interest in another "European War." England was the last enemy. If Germany defeated them, the war could be over. Of course, there had been casualties, and God bless every last man, woman, and child who had died, but if the war ended now, the casualty numbers would be a fraction of what they had been during the Great War. They would have rectified the unfair restrictions and repercussions of the Treaty of Versailles. They would have regained their honor. Germany would no longer be a laughing stock. They were a proud country, filled with history and tradition, who demanded and deserved respect. And they had earned it. And Reinhardt's promise to Mathias would be fulfilled.

Reinhardt locked in on a Spitfire plunging after a German dive bomber. He yanked the throttle, securing his grip as it shook violently. His face vibrated from the torque. The Spitfire weaved. Reinhardt studied its movement, gathering enough data to anticipate. Weave left. Right. Right. Left. Right. Left. Left. And Right. He fired his machine gun. Bullets punctured the Spitfire's left wing, so many that it splintered off. Black smoke billowed out. The Spitfire spun wildly, freefalling toward the choppy Channel, smacking into it, and blasting up a wave of water. The pilot struggled to free himself before the plane sank. It passed out of Reinhardt's line of vision. Bullets zipped past his canopy. Reinhardt dipped his head. He pulled on the yoke. The plane responded, rising higher and higher. The Spitfire behind him rose with him, firing. Reinhardt jerked the yoke forward. The plane speared toward the ground. The shrill and rumble of the engine signaled the plane had reached its limits. Reinhardt yanked up before he crashed into the water. The force of the plane lifted the water around it. One false move, one weave too great, and he would clip his wing, and he'd skip along the water like a smooth stone until he sunk.

A fellow Messerschmitt Bf 109 sped toward them and fired at the Spitfire chasing Reinhardt, shredding the pilot with bullets and broken glass. The Spitfire crashed into the Channel.

Reinhardt breathed a sigh of relief. He had run out of maneuvers.

With the bombers having dropped their loads, the attack was over. Messerschmitt pilots banked on the unofficial rule of half an hour of engagement. Any longer and the pilot risked running out of fuel over the Channel. Reinhardt and the *Luftwaffe* returned to the coast of France, and the wounded but skilled Spitfires returned to England.

Reinhardt landed his Messerschmitt on base and opened his canopy, breathing in the fresh air. His nerves were electric. It wasn't solely nervousness radiating through his body but also unadulterated adrenaline. An ultimate high stakes chess match. But it wasn't only your opponent across from you who could take your king; the threat came from all directions. They had been the most terrifying moments of his life, but he couldn't lie and say they weren't also the most thrilling. He'd never felt more alive than when he thought he might die.

Günter removed his flying helmet, smirking in a way that told Reinhardt he had experienced the same emotions. They clasped hands and spent the better part of thirty minutes detailing the sortie. The high faded slowly. Reinhardt had loved flying since the first time Mathias's father had taken them up. It provided a freeing feeling he'd never before experienced. Like being a bird coasting peacefully in the sky. But aerial combat proved to be a next-level drug. One you couldn't do recreationally. He'd sampled it, and now it would be a lifelong addiction. Up there, he hadn't been a dove sailing across the sky, he'd been a bird of prey. Want became desire, desire became necessity. Reinhardt Friedel needed to get back up into the air.

Sniper School

The train ride to Moscow felt like an eternity, like the ferry ride from this world to the next in the Greek myths Gerasim had told her. And as she pondered, it was. The Kira she'd been was dead. The one she was to be hadn't come. Throughout a person's life, there were moments before and moments after. There was before her mother's death, and there was after. And now, there was before her father and sisters' deaths, and there was after. She entered a nascent stage with no knowledge of how she would survive it. The Germans had ripped open her chest, torn her heart out, and stomped over it with the boots of 100,000 men. Everything hurt. It hurt to breathe, hurt to look. Even the sun caused her pain, shining brightly and trying to remind her of happier times. Questioning how she could be sad when it shone so brightly. She didn't want to be reminded. She wanted only darkness and to do nothing but sleep. Sleep was the only reprieve from the pain.

When Kira arrived, there was no time for sightseeing. She had no interest in it, anyway. She had no interest in anything except finding the man responsible for destroying her life, her world. She walked to the nearest recruitment center. Her ankle had gone back to its normal size, but now when she moved her foot, it popped and cracked. Once inside, an officer with an amputated right arm glanced at Kira, then grabbed a file.

"Nurses are in a different line," he said.

"I'm not here to be a nurse. I'm here to fight," Kira said.

The man stared at her. He wasn't laughing, but he wasn't amused with her, either. Kira could feel heat surging to her forehead and ears. She was not in the mood. She thrust the card Colonel Volkov had given her.

"Read it. I was told to speak with Colonel Volkov."

He looked at the number, then at her, then frowned for the extra work she had caused. He picked up the phone and dialed. When the operator connected the call, he introduced himself to the colonel.

"Comrade Colonel, I'm sorry to interrupt your day, but I have—" he covered the phone and looked to Kira for her name. She gave it. "Kira Kovalyova."

He'd expected to have to describe Kira or press her for more information, or worse, be laughed at for wasting the colonel's time. The call ended abruptly. Had Colonel Volkov not remembered her? Had he changed his mind? The Soviets had turned women away from combat roles as recently as the summer of 1941.

The recruiter slapped a file onto the table. "Fill this out," he ordered.

Kira grabbed the pen and filled in the information. Name. Birthdate. Home address. The address gave her pause. She had no home. It had been taken from her. She wrote 'destroyed by the enemy' in the address field. After it was completed, the recruiter reviewed it. He paused when he read her address. He looked up, and for the first time since their brief interaction, his eyes showed compassion. He approved the file and then swore Kira in.

"I, a citizen of the Union of Soviet Socialist Republics, entering the ranks of the Workers' and Peasants' Red Army, solemnly swear to be an honest, brave, disciplined, and vigilant soldier, and strictly preserve military and state secrets."

"Welcome to the Red Army, Comrade Kovalyova," he said.

When she stepped outside, an army green GAZ-M1, known more simply as *Emka*, waited for her. She sat in the back. The driver stayed silent on the minutes-only drive before he pulled to a stop. The driver stepped out and opened her door. Kira only knew where to go because the guard standing in front of a red door opened it for her. He, too, was silent. Inside, a woman sorted through documents. She was petite with blonde hair, no older than Kira, with grandmotherly kind pale blue eyes. She introduced herself as Veronika Kalashinka and asked if she could help Kira.

Kira stated her name.

Luckily for Kira, Veronika's eyes lit up with recognition. "Yes, you are here to see Colonel Volkov."

Kira confirmed with a nod. Veronika told her it would be a few minutes. She was overly kind, offering Kira tea, coffee, or water. Kira refused even though she was thirsty, but before she settled on changing her mind, the office door behind Veronika's desk opened.

Colonel Volkov dipped his head respectfully. "Comrade Kovalyova, I will see you now."

Veronika smiled encouragingly as Kira walked past and stepped into his office. She slid the rucksack and rifle from her shoulders to the floor.

"Please, be seated," Colonel Volkov said, gesturing to the chair in front of his desk.

Kira sat, sighing from the relief. It was the most comfortable she'd been since sleeping in her own bed days ago. Sitting reminded her how exhausted she was. The ashtray on his desk was filled with smoldering cigarette butts, giving the room an overwhelming smell of smoke. Colonel Volkov was silent as his eyes scanned her over. Kira hated the silence. Was what happened playing in her eyes for him to watch?

"I have come to fight," Kira said, breaking that uncomfortable silence.

But Colonel Volkov continued to ignore her, taking puffs of a fresh cigarette, giving the appearance of someone enjoying a sunset. After a long drag, he put the cigarette in the ashtray, leaned back in his chair, and crossed his fingers. "Something has happened to you."

Kira didn't meet his eyes and diverted hers to the floor. She bit her lip in a futile attempt to stop emotion from overwhelming her. Colonel Volkov rose from his seat, rounded his desk, and leaned against it. He locked his gray-blue eyes on Kira. She could feel the weight of that stare. Emotion was deemed a womanly response. If she wanted to fight, she would have to start by fighting those preconceived notions of what a female was and their supposed weakness.

"When I saw you at that factory, you burned so fiercely, I thought you might shoot that prick. But now ... you're still fierce, but there's something else there," the colonel said.

She lifted her head and pierced him with her gaze. "The Germans destroyed my home ... they killed my father ... they raped and murdered my sisters ..."

She had tried to be as stoic as she could, but she failed. Emotion curdled the words in her throat. She bent her foot to put pressure on her still-injured ankle so that pain would trump emotion. She deserved this pain for failing her sisters.

"I am saddened to hear of your loss," Colonel Volkov said. "Every day, thousands of Soviets experience the pain you now feel. Thousands more will experience it tomorrow. A thousand more the day after. I know revenge powers you. The Soviet Union certainly needs quantity. But what I want from you is quality. If what you want is to kill a German or two that is certainly possible. But I'm looking for someone to kill as many men as a plague. Someone to truly alter the war." He paused, bringing back that piercing gaze at Kira. "So, tell me, Comrade Kovalyova, have you come to fight, or have you come to die?"

Kira thought about his words. She had two thoughts after her sisters had been killed: *I want to die*, and *I want to kill every single fascist*. Those were the dominant thoughts since. Like two sides of a coin flipping through the air. So, the answer had been both. If she died, more Germans would live. She'd seen how evil they were, the unfathomable horror they were capable of. They did not deserve to live. She had failed her sisters, dishonored their dying father's last command. There was no changing that. But she could help prevent the deaths of further Noushas and Linas from ever happening.

"I want to kill fascists," Kira said.

Colonel Volkov grabbed a cigarette from the ashtray, not caring it wasn't the one he had been smoking. "If you fight, there will be more death. You understand this, yes?"

Yes, there would be more death. She would see to it.

"I serve the Soviet Union," Kira said.

Colonel Volkov put a fatherly hand on Kira's shoulder. "Let's get you situated."

He drove Kira to the barracks. He wished her luck and told her after her orientation was complete that she would be transferred over to sniper school. A uniform, sewn from khaki cotton, a forage cap, a tunic with a turn-down collar, trousers resembling riding breeches, Kirza artificial leather boots, a belt with a brass knuckle, and a SSh-40 helmet were issued to her. Classes filled the following day, allowing another day's rest and recovery for her ankle. The day after, she took and passed her physical test. She had spent her free time hiking for miles and dragging harvested animals from the woods. The only worry she'd had was if her ankle would hold up.

Colonel Volkov introduced himself to the twenty recruits of hopeful snipers. Kira was one of four women. The sixteen men had a silent swagger about them, an indifference exuding off them. Pilots were notorious for their supreme confidence. These men and women did nothing to distinguish themselves. It was Kira's first understanding of what made a great sniper. Snipers would never be those who walked into a room and were the center of attention. Great snipers were those who walked into a crowded room, and no one noticed. Chameleons.

Joining Colonel Volkov was Lieutenant Ruslan Orlov, a man six feet tall with large hands and gangly arms. He was far older than Colonel Volkov. Decades past fighting age. Lieutenant Orlov had been training soldiers to use the Mosin–Nagant since 1916. While some preferred the SVT-40, Orlov was a staunch believer in the tried-and-true three-line. Kira's father had sung the praises of the three-line, and it was the only gun Kira knew.

Lieutenant Orlov paced back and forth among the line of snipers, his hands crossed behind his back. "A sniper is no common soldier. A sniper is the most lethal predator in the history of the world. It camouflages into its environment. It studies its opponent. A sniper is lethal. The only difference between you and a tiger is that killing does not satiate your hunger. There will be no satiation. The hunger to eliminate the fascist enemy will never subside."

Orlov stepped in front of the largest of the new recruits. Private Pavlichenko, a stocky, barrel-chested man of thirty. Orlov handed a spade to him.

"Start digging," Orlov ordered.

Pavilchenko knew better than to question the command and stabbed the spade into the dirt.

Orlov addressed the group. "You are positioned 150 meters from an enemy soldier digging a trench. When do you shoot this man?"

"When he is alone?" a red-headed girl named Anna Alekseeva said.

"Wrong. He is part of an army. He will not be alone."

"When he is facing you, to insure it is a kill shot," the shortest of the men, Dobrow, said.

"Wrong. Why do you care if you provide a quick death? Let him cry out in pain. Others will come to help. Then you shoot them, too."

Kira studied Pavlichenko, his movement as he shoveled and dug the hole. The way his body torqued when he unloaded the dirt.

"You do not shoot him when he is facing you. You shoot him while he is turned away from the hole," Kira said.

Orlov looked to see who had spoken. He stepped toward Kira, his nose nearly touching hers. "Why?"

"Because if you shoot him while he faces the hole, he will drop the shovel in the hole. Shoot him while he is turned, the shovel falls to the ground. The next man up will bend down to pick it up. An easy shot."

Orlov nodded, a gleam of pride in his eyes. He wouldn't give her a full smile, but there was definitely a smirk. "Right you are, Comrade."

He told Pavlichenko to stop digging, then addressed the group. "Be cunning. Think ahead. Plan ahead. A sniper never reacts. He predicts."

Kira had thought the course would be exclusive to shooting. But learning to be a true sniper involved a level of detail she hadn't fathomed. There were twenty hours of politics classes, fourteen hours of parade ground drill, 220 hours of firearm training, sixty hours of tactics, thirty hours of military engineering, twenty hours of hand-to-hand combat, ten hours studying the Mosin–Nagant mechanism, and twenty-five hours devoted to the essentials of shooting. And then there was the need to achieve mastery knowledge in the laws of ballistics. Understanding the 'mil' in distance estimation, how to calculate range quickly according to angles by using a special formula and the reticles of PE telescopes, binoculars, and periscopes; determining how far a rapidly rotating bullet would drift laterally during its travel from muzzle to target, and the table of excessive deviations from average trajectories when firing cartridges with bullets ranging from light to heavy. It was not enough to know your weapon, part by part, but rather you needed to understand how the world around you impacted your shot.

The sniper rifle itself differed from Kira's father's rifle. It had an *Emelyanov* (PE) telescope mounted to the barrel. The scope prevented the rifle from being charger loaded, meaning each cartridge had to be entered one at a time. The sniper rifle handle of the bolt stem bent sharply downward so that the bolt was operable. There were also differences not seen by the human eye. The barrels for sniper rifles were made with the best steel, processed on precision lathes for greater accuracy—a task her father would have taken great pride in doing and would have thrived with. Colonel Volkov had known how special her father's rifle was to her, so with her permission, Colonel Volkov had it adjusted to the sniper specifications.

Orlov critiqued shooting motions, stating each one should last no more than eight seconds. Hold your breath. Take aim. Breathe out as you exert smooth pressure on the trigger. Shooting at moving objects was a skill every hunter must acquire. A shooter needs to calculate the time and distance where the bullet and the target will meet. This was termed the 'deflection of shooting.' Kira had been doing it her whole life, she just hadn't known the term for it.

Orlov continually shouted, "It's the barrel that fires, but the gunstock that hits!"

It meant much depended on the position a marksman adopted when holding the rifle. Though there were calculations to determine exact distances, an easy rule of thumb was that if the broad part of the horizontal crosshairs of the sight covered the target up to its knees, the range was 250 meters; up to the waist, 400 meters; and if the complete figure was visible, it was 750 meters away. One question on an exam proposed German machine gunners were in an armored transport six and a half feet above ground. You, the sniper, were in a trench with your rifle resting at 17.15 centimeters. 'What is the target angle?' was asked. Kira calculated the angle using the aiming line and the weapon horizon. The answer was thirty-five degrees. But Orlov threw a caveat. The transport vehicle was moving—currently 200 meters away. 'From the time the bullet fires, how far has the transport vehicle advanced?' At that distance, it'd take the bullet .25 seconds to hit the target. This equated to the vehicle traveling approximately four meters. And, ultimately, through this multistep question, she determined, using the concept of milliradians, that she had to adjust the windage drum of her rifle several units. With all those calculations, you'd expect they were trying to send something into outer space.

To Kira, shooting had always been instinct. A feeling in the air of when to shoot and when to pass. But through the course, she learned a sniper should know the result of the shot before he or she even fired it. It was all calculated. They were predators. They were tigers that knew a deer would travel at a certain speed, when it would change direction and how often. The tiger knew when it needed to take off and how fast it needed to run. It knew even as it stalked in the tall grass. There was no outcome other than its teeth tearing into its prey's throat.

But it wasn't all calculations and target shooting. After lunch, the recruits competed in a game called bottle base. An empty bottle was set on its side in a cleft stick. The neck of the bottle was pointed at the shooter some twenty to thirty meters away. To win, the shooter needed to shoot out the bottom of the bottle without damaging the sides. It was something they all considered impossible until Lieutenant Orlov succeeded. After knowing it was in the realm of possibility, each recruit attempted the feat. They scoured garbage cans for empty bottles after having destroyed their stock. Everybody failed and failed continually, but it was Kira who first completed the Artemis-type shot.

They learned about sniper hideouts and their variances: open, closed, base, reserve, and decoy. During the day on Tuesdays and Thursdays, Lieutenant Orlov sent them in groups to various construction sites around the city. For ten hours, they observed from a distance. Watching, learning, listening, scouting. How many people were at the site? Where did people enter and exit, and at what times? How much work was completed? Where were the windows and doors? If the foreman was the target, when was the most opportune moment to eliminate him?

This task proved to be anguish for Sidorov, Smirnoff, and Belyaev, the three recruits teamed with Kira. But to Kira it was a task she had perfected working at the munitions factory. The ability to let time slip by as you remained still. Ignoring your body's subtle hints of hunger and thirst and needing to go to the bathroom. Then overcoming them when they weren't subtle hints but what felt like resounding kicks and punches. When they returned to class the following day, Orlov surprised them with a quiz. Each recruit had to detail what they had observed the previous day. Kira wrote, disappearing into her mind as it replayed at fast-forward speeds those ten hours of observation. First, she sketched the layout of the building. Six unfinished stories. Seven windows on each floor. The first three floors had the glass block windows put in. She listed numbers and times. Sixteen workers plus the foreman. They had taken lunch at 11:45, with official smoke breaks every eighty-six to ninety-two minutes. One of the workers, a short, pudgy, and unmotivated man, had snuck extra smoke breaks. The foreman reviewed blueprints at a table away from the others. On and on she wrote, unloading all the data she'd stored.

Lieutenant Orlov read each of them out loud, adding to the nervousness of being graded by your peers. Private Gorkey, who was the unofficial runt of the twenty, had unofficially ended his chance at passing the final test. His shooting had been fair, but snipers only kept the element of surprise by shooting once. Follow-up shots could be pinpointed. It was no small feat to hit a target at 500 meters, but needing two or three shots threatened a sniper's objectives. Gorkey added to his mediocre shooting with a poor essay containing vague words like 'roughly,' 'approximately,' and 'either'/'or.'

"This is useless information," Orlov criticized. "Imagine if I told a general the enemy was maybe advancing with a force of either 2,000 men or 20,000 men. It changes things, does it not?"

Other recaps were overly brief. Stats. The number of men. What they did. But Kira's read like a book. Far longer than any of the others. She didn't just list the number of men; she had given physical descriptions of them. It was as if she had written a novel and introduced characters and established the setting.

"Excellent, Comrade Kovalyova," Orlov praised. "With this, you have detailed patterns, habits, mannerisms. These are all tools for the sniper. A sniper does not guess. He anticipates. The sniper fires the bullet, but the wind carries."

The test on course content took sixteen hours. There were four areas of testing: practical shooting, firearms mechanics, tactical training, and military engineering training. Sniping had proven to be the perfect blend of natural skill and passion. But Kira felt the overwhelming weight of responsibility. What she'd let happen to Nousha and Lina could not happen to other Soviet women. Guilt and vengeance fueled her. The other nineteen recruits were talented and worked hard, but Kira had more talent and worked harder. She was obsessed. She scored excellent in all four categories, garnering her recognition in city and district enlistment offices. Her certificate of completion was printed in black letters on coated paper and adorned with a round seal crest that included the subjects and her grades in them. Of the twenty in the class, nine passed. Private Gorkey was not among them. Tall and broad Pavlichenko and red-headed fellow-female Alekseeva were.

The nine gathered for the final words around a fire barrel. The night was dark, the air brisk but comfortable. The smell of burning wood clung to their clothes. It made Kira long for bonfires.

"Congratulations, Comrades," Orlov said. "I have but one final lesson to teach. It is one you must not forget." He let the gravity of his words sink in. "Snipers are not taken prisoner. The enemy will show you no mercy. If caught, you will be tortured. You women will be savagely raped. You will beg for death."

Orlov lifted a frag grenade. Though it looked like a pineapple, it was nicknamed the *limonka* (lemon).

"Roll the grenade under the feet of the approaching enemy." He drew his sidearm, a TT-30 nicknamed Tokarev. "The Tokarev contains eight rounds. Seven for the enemy. The eighth and final for yourself."

Lieutenant Orlov stared into the eyes of all nine recruits, ingraining the weight of his words into their memories. Kira disappeared into the memory of Nousha and Lina's death. Placing herself in their position. Would they have shot themselves if the Tokarev had been available to them? Would they have embraced death as they were sadistically raped, the constricting leather belt around their throats getting tighter and tighter? She had to believe the answer was yes. Rape was something that all women had thought of, but none could fathom until it happened to them.

Would she follow Lieutenant Orlov's advice if that German who had raped her sisters was in front of her? If there was only one bullet, who would she shoot?

Him. She would kill him and forsake herself to a horrible death.

Orlov wished them luck. New students would come, and Kira and the others would be just names on a list. Orlov had given them the tools to succeed, and the zealous belief that a shot was preordained to hit or miss before it was even fired. It wasn't just the class that was ending; it was the diversion it provided. Now, instead of spending her evenings calculating target angles, studying milliradians, and target shooting, horrible memories replayed cruelly on loop. Idleness was hell. She had to keep her brain busy, overwhelmed even.

1942 marked the third year since the war had started with the German invasion of Poland. The war on the Eastern Front was only six months old, but there had been few victories for the Soviet Union. Germany had punched the USSR in the face and, by the time it raised its hands to cover, Germany went for the ribs. 1942 needed to be the year the Soviet Union stopped the Germans' advance because if they did not, there would be no 1943 for the Soviet Union.

Pavlichenko was sent to fight in the Battle of Moscow. Two others of the nine had also been sent. But Kira saw no war. Her days were spent putting on shooting exhibitions for injured men. Pavlichenko was a formidable sniper, but Kira had scored better. Why had he been sent to fight while she wasted away? Was it because he was a man and she a woman? The weeks of inactivity were mentally grueling. Every night when she lay down to sleep, the German who had killed her family hijacked her dreams. The same memory of his pained yet pleasured face framed by the window. She'd studied *Schutzstaffel* and *Wehrmacht* ranks, gaining a detailed knowledge of what the insignia on their uniforms signified. The □□Armenian runes and three silver pips gorget patches had been on his. A *Hauptsturmführer*.

After weeks of being little more than a show pony, Kira asked for an audience with Colonel Volkov. She hadn't signed up, stayed up studying and practicing to become the top sniper in her class, to play bottle base for wounded soldiers. They could put on music to entertain the troops. The young and beautiful Veronika greeted Kira. Minutes passed until his door opened.

"Comrade Kovalyova, how may I be of service?" he asked.

"With all due respect, Comrade Colonel, I signed up to fight, not entertain men. I was top of my class. There were only nine who passed. Three women. The men have been sent to fight. Send me to kill fascists or I'll go myself."

The Battle of Moscow had been a Soviet victory, aided by a fortuitous early winter and a fortunate German decision. Snow had fallen in October, frozen, then melted, leaving a phenomenon known as *rasputitsa* (meaning a time without roads). German tanks and vehicles had a hell of a time traversing through it. Hitler had redirected his center forces from Moscow to the Ukraine in the south and Leningrad in the north. His decision was not unanimously agreed upon by Germany's generals. Many thought capturing the Russian capital would give an invaluable psychological advantage. But this wasn't to diminish the tenacious fighting of Soviet soldiers. Fighting Kira should have been a part of.

"Take it from an old man who has seen war. Enjoy these moments," Colonel Volkov said. "This war is far from over. Germany sets its eyes on conquering the entire Soviet Union. They push east toward Stalingrad and south toward the Caucasus."

Kira pushed through, ignoring those supposed wise words. "I keep replaying the day my father and sisters were killed. Thinking of the man who killed them. The look of enjoyment, of pleasure, on his face." She paused. *"Im Deutschen gibt es für solche Leute ein Wort. Schadenfreude."*

Colonel Volkov looked both uneasy and intrigued. "You speak German?"

"My mother taught me through reading. The man who raped and murdered my sisters took joy in what he did. One word has kept coming to me when I think back to that moment. *Schadenfreude.* Do you know what it means?"

Colonel Volkov shook his head, gazing intently at Kira.

"It is the German word to describe a person who takes joy in watching the pain of others. Hitler. Göring. Goebbels. Himmler. Heydrich. The *Hauptsturmführer* who killed my father, raped and murdered my sisters. They are all *Schadenfreudes.* They deserve to be killed. They need to be killed. Send me. Let me."

Colonel Volkov studied the resolve in her face and the pain underlying it.

"I must apologize, Kira," he said softly. "When I gaze upon you and contemplate sending you to war, I think of sending my own daughter. That is my shortcoming. You are a fine soldier, and I need to do better to treat you as such."

"You have treated me like a gentleman."

She wasn't naïve. He could have tried to force himself on her. Used his rank, threatened her with a court martial. But he hadn't.

Colonel Volkov dismissed the flattery. "I do not need to tell you how important Stalingrad is. The fighting will be street by street, building by building. Perfect warfare for a sniper."

"I serve the Soviet Union."

"Are you religious, Kira?"

Kira told him that in the traditional sense, no, she was not.

"You have brought a scripture to my mind. The Book of Isaiah. Chapter Six. Verse 8. *I heard the voice of the Lord, saying, Whom shall I send, and who will go for us? Then said I, Here am I; send me.*"

Kira focused her piercing stare on the colonel. "Here am I; send me."

Experten

The Reich gave orders to target London. If England was a body, then its capital city was its heart. The brave but outnumbered British Royal Air Force was its ribcage. The *Luftwaffe* bombed day and night, but with Britain's superior radar, they were seldom surprised.

Reinhardt spent the time between sorties reading and getting to know Günter and the others. He left poker to them, only weighing in on what certain objects were worth. They accused Reinhardt of being a shady pawn dealer more than once. He wrote to Mathias and relished reading the letters Mathias sent him. But often he couldn't sleep at night. He thought of how he had spent his time chasing lust and not love. He wasn't ready to call it a mistake yet, but he couldn't stop crippling doubt from spreading that he may never get the chance to entwine his soul with another.

Chasing sleep hadn't wiped those thoughts from Reinhardt's mind, but news that he would fly his first night mission did. He knew it would be different. He planned for it as much as he could. But in some ways, it was like studying how freezing the Atlantic would be in the heart of winter. He could read what the temperature was, what the frigid waters would do to his body. But it wouldn't prepare him for the shock of it once he dove in.

He and Günter shook hands and then climbed aboard their Bf 109s. The planes lifted off, crossing over the black water. Fear was always present, but at night, it was much more prevalent. At first, it was flying into blackness that caused it. Reinhardt squeezed his eyes, trying to better his vision. Night is not black, it's varying shades of blue, and as his eyes adjusted, he could make out shapes. The English coast lay ahead. Dots filled the night sky, looking like a cloud of mayflies. Growing larger. RAF Spitfires and Hurricanes soared to meet them. The German planes diverted, drawing the attention away from their bombers. Machine-gun fire pelted the night. Some planes used tracer rounds, igniting in greens, reds, oranges, yellows, and whites, making the scene look like the most dangerous firework show ever. It would have been beautiful if it hadn't been so terrifying. The bomber ahead of Reinhardt burst into flame, hit by machine-gun fire. A Hurricane crossed ahead. He squeezed the trigger, shooting to gauge how close he was to hitting the plane. The last couple of rounds strafed the Hurricane's right wing. He jerked his joystick left, then fired again. Pelting the plane from right wing to left wing. No smoke billowed out, none that Reinhardt could see at least. Had he missed? The Hurricane continued ahead but lost altitude. The pilot had been shot and killed. The plane dipped, the engine making a final rumble before it crashed into the inky blackness. Reinhardt followed one of his bombers toward London. Bomb after bomb whistled to the ground, then exploded in flashes of firelight. The city was under a 'blackout' policy. No lights were on, not even lamps in homes. They wouldn't give the Germans any beacons to bomb. Reinhardt didn't think about what the bombs did to the city below. What and who they hit. Who they hurt and killed.

His half-hour window was nearly up, meaning Reinhardt had to return now or risk running out of fuel. A flash of light exploded feet in front of his cockpit. Anti-aircraft artillery. Even a half second later and the flak would have destroyed the front of his plane and sent him spiraling into the Channel. His body tingled from the explosion that had rocked his plane. He rose higher, increasing his speed as he raced toward heaven. The city landscape below disappeared, replaced by murky water. His fuel gauge was lower than he was comfortable with. The flak faded as he left the English coast behind.

The Bf 109 next to him faltered; the propellers stalled. The plane dropped. They were halfway across the Channel. Even if the pilot survived the crash and escaped his plane before it sank, he would find himself in the middle of the Channel. The likelihood of rescue was slim. The water was fifty degrees. The pilot would die of hypothermia or dehydration. A slow death floating in the black expanse. Reinhardt prayed the pilot did not survive his crash. Was it Günter? Or Klaus or Uwe? Whoever it was, it was a son of Germany who wouldn't return home. Would his mother know? Would she wake in the night with a horrible feeling taking hold in her gut, constricting her chest? Like thinking about the bombing's effects on innocent people, Reinhardt had to force the German pilot from his mind. His fuel gauge neared empty, and there was nothing on the horizon but shades of dark blue. He may well face the same damning fate.

"Come on … come on …" he repeated, like it was a prayer.

Finally, there it was. The coast of France. The relief lifted the rock in his stomach. Flying at night was scary, but landing at night was terrifying. The altimeter showed how high you were, but it felt like at any second you and the ground would meet violently without warning. There was a desire to second-guess your instrumentation.

Many pilots had fallen to that foolish thinking. Eyes deceived. Reinhardt overcame the fear he was going to crash, trusting his instrumentation. The wheels dropped and then bounced off the runway. Pilots hopped down from their planes and scanned to see who had returned. Reinhardt looked for Günter and sighed in relief when he found him. His plane's left wing had caught fire and black smoke billowed out so thick it looked like a blanket blowing on a clothesline.

"I thought I had reached the end of my song," Günter said, after he and Reinhardt clasped hands.

Klaus and Uwe joined them, exchanging handshakes and smiles. It was the type of relief only those who had been in combat could understand.

"Where's Walter?" Uwe asked.

After looking for an answer from each other, they searched the runway. Sixteen planes hadn't made it back. And Walter Vorbeimann had piloted one of those planes. The four men faced the Channel, their flying helmets clutched against their chests. They stood in silence, honoring their fallen friend. Had he been the pilot Reinhardt had seen? Was he not yet dead? Instead, shivering in the sea? Nothing good could come from sharing that thought with the others, so he didn't. And as stupid as it was, Reinhardt thought of the first night Günter, Walter, Klaus, and Uwe had played poker, when he had been the unbiased third party brought in to measure the merited worth of a nude photograph to cover a bet. Günter had won that hand and kept his photograph. But had he not, Walter would have claimed the winnings and that photo would be floating atop the English Channel.

It was only natural to contemplate the randomness of death. To recount every near miss, every close call. It was only after the battle was over that Reinhardt's hands shook.

The following day, Reinhardt and Günter's sergeant, Karl Hartmann, a man of roughly thirty, summoned them. He always had time for small talk, something that may seem inconsequential to some, but helped men know they were more than just a number. A bit of normalcy in an abnormal situation.

"Well, I'll tell you why you're here and let you get on your way," Hartmann said.

Reinhardt's posture stiffened now that he'd transitioned from civilian small talk to military command.

"You both have now shot down five enemy aircraft. Though I'm sure you've been telling the women back home that you're already *Expertens*, I have the paperwork to prove it. Congratulations."

Reinhardt and Günter thanked him, saluted, and left. In all truthfulness, surviving had been the mission. Enemy kills had been a necessary byproduct of that mission. They both added to their number, reaching the milestone of ten, then twenty enemy planes downed. Despite that, there had been no successful sneak attacks, even at night. The British always knew when they were coming. The answer to how came in mid-August 1940, when the Germans realized the British were using radar to detect their approach. The British had codenamed them Chain Home stations. Reinhardt's next mission was to fly and destroy them. The stations were along the coast; their design reminded Reinhardt of the Eiffel Tower. To no surprise, the British Spitfires and Hurricanes greeted them.

The *Luftwaffe* fired. The RAF planes dispersed. Reinhardt shot down two, one with his dual machine guns, the other with his 20mm cannon, before he went from hunter to hunted. Bullets nipped his wings. He turned left, his plane perpendicular to the ground, then right into a barrel roll. His stomach rose into his chest. His body lifted from its seat. The ground AA guns battered the sky. Chain Home stations collapsed as German bombs found their marks. Reinhardt tugged on the yoke. In response, the plane climbed and climbed. The Spitfire rose with him, turning the speed advantage in his favor. 20,000 feet. 30,000 feet. 35,000 feet.

Reinhardt had been told the plane's max altitude was 41,000 feet. Both the German Messerschmitt Bf 109 and the British Spitfire approached their limit, risking stalling and losing their air speed. Whichever plane did so first would be in dire trouble. The Spitfire wobbled, drifting left and then right. Its engine groaned with finality and fell silent. The plane dipped. Reinhardt raced after the dead aircraft. He centered the plane's tail in his crosshairs and fired. The tail's tip burst off. Bullets ripped through the canopy. The pilot inside ducked for cover. Another burst of fire. This time, striking the engine. Black smoke billowed, poisoning its pilot inside. He struggled to open the canopy. But it was too late. The leaking fuel ignited and looked like dragon's breath as Reinhardt flew past. Its heat seared his eyes and flesh, then faded as if it were never there.

After the sortie was over and they had landed back in France, Reinhardt and Günter recounted the dogfighting with Klaus and Uwe as they changed out of their flight uniforms and washed their faces and necks. Then they enjoyed a beer.

"Stubborn bastards," Uwe said.

"They are defending their home. I hope we would be as stubborn," Reinhardt said.

"They surrender, the bombing stops. Churchill lets his people die," Klaus said.

"Surrender?" Günter asked. "Why would they surrender? We have no troops on the ground, and I'm not sure if you've noticed, but the Channel isn't exactly cooperative."

15 August 1940 had marked the heaviest fighting of the battle to date. The *Luftwaffe* had flown over 2,000 sorties and lost seventy-five aircraft. The British Fighter Command flew less than half that number, 974, and lost only thirty-four. Britain would call it 'The Greatest Day.' Germany referred to it as 'Black Thursday.' A day later, Winston Churchill uttered his famous words upon leaving a bunker at RAF Uxbridge, "Never in the field of human conflict was so much owed by so many to so few."

The air superiority Hitler and the Germans had desired over the British had never come to fruition. And on 17 September 1940, Hitler postponed Operation Sea Lion, the invasion of Britain, and set his gaze east.

Arriving at Stalingrad

Kira and red-headed Anna Alekseeva were on a train to Stalingrad. Alekseeva was a couple of years younger than Kira. She came from the city of Krasnoyarsk in Siberia. The only daughter of eleven children, Alekseeva's mother had been pregnant almost constantly from the age of sixteen to forty. Two children had died during infancy, another had been born stillborn. Brothers fight, and Alekseeva said her brothers treated her like a brother with long hair. Kira had only dressed femininely because of Nousha and Lina, otherwise pants had always been her attire of choice. Alekseeva had been raised a boy. She sat with her legs spread, she held her cigarettes with all five fingers rather than between two, she spit, farmer-blowed her nose, and cursed. Kira enjoyed her company, but growing up in a household of thirteen meant that there was never a quiet moment. Alekseeva did not do well with those, and she filled the silence by asking questions. Some of which she wasn't interested in the answers to. As an introvert, Kira was someone who needed silence to recharge. Alekseeva had a tremendous singing voice, though, and at night, she crooned songs from popular movies or songs popular during the Civil War, like "The Woman of Warsaw," "The Gun Carriage," and Kira's favorite, "The Blue Balloon Twists and Turns." With the constant need for speaking or singing, it was hard to believe Alekseeva could sit still and silent for hours on end when in a sniper nest. Hell, it seemed unlikely she could stay silent enough to go to sleep.

850,000 citizens called Stalingrad home, and that number greatly increased when Soviet troops entered the city. A defeat here could be the end of the war. Kira would do all she could to aid in a Soviet victory and send as many *Schadenfreudes* to hell as she could.

Not one step back.

Josef Stalin declared those words as part of Order No. 227. There would be no retreats or strategic withdrawals at Stalingrad. The Soviet Union would defend the city down to the last man, woman, and child. No civilians were allowed to evacuate. Stalin believed his soldiers would fight more ferociously if they knew women and children were in peril. It was a risk that didn't sit well with Kira. Thousands of *Schadenfreudes* were coming into the city. There was no act too vile for them to commit.

Kira and Alekseeva walked the city, studying the buildings, gauging potential sniper nests and bottleneck points. Alekseeva pointed to a fountain of six statues of children dancing the *Khorovod*—one of Russia's oldest dances—around a crocodile. The official name was Children's *Khorovod* (Round Dance). Kira stared at the crocodile looking behind itself, jaws open. A premonition of what was to come. Germany was that crocodile, and left to its own vices, it would kill all six of those jovial, dancing children.

Kira had trouble sleeping that night. War was on the doorstep. Most people don't truly have to contemplate it could be the last night of their life. But for those who fought in the fray, it was something they were forced to think of. Every single day of the war, people died. The next day would be no different. Kira thought of sniping, remembering calculations, and everything Orlov and her father before him had taught her. And she thought about her mother. Recalled all the books they'd read together, speaking German in secret. Of how frail she had become when she got sick. How the life had left her eyes long before she died. But she had never lost her smile when she looked at Kira. There was no face, no name of who had killed her. Just an invisible, ravenous, and unstoppable force. She thought of her father and all the times they'd hunted together. Less than a hundred words spoken between them combined during all those hunts, but it was their time to bond. And she thought about Nousha and Lina, her beautiful sisters. Thought of the missed memories and how she had failed them. Alekseeva hummed a song to herself, quiet but engaging. A sad soundtrack to add to the somber thoughts filling Kira's head.

"Does your mother sing?" Kira asked her.

"Shit, I'm sorry. Did I wake you?" Alekseeva asked.

Kira assured her she hadn't. Her body felt like it was one o'clock in the afternoon. Each breath she took was like a cup of coffee. Alekseeva's singing could get annoying, but not now. It soothed her.

"She sang us all to sleep," Alekseeva said.

Alekseeva held great reverence for her mother, obvious by the way she talked about her. She had red hair like Alekseeva and was nothing short of a folktale hero for the way she raised Alekseeva and all her siblings. Alekseeva said her mother had always been her best friend.

"Are your brothers fighting?" Kira asked.

84

Alekseeva beamed with pride. "Yes, those of age. I have not heard from them, though I feel that is better. No news is good news, yes?"

A blissful naivety Kira had not had since her mother died. Now, no news was awful news. It left the possibility that the worst had happened. But maybe that's how people could be divided. Not Jew and Gentile, man or woman. But those who had the blissful naivety of thinking no news was good news and those who knew the horrible possibilities of what that could mean.

The following morning, Kira and Alekseeva situated themselves in an apartment complex near the western end of the city. The sounds of war approached. The mechanical hum of tanks, half-tracks, and motorcycles. The clacking of boots against pavement. Kira stared at her father's rifle. How many men had it been the instrument of death to? How many men had her father killed? It was one of a million questions she'd never be able to ask him. She had added to the gun's total back home. With no one to witness those kills, her sniper tally stood at zero.

Kira readied the room for sniping. On the nightstand, she set her canteen and ammo. She dragged the twin-sized bed to the window. She opened the window, so the barrel of her rifle was unobstructed, and pulled the blinds to conceal the rest of the window. She went to the bathroom, and even though there was a toilet a few steps away, she wouldn't allow herself to get in the habit of being able to go whenever she wanted.

A new nervousness tingled throughout her body. A blend of fear and excitement she'd never felt before. Stalingrad was home to thousands of Noushas and Linas. Kira would defend them.

Through the scope of her rifle, the German Army advanced. The soldiers were in *Feldgrau* (field gray) uniforms. *Wehrmacht*. Many of those men had been conscripted into service. She let them pass. For now. She scanned the soldiers, studying the collar tabs and shoulder boards. Waiting for an officer. A soldier with shoulder boards of an opal-colored circle on the right and a gold-diamond shape on the left came into view. She had studied ranks by their insignia enough to recognize this soldier's rank as an *Oberleutnant*. A first lieutenant. She centered the crosshairs on the pale soldier's forehead. He was roughly 500 meters away, and she was in an elevated position. When shooting down from above, the air density is greater, but the velocity of the bullet increases at the same time. Gravity drags it down, resulting in the target's midpoint becoming higher. Kira needed to lower her sights or select a lower aiming point. She wanted this head shot. She wanted to create fear and chaos, and nothing did that like a perfectly placed shot. Let those around the *Oberleutnant* see the quality of marksman hunting them. Let them look around to see where the shot had come from and realize how great a distance it had come. Ponder the odds of being killed increasing with every step they took. Watch as they realized they had stepped through death's door.

Kira held her breath and then squeezed the trigger. The *Oberleutnant* dropped, his legs folding like an accordion. Kira brought her gaze to the *Oberfeldwebel*, a rank of master sergeant. He had enough time to look to see what had happened to the *Oberleutnant*, then his lifeless body landed atop the *Oberleutnant*'s. The men dispersed, diving for cover. Others thought the best course of action was to sprint ahead like a ship trying to power over the crest of a mighty wave. Brave but foolish. Kira fired. The bullet and the body traveled at precisely the speeds they needed to. The bullet ripped through the forehead of one of the brave but foolish soldiers, leaving a spritz of blood in the air where he had stood.

Those three successive kills froze the Germans. They clung to whatever cover they'd found like ticks to flesh. She waited for one to stick his head out. It would come. She only needed to capitalize on it when it did. A sniper's patience can be unfathomable. In the heat of the moment, half an hour felt like an eternity. To Kira, it was only seconds.

Bang!

Curiosity had gotten the better of him. His body slid down the wall, leaving a smear of blood. The survivors of the unit backtracked, clinging to cover.

An hour later, the next group came through. Another propaganda-fueled zealot. Another *Oberleutnant* standing tall, boldly barking commands. A *Schadenfreude*. She centered her sights on his chest, more specifically his left lung. Impossible for her to hear, it popped as the bullet ripped through the fragile organ. He'd drown in his own blood. A medic darted toward the wounded *Oberleutnant*. Given his role was to treat not harm, Kira intentionally missed her shot at him. Concrete shrapnel shot up in front of him. He stumbled backward to cover. Kira wouldn't allow the *Oberleutnant* to receive anything to ease his passing.

By the time darkness descended, Kira had killed eighteen enemy soldiers. She went away from the windows, stole a pillow from the couch, and slept on the floor. Before she could try to fall asleep, there was a knock on her door. Kira opened it. Alekseeva stood behind it, a pillow in one hand, her rifle in the other.

"Mind if I stay here?" she asked.

Kira allowed her inside and closed the door. Alekseeva rested her rifle against the couch, then laid down opposite Kira, so that her feet faced Kira's head.

"Productive day?" Alekseeva asked.

Kira told Alekseeva her number.

"Damn. I had nine."

Kira didn't say anything. Bragging about death wasn't something she wanted to do. She held no remorse for the men she had killed, but death deserved reverence. It was something she had to remember. That was the difference between her and the *Schadenfreudes* she killed.

"Strange trying to go back to normal after," Alekseeva said.

Kira knew what she was feeling. What was normal? They had spent all day killing, choosing their victims. Now, it was like two teenage girls staying overnight. The constant sound of gunfire and artillery made it impossible to relax.

"Sing one of your songs," Kira said.

Alekseeva obliged, singing so that only the two of them could hear. After, they talked about whatever came to mind. Alekseeva stated she had no desire for children, but should fate intervene, Kira knew she would be a great mother. She had a soothing presence. Her singing voice was medicinal. And growing up with ten brothers, she would know how to thrive in chaos. They talked about men, not in a yearning way. Alekseeva had showed as much interest in them as Kira. And it was different when you were a soldier. Respect as a female soldier was not afforded without merit the way it was for men. Kira and Alekseeva weren't going to offset whatever respect they'd earned by showing their male counterparts attention in that way. They were careful to never be around them alone. Lust is a poison men fall victim to all too easily. Alekseeva said she found Pavlichenko attractive. Kira had agreed to a degree. His height and size were attractive, but there was nothing the two had in common. Nothing about him that made her want to find something. Kira told her about Gerasim, detailing some of her favorite memories with him. And when tiredness consumed Kira, Alekseeva sang to help her fall asleep.

They sniped from the building one more day. Kira tallied twenty-three kills, Alekseeva seventeen. After killing nearly seventy men over two days, German paranoia of an enemy sniper or snipers would be extremely high. Fear that would make enemy soldiers advance slower or divert entirely. It was a good bet they would order their artillery to focus on the buildings ahead. Stalingrad was a massive city and Germany had brought plenty of its sons for slaughter. Day three was a Fall Harvest. Forty-six men between the two of them. Many of the Germans tried advancing under the concealment of darkness. For the most part, it worked. Kira could see scattering shadows jetting out behind cars, fences, and buildings, but only when the explosions lit the sky could she make out any targets to shoot.

On the sixth day, Kira set up in a different apartment complex while Alekseeva nested in an elementary school. Kira would miss her company and her nighttime serenades. Her morning was boring. Tanks had rolled through. To shoot at them would have been a waste of ammo and only give away her location.

Around mid-afternoon, a Soviet platoon of twenty men advanced down the main road, heading away from Kira and out of the city. She scanned ahead. Nothing but open, dust-covered streets and partially destroyed buildings. An hour passed, seeing no one within shooting range. But then a heavily guarded German platoon turned onto the street leading to Kira's building. Led by a Panzer tank and two *Sd.Kfz.* half-track vehicles with the death-dealing MG-42s, forty soldiers marched along. Kira debated on whether to shoot, and if so, who to shoot, and if who was singular or plural. Multiple shots were out of the question. It'd give away her location, and she'd face the retaliation of a tank and two half-tracks. However, she thought she could shoot once and create some carnage and chaos. Now, to find the highest-ranking officer amongst them.

But something else caught her eye.

Further ahead, five city blocks from where the Germans were positioned, the Soviet platoon returned. She scanned left and right. The other intersections were under unchallenged German control. These Soviet soldiers were advancing down a bottleneck straight into an ambush.

Four blocks.

Three.

Movement from the Germans. They were aware of the Soviet advance. The tank rolled front and center. The two half-tracks parked alongside it. This slaughter would be over in less than ten seconds.

Two blocks.

The only chance they had was if they were warned. But the entire city was in a constant drum of gunfire. If she wasted a shot, they may think nothing of it. To shoot close enough to scare them was a tremendous risk. You never knew what someone might do. She could aim away from the group only to have someone inexplicably sprint at that spot.

One block.

The two MGs were threat 1A and 1B. If they were manned, there'd be no chance for the Soviet soldiers. She settled her scope on the gunner on the left, then the one on the right. Rehearsing the movement. She'd have to be quick. Even one gun active for ten seconds was 200 rounds of fire. More than enough to kill all twenty Soviets. She centered her sights on the back of the gunner's neck. His shoulders were rolled forward, his helmeted head arched. Regardless, whether it was a kill shot, he wouldn't be firing with a bullet in his neck.

Gunfire lit the dusk sky like the flash of a welder's torch. The MGs' used tracer ammunition leaving streaks of green. The hailstorm of lead eviscerated two Soviets. Puffs of red vapor exploded into the air. Kira took a breath, held it, and fired. The MG soldier sagged, the green tracer bullets veering to the left. Kira worked the bolt, moving the rifle to the right. She fired a second time, killing the second machine gunner.

Now that the meat-grinder MGs were unmanned, the pinned Soviets volleyed a round of shots. Kira fired her three remaining rounds, then reloaded. There was nothing she could do about the tank, but she could keep the two MGs unmanned. She eliminated every German who tried to climb into the half-tracks. The Soviets glanced up toward her like devout Christians looking for their guardian angel. They finally realized their situation would not improve. If they waited, only more Germans would arrive. The Germans knew they had a sniper at their back and stayed covered. The Soviets sprinted, firing off to their sides. Two German soldiers stood to open fire. One to Kira's left, the other to her right. She killed both before they could fire their first round. The Soviets sprinted toward Kira and to safety.

But whatever joy and relief flooded through her faded as her eyes settled on the tank. It turned around, no longer facing away from Kira, but *at* Kira. The long barrel lifted. Kira's eyes widened. The chance it knew what window she was at was slim, but when a single round could destroy an entire section of a building, it didn't matter. Kira sprung to her feet, grabbed her rifle, and sprinted into the hallway. A terrible noise shook the building. Kira stumbled into the wall. A second and a third blast rocked the building. Kira was at the stairwell, reaching for the banister, but before she could secure her grip on it, a fourth explosion blasted her forward. She tumbled down the stairs, knees and elbows colliding against the unforgiving steps. Her rifle stock smacked her face. Her eyes filled with tears from the pain pulsating in her nose. Blood ran down, filling her mouth with the taste of copper. Her head throbbed, feeling like a beat drum, and her heavy eyes strobed closed.

Hunted

There was nothing but unconscious blackness. Slowly, the world returned to Kira. Blurry and indistinguishable. Voices carried up the stairwell. The desire to succumb to sleep was overwhelming. Even lying on the cold, hard stairwell was comfortable. She closed her eyes to surrender to it. But one word made her eyes snap open.

"*Schnell!*"

German.

She tried to stand. Every nerve ending in her body fired. Each one sending pain. Everything throbbed. She dabbed her nose. The blood had crusted. She used her rifle to help herself stand. Rubble covered the flight above her, the air smelling like singed wood, smoke, and smoldering stone. The voices below her advanced. Her only play was the floor she was on. She heaved the stairwell door open and limped down the hallway, checking for unlocked doors. There were none. She made it to the opposite stairwell, only to hear more German voices echoing up. She was trapped. Trapped wearing a Soviet Army uniform and carrying a sniper rifle.

Lieutenant Orlov's parting words came to her: do not get taken alive. Roll the grenade, then draw the TT-30. Seven shots for the enemy. One for her. Her Mosin–Nagant had two shots left. When it came to speed, her bolt-action rifle versus a submachine gun stood no chance. She was a rat in a maze, waiting for a mousetrap to snap her neck. She holstered the rifle strap over her shoulder and then drew her TT-30. She would fire those seven shots. She'd be reunited with her family soon.

The voices grew louder. They were on her floor now. It would all be over soon. She prayed to her mother and father and to her sisters for the strength to die well. To be defiant in the face of death. But just as she finished her prayer, the door to her left opened. An elderly woman waved Kira in.

"Come quick," she said.

Russian words were better than German words, so Kira rushed to the open door. The woman closed the door and fastened the dead bolt. Kira had no reason to presume to know what or who she'd find toiled away in the apartment, yet she was shocked to see six women of varying ages squeezed together on and in front of a sofa. The woman who had offered sanctuary put her hand on Kira's shoulder.

"We must hide that," the woman said, nodding at the rifle.

Kira nodded and handed the rifle over. The woman looked to be in her late seventies, and Kira had her doubts if she'd be able to even carry it. But the woman took it in her arms and carted it into her bedroom. She stashed the rifle amidst a stack of blankets. When she returned, Kira asked who she was. But the woman was too busy examining Kira's nose. Her touch was gentle, but the pain was enough to make her eyes water. With a wrinkled hand, she grabbed Kira's and shepherded her to the sink. She took a washcloth and dabbed Kira's nose with it.

"I am Galina," she said, as if it were an unimportant side note. "We need to get you out of this uniform."

Her grip on Kira's wrist was supportive yet firm. In the bedroom were stacks of folded clothes. All the women's possessions had been stockpiled into the lone room. Galina grabbed a shirt from one stack and held it up against Kira's body. It was a close enough fit. From a different pile, she grabbed a dress, light blue in color. Kira had waited for her to leave, but she aggressively nodded at the clothing.

"Change, change!"

Galina grabbed clothes from other piles and created a new pile. Why, Kira couldn't say. She stripped down out of her uniform and stepped into the dress. Galina examined the fit, then pinned alterations to tighten up around the stomach. The bust was too tight, but there was nothing she could do about that. It wasn't a perfect fit, but it was a passable hand-me-down. Kira and Galina stepped out of the room. The six women stared at Kira. They were so close together it gave the impression the couch was a piece of driftwood they were clinging to out in the middle of the ocean. Galina lifted Kira's two braids, then called to one woman by the couch. A quick rundown of names came. Olga was Galina's daughter and the woman she had called for. Nadia was Galina's sister, only slightly less wrinkled. Her hair had the bluish white color of snow at night, whereas Galina's had stayed a dirty gray. Galina's daughters, Olga and Dasha, were both older than Kira by ten years. They must have looked like their father, but shared their mother's disheveled, gnarly hair. Nadia's daughter, Nadine, was a robust woman in her early thirties. The two children were Doroteya, twelve, Olga's daughter, and Dasha's daughter, Feodora, only six. She clutched a small doll with a distorted face.

Olga snapped to action, undoing the braids Kira had kept her hair styled in since she was a young girl. Nousha and Lina had always styled, combed, and braided each other's hair. Kira had never had an interest and, after turning down their offers for fifteen years, they had stopped trying. Even with the fear and anxiousness of her current situation, regret still found a window to sneak in through.

Olga gave an apologetic smile, one that meant she knew it was rude, but she had no choice. After separating the braids, Olga brushed Kira's hair, taming it and giving it a more feminine, nurtured look than Kira had ever had. She felt like an impostor.

"Hungry?" Nadia asked.

Funny how sometimes a person only becomes aware they're hungry when they're asked. But at the contemplation, her stomach rumbled. But like with any grandmother, no wasn't an acceptable answer. Nadia filled a bowl with pea soup and looked on encouragingly as Kira ate it. The soup was thick, hearty, and spicy. Kira slurped every possible spoonful. Everyone watched her, making her feel like an animal in the zoo.

Olga, Dasha, Galina, and Nadia sat and played *durak*, a popular Soviet card game. Kira had played it against Nousha and Lina. A player's goal was to get rid of all their cards. The last player to do so was the *durak* or fool. The kindness and selflessness Galina and Nadia had exhibited before was gone when they played. They were ruthless and had one objective: absolute victory. After the two women won, they insisted Kira play. Now, instead of teams of two, it was every woman for herself. Kira felt Olga and Dasha were at a disadvantage, having Doroteya and Feodora asleep on their laps. Dasha lost the first game, Kira the second, and Nadia the third. Kira loved how upset Nadia was at losing. Before a fourth game could be dealt, German voices sounded outside. A loud bang rattled the door, waking Doroteya and Feodora. The second knock came before the door had stopped rocking from the first. Galina wobbled to the door and opened it.

A German officer barreled inside, shouldering Galina out of his way. Kira studied his gray uniform. Shoulder boards with three dots on the left-hand side and a lone, larger one on the right. A *Stabsfeldwebel*—a sergeant major. Given the amount of grime stained on his face, his age was hard to ascertain, but Kira guessed him to be in his mid-thirties. He held a Sauer 38H. Though it looked pathetically small in his large hand, it had enough ammo to kill everyone in Galina's family. Lower-ranking soldiers piled in, hands resting threateningly on their Gewehr 43 rifles. The *Stabsfeldwebel* studied the women, the deck of cards, and the apartment.

"*Wer lebt hier?*" he asked.

Kira acted as though she didn't know he had asked who lived here. But reacting as if you didn't understand was tricky. Reaction was hard to control. Galina spoke, telling him she didn't understand German. The *Stabsfeldwebel* looked at her in a way that showed that was her problem, not his.

"Search the place," he ordered his men.

They rushed forward, storming into the bathroom and bedroom. They reported there were no men in the apartment. Kira knew they were looking for the sniper who had decimated their ranks. The *Stabsfeldwebel*, unsatisfied with their summation, searched the rooms himself. He noted the stacks of clothes, counting the number of piles. He grabbed from each pile, then tossed them aside. He picked up the deck of cards and sifted through them. Finished, he tossed them to the ground, the fifty-two cards floating every which way. He glared at each of the six women. Young Feodora had her head buried in her mother's chest, terrified. The *Stabsfeldwebel* slid the hair from her face with his pistol. Dasha pleaded for him to point his gun elsewhere. He did not know what she said, nor would he have cared if he had. He made a clicking noise with his mouth, like a cowboy trying to settle a neighing horse.

"What a beautiful child," he said.

Even if she hadn't understood German, his body language was threatening enough. "She is too young to have had her first bleed, but this one isn't." He stroked Doroteya's cheek with his leather-gloved hand. "Should I find any evidence that you are harboring an enemy of Germany, we shall make her a woman. Again and again and again. And you old, decrepit women … we shall find out just how dried up you are."

He looked at each of the women, studying for any subtle signs they had understood his words. His eyes lingered on Kira. Her nose no longer bled, but it must be bruised. The *Stabsfeldwebel* lingered, allowing his men to leave the apartment first. Finally, he stepped out and closed the door. The moment he did so, the weight in the room lifted. There was a collective deep breath taken.

"It isn't safe for you if I stay," Kira told them.

"Even less safe if you leave now," Galina said.

"You don't know what they threatened to do."

"We are women. They are men. I can guess."

There wasn't a good decision to be made. Stay and risk their safety. Leave and risk their safety.

They slept on the floor, one lined up after the other. The two children were the first to fall asleep, cuddled between their mothers. Kira lay wide awake. What if the *Stabsfeldwebel* had seen something while he searched? Her rifle or uniform? But she told herself she was overthinking. Had he seen something, they wouldn't have left. But she couldn't help but feel like the front door would blast open at any second. She thought about the eighth pile of clothes Galina had created. Genius. Had she not, the *Stabsfeldwebel* would have noticed it.

Somehow, Kira went from a restless mind to asleep and back to awake as if no time had elapsed. When she opened her eyes, Galina sat at the windowsill watching the green and red tracer rounds zip through the black night. The thunder of artillery never stopped. Kira stood and joined Galina.

"Do you have family fighting?" Kira asked.

Galina kept her eyes trained on the battle lighting the darkness. "Three sons. My daughter's husband, too."

"This city isn't safe for you," Kira said.

"No, it's not."

Before Kira could ask why she had stayed, or plead for Galina and her family to leave, the horror of why they hadn't came back to her. Stalin's Order No. 227. He would not allow citizens to evacuate. It had been a decision she had disagreed with when citizens were just a number, just a stat. But now that she knew that in those numbers were two sisters, their daughters, and granddaughters, and that they were kind, excellent cooks, ruthless card players, and stoic in the face of fear, the order wasn't only ruthless; it was heartbreaking. How could Stalin forsake his own people? He knew the wolves were coming, and he had left his sheep to slaughter.

"I wish I could fight as you do," Galina said. "I was not made to sit and wait."

Kira wished she had something profound to say, some balm-like words. But she had none. How often throughout history had women wanted to fight but been deemed unsuitable to do so? The shield maidens of Viking lore had shown how tenacious women could be, but history views them as barbarians for it. Throughout history, wars had been fought by men, but war didn't affect only men. Why should women be resorted to the sidelines? For the first time, she recognized the honor and gift of being able to fight. That choice wasn't afforded to Galina when she had been of fighting age. It wasn't a choice for many nations fighting in this war. The British and Americans were adamant that war was no place for a woman. Kira would rather die fighting than hide in a basement waiting for a bomb to bury her in rubble. Galina had to fight in other ways, and she had. She had gambled her life to save Kira when there was only risk and no reward in doing so. But Kira couldn't stay here any longer.

"I have to go," Kira said.

Galina nodded, a wise grandmother who knew what would be said before it was said. Kira grabbed her uniform and rifle. She emptied her food rations onto their counter. Galina motioned to refuse, but Kira stopped her.

"You will need it more than me. You must ration your food. Supplies will be hard to come by," Kira said.

She didn't have the heart to tell her that there wouldn't be *any* supplies. Kira disassembled her rifle and stashed the bolt, scope, receiver, barrel, and the TT-30 into a bag. Galina went to her fireplace and grabbed two unburnt cuts of firewood.

"Conceal rifle," she said.

Kira held the firewood in her arms, the rifle hidden behind it. It wouldn't pass a check, but she hoped that at a glance the Germans wouldn't think anything of a woman transporting firewood from one location to another. But the fear of what the Germans would do to a young woman alone terrified her. Kira rubbed soot on her face, doing anything she could to make herself appear undesirable. She headed to the door. Hand on the handle, she paused.

"You saved my life."

Galina required no thanks. It was the role she had been reduced to. Years younger, Galina would have carried a rifle alongside Kira. Galina only nodded, but there was so much packed into it. There was the unspoken plea to fight on her behalf. Kira found her brown eyes and nodded. She opened the door and left.

There were no Germans in the hallway. But something in the hallway caught her eye. A mass sprawled on the floor. She continued toward it. The body of an elderly man with a white beard. His throat had been slit. The blood around his body was dried and tacky. Less than ten feet from the old man was a boy who'd barely reached puberty. He'd been beaten to death. At the stairwell lay the mangled body of a man in his sixties. He'd been thrown from the stairwell above. His left leg had snapped, and now grotesquely pointed above his head. Down the stairs, two more bodies lay. On the ground floor, four men lay beaten or stabbed to death.

The horror of realization hit her squarely in the chest. The Germans had been looking for the sniper. They'd killed anyone they thought it could be. These were men murdered for Kira's actions. Their killings had not been quick. These innocent boys and elder men had died cruelly. How many lay dead on the floors she had not traveled? The answer was every boy and man in the apartment complex. A number too painful to contemplate.

Kira pushed the front door open with her shoulder and stepped outside. The sky was ablaze in orange and purple, the air congested with toxic smoke. Stone and brick rubble littered the ground. From what she could see, there were no Germans. But they were here, somewhere. Kira considered which way she should go. The main road would be quickest, yet the riskiest. Traveling through alleyways would be the safest, yet slowest and most suspicious. So, she settled on something of an in between. A path a civilian woman would take to avoid harm yet get to where she was going as quickly as possible. Her next inner debate was how fast to walk. How to look rushed, not hurried. Worried but not guilty.

She traveled three blocks without incident. But when she stepped out from the cover of a building, the Germans saw her before she could turn away.

"Halt!" a voice commanded.

Kira froze. Even from across the street, she could make out his epaulettes and insignia reflecting the rank of an *Unteroffizier*—a sergeant. The man next to him was an *Obergefreiter*—a corporal.

"What are you doing?" the *Unteroffizier* asked, flicking his cigarette to the ground.

How to respond? Run? They'd catch her. They had a jeep parked beside them. Pretend she hadn't understood the German they spoke? If she did, they would cross the street and check what she was carrying. Or thirdly, respond to him in German and attempt to talk her way out? When presented with three bad choices, it bodes well to realize that one is the best choice and, therefore, a good choice. Or something like that … You also had to forget that you wouldn't know if you hadn't chosen right until after it was too late.

"I am delivering wood to my aunt," Kira shouted back in German.

The *Unteroffizier* had not expected to hear his native language shouted back.

"You speak German?" he asked, bewildered.

"My mother taught me."

The best way to lie was to dash bits of truth in it.

The *Obergefreiter* cared significantly less about a Russian woman speaking German. "It is the heart of summer, yet your aunt requires wood for burning?"

There was no time for hesitation, planning, or thinking.

"She is very old. You will never see her not wrapped in a blanket."

"It is not safe for you to wander these streets," the *Unteroffizier* said.

"I know, but it is my responsibility to take care of her. War does not change that."

A German jeep sped past them. Kira wished she could perform one of those disappearing acts like in the American movies, but when the jeep passed, she was still rooted in place.

"It is summer. Why the need for a fire?" the *Obergefreiter* asked.

"She is old and always cold," Kira replied.

"Two logs will not last you long," the *Obergefreiter* said, his condescension thick.

"No, it will not. I carry what I can find. Perhaps you'd like to load your transport trucks with firewood and drop it off."

She was unsure if she had gone too far. The *Obergefreiter* stepped out into the street, but before he could march toward Kira, his superior put a hand on his chest to stop him.

"Hurry to your aunt's. I recommend finding more blankets rather than firewood," the *Unteroffizier* said.

Kira nodded, thanked him, and turned right, trying to impress she had always intended to go this way. She clenched the wood in her hands so hard she gave herself a sliver. But even as she stepped away, she could feel their eyes upon her.

Chess

Reinhardt had shot down thirty-three enemy aircraft by the time the Germans had abandoned the planned invasion of England. Hitler issued *Führer* Directive 21—code named Operation Barbarossa. In the 1930s, Stalin had ordered Soviet purges—including the killing of many experienced military officers. And now, the Soviet Union paid for that self-mutilation. The Russo-Finnish War had also unimpressed the Nazi High Command of the Soviet Air Force's skill. All factors adding to Hitler's hubris.

Even before Reinhardt got into the air, he could tell the fighting over the Soviet Union would differ drastically from the fighting over the Channel. The most obvious difference was the scale. The Soviet Union was massive. Reinhardt's single-engine Bf 109 had less range than twin-engine aircraft, something that could prove to be a problem. Reinhardt's unofficial flight time of thirty minutes had been enough to fly across the Channel, fight, and fly back. Now, he could fly for hours over a single stretch of grassland. Russia alone was seventy times larger than England.

Most countries' air forces used the Vick formation—three planes forming a triangle. The problem with this was that only the lead plane could spot danger. The *Luftwaffe* increased spacing between planes and added a fourth fighter plane, resulting in a four-finger shape that could separate into two pairs. The *Luftwaffe* added to their air superiority by destroying a large number of Soviet planes before they even left the ground.

Reinhardt and Günter led a four-man team, Klaus and Uwe joining them. The open fields swept by below them. Soviet troops marched, looking like miniatures. Reinhardt and the others opened fired on the Soviet ground forces. The Soviet planes, late in response, now flew to meet them. Some of them were relics from the end of the Great War. Reinhardt split with Klaus; Günter with Uwe. Reinhardt had the advantage of aircraft, experience, and confidence. He shot down one, two, three, and a fourth. One more and he would achieve the prestigious title of *Experten* in a day, or as the Allies called it, ace in a day. He fired from his double machine guns at the ground forces. They dove to the ground, covering their heads and necks with their hands.

"One's on my tail!" Uwe shouted, his voice distorted through the radio.

Reinhardt looked through his canopy, left and right, trying to find Uwe. A Soviet fighter mimicked every move Uwe made.

"I'm coming. Stay calm. Don't freeze," Reinhardt said.

His Bf 109 hummed as it soared after Uwe's attacker, rising to 30,000 feet. He glanced below. Uwe flew past. Reinhardt plunged. The Soviet fighter flew parallel, Reinhardt perpendicular. Advancing toward a violent intersection. Reinhardt fired his cannon. The hit ripped off the front of the Soviet plane, its detached propellers slicing through the air like lethal boomerangs. Uwe screamed his appreciation.

"Good move, Friedel," Günter said.

"Nothing but tanks, let's return to base," Klaus said.

The others agreed, but Reinhardt didn't answer. Günter called his name. Reinhardt silently debated his next move.

"I'm going after the tanks," Reinhardt said.

"Okay, someone's a little sky drunk," Klaus said.

Radio silence, then crackles. "Alright, Friedel, you've piqued my curiosity. Let's go wake the sleeping dog," Günter said.

Günter followed Reinhardt's lead, swooping high overhead and clear of the troops below. They sped from behind. Lower and lower. The tanks and troops no longer looking like figurines. Low enough to see individual blades of grass swaying. Soviet troops turned toward the sound of rolling thunder.

Both Reinhardt and Günter fired their cannons. The tanks exploded in balls of fire. Those inside struggled to escape before the flames engulfed them. The Soviets fired their rifles, but Reinhardt and Günter were too far away and too high to be in any danger. It was frustration fire.

When they landed, pilots applauded, patted their backs. One called the two of them mad fucks for going after tanks. Major Hartmann joined in the applause.

"Gentlemen, gentlemen," he said, waving his hands to silence them. "Reinhardt Friedel, you have achieved five downed enemy aircraft in a single day."

"*Experten* in a day!" Günter yelled.

The men cheered and whistled. Reinhardt had forgotten the number. All that had mattered was getting that fifth Soviet plane before it got Uwe. Hartmann shook

Reinhardt's hand, but no one was more ecstatic than Uwe. He had evaded death because of Reinhardt.

The following day, Reinhardt was promoted to the rank of *Leutnant*. The sorties that followed the next days and weeks were even more bountiful. Reinhardt's strategy was to hold his fire until he was twenty meters away, an extremely close distance. He unleashed a brief burst at point-blank range. This strategy accomplished several things. It revealed his own position at the last moment, preserved ammunition, and prevented the enemy from attempting evasive maneuvers. Quick thinking. See. Decide. Attack. Reverse. And Restraint. He'd seen many pilots miss their shot and foolishly continue on instead of retreating. Just like chess. If you miss your chance at the queen, don't continue with it and open yourself up to attack. Once the attack was over, Reinhardt vacated the area. If attacked, Reinhardt's go-to evasive maneuver was to use the rudder to mislead his attacker in the amount of deflection needed when firing. Then he flew into an oblique loop. His ambush tactics resulted in quick enemy eliminations.

During the nights and respites from battle, Reinhardt longed for quiet moments where he could read his book. The others played poker.

"How come you never play cards?" Günter asked.

"Too much luck involved," Reinhardt answered, his eyes staying on the page.

"So, all you do is read? No wonder you signed up for war, you poor bastard."

Klaus, Uwe, and a fresh-faced pilot named Adenauer laughed.

"I play chess."

"Oh, one of those high and mighty intellects," Günter joked.

"Yes," Reinhardt deadpanned. "Never played?"

"Nope."

Reinhardt made it his unofficial mission to find a chessboard. Günter won a checkerboard during a game of poker. The board had sixty-four squares—the same amount needed for chess. But finding actual chess pieces proved impossible. After all, it wasn't like people carried around bishops or rooks. So, they had to get creative. They used checker pieces as pawns. Spent casings were colored and taped to signify the rooks, knights, bishops, and king. A 7.92x57mm Mauser cartridge from the lethal MG-42 was used as the queen. Reinhardt explained the names of the pieces and how they moved. Günter nodded in a 'let's just play' way. He was a 'learn-by-doing' type of person. Reinhardt beat him in two moves. Then three and four. The look of annoyance told Reinhardt that Günter was hooked. No one enjoyed getting their ass kicked. There were only two results from it. Quit and don't play, or practice and vow to never get man-handled like that again. They played every chance they could. Sometimes, the moon illuminated the board enough to play. Other times, they used their lighters to see.

"I don't know if you're setting me up for something," Günter said.

"Yes, that is the conundrum," Reinhardt said. "Knowing when your opponent has actually made a mistake and when he wants you to think he's made a mistake."

Günter smirked. He loved that psychological warfare aspect of it. Getting into the mind of your opponent. Making him second-guess everything. A move wasn't complete until the player took his hand off the piece, and you wanted your opponent to fear removing their hand. They shared a good laugh when Günter mentioned the knight's irregular movements of two up and one over, or two over and up, and how he failed to anticipate these moves.

"I keep getting fucked by knights," he'd said.

The phrase would come to them, even at night, and they'd fail to stifle their laughter.

Reinhardt had always considered air combat to be like a massive chessboard, and now Günter did, too. Anticipate. Attack. Retreat. Your plane was your king. Protect it. Your plane was your queen. Attack with it. Your squadron were your bishops, knights, and rooks. Set them up. But unlike chess, in air combat, there were no pawns. None of your brothers in arms were sacrificial.

For Reinhardt and the *Luftwaffe*, the Soviet campaign had been a never-ending series of checks. But the Soviets had a seemingly unlimited number of pawns at their disposal and Stalin had no qualms about sacrificing them to prevent a checkmate. Stalin famously stated, "Quantity has a quality all its own." He was sending his unending pawns into the fray, buying time to build up his own backline pieces.

Massacre

Colonel Volkov took in Kira's disheveled appearance. She was still dressed in the clothing Galina had given her. Her two staple braids were absent, and black soot covered her face. She explained what had happened.

"The Germans looked for the sniper ... for me." She paused. Colonel Volkov had treated her as a soldier, but all removal of gender would end if she couldn't keep her emotions in check. All the anti-women-in-combat-role believers would have plenty of fuel for their arson.

"They killed all the men," she said.

Colonel Volkov peered at her. Was he looking for weakness? She didn't think so. He had a kindness in his eyes that made her trust him.

"We are only responsible for our actions and our actions alone," he said.

Kira nodded, keeping her gaze on him, but struggled to show the conviction she wanted to.

"Speak freely to what is on your mind," Colonel Volkov said.

"I believe what you say. But it is a truth with a caveat."

"How so?"

"Cause and effect. Had I chosen a different building to snipe from, they'd all be alive."

"You believe that?"

"Yes, Comrade Colonel."

Volkov thought on it, a pensive look in his piercing eyes. "Perhaps. Say you chose a different location. Do you not think they would search that building? Would you trade lives? Would any scales be balanced?"

Before Kira could speak, he continued.

"The soldiers you eliminated. Say you spared them, or you had missed. One of these men calls in an airstrike and the building is destroyed. Now, instead of only the men killed, the women and children are, too. Or perhaps had I not ordered you to fight, they'd still be alive. Had I not met you in that factory, had the Germans not killed your family, had Hitler stayed out of Russia, had the Treaty of Versailles not left Germany in runes to allow Adolf Hitler to ascend to power, had that young Serbian stayed his pistol and not killed that archduke, had there been no Great War." He placed a comforting hand on her shoulder. "It does not bode well to pluck the wings of butterflies."

Kira forced herself to nod. Volkov poured a shot's worth of vodka into a tin cup and handed it to her. Kira sipped it. The fiery delicacy burned away the emotion curdled in her throat. Colonel Volkov enjoyed his own drink and sighed.

"A major passed through here after dusk speaking as if he'd witnessed a miracle," Volkov said. "He said that he and his men had been pinned down by a tank, two MGs, and a horde of enemy troops with no chance of escape. He had given up hope when, from on high, a sniper opened fire. Raining death from the exact building you just described. He said the Angel of Death had protected them." He paused and focused that intense, penetrating stare on Kira. "Comrade Kovalyova, there are men who thank God you were in that building."

He fixed his gaze on Kira, willing her to understand his words, as if the meaning of them could be transferred from his eyes to hers. Then he broke that intense gaze. "Comrade Kovalyova, I promote you to sergeant. Congratulations."

Emotions swirled inside her, blending into a volatile cocktail. But most dominant was pride. Pride in herself, but also the pride she knew her father would have in her. His pride in her had never been a dominant, boastful display. It was the ever so slight nod, a barely seen gleam in his eye.

"See yourself to a meal and some rest," Volkov said.

Kira thanked him, then headed downstairs of a department store being used as headquarters. She washed her face and hands, ate her breakfast rations, and then crawled onto a cot. There were a hundred others sleeping, staining white sheets with grime, blood, dust, and dirt. Somehow, even with the constant gunfire and artillery, and the occasional hum of fighter jets, it was the snoring that woke her. When she stepped out later that day to rejoin the fight, Alekseeva's hug nearly tackled her.

"I thought you had died," she said.

Kira explained what had happened, but with less detail than she had to Colonel Volkov, and leaving out the sacrificial slayings entirely. It wasn't something that Alekseeva needed to hear, needed gnawing at the back of her mind. A thought that could come at the worst time. They stayed together, nesting in a grade school. They ascended to the top floor, fifteen stories high. It was a massive school, especially for Kira, who had gone to a small single-story school. The school had an eerie aura to it. Open books and unfinished quizzes were on classroom desks, and chalkboards had incomplete formulas scrawled on them.

"There must be a hatch to the roof somewhere," Kira said.

They searched for a custodian's closet and found it, but the door was locked. Though it most certainly was always kept locked, Kira smiled at the thought that some custodian had thought the Third Reich had invaded the Soviet Union for the mops, brooms, and cleaning supplies stored inside this closet. Alekseeva dug the blade of her knife into the keyhole and worked it loose. A metal ladder merged into the wall led up to an access hatch. They climbed it and crouched along the roof. The sight before them was truly apocalyptic. Smoke and fire. Smoldering ruins. Corpses littered like stones on a beach.

They got into position and then watched the battle play out through the lens of their scopes. It lessened the scale of the battle, but made it personal. Now, Kira could make out faces, see the mists of blood as bullets eviscerated men.

Angel of Death.

A moniker she took pride in. Soviet soldiers felt safer, more willing to venture forth, knowing some angelic force protected them. Alekseeva sniped; Kira studied the other buildings.

"Stop," she ordered Alekseeva.

Alekseeva crouched for cover and looked to Kira for an explanation.

"Enemy sniper," she said.

They crawled to the access hatch and climbed down. Kira had seen the glint of a scope. If she had seen him, he most likely had seen them. Kira readied her three-line and focused her gaze on the buildings some 400 or 500 meters in the distance. She ignored the fighting on the ground. Scanning window by window. Alekseeva looked through her scope, calling out floors she cleared.

Kira's eyes widened in recognition, seeing the barrel of a Karabiner 98k and the tip of a man's head.

"I found him," Kira whispered softly, so that the rifle didn't move. She told Alekseeva the window, building, and floor he was on. She readied her sights, took a collective breath, and then fired. Sniper eliminated. The Soviets on the ground didn't know that they were being hunted. If Kira hadn't killed the sniper, a few of those Soviets would be dead.

Kira and Alekseeva returned to the roof and rained down on the unsuspecting Germans. Not even the shadows were safe. When darkness descended, they turned their attention from the battle to the stars.

"Do you ever wonder where they all came from? What they are?" Alekseeva asked.

"My friend knows all the stories about the stars," Kira said, the thought of Gerasim making her smile.

Alekseeva asked to hear some of them, and Kira did her best to tell them, but they lacked the flair with which Gerasim had told them. Alekseeva fell asleep before Kira. Kira had too much on her mind. Gerasim mostly. Where was he? Was he alive? Did he know what had happened at home? Then her attention drifted to Galina and her family. And then Colonel Volkov's advice replayed in her mind: it does not bode well to pluck the wings of butterflies. But she had killed the sniper. She could pluck those wings. How many men had been given a second chance of life? If Kira wasn't here at this battle, more Soviets would be dead.

The fighting grew more ferocious, more ruthless. But the only thing that surrendered was summer to fall. Wintry winds advanced like an invading army. But this army couldn't be stopped with bullets or tanks. It was the true master of *blitzkrieg*. Who controlled which parts of the city shifted block by block, day by day. When Galina's apartment building was back under Soviet control, Kira took Alekseeva to meet Galina. She had gotten her hands on two chocolate bars she'd taken off dead Germans to give to Feodora and Doroteya.

Kira paused at the entrance door. Cowardice crept in her chest. Would the bodies still be there? A month and a half later? She opened the door before Alekseeva could ask what was wrong. Concrete dust and debris covered the inside, but there were no bodies. Water dripped from busted pipes with that methodical *drip, drip, drip* that could drive people mad. Because of it, the apartment block had taken on a musty smell. Getting to Galina's door was a maze. One stairwell would be blocked, forcing them to walk the length of the hallway, only to find that the stairwell was only clear for one level before they were forced to use another one.

Finally at Galina's door, Kira knocked, notifying those inside who she was. No answer. No sound of movement inside. Kira tested the handle. Unlocked. The first bubble of worry gurgled in her stomach. Galina had kept the door deadbolted. She removed her TT-30. Alekseeva did the same. Kira opened the door, but something was lodged in front of it. Kira banged her shoulder into the door for added force. Whatever was behind it rolled away. Alekseeva shrieked. A nude woman lay face down. Kira turned her over. Dasha stared up at her with lifeless eyes.

Nadia was seated on the couch, hunched forward, head down. Alekseeva lifted her head and brushed aside her bloodstained, snow-white hair. Her throat had been slit.

"This one's dead, too," Alekseeva said.

Olga was on the kitchen table. Nude, her legs spread. Bite marks covered her breasts. Her throat had been slit, too. Nadine was on the floor in the same horrible condition. Kira crept into the bedroom. A circle of blood stained the carpet. Sprawled on the bed, dress torn open, was Galina. A bottle of wine shoved deep inside her vagina. A bloody chef's knife close by. Kira stood by her in abject horror, deducing Galina had stabbed the first German to come near her and had then been overpowered.

"Oh my God …" Alekseeva's voice came from the living room.

Kira rushed to her and instantly wished she hadn't. Young and innocent Doroteya and Feodora had not been spared. Their deaths were not merciful. They were merciless. They were naked, bloody, and bruised. Their virginal wombs viciously defiled. They hadn't died from bullet or blade, but fists. Beaten to death.

Schadenfreudes.

Rage consumed her. Burning away every pure emotion she'd ever had, leaving behind only the charred remains of vengeance. A whole family killed. Had it been the *Stabsfeldwebel?* Had he returned because he found out Kira had been the sniper he was searching for?

"I'm sorry, Kira," Alekseeva said.

Tears burned Kira's eyes. She dug her fingernails into her palms until crescent moons appeared. She deserved to feel some small measure of pain. Alekseeva said something, but Kira didn't hear. She wandered about the apartment gazing at each hell-earning atrocity. She didn't know where Alekseeva had gone. Right now, Kira could only think about Galina, Nadia, Olga, Nadine, Dasha, Feodora, and Doroteya. These women had saved her life, and it had cost them theirs. Kira covered their bodies with blankets and placed the chocolate bars on the young girls' laps. Footsteps clambered outside. Kira raised her pistol to greet them. But it was Alekseeva, returning with Soviet troops to help collect the bodies. The two soldiers who took Feodora and Doroteya confiscated the chocolate bars. Kira couldn't blame them. The dead had no use for them, and these men had fought valiantly.

Kira didn't stay to see where the soldiers took Galina and her family. She didn't want to see them burned or dumped into some mass grave. Kira left them behind, taking refuge against a building in an alley. She propped her foot against the opposite building and puffed away on a *Belomorkanal* cigarette to steady her nerves. Her hands shook not from fear, but from rage. It hadn't been enough to kill Galina; they had to humiliate her first. Rape was never acceptable, but Olga, Nadine, and Dasha were grown women. Little Feodora and young Doroteya? Children. Grown men had raped them and then beaten them to death.

Schadenfreudes.

Kira's father had taught her how to shoot, so that her prey received a merciful death. But her prey was not a deer grazing upon an open field. Her prey was the *Schadenfreude*. A vile predator who killed and raped for sport. To hell with quick deaths, she would grant them death slow as starvation. Painful, too. Suffering. Merciless. Destroying organs, so that the body was poisoned from the inside out. Yes, there would be adjectives the Germans would come to know well.

Langsam. Schmerz. Angst. Und Tod.

Slow. Pain. Fear. And death.

The days turned to weeks and the crisp chill of November came and went. Snow dusted the ground, mixing with ash. A private told Kira Colonel Volkov wished to see her. Kira grabbed her rifle and strapped it over her shoulder. As she walked through the streets, Soviet troops nodded respectfully toward her. Her reputation as the Angel of Death, protector of men, had spread. They all felt better knowing Kira was perched on a roof somewhere. Soviet soldiers pushed, kicked, and smacked captured German soldiers to keep them moving in line. It was a long line of unknown faces. Except for two. The *Unteroffizier* who had let her pass and told her to be safe when she left Galina's apartment and the *Stabsfeldwebel* who threatened to rape her and every member of Galina's family, including the children Feodora and Doroteya.

"Stop," Kira said.

The Soviet sergeant re-uttered her command to his troops. Kira stepped before the Germans. Both the *Stabsfeldwebel* and *Unteroffizier* recognized her. But the looks on their faces varied. The older, fouler *Stabsfeldwebel* looked at her with disgust and a hint that he should have known. The *Unteroffizier* looked at her with something resembling a smirk. He had gotten fooled but reacted as though he had been the butt of a joke.

She stepped face to face with the *Stabsfeldwebel*. Close enough to smell his waning cologne, and the overwhelming stench of cigarette.

"You remember me?" she asked in German.

The *Stabsfeldwebel* glared. "I remember you, *Schweiner.*"

"You remember what you said you would do to me?"

"Do not flatter yourself, *Fräulein*. We would share equal enjoyment in me fucking you."

"Go. Run," Kira said. The *Stabsfeldwebel* hesitated. "I will count to thirty. At thirty, I shoot." She worked the bolt. "Thirty. Twenty-nine." The *Stabsfeldwebel* ran. He didn't waste time looking over his shoulder. He just ran as fast as he could. Internally, he kept time. The Soviet sergeant looked at Kira nervously. The Nazi was over 200 meters away. Now, he ran in a serpentine pattern. Kira raised the rifle. She steadied her breathing, calculating her target angle. Her target was now over 250 meters away. She squeezed the trigger. The shot rang out. A moment later, the *Stabsfeldwebel* fell face forward. His body spasmed violently. The bullet had shattered his vertebrae, paralyzing him. His screams had no trouble reaching Kira. No one spoke, only listened until minutes later, the screams ended.

She faced the *Unteroffizier*. That smirk was gone. Replaced with fear. He was a cute boy, one both Nousha and Lina would have taken a liking to. Had one of them brought him home to meet Papa and her, Kira would have approved. The *Stabsfeldwebel* had threatened rape. This man had told her the road wasn't safe and that she should get to safety.

"You will tell your *Schadenfreudes* that Soviet citizens are not to be touched," Kira said. "I will be watching, and I will kill each and every one of you slowly. You will beg for death before it comes." Kira turned to the Soviet sergeant. "Let him go."

The *Unteroffizier* looked relieved and horrified. He would leave his friends behind to die, but his desire to live made him shuffle his feet. He paused. How could he trust Kira wouldn't shoot him? Ultimately, he ran. Once he reached the dead *Stabsfeldwebel*, he turned to see if he would be killed. No bullet came. He turned and ran as far away from the Angel of Death as fast as his legs could take him. But it wasn't the Angel of Death the Germans would come to know her as. Tigers are vengeful animals. Once they have been wronged, they do not kill quickly. They maul, digging their claws into an animal's spine, severing vertebrae. They lacerate flesh. They eat you alive.

From that moment, the *Stabsfeldwebel* would bring voice to a new moniker for the lethal Soviet sniper: The Winter Tiger.

R&R in Italy

Reinhardt continued to excel, tallying up an impressive seventeen kills in a single day spaced out over three sorties. Günter had achieved fifteen. Promotions followed. Reinhardt to *Hauptmann* (captain) and Günter to *Oberleutnant* (first lieutenant). Over the holidays of 1941, Reinhardt, Günter, Uwe, and Klaus were sent to Rome for a reprieve. A wonderful surprise awaited Günter: Klara. Her creamy blonde hair was styled in brushed-out finger rolls. Günter stared at her in disbelief. Reinhardt, however, was not surprised. He had orchestrated this Christmas gift.

Günter picked her up and spun around with her in his arms. He stared into her eyes, his own eyes twinkling. "How the hell?"

Klara nodded at Reinhardt through her fits of laughter.

"You spy!" Günter joked, as he hugged Reinhardt.

Klara hugged him, too. It was slightly awkward when you'd only written letters with someone and were now meeting them in person. Uwe and Klaus were afforded smiles. But it was enough. Klara was the most beautiful thing they'd seen in months. The two of them set out with a group of other soldiers, no doubt looking for alcohol and women, leaving Reinhardt, Günter, and Klara.

"I have a gift for both of you," Klara said.

"Is it a photograph of you?" Reinhardt joked.

Klara held up a wrapped box, a gold bow in the upper left-hand corner. Günter deferred to Reinhardt to open it. Günter's hands were wrapped around his true gift. Reinhardt ripped the paper off. It was a travel-size chessboard folded together. He opened it. The ivory and ebony chess pieces were snuggly placed in the black felt. He thanked Klara. Günter talked her into allowing one three-minute match. She dutifully kept time. The game went unfinished; Reinhardt had a plus four advantage at the conclusion. At the behest of Klara, they packed the chessboard up and toured the historic city. The sun had set, the smell of roasted coffee beans caressing their noses.

They stopped at the Trevi Fountain and gazed upon Neptune, the Roman God of the sea, seated on his seashell-shaped chariot. Two horses, one calm, the other unruly, pulled the chariot and represented the different moods of the sea. Roman mythology fascinated Reinhardt (even if they had stolen all their gods from the Greeks).

Günter stood behind Klara, his chin resting on her shoulder, his arms wrapped around her waist. Reinhardt beside them.

"There is a legend that if you throw a coin from behind your back into the fountain, you will return to Rome," Reinhardt said. "Two coins and love will find you. Three assures you marriage." He paused, bringing his eyes to Günter and Klara. "Or divorce."

They laughed.

"Good thing, darling, that I only have two coins," Günter said.

"Give them to Reinhardt," Klara said.

Günter did, and under their encouragement, Reinhardt threw the two coins in.

"Now pray that the love that finds you is not a husky, bearded Russian," Günter said.

"I think it may increase my chances if I wander the city," Reinhardt said.

Reinhardt said goodnight to them, granting them the privacy they deserved. They both pleaded with him to stay, but Reinhardt knew it was simply to be nice. It'd been a year since they were alone. The desire to embrace one another as man and wife must have been cataclysmic. He strolled the city, stopping at a bar for an espresso. It was a perfect night for a stroll. Klaus and Uwe had planned on finding a brothel, and though being with a woman enticed him, it was the thrill of enticing a woman that excited Reinhardt. Paying for a woman's company was like paying for someone to hand over a trophy fish instead of luring it in yourself. He thought about Mathias and what his best friend was up to. His next letter to him would detail Rome and its beauty.

As he toured the historic city, he couldn't help but note how many wars the Roman Empire had fought in. History was forged by war. War was never new, only the weapons that waged it were. The respite from war had afforded him time to contemplate. It proved to be a blessing and a curse. He thought about home and how much he missed it. He thought about the pilots he had killed. Forced to contemplate the effects of war and ponder how long they would linger.

Over the following days, he, Günter, and Klara toured the Colosseum, St. Peter's Basilica, and the Sistine Chapel. The Colosseum was truly a marvel, but a sad reminder of how little mankind had advanced. Thousands of years ago, men killed each other with swords and spears. What would they think of the aircraft Reinhardt and Günter flew? Would they think they were the gods? Aliens?

Reinhardt, Günter, and Klara returned to the Trevi Fountain. How could you not? It was breathtaking. A photographer took their picture. One with all three, one of Günter and Klara, one of Günter and Reinhardt, and one of only Klara. A final Christmas gift for Günter. They went to a restaurant that served family-style servings. They ordered spaghetti with meatballs, basil pesto noodles, and noodles drenched in butter and olive oil. All three ate past the point of being full. The smell of simmering oil, melted butter, fresh bread, and pureed garlic was enough to make them drool, and then, after being disgustingly full, gag. Tomorrow, it would be back to rations. Not just for Reinhardt and Günter, but for Klara back home in Germany. It was heartbreaking they couldn't eat more.

Afterward, Reinhardt wanted to do nothing but nap. He had a bowling ball amount of pasta in his stomach, but they stayed to listen to a woman sing and play a harp. Her voice was angelic, the harp even more so. After, they picked up their photos from the photographer. And then it was time to say goodbye. Reinhardt hugged Klara and wished her well. Günter kissed her long and good. When he stepped aboard the train, she lunged through the train window and kissed him again. Günter hung so far out of the train that Reinhardt had to grab the back of his uniform to prevent him from falling out. Günter and Klara laughed as they kissed. When the train moved, Reinhardt pulled Günter back in before he would have kissed the cement tunnel wall. Klara lingered, watching the train leave the station, blowing kisses to Günter.

The reprieve from battle had been a gift. No fighting. No bullets or bombs. Great food, even better company. A chance to see an iconic city with someone who had become a great friend and his beautiful and kind wife. A comfortable bed to sleep in each night. Food to fill his stomach and ignite his taste buds, and wine to wain worry. But it had also been a curse. It offered a glimpse of normal life. It made him aware of how much he wanted this pestilential war to end. He loved Rome, but he missed having Mathias there with him. He missed him. And though he was happy Günter could see Klara, it had unleashed an internal longing, a missing void. A jealousy. Not of Klara herself, but the idea of Klara. Had the war given him a ticking clock? The sands of an invisible hourglass counting down until his time was at an end? He'd tossed two coins into the fountain as a joke, crossing off one part of a tourist's to-do list. But maybe he'd also thrown those two coins as an offering to the gods that there was someone out there who could make him feel the way Klara made Günter feel, and that he would live to be able to find her.

Inferno

Kira and Alekseeva moved from the roof of a grade school to a high-end hotel, nesting on the top floor. The carpet was green with red swirls, giving the hotel a permanent Christmas aesthetic. The lights lining the hallway looked like lampposts. Alekseeva used her knife to unlock a door. The room was larger than Galina's entire apartment had been. All over the world, the rich couldn't be expected to sleep in something so small for a day while the poor had to live their entire lives in it. A small kitchenette was to the left, sofa and chairs lay ahead of it. The lone bedroom, equipped with two double beds, was off to the right. Alekseeva tossed a pillow beside the main room window and knelt on it while Kira set up position in the bedroom. Kneeling on a pillow, Kira scanned the distance. She gauged wind direction and speed by studying how the debris on the ground blew in the wind. She searched entrances and windows. A glint caught her eye. She scanned back to it, but there was nothing. Had her eyes played a trick on her? She was about to move on until something moved. Not something, but *someone*. A German soldier wearing a *Stahlhelm* turned his head to crack his neck. The most marginal of movement. But Kira had caught it.

"Enemy sniper," Kira called out to Alekseeva. "Red brick building. Eighth floor. Fourth window from left."

"That has to be 900 meters," Alekseeva said.

Kira put it closer to 915.

"Too far away to be a threat," Alekseeva added.

Kira calculated the milliradians and adjusted the windage drum on her three-line. Alekseeva watched her, realizing that while the enemy sniper wasn't a threat to shoot, Kira was. Kira took three deep breaths and then held it. The enemy sniper didn't offer much to shoot. She could only make out the left side of his face. The room he was in was dark, and she couldn't differentiate his face from the backdrop. Still, the average deer measured eighteen inches belly to back. She had perfected small shooting windows long before Orlov had trained her. She squeezed her eyes shut, then opened them wide, making sure an untimely blink wouldn't impair her shot. Sniper school had taught her much, but what it didn't need to teach her was intuition. Ever since her father had taught her how to shoot, there had been some unexplainable force that told her when the time was right to fire. A sense that told her when it wasn't. Some people tried to refute its existence. But it was there, like people who could pick up a pencil and draw. She waited for that silent voice to whisper, *Now!* When it came, she squeezed the trigger, releasing her breath. Watching through the scope. The German's head snapped backward, and he fell from sight.

A brief silence, then Alekseeva exclaimed, "You got him!"

Kira's longest confirmed kill. 915 meters. Over half a mile. Alekseeva left her post and hugged Kira, beaming at her friend's accomplishment. The fact that it was an enemy sniper she had eliminated made it all the more meaningful. He wouldn't be able to prey on her countrymen.

"The Angel of Death!" Alekseeva boasted.

It was too dark to see any other potential targets, so they sat on the floor, their backs resting against the couch. Alekseeva kept repeating the distance of 915 meters.

"The Angel of Death ... how come I do not have a nickname?" Alekseeva asked.

Kira blushed, then turned the attention back on Alekseeva. "I will give you one. Let me think."

Alekseeva sat straight and prodded her chin out in exaggerated stoicism, like a Roman emperor having his face chiseled into marble.

"Red Death," Kira said.

Alekseeva thought about it. "I like it. But it's not a nickname if only one person uses it."

"It will spread," Kira said.

At eleven, they dragged the mattresses off their frames and positioned them away from the windows. Kira was grateful for a mattress to sleep on, knowing thousands, if not millions, of soldiers slept on the ground. And she had blankets. There was something about the safety and comfort a blanket provided.

What felt like both days and seconds later, the need to use the bathroom woke Kira. With a tiredness mirroring drunkenness, she stumbled into the bathroom. Once finished, she leaned into the sink and slurped a mouthful of water, blinking slowly.

A bright light flashed, followed by a thunderous boom. Kira shielded her eyes. An explosion rocked somewhere below them. Alekseeva woke, jumping to her feet. A second barrage struck above them, rupturing a pipe. Water blasted out. Kira ran to Alekseeva. Inches from reaching her, the floor gave way in the middle, slanting dangerously. The couch slid down first, then Kira and Alekseeva. They crashed to the floor below them. Before they could get to their feet, the floor snapped in the middle. The room's furniture slid down after them. Couch, dressers, a refrigerator. Any of them heavy enough and falling fast enough to kill them. Alekseeva got to her feet first. She dragged Kira out of the way just before a dresser splintered apart. The room caught fire. The heat of its flames licked their flesh, so hot their skin nearly sizzled. They had to act fast. Flames engulfed the walls. The center of the floor was a black hole that descended an unknown number of stories.

"We have to climb up!" Kira shouted over the swooshing flames.

She was taller than Alekseeva, so she would have the best chance of reaching the dilapidated floor above them. Had the floor been level, she never would have reached it, but the slant was extreme enough that she could reach a protruding piece of floorboard. It felt like two 100-pound weights were strapped to her feet. An undeniable gravity sucked her down. Water from busted pipes dripped down, making her grip falter.

She was about to fall.

But Alekseeva wrapped her arms around Kira's legs and heaved her up. Kira lifted her feet over, then reached for Alekseeva. But as Alekseeva prepared to jump, the floor gave way. Their fingertips grazed. Alekseeva's eyes widened, the fire reflecting in them. The swooshing flames swallowed her screams as Alekseeva disappeared into the fiery chasm.

No Pawns

There was something about having an official chessboard that made their games more legitimate. And now that they weren't using bullets and checker pieces, but actual chess pieces, Klaus and Uwe were willing to learn. Klaus used to play against his grandfather. Though that had been fifteen years ago, he was at least familiar with the game. Uwe knew nothing but the phrase 'checkmate.' Sometimes they played doubles, alternating moves. Reinhardt and Günter against two schmucks. It didn't take long for them to think as one, knowing how to set each other up. This also led to long stalemates in their one-on-one matches, both recognizing what the other was attempting to set up. Yet throughout these epic chess matches, there was still a war to fight.

Fall Blau or Case Blue was the name for the offensive in Southern Russia. Launched on 28 June 1942, the objective was to capture the Caucasus—the oil-rich lands of the Soviet Union that included Azerbaijan. War was paid in blood, but it ran on oil. Capturing the Caucasus would fuel the German war machine while simultaneously hindering the Soviet Union's ability to wage it.

With luscious green fields and the gradient of gray of the Caucasus Mountains looming in the distance, the area was breathtaking. Reinhardt continued his strategy of flying high, then diving like a bird of prey. His strategy, skill, and superiority had given Reinhardt a nickname. *Der Kriegsadler.* The War Eagle. The Soviets knew his nickname too and had come to fear it.

Reinhardt respected any man who took to the skies, but one RAF pilot was worth five Soviet pilots. Yet Reinhardt had to admit they had gotten better. And many of their shortcomings could be blamed on their aircraft. The industrial might of the Soviet Union had worked day and night to produce aircraft that could rival the *Luftwaffe*'s. There weren't many advantages to having a war waged in your own country. But there were some (hard to see when your homes were destroyed, and your cities left as smoldering rubble). If a German pilot was shot down and survived, he was killed or taken prisoner. But if a Soviet pilot was shot down and survived, he was treated and back in a plane as soon as he was ready. The Germans destroyed a high percentage of Soviet planes before pilots could even climb inside them. That had been an early advantage for them, but that advantage had shifted in favor of the Soviets because no pilots had been killed, just the machines. And outdated machines at that. The summer waned into fall.

The gorgeous landscape was tough to ignore, but it had to be. Distraction equals death was a formula Reinhardt warned all new pilots about. In the four-finger formation, twelve to a squadron, Reinhardt and his fellow Germans flew through the murky gray sky. Visibility was poor. Sight was obviously a pilot's primary sense. Because of the humming of not only his own engine, but his squadron's, Reinhardt couldn't hear anything else. Taste and smell were useless. So, it was feeling he relied on. Not a physical touch, but an awareness of the world around him. It was something impossible to explain until you gained that awareness. Reinhardt had it. Günter, too.

A hundred *Luftwaffe* planes soared south. The Soviet planes broke through the fog. Reinhardt hardly had time to count, but it was a puny counter offensive, considering the numbers of the *Luftwaffe*. Of the twenty Soviet planes, all but six were shot out of the sky.

Klaus cursed on the radio, his shots narrowly missing a retreating Soviet fighter.

"Going after him," Klaus said.

The Soviet plane weaved in the sky. Each time Klaus zeroed in, the Soviet rolled and spun out of the way. Reinhardt followed the chase. Luck was on the Soviet's side. But the more Reinhardt watched, the more obvious it was that luck had nothing to do with it. It was skill. The pilot goaded Klaus into following. With the skill set he possessed, he could create enough separation to remove any possibility of Klaus having a shot. But he wanted Klaus to think he had the shot. That it was only a few seconds, a few meters away. Reinhardt thought of the great chess dilemma he had instilled in Günter early on: How do you know when your opponent has actually made a mistake and when he wants you to think he's made a mistake? Reinhardt didn't always know the answer in chess. In the skies, he relied on the roiling in his gut. That indescribable feeling that tells us something isn't right.

Reinhardt had that feeling now.

"Klaus, pull back. Abandon the hunt," Reinhardt called.

"No, I can get him. Just a few seconds," Klaus said.

"It's a trap!"

The seconds Klaus pondered were too long. He flew through the veil of fog. The visible ground revealed an unending stretch of anti-aircraft guns. Hundreds of them. The sky exploded with flak. So violently loud it felt like Reinhardt's eardrums would shatter. He was out of range, but Klaus and twenty-some pilots had flown into the kill zone. By the time Klaus's plane fell to the ground, it was in two dozen smoldering pieces.

Günter retreated, but a perfectly placed shot struck his engine. It smoked, then flickered on and off before sputtering its final breath with a cloud of gray smoke.

"Shit, I lost my engine!" Günter said. He read his instrument panels. "I'm losing fuel!"

Reinhardt gazed out his window at Günter's plane. Fuel wasn't leaking out; it was flooding out.

"I'm going down," Günter said.

Delivered in a way that was both calm and shocking. Panicking would do him no service, so he didn't. His plane swooped as he tried to control his descent. He soared over the anti-aircraft guns, so low that the gunmen ducked. Günter's plane bounced on the ground, tearing up the grassy field.

Günter called for Reinhardt over the radio. "Tell Klara I'll do everything I can to come home to her. Everything. You tell her I love her more than anything."

Reinhardt gazed at the scene below. Günter was not the only downed pilot still alive. He and the other Germans struggled out of their cockpits. Soviet troops advanced toward them. Their firepower was superior to the pistols the *Luftwaffe* pilots wielded. The *Luftwaffe* pilots had three choices: flee, fight, or forfeit. Sure, they could run, but to where? They could fight, but they would lose. They could forfeit, throw up their hands in surrender. But it was an all-or-nothing choice. If one pilot shot, the Soviets would kill them all. And 'prisoner of war' meant being a prisoner for as long as the war lasted.

Maybe even longer than that.

Or maybe they wouldn't take any prisoners …

Shoot them dead. Ransack them for cigarettes, rations, and ammo. They'd find the picture of Klara in front of the Trevi Fountain. Pass it around, each man telling crude stories of what they would do to her.

Reinhardt wouldn't sit idly by, watching like a seagull floating over the beach as a shark tore into a seal. Because Reinhardt wasn't a seagull; he was the shark. The War Eagle who instilled fear in his enemy. A cold chill, as if death's hands had wrapped its skeletal fingers over their shoulders.

Günter cocked his Luger. The surviving pilots took cover around his plane. The advancing Soviets were 900 meters away. Two jeeps and an armored truck leading them. Günter stared at his picture of Klara. He'd burn it before he let strangers use it to pleasure themselves. He struck his lighter. The flame longed for the photograph, reaching out to touch her. His eyes stayed locked on Klara. Thoughts about his last embrace with her in Rome filling his mind. The way she felt, tasted.

Before the flame kissed the photograph, a mighty wind extinguished it. A German fighter plane roared above. Reinhardt flew at the approaching Soviet vehicles, firing from his machine guns and cannons. One jeep flipped end over end; the second was eviscerated by cannon fire. The armored truck skidded sideways and flipped onto its side. Reinhardt swung tightly, flying back toward Günter and the other survivors. He dropped his landing gear and then braked as fast as he could.

He opened his canopy and shouted, "Come on!"

Günter and the others sprinted toward him. The Messerschmitt Bf 109E was a single-seat aircraft, so where seven pilots were supposed to go, they'd worry about when they got there. If they got there ...

"Get on the wings," Reinhardt ordered them.

Günter took a breath and jumped on. Some of the other pilots looked at the wing, then at the approaching Soviets, debating on the best choice.

"Choose," Günter told them.

Almost as one, they climbed on. The max weight the plane could handle was 5,000 pounds. It could handle these men. More Soviet jeeps and transport trucks raced toward them, less than 400 meters away. Reinhardt accelerated the throttle. Speeding across the open field faster than any car or train Günter and the others had been on. The plane took off. Reinhardt kept the plane as flat as possible, to help offset the risk of Günter and the others falling off. Gunshots erupted behind and below them. Reinhardt kept the plane low, but the wind was ungodly powerful and loud. Lower still, less than twenty-five feet above the ground. Once clear of the Soviet threat, Reinhardt checked his fuel gauge. It neared empty.

Just a little bit further.

He lowered the plane; the ground rising to meet them. His head jerked upon impact. German troops stared, dumbfounded at seeing pilots clinging to the wings. The plane sputtered and came to a final rest shy of the German defense. Reinhardt climbed out of the cockpit. Every pilot he'd saved embraced him. Some smiled, some laughed, some cried, and some did all three at once. Günter stared at him, trying to think of something worth saying. He shook his head, overcome by the moment.

"I ... I don't know what I could ever say or do to convey my gratitude for what you just did."

Reinhardt preemptively dismissed whatever further thanks Günter wanted to give.

"There are no pawns in war," Reinhardt said.

Günter nodded and hugged Reinhardt, whispering his thanks.

Reinhardt had previously received the Iron Cross for having accumulated well over twenty points. The point scale was simple enough: one point awarded for shooting down a single-engine plane, two points for a double-engine, three for a four-engine, and all points were doubled at night. But two days after his rescue of Günter and the others, Reinhardt received notification that he had been nominated and approved for the Knight's Cross. An award that needed approval from the *Führer* himself.

The Treaty of Versailles had forbidden Germany from issuing any military medals. The Iron Cross was a famed symbol awarded to Germany's bravest sons. Hitler had reintroduced it in 1939. Not only had Hitler approved Reinhardt for the Knight's Cross, but after reading about Reinhardt's exploits, Hitler awarded Reinhardt the Knight's Cross with Oak Leaves. A medal Hitler would present himself.

The memo had a Nazi war eagle with a swastika enclosed around it and bore the *Führer*'s signature. The text ran almost in a vertical orientation rather than horizontal. Reinhardt didn't feel like telling Uwe or Günter, so he handed the memo to them.

"Reinhardt ..." Günter said. "This is a tremendous honor."

"It's not right that I get leave," Reinhardt said.

The battle had ended on 24 November, and Günter and the others awaited their orders. Still, they'd be here somewhere in the expansive Soviet Union. The letter had invited Reinhardt to Berlin to meet *Luftwaffe* Commander-in-Chief Hermann Göring, then to Hitler's Eagle's Nest in Austria to meet the *Führer*, and ultimately, leisure in Paris for Christmas.

"There'd be seven people who may not even be alive if it wasn't for you. You deserve it." Günter put his hand on Reinhardt's shoulder. "Make the most of it."

Reinhardt packed his things in his duffel bag and took note of the men he left behind. They wouldn't all be here when he returned. That was the brutal reality about war. Reinhardt had no plans to say goodbye. He snuck away in the twilight hours, forcing himself not to look behind, but ahead.

Novice Spy

Kira stared into the fiery chasm, unable to believe that Alekseeva had disappeared. Forever. The world would never hear her wonderful voice again. The horror of what had happened wouldn't let her turn away, as if it were some black hole with its own gravitational pull. She didn't want to leave. She wanted to jump in after her. It wasn't until the flames lashed, signaling their final warning, that she left.

She lumbered to the department store Colonel Volkov was stationed in. Was she cursed? Did her father condemn her for letting another woman die? She'd failed Nousha and Lina; Galina and her family. And now, Alekseeva, too. Alekseeva had saved her. Kira had thought she was tall enough to climb up. But she hadn't been. Deep down, had she known that? Embraced her cowardice? Why hadn't Kira offered to help Alekseeva first? Neither of them was tall enough on their own.

Red Death. The nickname would never spread. It had been uttered once, and now forever swallowed up in that inferno.

Colonel Volkov was in the basement. The windows were too high for Kira to see out of them. She wasn't fond of this type of setting; it made her claustrophobic. To consider that any moment the building could be bombed and bury them in rubble was enough to make it hard to breathe, like being in a coffin. She belonged in the open air. At the entrance to a supply closet turned office, Veronika sat behind a desk, beaming a friendly smile.

"It's good to see you again!" she said.

Kira forced a smile. Veronika asked if she could get Kira anything. Kira refused, but Veronika poured her a glass of water regardless. Kira hadn't seen her reflection in hours, but she knew soot covered her face, and more than likely, some crusted blood. Veronika handed the water to her with a smile that said, 'Don't worry, everything will be alright.' Kira sat in silence, Alekseeva on her mind. Her red hair, the traces of freckles on the bridge of her nose. How close Alekseeva had been to her mother. Roughly ten minutes later, Colonel Volkov opened the door and waved Kira inside.

The supply closet was larger than expected, wreaking of cigarette. All the shelves and supplies had been emptied from it. Five men sat at a long, rectangular oak table in the center of the room, the epaulets and chest insignia revealing the ranks of the men. Kira saluted them as Colonel Volkov made the introductions. The robust, mustachioed general major was Mikhail Turgenev. The tall, gaunt man was Colonel Chernyshevsky. Oblonksy was a barrel-chested lieutenant colonel, and the lowest ranking of them was Captain Yahontov, a man a week behind his shave and weeks behind his meals. For some of them, women soldiers were a gimmick to draw support from the Americans and English. But soot-covered, bloodied, and bruised, Kira wiped that foolish assumption away, taking a couple of them by horrified surprise.

"So, you are the famed Angel of Death," General Major Turgenev said, bowing his head.

Kira nodded, the moniker making her blush. Colonel Volkov gestured to the empty seat. The five men were on one side, Kira on the other. No expression she gave would go unnoticed. Captain Yahontov slid a folder to Kira. She looked to Colonel Volkov for permission to open it. He granted it with a nod. A glossy eight-by-ten-inch photograph sat atop a series of documents. A high-ranking *SS* officer, clad in black, his arm raised in a Nazi salute. He appeared to be in his mid-forties.

"The man in the photograph is *SS-Oberst-Gruppenführer* Jürgen Wolff," Colonel Volkov said.

"Jürgen Wolff was born in Würzburg, Germany. He served in the Great War under the 16th Bavarian Reserve Regiment," Colonel Chernyshevsky said.

Kira read through the biography spanning the length of one type-written page. She didn't know what significance the 16th Bavarian Reserve Regiment had, but since it had been referenced, it must have some.

General Major Turgenev explained, "The 16th Bavarian Reserve Regiment is the very same division Adolf Hitler served under. Hitler saved Wolff's life at the Third Battle of Ypres. Wolff has been as loyal as a dog ever since and has been by Hitler's side through Hitler's ascension of power, including executing the Night of the Long Knives."

Nacht der langen Messer. Kira knew the significance of the Night of the Long Knives. From 30 June to 2 July 1934, the Nazi Party purged current conservatives, past enemies, and future rivals. It established Hitler as the supreme leader of the German people.

"A more devout follower of Hitler you will not find," General Major Turgenev continued. "There are few generals Hitler listens to, and even fewer who are damn good military strategists. Wolff is among them."

A thick pause filled the room. Each man stared at her unabashedly. Kira cheated her eyes to Colonel Volkov, hoping he would break the silence.

"We want you to kill him," Colonel Volkov said.

If this man was a devout believer in Hitler and all the Nazi Party stood for, then he was a *Schadenfreude*. And *Schadenfreudes* deserved to die.

"He is in Stalingrad?" Kira asked.

Even before they answered, her mind raced through the possibilities. Wolff was a general. He wouldn't be out in the fighting. He'd be held up somewhere, hidden in a basement like this one. How could she get a shot at him? The windows would be well above his head. The building itself would be centrically located in a German-controlled zone of Stalingrad.

"Wolff spends his Christmases in Paris," Colonel Volkov said.

Kira tilted her head, confused. "You are sending me to France?"

Colonel Volkov answered, "Yes, under the guise of a student."

"A student? A student of what?"

"Music," General Major Turgenev said. It was hard to know when he spoke because his lips were hidden by his bushy mustache.

A dozen initial questions spawned a hundred more.

"Live the life of a single woman in Paris. Tour the city, drink coffee, read books. The more visible you are, the more invisible you will be," General Turgenev said.

They didn't need to tell her. Kira knew that it was an invisibility only offered because she was a woman. A woman was assumed to be innocent, docile. Someone who posed no threat. But no matter what her reservations were, and she had them, she was aware this wasn't a request. It was a command.

"When do I go?" Kira asked.

"Today," Colonel Volkov answered.

"I serve the Soviet Union," Kira said, but her mind raced with a hundred thoughts. A strange nervousness took hold. She'd never left Russia before. Nor did she speak French.

The meeting ended, and the men dispersed. Once the door opened, the trapped cigar and cigarette smoke billowed out into the open space. Colonel Volkov lingered behind. He waited for Kira to process what she had just been ordered to do.

"Colonel, was I chosen because of my ability or because I am a woman?" she asked.

"General Turgenev asked for my best. I must admit being a woman grants you advantages men do not possess. It will help you get a shot, but there is no one else I would want to take that shot. You are my best, Kira."

Kira couldn't even show her appreciation with a fake smile. There were too many questions. Traveling abroad would be a nerve-wracking experience. Factor in that she'd be a spy, and it added a whole other level of stress.

Colonel Volkov escorted her to the door. "Veronika will assist you."

Veronika rose at the mention of her name and smiled apprehensively. She led Kira to another room. What it had once been used for, Kira couldn't say, but now it was an impromptu washroom normally reserved for high-ranking officers like the men who had been in the meeting. A galvanized tin tub sat in the middle of the room, in front of a sink and mirror. A bottle of shampoo and a bar of soap sat on a ledge. A towel hung on a nearby rack.

"Do you know your size?" Veronika asked.

That was something Lina and Nousha knew. Kira, however, had no idea. She wasn't overweight, and she wasn't rail thin. That had been enough. There'd never been a reason to get any more precise.

"It's okay if you don't," Veronika said. She held up a seamstress tape measure. "May I?"

Confused, Kira nodded. Veronika straightened the tape, then wrapped it around various parts of Kira's body. After jotting down the measurements, she told Kira to bathe and that she would knock when she returned. Even more confused but enticed by the idea of a hot bath, Kira stripped. It'd been weeks since she had undressed. Men would take moments to strip their shirts and wash their armpits and groin. But for a woman, there was never the privacy necessary to do such a thing. War released a primal quality in those who waged it. She and Alekseeva would never risk enticing them by showing skin.

Alekseeva.

Her burned body was buried under rubble while Kira prepared to take a bath. The guilt felt like battery acid in her stomach.

The mirror across from her cast the glaring difference between the pale skin covered by clothing and the grimy black skin that hadn't been. She unbraided her hair with difficulty; they had woven together like two vines. She climbed into the washbasin. The water wasn't as hot as desired, a few degrees warmer than lukewarm, but she knew better than to complain, as thousands of soldiers hadn't had a bath in weeks. The water turned murky. She dunked her head, then scratched the shampoo into her scalp. The comfort relaxed her so greatly that her eyes grew heavy. Tiredness like a drug, sedating her. Veronika's knock and call woke her.

"A few minutes please," Kira said.

She rose from the tub and grabbed the towel off the rack close at hand. She dried herself, then wrapped it around her body. Kira opened the door, expecting to see Veronika's petite frame. Instead, a wheeled rack of dresses steamrolled in.

"These all fit your measurements," Veronika said. "I'll let you pick one and dress."

Veronika left again, leaving Kira to gaze upon the rack of dresses. Thirteen in all, varying in necklines—square, sweetheart, keyhole, slit, V-neck, and round. Most of the dresses were shirtwaist, a few button dresses, and two were wrap dresses. The colors varied from pale pink to cornflower blue to black. But it was the rich emerald dress that caught her eye and kept demanding her to return her gaze to it. Veronika had also found undergarments for her. Kira dressed, instantly feeling self-conscious that she did not do the dress justice.

Veronika knocked and entered. "Oh, you look great!" she said, her voice scandalous.

Kira smiled to show her appreciation. Veronika grabbed a towel and dried Kira's hair. Kira studied her reflection in the mirror. All the grime and dirt, soot and blood, were gone. Her alabaster skin tone had returned, appearing as if it had been polished. Her thin lips were barely visible. Veronika combed through Kira's damp tangled mess of hair. Hair enslaved in braids now liberated.

"Do you have a preference on how to style your hair?" Veronika asked.

Kira bit her lip. Whenever Nousha and Lina talked about hairstyles, it always sounded like some foreign language. One Kira never wanted to learn. Veronika assured her it was fine. She listed off the possibilities: bouffant, curls, victory rolls, and pompadours. Each more foreign and unknown than the last. What was the name of the style that Nousha and Lina had styled their hair in? She could picture it. But would that fade?

"May I choose?" Veronika asked.

Kira nodded, relieved to defer. Veronika combed, brushed, and applied hot rollers, styling Kira's hair in a style known in the West as victory rolls. The curls were tight around her face and the crown of her head. Her long dark hair, that fell to below her shoulders, was now curled to the middle of her neck. Veronika picked black slip-in pumps that angled her feet and increased her height a few inches. What impractical footwear. The last piece to her makeover was makeup. The 1930s had focused on reshaping eyebrows and contouring the face. The 1940s favored a more simplistic approach, or so Veronika explained. Nousha and Lina would have gotten along grandly with Veronika. The thought brought a heaviness to her heart.

Much of the reason that women in the Forties preferred a more simplistic look was that they faced cosmetic shortages as petroleum and alcohol, main ingredients in makeup, were needed in the war effort. Veronika explained she had gotten creative, using beet juice to stain her lips and petroleum jelly to darken her lashes and shape her eyebrows. But now she didn't even have that at her disposal. Kira knew how much makeup meant to some women, her sisters included. But like her sisters, Veronika didn't need it. She had a gorgeous face and long, fluttering eyelashes.

"Less is more," Veronika warned Kira.

There was as much involved with applying makeup as calculating a long-distance shot. Baby oil was applied first, then foundation, powder, and rouge. Veronika used a dark pencil to shape her eyebrows, and gray eyeshadow to make Kira's green eyes pop.

"But in the evening, you can use silver or gold," Veronika said.

The lipstick was a rich matte red. The final touch was nail polish, also red. Kira stared at the stranger in the mirror. She'd never paid attention to her body before, but now she noted the way her breasts filled out the front of her dress, and the curviness of her hips. And for the first time, she could see her mother in herself the way her father always could. She had to fight the sensation to reach out to see if the woman in the mirror would reach out in response. Nousha and Lina had always enjoyed styling their hair and applying makeup. Kira had considered it painful, but this hadn't been. Not the actual application, at least. The pain she felt came from realizing the memories she had missed out on, and that realization ached in her chest. She could never rectify them. They would never exist.

"Well … how'd I do?" Veronika asked.

"I don't even know who this woman is …" Kira uttered.

"Please. This beauty was always here. Makeup never makes a woman beautiful. It simply accentuates."

Kira turned her gaze from the mirror to Veronika. "Thank you."

"It's the least I can do for the Angel of Death."

Veronika explained every step of styling her hair and applying makeup, and Kira listened as intently as she had in sniper school. Veronika helped Kira slip her long gray wool coat on, then left the room. Kira lingered to examine herself in the mirror a moment longer. Not for vanity, but for the palpable feeling that it was her mother gazing back at her. If Gerasim had seen her, he would have accused her of being Narcissus from Greek myth who fell in love with his own reflection. The thought brought both joy and worry, and her mouth was caught somewhere between a smile and a frown. Where was her best friend?

Kira stepped out of the room. Colonel Volkov gazed at her like a father seeing his daughter on her wedding day, a coy smile forming in the corners of his mouth. Kira had a gruffness to her, but now, makeup concealed it. The woman before him was feminine with enough sex appeal to disarm men.

Colonel Volkov lifted a large black case onto Veronika's desk. It resembled a guitar case, but it was much larger. He flipped open the locks. It wasn't a guitar but a different string instrument. One Kira didn't know by name.

"Double bass," Colonel Volkov said, as if he had read her mind.

He lifted the instrument out of the black felt and handed it to Veronika. He ran his fingers along the edge of the case and removed a false bottom. Underneath it was her disassembled rifle, a cloth coin purse filled with all the bolts and screws for it, a box of ammo, and a small screwdriver. Volkov lifted her TT-30 pistol and placed it inside a black purse. Veronika had packed a suitcase with more dresses, socks, undergarments, and a single pair of pajamas.

"There is money in the purse. *Reichsmarks* and *Francs*," Colonel Volkov said.

Veronika lugged the suitcase, Kira the double bass case, and together, they toiled after Colonel Volkov up the stairs. The sunlight refreshed Kira, powering her as if she were a cold-blooded animal. Sometimes, we all just need to feel the sun on our faces. And for Kira, it was escaping that claustrophobic feeling the basement afflicted her with.

Kira and Veronika loaded the luggage into the back of a GAZ-67 jeep. Veronika surprised Kira by hugging her.

"Good luck. I will see you when you return."

Kira thanked her and then sat in the back seat, while Colonel Volkov took the passenger seat. The driver stayed silent on the drive east out of the city. Colonel Volkov explained her itinerary. She would fly to Sweden, then fly to Spain. From Spain, she'd take a train to Paris. Both Spain and Sweden were neutral, meaning it was far easier to land there than occupied territory. She reviewed all the forged identification papers, documents, and photographs in her purse, and then slipped them back in her bag, ensuring nothing had fallen between the seats or onto the floor.

When the car stopped and they stepped outside, it was the complete opposite of Stalingrad. The war hadn't happened here. The air was pure, and trees in the distance provided the freshest and deepest breaths Kira had had since she had read on the bluff back home. The grass was vibrant green, giving a different sensation than walking around the rubble of Stalingrad. It was spongy. Her feet bounced into the next step. But for how beautiful it was, a winter storm loomed. One you could feel coming in your bones.

Kira's driver loaded her luggage onto the plane.

"Your mission is to kill Jürgen Wolff and return. Understood?" Colonel Volkov said.

Return. This was not to be a suicide mission. She couldn't deny that him saying that meant something. That she was more than just a number.

"I will do my best, Comrade Colonel," Kira said.

Colonel Volkov got back into the GAZ-67 and returned to Stalingrad. In what felt like minutes, the weather turned mean. The wind nipped. Snow started to fall. A slender man wearing a *ushanka* stepped toward Kira. His cheeks were flushed red from the cold.

"My name is Semyon Peukhov. I will fly you away from this frozen piece of shit to an equally frozen piece of shit," he said.

130

Kira had her doubts if he would return to Russia after he flew her to Spain. He looked miserable and winter hadn't even started. He may stay in Spain for the rest of his life. The plane they were flying in was a Yakovlev Yak-6. Semyon affectionately referred to it as 'the Yak.' Semyon's co-pilot, Yuri Genrich, finishing the preflight inspections, chimed in that that wasn't the most charming of nicknames.

"We are all set," Yuri said a few minutes later, blowing on his hands.

Semyon helped Kira climb aboard. He and Yuri took their seats, bringing the plane to life one switch at a time. Leading up to the flight there had been too many questions to ponder for Kira to get nervous, but they now all lined up neatly for her to worry about them one at a time. She'd never flown before. The only truth she knew was gravity. What went up came down. It didn't matter what it was. Even a feather fell. Now, she was in a hunk of aluminum that weighed thousands of pounds. *How in God's name could this stay suspended in the air?*

The front propeller hummed, a rotating blur. Semyon pushed on the throttle. The plane rushed forward, faster and faster. Kira clutched the sides of her seat, digging her freshly polished nails into the fabric. Her stomach felt like a volcano moments before eruption. An invisible force shoved her back into her seat. A temporary weightlessness filled the plane as it defied logic, resisted gravity, and rose higher and higher into the sky. A horrifying exhilaration and an exhilarating horror. The plane rose to 10,000 feet before leveling off. Kira released her death grip on the seat cushion. She gazed at the world outside her window. A child gazing upon a doll house. Stalingrad loomed out of the left window, flashes of light visible even from this high and this far away. *Is this what the battle looked like to God?*

A while later, Semyon leaned back toward Kira. "We must refuel. We will land in Kostroma."

It was a city east of Moscow. But it wasn't the city that had gotten her attention, it was the word 'land' and its troublesome definition. The ground grew out of the cockpit window. Her body shifted forward. Her nails dug into the seat cushion in response. This was no longer horrifyingly exhilarating or an exhilarating horror. It was sheer, undiluted terror. She debated closing her eyes. Even the sounds the plane made were cause for concern. The hum of the engine reached some musical crescendo. The plane jerked and shook, as if the hull would snap away at any moment. Her breathing raced. The ground was upon them. The wheels of the plane bounced on the runway. Kira expected the plane to roll over onto itself, snapping its wings. The brakes screeched, but the plane still traveled deathly fast.

Finally, by the grace of God, it slowed and came to a stop. Though the plane had stopped, her stomach still sloshed about. She deboarded and then asked the first person she saw for a bathroom. Inside the bathroom, she leaned over the sink and slurped water to get the taste of bile out of her mouth. After wiping the sweat from her neck with the hand towel, she stepped back out.

Semyon offered her a cigarette to calm her nerves, and the two smoked while the flight crew refueled. She'd have preferred it if the flight had been broken into sections days apart. But maybe it was for the best that it wasn't. She had hated the landing. Having a day or two to think about it would have been torturous. The winds were frigid, so after she finished her cigarette, she waited in the plane while Yuri and Semyon went through the preflight checklist. She sandwiched her hands between her armpits for warmth. Dresses. What a ridiculous thing to wear in winter.

In less than thirty minutes, they were back in the air, soaring toward Sweden. The entire sky looked frozen. Even over the noise of the engines, the winds sounded like a swarm of wasps. Kira swore she could hear ice breaking as the wings sliced through the frozen air.

She didn't want to ask for a blanket; she already looked like a damsel in distress in that stupid dress of hers. She wrapped her wool coat tightly around herself, ensuring her legs were covered. She had hoped she'd be numb to any aches. She was wrong. Terribly wrong. Her lower back, knees, and butt all throbbed. Being this tense was physically draining.

Near Stockholm, they once more descended for landing. This one was not any easier for her. Landings seemed more like controlled crashes. Kira questioned their route. Surely there was a quicker way. Semyon answered that yes, there was, but it was too dangerous. The Allies and Axis fiercely fought over North Africa and Italy. Sweden was Pro-German but at least neutral, meaning the skies would be free of fighting.

"What about taking a ship from here?" Kira asked, as the three sat for a quick supper of lentil soup with the most infinitesimal bits of ham, along with a piece of stale bread. In these chilly temperatures of less than thirty degrees Fahrenheit, the soup went cold halfway through finishing it.

"U-boats in the Channel," Yuri said, chomping through his hardened piece of bread.

Passenger ships shouldn't be targeted, but no one with a straight face could tell the Germans that the Americans and other anti-Axis nations didn't use transport ships to smuggle weapons, food, and supplies into England. Of all their sins, Kira didn't blame the Germans for this tactic; she blamed the Allies for risking the lives of innocent people.

Even with a mind full of thoughts of crashing, her shivering, and the sheer uncomfortableness, Kira fell asleep on the plane. A pure sleep undiluted with dreams. But something woke her. The sound of a million angry bees defending their hive. The sound grew louder. The air vibrated.

"What is that?" Kira asked.

"I don't know, but it's getting louder," Yuri answered.

Semyon told Kira they were over the English Channel. It looked like a sheet of black marble from this height, the horizon a cerulean-tinted black. A mass cloud of mayflies soared toward them.

No ...

The horror of what was beyond the cockpit crashed over her. It was no swarm of insects. It was the mighty German *Luftwaffe*.

Heading right toward them.

The Eagle's Nest

It didn't sit well leaving the others behind. But Reinhardt couldn't deny there was an aching in his bones to return to Germany. It was where he belonged. He was allotted a guest on his tour of Berlin. And a much-needed face from his prewar life awaited him outside the airport. Mathias hugged Reinhardt. The war had aged Reinhardt; his handsomeness was more refined now. Mathias looked older, marginally so, but older. The last time he'd seen him, Mathias had been on his knees in front of a toilet.

"Reinhardt ... your accomplishment ... it's unbelievable. I'm proud of you," Mathias said.

Reinhardt shrugged at the praise. "What about you? Clocking sixty hours a week yet?"

The last he'd written, Mathias stated he worked ten-hour days Monday through Saturday.

"Seventy-two," he explained.

"Building airplanes?"

"Messerschmitts and Junkers."

"How about you build one that can't get shot out of the sky and that repels bullets?"

Mathias chuckled. "I think the one you have has done quite well for you."

The chilled air was refreshing, not debilitating. Perfect for an afternoon walk. Reinhardt told Mathias about his trip to Rome with Günter and Klara, and all the chess he'd been playing.

"Still pushing the queen's gambit?" Mathias asked.

"You know I like strong women."

The Reich Chancellery was an elegant sight to behold. Biased as a German may be, Reinhardt felt it was worthy of recognition to be called a wonder of the world. Had Alexander the Great still been alive, he would have visited the immaculate building.

Reinhardt stated his name to the guard. The guard allowed them to enter. Another guard led them through the ornate labyrinth too quickly for them to admire all the marble, statues, and paintings. In an office larger than a classroom, Hermann Göring sat. He was shy of six feet, cleanly shaven, and hefty. Reinhardt and Mathias sprung into the Nazi salute, shouting Heil Hitler. Göring reciprocated the greeting.

"Reinhardt Friedel, I have heard of your heroism in Russia. Germany is honored to have a son like you defend her," Göring said.

"Thank you, *Reichsmarschall*," Reinhardt said.

Göring's eyes drifted to Mathias. "And who is this?" he asked, unable to withhold judgment of the scrawny, short, bespectacled boy-man.

"My best friend, Mathias Holdenbrücke. He has worked all hours, day and night, building the finest aircraft in the war," Reinhardt said. "We must not forget the sacrifice all Germans make."

Göring smiled, though it was obvious he didn't share the same praise for the men and women toiling away in factories or the farmers feeding their country. It was the headlines the Reich wanted.

Göring asked how the war in the East waged, and Reinhardt was savvy enough to know what he wanted to hear. A photographer took a picture of them shaking hands and then Mathias and Reinhardt joined Göring for a dinner of Viennese chicken and crab deep-fried in its shell and served with spicy sauces. Göring ate with frenzy, his eyes wide with excitement. Reinhardt did not indulge in the crab—the animal terrified him. The look, the scamper. Just looking at it was enough to make him shiver. And Mathias knew him well enough to know that just having the crab at the table made Reinhardt uncomfortable. Mathias fought off his grin by keeping his mouth full.

Bienenstich (bee sting cake), sweet yeast dough topped with caramelized almonds and filled with butter cream, was served for dessert. Reinhardt and Mathias, both restricted to rations, salivated from the explosion of flavor. For Göring, this caliber of meal was always available. But for Reinhardt and Mathias, it was a reprieve from monotony. Whatever medal the *Führer* would give him, he could keep it. Reinhardt would gladly take a second helping of dessert instead.

After the dinner, Göring excused himself for a meeting but thanked Reinhardt again for his service. Bloated and full, Reinhardt and Mathias left the Reich Chancellery.

"Did you see Ilse this summer?" Reinhardt asked.

Ingrid's attractive face, then body, flashed in his mind. She was most likely married now to a man Reinhardt had seen but couldn't recall what he looked like. Mathias's face drooped into a frown. Not uncommon when it came to Ilse. But as Reinhardt stared at him, this frown was different.

"What is it?" Reinhardt asked.

"They took her," Mathias said.

"Took her? Who took her?"

Mathias cast a 'you know who' look. "Her and her whole family."

"East? To Poland?"

Mathias shrugged. "I don't know."

Reinhardt had known Ilse was Jewish, not overly devout, but it'd never mattered to him. He'd heard all the propaganda about the Jews, but he didn't know what to think. The Nazis seemingly had proof that they caused all of Germany's hardships, but he knew Jewish families. Families like Ilse's. To Reinhardt, they were no more to blame for Germany's hardships than he was. *Lebensraum* was the name given to the reasoning. Living space. A designated area for undesirables.

How was Ingrid? Had her mind about the Reich changed? How was married life? He had enjoyed their moments together, but he wanted more. And so had she. He wanted a woman to share more than a bed with. He wanted someone who challenged him, inspired him to ascend beyond what he was capable of alone. Watching Günter and Klara at the Trevi Fountain had sparked something inside him. A *Wanderlust* feeling to find his own Klara.

"I'm sorry about Ilse," Reinhardt said.

"I'm sorry for her, too," Mathias said.

Reinhardt asked if there had been any women since he'd been gone. Mathias let out a sigh. "Loads," he joked. "What about you? Violate Rome enough?"

Reinhardt smirked. He told him the truth. There'd been no women. Mathias didn't need an explanation. The war had shifted desires inside Reinhardt. Rearranged priorities.

The Reich had set Reinhardt up in a room at Hotel Kaiserhof. It was the first hotel in Berlin in which every room had its own bathroom and telephone. Once inside their room, Mathias dug into his suitcase and withdrew a chessboard. Mathias played as white and, therefore, was given the first move. All of Reinhardt's attempts at taking Mathias's queen were thwarted; Mathias was no novice. Mathias gathered a plus three advantage and then devastatingly took one of Reinhardt's rooks with his bishop. Reinhardt thought ahead one, two, three, and four moves. But no matter how many scenarios he tried, he couldn't get past four. Mathias had him.

"You smug bastard," Reinhardt said, tipping his king over in forfeit.

"You're easy to entice. Always chasing a good-looking woman," Mathias said.

During the second game, Reinhardt exacted revenge, launching a devastating bishop and knight attack. Once he moved his knight, Mathias was in check. He had to move his king, leaving his queen to be captured by Reinhardt's knight. Seven moves later, Mathias surrendered.

"Now who's the smug bastard," he said.

The third game was a defensive battle, ten moves in and each had lost only a pawn.

"Are you scared over there?" Mathias asked.

"About this game?" Reinhardt asked, deciding on where to move his queen.

"No, *over there*," Mathias clarified.

"Yes, and no … you're aware of death, but you can't stop it … You just learn to exist in that world," Reinhardt said.

"I don't think I could have done what you did. Saving all those people."

"Yes, you could have." Reinhardt slid his bishop into check.

Mathias blocked it with a knight. "No, I don't think I could."

Reinhardt advanced a pawn. Mathias put his hand on one of his own pawns, unsure whether to commit to the move when Reinhardt grabbed his hand.

"Yes, you would have. Everyone gets a moment in life to prove it. You'll surprise everyone. Everyone but me."

Mathias nodded, clearing his throat from the swell of feeling in it. "I wish I could be there with you."

"You are. I wouldn't have joined if not for you."

But the truth was it elated Reinhardt that Mathias couldn't be there. War is glorified. It's easy to fall into its allure. The sharp uniforms, the parades, the medals, the songs. But the reality of it is blood, fire, and death. No more. No less.

The chess match was balanced, each having lost the same value of pieces. When Reinhardt reached to move, Mathias waved him off.

"We'll finish later."

He wouldn't say when, but Reinhardt knew what he meant without it needing being said. It was to be continued when Reinhardt saw him next. *If* he saw him next. No matter how trivial, this chess match was some manner of unfinished business that would help keep him alive. Or so Mathias thought. But none of those things matter in war. It doesn't matter what your plans are.

"When we write, include your next move," Reinhardt said.

Mathias sketched the board and where each remaining piece resided. Reinhardt studied it to make sure his drawing hand didn't go from realism to expressionism in terms of where the pieces lay on the board.

The hotel had mastered comfort. Reinhardt had no trouble falling asleep. But *staying* asleep proved difficult. Ilse flashed into his thoughts. Forced to move because she was Jewish. His thoughts went to Günter and Uwe. Were they alive? Did they keep up chess without him? He missed them. But there was another absence he felt. One that scared him. Battle. He missed it. The speed of his Bf 109, the way all his senses amplified in the air. The way the tiny hairs on his arms and neck stood. The adrenaline. The camaraderie of us versus them. It was the ultimate chess match. Reinhardt had never felt more alive than he did on the cusp of death. It was the ultimate drug.

Reinhardt's bus to Alderhurst left at seven. Like he had before, he'd planned to sneak off before Mathias woke. But Mathias was seated in the chair, waiting for Reinhardt to wake.

"I thought about sneaking out on you. See how you like it," Mathias said.

Reinhardt gathered his things, and Mathias followed him to the bus stop.

"So, I had you in check, right? My pawn one move away from promotion?" Reinhardt asked.

Mathias rolled his eyes. "Cheating's beneath a Hero of the Reich."

"No, it's not."

They shared a quick laugh as the mechanical shifting of the bus grew louder. It let out a puff of smoke as the hydraulics sighed, and the bus came to a stop.

"Work on that unshootable airplane, yes?" Reinhardt said.

"Will do," Mathias said.

Reinhardt paused. Goodbyes forced him to contemplate whether they would be temporary or permanent. "Tell my family I love them."

"I will."

The possible finality of it was impossible to ignore. But to give voice to that possibility seemed like it would jinx it. So, neither did. They hugged and then Reinhardt stepped onto the bus. The door closed, and the bus shuddered forward. The bus ride was long and uncomfortable. Reinhardt had wanted to stay awake to watch Germany outside his window, but the lack of sleep and boredom of the drive coaxed him to sleep. Some six hours later, Reinhardt's stop had come. A soldier of the *SS* waited for Reinhardt and drove him to an empty parking lot, where four other servicemen waited.

Commissioned in 1937 by Martin Bormann, the *Kehlsteinhaus*, or Eagle's Nest, was near the town of Berchtesgaden and erected on the summit of the Kehlstein. Reinhardt and the others separated into two black Mercedes-Benz 770s. Sleek and gorgeous. It added to the infinite list of reasons Reinhardt loved Germany. The drive covered over four miles and ascended 2,600 feet. A 407-foot tunnel, lined with marble, lay ahead. It was prime real estate for people afraid of enclosed spaces to freak out. Reinhardt was okay in the tunnel. It wasn't like his Messerschmitt cockpit was spacious. The sailor next to him had served on a submarine. He'd be fine in here for years, but the soldier next to him looked to be on the verge of a panic attack. At the end of the tunnel, Reinhardt and the others stepped out. There was no room for the cars to turn around, so the two black Mercedes-Benz retreated in reverse. Reinhardt and the others stepped into an elevator. The interior was green leather, polished brass, and Venetian mirrors.

"Hope this doesn't get struck by lightning," a sinewy soldier said.

The sailor next to him looked at him to see if it'd been a joke. It hadn't been. The threat of this metal box 1,800 meters above ground being struck by lightning was a legitimate concern. The elevator door opened and every single one of them experienced some level of relief, spoken or otherwise. A short man with thin lips and a sunken mouth greeted them. Reinhardt recognized him; it was Joseph Goebbels, dressed in a gray suit with a swastika patch on the left arm.

"Welcome, heroes of the Reich!" he said.

He introduced himself and shook hands with his distinguished guests.

"The *Führer* has business he must finish," Goebbels said. "But perhaps you'd like to see the view."

He gestured for them to follow him outside. The air was thin and freezing. The walkway was tan stone. Reinhardt's mouth opened in response to what he saw: a breathtaking 360-degree view of the Bavarian Alps. The sort of views he saw in his Messerschmitt, but unlike in his plane, where he traveled at hundreds of miles per hour, here, everything was still. A glimpse of a world that no longer existed. The beauty of the landscape transcended anything Reinhardt had ever seen. Hitler, afraid of heights, limited his time spent at the *Kehlsteinhaus*. What an incredible waste.

"Tell me, gentlemen," Goebbels said, spreading his arms toward the view worthy of being painted a thousand times. "Have you ever seen anything as magnificent?"

No. Germany was gorgeous. Reinhardt had never taken its beauty for granted. He longed for it in his bones. No other place in the world could hold a candle to this place. He had thought he'd remembered it well. But memories can never capture the awe the way experiencing it does.

Goebbels left Reinhardt and the others to see how the *Führer* was coming. Reinhardt took deep, meditative breaths. Clean. Crisp. Cold. The other four continued talking amongst themselves, but Reinhardt paid little attention to them. Whatever they had to say paled in comparison to the beauty of this serene scene. Fall silent in nature and you will hear it speak to you. This view had existed for thousands, millions of years, and if man didn't destroy it, it would exist for millions more. The scope of it put your own existence into perspective. In hundreds of years, maybe less, no one would even know or remember that Reinhardt Friedel from Rastede, Germany, had stood in this spot waiting for a medal. Maybe that was why the *Führer*, a larger-than-life person, didn't like it. It made him realize he was only a man. Mortal. Temporary. That even if his dreams of a thousand-year Reich came to be, it'd still be a blink in the eye of this place.

Minister Goebbels announced the *Führer* was ready, and Reinhardt and the others followed him inside. A dinner table was in front of a red-brick fireplace—a gift from Benito Mussolini. Reinhardt and the others sat, waiting for Hitler and the food that would follow. When Hitler gaited in some five minutes later, they stood, snapping into the Nazi salute.

"*Heil, mein Führer!*" they shouted.

Hitler smiled, patting his parted hair flat. Goebbels made the introductions. The sailor from the *Kriegsmarine* was Rudolf Blaustehl. The sinewy soldier who had made the comment in the elevator was *Rottenführer* Hans Heinrich. The short, stocky blond was *Oberschütze* Leon Nachtnebel. And Johan Betzer was a tall, quiet *Hauptsturmführer*. Goebbels introduced Reinhardt last.

"*Mein Führer*, an honor," Reinhardt said.

Once Hitler sat, the others did, too. Reinhardt's stomach rumbled at the unlimited possibilities of what would be served. Rationing did not exist for the highest representatives of the government. Steak and potatoes. Pork chops and sauerkraut. Sausage and cheese. Beer and pretzel. Bring them all. But Reinhardt struggled to feign his disappointment when the first dish was vegetable soup. No beer, but at least it was lemonade. The next course was a salad with hard-boiled eggs sliced atop it. The main course was a dish called *Eiernockerl* (egg dumplings), one of Hitler's favorite dishes. It left Reinhardt disappointed. After eating dinner, he normally smoked a cigarette, but the guard had warned them the *Führer* was vehemently against smoking. Hitler asked questions throughout the early supper. Some about the war, but more about the cities the men came from and their families. After the plates and silverware were cleared, gloved guards brought the medals out in black presentation cases. Photographers and journalists, handpicked by Goebbels, snapped photographs and jotted notes. Reinhardt and the others lined up; Reinhardt was last in line.

Hitler read through their exploits. Leon Nachtnebel had stormed a machine-gun nest in Libya, eliminating the enemy who had gunned down countless German soldiers. *Rottenführer* Hans Heinrich had jumped on a grenade to save his fellow soldiers. The grenade had not gone off, but he hadn't known that when he leapt on top of it. Rudolph Blaustehl's U-boat had been sunk in the North Sea. He pulled nine sailors from the water and into a life raft, then dragged the raft as he swam three miles to shore. Johan Betzer was a sniper commended for killing twenty-six Soviets in a single day of combat, and fifty-three over three days.

"Reinhardt Friedel flew bravely against the Soviet savages, already a recipient of the Iron Cross First and Second Class for his superiority in the sky, shooting down Soviet after Soviet after Soviet."

It was a glimpse of the fanatical passion Hitler exuded during his speeches. His face reddened, his hands jutted demonstratively, and spittle slung.

"He had earned the right to return to base. But several of our valiant soldiers of the sky were not afforded such a fortunate outcome. Stranded, injured, outnumbered, they faced certain merciless slaughter. But in the sky was a war eagle. Reinhardt Friedel swooped down and obliterated his enemy of vermin. He landed his plane, and on the wings of his Messerschmitt, he transported seven of Germany's sons to safety. For his valor and intrepidity, I award Lieutenant Reinhardt Friedel the Knight's Cross with Oak Leaves."

Reinhardt bent forward. The Iron Cross First Class was worn on the left breast pocket, but the Knight's Cross was worn around the neck. The black Iron Cross was inscribed with the swastika in the middle and the year of the medal's inception—1939. The silver Oak Leaves were attached to the black, white, and red ribbon.

"But after hearing his story," Hitler continued, "I determined his gallantry and leadership are the exact caliber our *Luftwaffe* needs. Therefore, I promote Lieutenant Friedel to Major."

He patted Reinhardt's shoulder, and then Reinhardt stepped back into row with the others.

"You men have epitomized the courage and sacrifice Germany is capable of and must reach. When all of Germany rises to your caliber, victory can reside in no country but Germany! *Seig Heil!*" Hitler shouted.

The five recipients threw their hands up, repeating "*Seig Heil!*" three times. Hitler stood between the men for a picture, shook their hands once more, then disappeared into another room. Minister Goebbels smiled, thanking them before sending them to the elevator. Reinhardt longed for another look outside. Of all that had happened, it would be that view that would stay with him the rest of his life. As he walked, he could feel the Knight's Cross pressing against his uniform. Every German had heard stories of relatives or men from their hometowns who had earned the famed Iron Cross. Knew the level of pride in which they were held. And now, the name of Reinhardt Friedel would be held in such reverence.

In Foreign Territory

The buzzing grew louder. It no longer seemed like bees were flying at them, but they were flying into the hive. Yuri cursed. Kira looked on helplessly. Ahead, planes rose, fell, and swerved. Sheer chaos.

"Hold on!" Semyon told Kira.

Unnecessary advice. Her fingers were dug into the sides of her seat. Their plane was used for transport and had no weapons. It wouldn't matter. There had to be over fifty German planes. The prospect of outmaneuvering them was as improbable as fighting them. Sirens wailed along the English coast, warning its citizens bombing was imminent. How terrifying for those poor people. Cowering in basements, keenly listening for the whistling of falling bombs. Whose home or business was about to be destroyed? How many deaths? How many people would be buried under stories of rubble and have to wait to die? Kira's stomach churned at the thought.

The valiant RAF pilots stretched out from the English coast. The sky erupted with the sounds of gunfire and the mechanical hum of maneuvering planes. The tracer rounds of fire flashed like strobe lights. Semyon rose and dipped, doing whatever he could to not be an idle target. But they were at a severe disadvantage. The German *Luftwaffe* knew the Royal Air Force was its enemy and vice versa. But to both, this strange unarmored plane was a dangerous anomaly. A spacecraft from a distant galaxy. No sooner had Kira pondered that, than machine-gun fire ripped through, dotting the side of the plane.

"Are you okay?" Yuri shouted.

Kira shouted she was after checking herself for blood. More gunfire speckled the plane. A swooshing noise came from the engine. It was on fire, and flaming like a comet.

"Lost right engine!" Semyon shouted.

Black smoke billowed out, a warning that the plane neared its end. Yuri and Semyon shouted an ever-growing list of problems. Bullets pierced the cockpit glass. Kira leaned forward, covering her face with her hands. A bullet struck her headrest where her head had been a mere second ago.

"Yuri! Yuri!" Semyon repeated.

Kira leaned forward. Yuri slumped in his seat, his head tilted to the right, and three baseball-sized holes in his chest.

"Yuri ..." Semyon lamented.

"He's gone!" Kira shouted.

Semyon needed to stay present. Grief needed to be experienced, but not here and not yet. Because if he experienced it now, he and Kira were dead.

"Semyon. Focus," Kira said, as calmly as she could.

He nodded to show he understood but also to encourage himself. "I have to bring the plane down!"

Kira knew he had to, but hearing that need out loud terrified her. Landing had been scary enough when Semyon was calm and the sky wasn't a battlefield. But now there were a hundred and one things that could go wrong. The right engine puttered then died. The plane dipped to the right. The lone engine struggled to keep the plane airborne.

"Grab the parachutes! We must jump!" Semyon yelled.

Those words shook her whole soul, but she snapped into action. There was no time for hesitation. She took a deep breath in through her nose, held it for a few seconds, then released it through her mouth to calm her shaking nerves. The plane spun. Semyon abandoned the cockpit and helped Kira into her parachute before fastening his own. He opened the side door. The wind rushed in, sucking their breath away.

The plane's left wing snapped off, flinging Kira and Semyon to the opposite end and then back to the right. The double bass case, black purse, and suitcase flew out. Kira hit the wall. Semyon stumbled out of the open door, leaving her alone. The overwhelming fear of being alone in a crashing airplane consumed her. The whole cabin vibrated as if it would implode. But fear had never paralyzed her like it did most people. To Kira, there was always a voice whispering in her ear what she needed to do. Right now, that voice told her to escape. She crawled to the opening, took a deep breath, and flung herself out. She hyperventilated, unable to draw in breath. The wind felt like being slapped with a notebook. Beneath her was a black unknown. All thought was wind-stripped from her. Sea mist pelted her face, saturated her clothes. The force and speed were nearly enough to knock her unconscious. She reached for the parachute chord and yanked it. The parachute rose, lifting her just in time to avoid the canopy of trees. But only temporarily.

She braced for impact, arching her toes down, drooping her head into her shoulder. Leaves slapped her face and body; the thinner twigs scratched her hands and face, caught her clothing, and snapped off. Branches punctured the parachute. The boughs bludgeoned her shins and elbows. The straps tightened, and she jerked to a stop, dangling twenty feet from the ground. The nearest bough was two feet below her. A fall to the ground would at a minimum break her legs. To hope that if she released the straps, she would land on the bough two feet below her was a foolish optimism she couldn't fall victim to. She reached for the branch ahead and above her. Her fingertips grazed it. Once. Twice. She swung her legs to create momentum, then secured a grip around the branch. With her other hand, she freed herself from the parachute vest. The moment it was free, gravity seized her. Her grip slipped and she fell onto the bough two feet below, bruising her butt. But all things considered, it could have been worse. Much worse.

She'd climbed hundreds of trees growing up but never in a dress and shoes like this. Still, the principle was the same. Secure a hand or a foot and move the other, keeping as many points of contact as she could. She kicked off her shoes; they couldn't be trusted. When she was five feet from the ground, there were no more branches. She had no choice but to jump. The impact felt like the ground swung up to hit her feet. She spun around, trying to figure out where she was. Where was Semyon? As her adrenaline faded, pain took its place.

She limped ahead, feet throbbing, ass aching. She gasped. Ahead, a corpse swayed from the trees. Semyon. She stumbled to him. Blood covered his lacerated face. At the speed he'd crashed through the trees, the branches had been as lethal as knives. His shin bones had broke through his skin. She reached for him, calling his name. But he was gone. His parachute hadn't opened in time. She put a hand on his chest and recited a prayer for him and Yuri. She hated leaving him hanging from the tree, but he was too high to cut free.

She tried to get her bearings. The sky lit with flashes of light and booms of thunder. She grabbed her shoes, not because she wanted them but because it was something to do. An objective to accomplish. She continued searching for the black case, her suitcase, and her purse. All her forged documents were inside it as well as her pistol. A surge of heat swarmed the salty sea air. She descended the small hill. Plane wreckage burned. Black smoke seared her lungs, stung her eyes, and stained her face and dress.

How far away from a city or town was she? Was she not in England? Or some uninhabited island nearby?

The sound of a car engine drifted toward her. Headlights pierced the fog then blinded her. Doors opened and closed. A man spoke. She had no idea what his English words meant, but it was a safe assumption she should put her hands up. British soldiers advanced toward her. The flaming wreckage had been what sent them out. Either to save any British pilots or make sure no surviving enemy soldiers were left unaccounted for. The soldier who approached Kira was older than she had expected. A man well past his fighting prime. Perhaps he was a volunteer. When war was on your doorstep, everyone served.

Kira spoke; he wouldn't understand anything she said, but hopefully he would recognize the language. He must have, because he was even more confused now that the strange woman out in the wee hours of the morning near a burning plane crash was Russian. A younger man returned to them. He spoke to the older man then returned to searching the area. The old man pointed to the truck. Kira followed him to it and sat in the back. She stared out the window, waiting for trees and grass to turn into buildings and homes.

"*Ich spreche auch Deutsch,*" Kira said.

Not a popular language to speak in spy-worried England, but there was a far greater chance of someone here speaking German than Russian. The old man spoke into a radio then smiled. A universal gesture to instill comfort and calmness. Kira didn't fall for it—genuine or otherwise.

The sun peaked over the horizon, dull enough to be able to gaze upon the wash of purple and orange. As they entered a city, the name Kira didn't know, the fire brigade put out fires, and volunteers sorted through rubble searching for survivors. The German bombers had penetrated through the RAF defenses. What was the tally of dead? How many were buried alive and dying?

The truck stopped. Kira followed the old man inside a stone building. Kira couldn't help but notice they walked in the formation of the number five on a die, with Kira being the dot in the middle. Kira wasn't under arrest, but she wasn't trusted, either. Inside, it appeared to be a government building of some kind. The old man reported to a makeup-free elderly woman at the front desk. She made a call and less than a minute later, a man in a black suit and fedora approached. He removed his hat and extended his hand to Kira. Roughly thirty years old, he had a cleanly shaven face, dark eyes, and a strong, stocky build.

"James Wesley, mam. I understand you speak German?" he asked in German.

"I speak it," Kira said, then gave her name.

"Are you hungry, Ms. Kovalyova?"

It wasn't a question she had expected to be asked and one she hadn't even considered. But now that they had asked it, her stomach rumbled. It'd been hours since the small bowl of soup. Her pause was answer enough. Wesley smiled and told her to follow him.

He held the door open but stopped her before she walked out. "It may be best not to speak German on the streets. Wouldn't want to scare anyone, understood?"

Kira nodded. War caused paranoia. If someone heard the two of them speaking in German, it would cause a panic. At worst, a violent panic. Wesley smiled and then they walked a block to a small restaurant. Rations had greatly limited restaurants, but Kira had the feeling a special arrangement had been made on her behalf. Her choice was limited to cod or haddock. Fish had never been a staple of her diet. She was a hunter, not a fisherman. The smell wafting off her plate vanquished her hunger. The fish was pale and pungent. Maybe special treatment hadn't been given to her after all. Maybe they couldn't pay people to eat this. She gave it a try and found the secret to eating it was to not breathe when you chewed or swallowed, and then to wash it down with lemon tea before you could even taste it. Tea ... Good God, that wasn't much better.

"I hope you don't mind if we talk while we eat," Wesley said.

Kira shook her head.

"How is it you have come to England?"

Kira told him as much truth as she needed to. They had found the wreckage and certainly Semyon's body; perhaps Yuri's, too. Her reasoning for being sent to France was left redacted. She explained her flight from Sweden to what should have been Spain.

"I can only say that our countries are allies and what I have been ordered to do will benefit both our countries," she concluded.

Wesley thought on it, sipping on his water. He smiled and wiped his face with a serving napkin. "Then let's get you to France."

They returned to the government building to determine exactly how they would get Kira to France. Kira's black bag and suitcase had been found and looked exactly as you'd expect luggage pulled from a plane crash to look—covered in black stains and coated with ash.

"Found close by to where you were picked up," Wesley said. He flipped a light switch, revealing a washroom. "I'll grant you some privacy to clean up. If you require anything, please be sure to let me know."

He flashed a hospitable smile then left the room. Kira examined herself in the mirror, bashful at how she looked. Her victory rolls had been defeated, her lipstick smeared, and her ravishing green dress stained with dirt, blood, smoke, and grass. And upon closer examination, flecks of fish. Even her vivid green eyes had not been immune. They were bloodshot from the smoke. She changed out of the dress and patted her body with a moist washcloth, and then slid into a black dress. She recalled what Veronika had told her as she reapplied her makeup. The result was fine, but Veronika had made it look so simple. After, she worked at styling her hair. The result should be called the *Tie*, for the roll was neither victorious nor defeated. She opened the door, self-conscious of how she looked. Wesley nodded, a professional gentleman's gesture to show he liked what he saw. He stepped into the room.

"So, you're to be a musician?" Wesley asked.

Kira wanted to scoff at that but settled for a nod.

"Do you know how to play?"

Kira hesitated, then answered truthfully, "No."

"The Germans are no fools. It'd be wise to learn a few key notes. I can show you."

"You play ... this?" Kira asked, forgetting the instrument's name.

"It's called the double bass," he said, with a deserving smirk. "May I?"

Kira nodded; Wesley removed the double bass. He explained that this model was the 3/4, the most common variation. It was tall, making Wesley look like a doll with a guitar. He pointed to the four strings and labeled them: E, A, D, and G.

"If you learn just a few key chords, you can play a lot of music."

His fingers were surprisingly delicate. The bow moved fluidly. He called out each chord as he played them. Then he helped position the instrument in front of Kira and set her hand at the starting position. She visualized the way his fingers had moved, and the way the bow glided across the strings, then played. A painful shriek wailed out.

"Caress the strings, don't pull," Wesley said.

Kira kept it in mind and tried again. She came to an understanding. You freed the music the instrument possessed, and with that understanding, the sound emanating improved. Tranquil. Beautiful even.

"How did you learn?" Kira asked.

Wesley sighed, a noise that told Kira it was a long story, one starting when he was a child. "My grandmother taught me. I played at school, church, family weddings, holidays."

"And learning German?"

"I studied at the Hoch Conservatory in Frankfurt."

His many talents impressed Kira. "People don't think you're a German sympathizer?"

Wesley raised his eyebrows. "There are some. For certain. And you? How was it that a Russian woman learned German?"

"I read German books." Kira elected to keep the truth of her mother to herself.

"Self-taught?" An impressed look. "Are there many lady soldiers?"

"Some. The Germans attack both genders. Since you English and Americans have not opened a second front, we are all that stand in Germany's way."

Kira enjoyed watching and listening to Wesley play music. She found his ability to create melodies attractive. She focused on the movement of his hands. If the world had been different, would Wesley have pursued his love of music? A teacher or member of an orchestra? But like millions of others, his dreams had been put on hold. And for some, they were put on hold forever.

Kira played for three hours. Wesley called out the chords and Kira played them. After, they shared lunch. More fish. Lemon tea helped mask the taste. But nothing helped mask the taste of the tea. Afterward, Wesley drove Kira to the shore near Portsmouth. Small boats buoyed beside a wooden dock that had seen too many storms.

"We're taking one of those?" she asked.

The boat looked like a larger version of a child's bath toy. The Channel loomed ferociously, the shore foaming like the mouth of a rabid animal.

"Would you prefer to swim?" Wesley asked.

"I think I'll have to swim regardless," Kira said.

Wesley introduced Kira to the small crew. A grandfather, son, and grandson. They powered the meek engine and patiently waited for her to step aboard.

"Well, this is where I leave you," Wesley said.

"Thank you for your help."

"A pleasure."

They shook hands, Wesley holding her hand longer than customary.

"Oh, should you require anything …" He handed a white card with a number typed onto it. "Tell the person who answers that you're looking for someone to replace your shingles."

Kira pocketed the note and stepped aboard. The white boat left the dock; waving Wesley faded away. The sun had set. Darkness descended. Crossing the Channel at night wouldn't have been her choice. Then again, in this boat, no time would have been suitable. It took all of ten minutes for seasickness to inflict. Everywhere she looked, it was black. The ship sloshed and rocked. She focused her gaze on the stars. They were the only thing that broke up the blackness. She thought of Gerasim and what story he would have told if he were with her. Surely, it would have been something about Poseidon—God of the Sea. The waves washing upon the ship were their own music. But beneath the waves were monsters worthy of Greek myth—the German U-boats. But it didn't do any good to contemplate them. She had to hope the shark-like U-boats didn't notice the seagull-like boat resting on a piece of driftwood.

There was nothing for her to do but think and reflect. So much had happened in the last few days. Alekseeva's tragic end still stung. She could use her company and the soothing comfort her soulful voice provided. But sadly, her death felt like years in the past. Her contemplation made her feel guilty. Kira was alone. She'd traveled to Sweden and then to Great Britain. The ticket in her bag was for a train in Spain she would never board. Semyon and Yuri were both dead. Not dying for their country, but to fly Kira to Spain, and no one back home even knew they had died. And, as always, there was the permanent ache in her chest when she thought of her parents and her sisters. Its blade would always be sharp. She owed it to all of them to complete her mission. It hadn't started to plan, but no matter the setbacks, Kira was still on her way to France.

Train Ride to Paris

The train ride from Germany to France was coaxed in comfort. His cabin wasn't cramped at all. It had a private bathroom, a most fortunate amenity, as there was always a line for the public one. Servers fixed his drinks first, and the food was diverse and delicious.

The route didn't go directly west. Instead, it went along the Alps and then northwest toward Paris. Reinhardt was glued to the window. It seemed as if Hitler and Goebbels had noticed the awe in his eyes at the *Kehlsteinhaus* and rewarded him with this scenic train ride. Was this long, scenic route a thank you? If it was, Reinhardt didn't think the gesture was without ulterior motive. Perhaps they thought it would remind him of what he fought for. Where he was from. Further encircle themselves into the moldable minds of young men.

Around six in the evening, a servant knocked on his cabin door.

"Excuse me, sir," a cute young server said. "You have been invited to dinner."

She handed a small placard to him, curtseyed, and left. On the front of the placard was an embossed black swastika. A handwritten note was written on the back: *Honor us with your presence. Oberst-Gruppenführer Jürgen Wolff.*

Reinhardt knew better than to consider it a request. It was an order. So, he slid his Iron Cross First Class into his book as a bookmark and snapped it shut. He checked over his uniform in the mirror, ensuring it was wrinkle-free and that all the creases were in the right spots. He left his cabin and navigated the narrow hallway toward the dining cart. Every now and then, a rumble knocked him off balance. He ducked his head and opened the door to step into the next cart. Reinhardt looked at the tables, trying to decide if he would know Wolff when he saw him. But it took a wave for Reinhardt to know. Jürgen Wolff had dark blue eyes, and his graying hair was styled in a bald fade and slicked back on top. He wasn't alone. A woman a handful of years younger than him with striking blonde hair and olive-green eyes sat beside him, and to each side of them were two young children—a girl no more than twelve and a boy only eight. Reinhardt rose his arm in the Nazi salute.

"Major Friedel, it is an honor to meet you. May I introduce my wife Christiania and our children, Susanne and Manfred. And I am Jürgen Wolff," Wolff said.

Reinhardt nodded respectfully at Christiania and smiled at the children, then took the offered seat.

"I hear you came from visiting the *Führer*," Wolff said.

"Yes, *Oberst-Gruppenführer*," Reinhardt said, buttering a piece of bread.

"Really? What for?" *Frau* Wolff asked.

"A ceremony."

"Ah, a modest man," Wolff said. "Major Friedel received the Knight's Cross with Oak Leaves from the *Führer* himself. A tremendous honor."

The Wolffs focused their gaze at Reinhardt's neck.

"What'd you do?" young Susanne asked.

Reinhardt looked for the words, regretting answering the knock on his door. He hadn't even been able to finish his chapter, a major pet peeve of his. But luckily, Wolff answered for him. Detailing with a showman's flair Reinhardt's exploits in the West and East. The way he explained it made it seem worthy of being retold on the big screen. Wolff's wife and children stared at him in amazement.

"I want to be a pilot," little Manfred said.

"The greatest pilot who ever lived had your name," Reinhardt said.

"Really?"

"Yes, Manfred Von Richthofen. The Red Baron."

"I have heard of him! Papa told me!"

"Your father may know more than me given his rank, but I believe all parents are required to have permission to name their sons Manfred. It's a great honor and only those capable of living up to the name may have it."

"Seriously?"

Reinhardt nodded as he placed his hand on his heart. Manfred turned to his father and asked him if it was true. Wolff smiled as he nodded.

Manfred's smile changed to confusion. "But I'm named after an uncle. Mama says he's useless."

Wolff and Reinhardt burst into laughter. *Frau* Wolff looked aghast, turning the color of her wine.

"So, Reinhardt, where are you off to now?" she asked, desperate to change the topic.

"Paris, *Frau* Wolff. The Reich has given me a reprieve."

"We'll be in Paris for Christmas," she said.

Reinhardt's face showed his confusion. Were they not on a train heading to Paris?

"I have orders in Geneva. We get off in the morning," Wolff explained, catching onto Reinhardt's confused look.

A few moments of silence descended as they studied the menus. Snow slowly danced to the ground outside the train's windows. The special was *Sauerbraten*, pickled roast; this one, *Schweinebraten*, was served with braised cabbage and *Knoedel* (dumplings).

The Wolffs were pleasant company, hospitable, treating the train as if it were their own home, and offered Reinhardt the same advantage. Reinhardt wasn't a wine connoisseur, but he knew the bottles they drank were expensive.

"You saw the *Kehlsteinhaus*?" Wolff asked.

"Yes, *Oberst-Gruppenführer*. It was … unbelievable."

"Oh, it is breathtaking!" *Frau* Wolff said.

Manfred finished his dumplings and, possessing the normal amount of tact a child has, hijacked the conversation.

"Do you get scared?" he asked.

Reinhardt chewed on the thought, buying time by sipping his Riesling. He knew what the Reich wanted him to say. That no, he does not. He wasn't here to be a propaganda puppet, but he also didn't want to scare the boy. The answer required some thought.

"Of course. Everyone gets scared. But you have a job to do. Other people depend on you. You're never alone."

"Should I be afraid?"

Reinhardt shook his head with no hesitation. "No. The war is far from you. Hundreds of thousands of soldiers defend Germany."

Wolff nodded at Reinhardt with gratitude. A father's thank you. "I'll always be here to protect you and your sister."

After dinner, Manfred and Susanne returned to their rooms. Manfred insisted he wasn't tired, even as he spoke through a long yawn. Wolff, *Frau* Wolff, and Reinhardt smoked cigarettes, sipped on whiskey (wine for *Frau* Wolff), and watched the snow fall through the windows. Soon, the rest of the train car emptied. *Frau* Wolff sighed and rose. She kissed her husband's forehead, bid goodnight to Reinhardt, and left to join her children.

"Thank you for how you handled Manfred's questions," Wolff said.

"Of course," Reinhardt said.

Wolff took a long drag from a freshly lit cigarette. "Do you remember the Great War?"

Reinhardt shook his head. He'd been too young. But no German grew up without hearing the stories.

"War weighs on all. The soldiers certainly. But mothers and fathers, too. Wives. Children. What we tell the people is for their benefit. So is what we do not tell them."

Reinhardt only listened, taking relaxing drags of his *Eckstein*. A server checked on them. Wolff ordered whiskey refills for both of them.

"The *Führer* saved my life during the Great War," Wolff said.

Reinhardt raised his glass to his mouth but paused briefly after Wolff spoke.

"Battle of Passchendaele. You have heard of it?" Wolff asked.

Reinhardt had. Sometimes known as the Third Battle of Ypres, it had been fought from July through November 1917. His maternal uncle had died fighting there.

"The Earth had been destroyed," Wolff said. "Barren trees, scorched mud. As we repositioned across a floodplain, a bullet ripped through my shoulder. And then another through my left leg. Fear ... you spoke of it. We cannot help but feel it, can we?" He took a long puff of his cigarette, his fingers massaging it. A calming sensation. During war, cigarettes are the only thing to stop the shaking. Whether instinctively or by choice, he performed the action now. "I felt it, more than I felt the cold water drenching my uniform, more than I felt the stinging pain of the gunshots, or the warmth of my own blood. Many people don't know what it's like to see death lurching toward you. To this day, I swear I could see a faint figure cloaked in black. My heart raced. Fear raised the hair on my arms. But a man I only knew as Adolf dragged me out of the water. He risked his own safety to help me escape death's caress. If not for Adolf Hitler, I would have died in that muddy water. My body, my bones eroding in the soil. I never would have met the love of my life, never would have had my wonderful children. My shoulder, my leg, they still ache every day, reminding me of the debt I owe." He took a hearty swig from his tumbler.

"To the *Führer*?"

Wolff nodded, putting out his cigarette in the glass ashtray. "Yes, but to Germany as well. Over 2,000,000 Germans died during the Great War. Their sacrifice disgraced by weak men. We will honor those who have fallen and those who join them with absolute victory. Remove the Jews and communists who brought weak men into our government."

"A thousand-year Reich," Reinhardt said, raising his glass of whiskey in a toast.

Wolff did the same. "A thousand-year Reich."

Reinhardt returned to his cabin after their drinks were depleted. He removed his uniform and washed his face. He crawled into bed, turning onto his side to watch the snow through the window. The Great War had always been a looming figure, not hidden in the shadows, but ever-present over Reinhardt's entire life. He didn't know anybody who hadn't lost someone in the war. Weakness in leadership, Wolff had said. Reinhardt could never decide what it was he believed. He loved Germany. It could not endure another defeat. Its people couldn't live the way they had in the interwar years. If Germany lost the war, it may fade into the pages of history like Sparta and Rome before it. Reinhardt wouldn't let that happen. Reinhardt *couldn't* let that happen. Germany now. Germany forever.

The Givre Strudel

Kira fished the *Francs* from her purse and paid for her train ticket. Luckily, uttering "Paris" sufficed. Kira strolled through the station's gift shop as she waited for the train. The small shop was filled with postcards, books, and trinkets. Among the books was a German/French dictionary. She paid the woman at the register and started reading at A, whispering the words to herself.

The air had a damp chill to it. But to Kira, who had grown up and survived harsh Russian winters, this cold wasn't a legitimate danger but only a minor annoyance. The *thud thud thud* of the train approached. Waiting passengers turned toward the noise. Those closest to the tracks stepped back and those farther back stepped forward. A voice rang through the speakers. Kira followed the crowd onto the train. A few moments later, the train left the station. France had been the sight of many Great War battles, and its people had sacrificed tremendously. Nearly 1,500,000 deaths. Millions more casualties. These unfortunate men, missing limbs, afflicted with shell shock, had fought from the first day to the last day of the four-year war. But during the Second World War, France had broken and bowed to Germany in a matter of weeks. The city of Paris had fallen to the Germans by 14 June 1940.

Paris was a city everyone in the known world knew of. Kira knew of its history, its glamor, and its prestige. A strong sensation stirred in her stomach. Not nervousness, but excitement. *What a foreign feeling!* Until the war, she had never left her hometown. Now, she was moments away from visiting one of the grandest cities in the world. A place she thought she'd only ever experience by reading about it in novels. Filtered by fiction. Now, she would breathe the city. Be a part of it.

A while later, the train shrieked, slowing to a sparking stop. Kira grabbed her double bass case, suitcase, and purse, and stepped off. She didn't know where she was going, but figured other people knew where *they* were going. She followed them away from the train station into the epicenter of Paris. She dug into her purse and drew out the note with the scribbled address of where she would stay. She read the street sign, translated it into German, then to Russian. The building was antique tan brick with a glass entrance door on a stoop. Kira knocked and waited. An elderly woman with blue-white hair answered. Kira gave her name, and the hunchback woman arduously climbed the stairs all the way to the top, her ring of keys clanging against themselves. She wasn't an overly pleasant woman. Maybe she would have been if Kira's room was on the first floor. When the woman spoke, Kira simply smiled and hoped whatever foreign words she spoke warranted a smile. The room smelled of faded lavender, its potency weak, replaced by the smell of a long vacancy. There had been nobody to add smells of scented soaps, freshly laundered clothes, and cuisine.

The apartment was undoubtedly small. The kitchenette was to the right. Against the far-left wall was a mattress. There was a sofa, and a small kitchen table around which could maybe squeeze four people. Only the bathroom was its own separate room. It was small—a sink, toilet, and bath. The two windows in the apartment bathed the room in sunlight. Dust particles floated in its light. Kira made a mental note that the apartment needed to be dusted.

"*Merci*," Kira said.

The elderly woman held up two wrinkly fingers. "*Deux Semaines.*"

The gesture was blunt aggression, yet helpful in translating. Two weeks. Kira struggled to remember how to say, 'How much?' The old woman read her mind and requested the amount. Kira paid her, quite certain she was entitled to some change, but the old woman offered none. Change was apparently something lost in translation. The old woman handed her the bronze, jagged-tooth key and uttered a phrase Kira translated to, 'Have a day.' After consulting her German/French dictionary, Kira was certain the word good was not included, allowing Kira to have whatever day she saw fit. She locked the door behind the elderly woman and lugged the cumbersome double bass into the corner next to her bed. She tested the mattress to gauge how much sleep she could expect to get. The answer was a lot. By far the most comfortable bed she'd ever laid on. Even in the brief seconds she had laid down to test it, the mattress drugged her with sedatives. If she didn't sit up, she'd be asleep in minutes. And she couldn't afford to sleep.

Kira opened her purse and read through the files on Jürgen Wolff, but even sitting on the bed was too comfortable. She moved to a wooden chair at the kitchen table. The date was 12 December; Wolff was scheduled to arrive a week before Christmas. Kira studied the dates and facts, and stared at the photographs, trying to visualize what he looked like from different angles.

After reviewing them, she slid the folder under the center of her mattress. Paris had some of the best bakeries and cafés in the world. It'd be a war crime not to try them. She had dreamed of seeing Paris. She couldn't stay cooped up in the apartment for a minute longer. She stashed her TT-30 pistol in the toilet's water tank and then grabbed a handful of *Francs*. A light snow dusted the sidewalks. Cafés were everywhere, and the smell of fresh bread and coffee hung in the air, but there was one close by that had caught her eye and her nose: the Givre Strudel. The outdoor section was closed for winter, but the smell of freshly baked breads and pastries exhaled from the building like smoke from its chimney. The smell was enough to make her salivate.

Kira opened the glass door. Laughter and conversation struck her immediately, but more so the smell. She'd craved food before, but these smells had unleashed an animalistic craving with the slobber to boot. The café was packed. Servers delivered food and drinks, cleared tables. A woman with olive skin and pale-green eyes manned the register and greeted Kira, who was ready to deliver her first French sentence.

"Sorry, I do not speak French," Kira said.

"*Quelle langue parlez-vous?*" the woman asked, delivering each word slowly.

"*Allemande.*"

German.

The woman hid her expression well, but Kira saw a glimpse of how she truly felt. Almost imperceptible. This woman had mastered her ability to diminish what she thought. A less observant person never would have been able to catch the slight narrowing of her eyes. The slight tensing of her fingers, and the way her upper teeth slid over her bottom lip.

"Just you?" she asked.

Kira nodded and then followed the woman through the café. The woman had a fierceness to her, a silent strength. Writers are observant, snipers, too. Most people would have missed the subtle signs she exuded when she talked with a German officer. A hurricane inside, clear skies outside. It was a mastery Kira needed to emulate if she was to be successful in her mission. The woman's name was Josephine, and it would be easy to remember because everybody from staff to guests greeted her as they passed by. She was famous.

Josephine probably assumed Kira was here to see her German husband for the holidays. Kira wished she could tell her otherwise. That she was here to assassinate a high-ranking fascist pig. But of course, she couldn't. Yet Josephine was so great at keeping her hatred hidden, it made Kira question if it was even there. Josephine set a menu on a circular table meant for two. Kira thanked her and sat. Josephine left.

Judging by the way everyone stopped her to talk to her, it could take her an hour to get back to the hostess podium. Kira dug in her bag and removed her German/French dictionary, cross-referencing the menu items with it. Old couples, single French women, and German soldiers and officers occupied the café. Seated in the back corner alone at a table meant for two was a man in a dark gray uniform. He held a lit cigarette in his left hand, rubbing his thumb against it. In his right hand, he held a cracked book. On the table was the Knight's Cross.

A *Schadenfreude.*

The book obscured his face. Kira couldn't help but try to decipher his rank based on the patches and medals, but she didn't recognize the medal dangling from his neck. A wreath of half laurel and half oak leaves with a winged eagle clutching a swastika in its talons. What was that? She stared too long. The man felt it as if she had tapped him on the shoulder. He lowered the book and looked at her. His eyes were the most brilliant shade of blue she had ever seen. His wavy black hair was parted to the left. Kira looked away, but not before catching his smirk. She was equal parts embarrassed and angry with herself.

He rose from his seat. Kira focused more intently on the menu than natural, hoping to avoid his gaze as he left. But he didn't leave. His long, powerful legs had taken him to her table, and not a step further.

"May I?" he asked.

Before she could answer, 'No, you cannot,' he sat. Kira met his eyes. He smiled. Something strange happened in response to it. A sudden explosion of nerve endings firing through her body. Nervousness and excitement. The sensation of fireworks erupting in places she'd never felt. Her body temperature rose; her face felt like a lit candle. There was no lying. There was no denying. This was the most attractive man she had ever seen. Yet no matter how charmingly handsome he was, the uniform he wore instilled a passionate hatred. The chosen skin of a *Schadenfreude.*

"I believe I may be of help in translating these texts," he said.

Kira scoffed. "Texts? These aren't ancient hieroglyphs."

The man flashed a charming smile. "No, but I imagine it'd be easier for you if they were pictures."

"I don't need help," Kira said.

He smirked. The opposite effect Kira had intended. Instead of being intimidated, he was intrigued. And his smirk made her want to smile. She had to bite her lip to stop it from spreading.

"Of course not. I trust you can figure it out. My only worry is that the café will be closed by the time you do."

And now it was Kira who reacted the opposite way than intended. She wanted to scowl, but instead she smirked. He put a cautious hand on the dictionary and then lowered it to the table.

"Please, let me help."

It wasn't a request so much as it was a genuine offer.

Kira sighed. "Fine."

The delicious smell of melted butter, baked breads, brewed coffee, and frosted pastries was the best advertisement a café could have, and she longed to try all of them. Translating a menu was time her urges wouldn't allow for. He took the menu and displayed it to her like a parent reading a picture book to their child. Had the menu had pictures, he'd still be seated in the corner reading. He read off all the pastries, strudels, croissants, and drinks available. His voice was deep and smooth.

"So, what will it be?" he asked.

"The frosted apple strudel," Kira replied.

Before she could tell him he could go back to his corner, Josephine returned. Kira ordered the strudel, and the German ordered the same. He thanked Josephine.

"What's your name?" he asked Kira, after Josephine took the menu and left.

"Kira."

"What brings you to Paris, Kira?"

"You're not going to tell me your name?"

"You didn't ask for it."

Kira hated the way her own body betrayed her. What the hell was happening? My God, was she flustered?

"It's Reinhardt."

Kira nodded, hoping she wasn't blushing. "You were right. I didn't ask for it."

Reinhardt smirked. Those star-blue eyes glistening, moving as if they were a blue body of water. "What brings you to Paris?"

"The strudel."

Reinhardt laughed.

"What brings you to Paris?" she asked.

"The war."

"You Germans seem to bring that wherever you go."

Reinhardt did his best to ignore her comment. He lit another cigarette and offered one to Kira. She refused, but only because she didn't want to be in his debt. He snapped the silver cigarette case shut and pocketed it.

"You're not French. You're not German. So where is it you're from? I hear a bit of an accent."

"You wouldn't hear it back at your own seat."

Reinhardt chuckled and nodded at her jest. "True, very true." He paused, his eyes sparkling like topaz, his lips smirking. He scrunched his eyes, studying her as if her hair or eyes or lips would divulge her homeland. "Russian."

Kira neither confirmed nor denied. But it didn't make her feel very confident with her spy skills.

"Teach me a Russian phrase," he said.

Kira spoke one.

"What does that mean? 'Hello, beautiful?' Or 'Good afternoon? Please sit here with me forever?' 'Take me right here on this table?'"

Kira rolled her eyes. "Where is the toilet?"

Reinhardt laughed, making his eyes look like Christmas bulbs. He took a drag from his cigarette. "Your wit is as sharp as a knife, Kira."

"Not sharp enough to make you bleed. So, do I need a translator to eat French food?" Kira asked.

Reinhardt nodded in surrender. "Duly noted."

162

He rose to reclaim his corner spot, but two elderly French women had claimed it. Had Kira set the *Schadenfreude* off? Would he demand these geriatric women leave his seat?

No, he did nothing of the sort. Reinhardt smiled at them, then turned back to Kira.

"Would you be so kind as to allow me to eat my strudel before sending me out onto the street?"

There was certainly some gratification to be had in saying no. Though Reinhardt had asked for permission, some of the other high-ranking Nazis may intervene if she refused.

"Fine," Kira said, trying to land in the middle of irritated and indifferent.

"You're too kind."

Kira couldn't help but sneak a peek at the book he had been reading. *The Trial* by Franz Kafka. A book she'd read and enjoyed.

"You've read it?" Reinhardt asked, not missing the glance.

"I have."

A server delivered their strudels. Each topped with a dollop of frosting that made their plates look more like art than food. Kira dug her fork through it, scooped up a piece, and took a bite. Her eyes widened in shock. How could something taste so good? No, good was too short a word. Delectable. Mouthwatering. A firework grand finale of flavor exploded in her mouth. Reinhardt savored it equally. A supreme satisfaction that mimicked a Zen-like state. His eyes rolled back as he chewed.

"Imagine how many wars could have been averted if both sides sat down for strudel first," Reinhardt pondered.

Kira fell more in love with Paris with each bite. The experience was too short-lived. Reinhardt's plate didn't have one fleck of strudel or a smear of frosting left. It could have gone back into circulation with no one noticing. He stood and removed enough *Reichsmarks* to cover both strudels and leave a generous tip.

"Well, Kira, I hope you find whatever it is that has brought you to Paris. Perhaps we will see each other again," Reinhardt said.

He straightened his uniform and grabbed his book, and with long, proud strides, left the café. There were far too many people waiting for a seat for Kira to stay any longer. She left enough time that Reinhardt wouldn't be anywhere near the Givre

Strudel. But she couldn't deny there was some unexplainable desire to sprint out the door after him.

She thanked Josephine then walked the city. There was no greater way to learn and experience a city than by walking it. She remembered not street names but buildings. Memorizing the route from her apartment to the Givre Strudel. She set out toward the Eiffel Tower. No set route but to continue walking in the direction to which the Eiffel Tower grew. She sat on a bench and gazed at the marvel. Most of the French found the weather chilly, but winter was bred into her bones. The chilled air filling her lungs only soothed her.

The city had a curfew of 8 p.m., and Kira was sure to be back at her apartment well before then. She had walked over thirty kilometers and her feet let her know it. She opened the apartment door, expecting to find that the room had been ransacked by Nazis. But if someone had, they had also taken the time to put everything back and neatly fold her clothes and make the bed. She verified the TT-30 pistol was still stashed in the water tank. Then, because she had nothing to do, she removed the double bass and practiced. She turned the radio on for soft background noise. She visualized how Wesley's hands had moved when he played. Creativity had never been Kira's specialty. Creativity was subjective. No right or wrong. A gradient of gray, not the black and white world she craved. Gerasim had always been in awe of how Kira could shoot. But she had only watched her father, and now, after sniper school, it was math and instinct. Her thoughts drifted to Gerasim and the stories he had told. She stopped playing and stared out into space. How was he? She couldn't remember the last time she had seen him. She tried convincing herself that she would have known if something had happened to him. But what a naïve thought that was. Gerasim Petrov was a stat—a prospective name on a casualty report. The war claimed hundreds, thousands of Soviets every day. It was absurd to think that the Soviet Union could alert everyone of a loved one's passing. Would they even know? Could they even know?

Kira forced the cancerous thought from her mind. No good could come from it. Back to the literal task at hand. She didn't need to create the music herself. She simply needed to replicate it. She listened to the music playing on the radio and tried to mimic it. After an hour, her fingers stiffened and ached. She needed to stop anyway. The last thing she needed was a noise complaint. The kilometers of walking exacted its toll. Her feet ached; her lower back was stiff. She sat on her bed and gazed out the window. There were hardly any lights on throughout the city, robbing her of a tremendous view, but even so, the city was a dormant transcending beauty.

Her body was exhausted, her mind tireless. There are years packed into a day sometimes. A curtain call of characters came to her. Yuri and Semyon. Alekseeva. Nousha. Lina. Her mother and father. Gerasim. Galina and her family. And the German with striking, star-blue eyes and wavy hair black as space.

Exploring Paris

Though there were hundreds of cafés in Paris, Kira had no interest in going anywhere but the Givre Strudel. Addiction. That's what her relationship to the strudel was. A onetime consumption and hooked for life. She woke later than she had wanted to. Those 'just a few more minutes' had turned into an hour. fShe washed her face, fixed her hair, and applied a 'more is less' amount of makeup.

At the Givre Strudel, Josephine greeted her, somehow looking gorgeous with a dusting of flour in her hair and frosting staining the cuticles of her fingernails. They exchanged pleasantries and then Kira followed her to a vacant table for two. She had expected the menu, serving napkin, and silverware. What she hadn't expected, yet some physiological response certainly had hoped for, was the handsome German seated in the corner reading and sipping an espresso. Her eyes found him, then fell to the book. He hadn't even been halfway through it, but now he had only three or four chapters left.

Kira sat, lifting the menu to create the walls of Troy.

Too late. Achilles had come calling.

"I had taken your comment that the strudel had brought you to Paris as a joke, but I see it was the truth," he said.

He was smooth. Confident. No matter what looks of disdain she cast, Reinhardt was unfazed. He slipped his Iron Cross ribbon into the book and stood near the unoccupied chair opposite her.

"Do you spend your whole day here reading?" Kira asked.

"No," he said, but added no elaboration.

Kira looked over the menu, remembering only a handful of translations. But it didn't matter. Who was she kidding? She would order the apple strudel. Reviewing the menu was a desperate act of diversion, a pathetic attempt to keep her eyes on the alluring foreign text instead of the alluring foreigner's eyes and smile.

He was comfortable with uncomfortable. He stood there as she scanned the menu for a small eternity. One of them had to feel awkward in this situation and it looked like it had to be her. She set the menu down, feigning a sigh.

"So, while the war rages in the East, you get to stay here and eat strudel?" Kira asked.

Delivered in a far colder and more insulting way than intended. But no matter how pleasant his looks, that uniform ruined it all.

His smile was absent. No glimmer in his eyes. "The Reich feels I have earned a reprieve."

His face made it clear he hadn't asked to come, that a large portion of himself felt guilty about it. And now she felt bad about her comment. *What the hell was going on?*

"If you stand any longer, I'll make you take my order," Kira said, pushing a chair out with her foot.

Reinhardt chuckled, then sat. His eyes were hawk-like, locking onto hers. Studying her. Deciphering. Deducing. But never critiquing, never assuming.

"And what has truly brought you to Paris?" he asked.

"Music."

"Music ... you play?"

"Well, I don't eat it," Kira said. "Double bass."

An involuntary truth, even though it was no truth at all. What if he knew music like Wesley had?

"How extraordinary," he said.

Josephine stopped to take their order. Both elected for the apple strudel. An uncomfortable silence hung between them as they waited for it to arrive. She could feel his stare. Anxiety assailed her. What if he could sense what she had truly come to Paris for? But that was utter nonsense.

Or was it?

"What are you doing tonight?" he asked.

Kira shook her head. "Nothing. There is a curfew."

"Meet me here at seven."

"Why?"

"I want to show you something."

"What?" Kira annoyed herself with her single-word questions.

"Paris."

"I have seen Paris."

Reinhardt shook his head, leaning back in his seat. "No, you haven't."

A server set their strudels on the table. Both lifted their forks like sprinters waiting for the starting gun. It was even better than yesterday's. Compared to her army rations, it was as glaringly different as having seen only black and white and suddenly seeing the full spectrum of color.

Reinhardt finished his strudel first, wiped his mouth, and then stood. "I tell you what, Kira. I will be here at seven. If you choose to come, wonderful. But if you choose to lock yourself away and gaze down upon Paris like a caged bird, that is your right to do so."

"And let me guess … you won't judge me for it?"

"No, I absolutely will judge you for it, but I'll wish you a splendid evening all the same." He leaned forward and whispered in her ear. "*Oser Vivre.*"

His scent of anise, fennel, tarragon, and leather intoxicated her, causing tingles to pulsate along her body. Kira bit her lip to stop her smirk from becoming a full-fledged smile. Reinhardt—tall and broad-shouldered—strutted out of the café. Kira paid for her strudel, then left the Givre Strudel.

Show her Paris. That thought had been a virus, infecting and inflicting all other thoughts. Her stomach was a nervous wreck. But a good nervousness. A jittery feeling. Reinhardt intrigued her in a way no other man had. A handsome blend of rugged and refined. An avid reader. At five feet nine inches, Kira was taller than a lot of men she knew. Men didn't like that. She didn't like that. But Reinhardt was much taller. Not that she needed it, but she felt safe in his presence. Yet his uniform. Reinhardt was dangerous. As a person it remained to be seen. But dangerous for what he represented. Diversion. Distraction. Disorientation. Yet that only added to his allure.

She thought about not translating what he had said, but that lasted all of a minute. She scoured through her dictionary.

Dare to Live.

That suave son of a bitch.

Kira returned to her apartment and read through Wolff's files again. It was exactly what she needed. Details of a *Schadenfreude*. An ardent Nazi, a man who helped run Jews out of his country. A man who helped orchestrate the actions that brought the world back to war. She studied his face. Her mind sketching it. First, a long, oval-shaped face. Then narrow, fierce, dark sapphire eyes. Far darker than the brilliant star-blue of Reinhardt's.

Stop.

But even though she detailed silently to her mind Wolff's appearance—the long, oval-shaped face, sapphire eyes, graying hair slicked back on top with bald-fade sides, smug narrow-lipped expression—when that imaginary artist showed her its canvas, it was Reinhardt on it. His wavy space black hair styled in a bald mid-fade comb-over, his blue eyes that looked like they had been plucked from the night sky. Alabaster skin. Smooth, lean jaw. Tall and broad-shouldered.

Stop. Stop. Stop.

She ran an eraser through the imaginary sketch, but to her abject horror, the sketch was no longer pencil but ink. She placed all the files in the folder and slid it back under the center of the mattress. She verified her door was locked and her blinds shut before removing the fake bottom of the double bass case. Resurrecting the rifle like it was an artifact freed from a sarcophagus, she cleaned it, then assembled it piece by piece, bolt by bolt. She set a timer, challenging herself on how long it would take her. After assembling it, she timed how long it took to disassemble it. In theory, she had all the time in the world to assemble it. It was the disassembling that would be limited. Her own shot would condemn her by revealing her location. The easiest thing would be to leave the rifle. That was a last resort. This was her father's rifle. The only family heirloom she possessed. She assembled and disassembled it three times. Finished, she stored it securely under the false bottom of the double bass case.

Reinhardt had told her seven. The clock on the wall betrayed her. 3 p.m. to 4 p.m. took hours. Five to six, all of fifteen minutes. She read a book, but her mind was elsewhere. To pretend to read cheated the experience of reading. She couldn't go. It was as simple as that. Curfew for one. Mission another.

But how she wanted to see Paris. Truly see it. Experience it. Smell it, feel it, taste it, breathe it in. Yet there was some unexplainable desire to want to be around Reinhardt. The clock ticked abnormally loud, making sure Kira was aware of every second that passed.

She couldn't go. It was as simple as that.

Concentrate on your book. But her eyes kept glancing toward the clock. Minute by minute. Until finally at 6:30, she tossed the book onto her bed and stormed into the bathroom. She reapplied her makeup—burgundy lipstick and a light blush. She picked out her black winter dress. She knew the walk to the Givre Strudel would take less than seven minutes, but still she felt late. She didn't know what had made her change her mind. She liked to think it was the advice 'be invisible by being visible.' But she couldn't deny Paris had woken a dormant *Wanderlust* spirit in her. Nor could she pretend the charming German hadn't played a part in her spontaneous change of mind.

As expected, yet somehow a surprise, she arrived at the café in seven minutes. Early. Now, she was waiting for him. *Fantastic.* Josephine was inside, talking to a dark-haired man with a thin mustache sipping coffee. There were a few other guests inside. Closing time was mere minutes away. Kira discreetly checked the clock inside, hoping Josephine didn't see her.

What if he didn't show? Shouldn't he be early? She cursed herself for her current predicament. She still had an opportunity to leave. That's what she'd do. Maybe stop inside quickly and bring home whatever pastry Josephine had left over. She stepped toward the door, but a figure caught her eye. A man leaning against the brickwork, reading a few pages from his book.

Reinhardt.

Every now and then, he glanced around. It took a double take for him to notice Kira. He tossed his cigarette, squished it with his boot, then marched to her, slipping the book into his pocket. He tried to pass off his walk as normal, but there was excitement in his step. Dare she say a giddiness?

"You're early," he said.

"And so are you ... sort of," Kira said. Technically, he hadn't arrived at the Givre Strudel.

"Full disclosure. I did not expect you would come. I did not want my shame on full display for Josephine and her customers," Reinhardt said.

Kira politely laughed. "I could still walk away."

"You could." His gaze on her was fierce.

Had she overdone the makeup? Or not enough? Kira looked down at the sidewalk. But even though she couldn't see his gaze anymore, she could still feel it.

"Is something wrong?" she asked, summoning the courage to turn her head and meet his eyes.

Reinhardt didn't break his gaze when he shook his head. "No, but I'm afraid I must make you even more uncomfortable, Kira, because I must say, you look marvelous."

Kira blushed, feeling as if the color of her cheeks matched the Soviet flag. The sudden surge of heat made her feel overdressed.

"So, Kira," Reinhardt said, finding her eyes. "Are you ready to see Paris?"

Kira shrugged. It was all she could do. She still couldn't believe she was here with him. A German. A German soldier. Her intrigue was inexplicable.

"I will take that shrug as a yes," he said, his lips curling into a smirk.

He gestured for her to walk, and she did. Reinhardt ensured he was on her outside. The air was frosty. Kira dug her hands into her pockets as deeply as she could.

"So, how is it a German knows so much about Paris?" Kira asked.

"My aunt lived here. She died shortly before the war. My sisters and I visited her during the summer and holidays."

Kira imagined what his sisters looked like. Most likely beautiful.

"Do you like art?" Reinhardt asked.

Kira struggled for an answer. She didn't love it. She didn't hate it. Indifferent? Didn't care enough to even look was the most apt explanation. But she could appreciate the skill. The precision of drawing or painting a portrait. Tossing paint on a canvas and pretending the blobs and smears mottled on it held some deep meaning wasn't art.

"I wish I could show you the Louvre," Reinhardt said.

He explained that the French, anticipating an invasion of Paris, had evacuated the historic art museum's displays and pieces.

"Smart, given the Nazis' propensity to destroy," Kira said.

Reinhardt looked at her with a frown. "You should be careful saying something like that."

"Around other people or around you?"

Reinhardt met her eyes for a moment, then stepped back and arched backward, gazing up at the Haussmann-style building. He stepped onto the stoop and knocked on the door. A middle-aged woman with ash-brown hair cautiously answered. Reinhardt greeted her in French. Kira had studied her German/French dictionary and could translate "Good Evening, please," but one word she thought she must have misheard. *Les Catacombes.* A French word eerily similar to the German word *Die Katakomben.*

The woman nodded, recognizing Reinhardt. He must have stopped ahead of time and talked to her. It made Kira feel better about him and about being out with him. He was a German; asking permission was not required. The woman opened the door; Reinhardt gestured for Kira to enter first, holding it open for her.

"*Merci beaucoup,*" Kira said.

The hallway was so narrow they were forced to walk in single file. The French woman unlocked a wooden door and heaved it open. It revealed nothing but blackness. Reinhardt fished in the pockets of his gray greatcoat for a rectangular-shaped flashlight.

"Ready?" he asked.

She was intrigued before. But nothing intrigued like opening a locked door to reveal a strange staircase winding down to blackness. Kira felt like a treasure hunter. Confusion and intrigue demanded she nod. Reinhardt thanked the woman. Kira repeated his words. The French woman closed and locked the door behind her, which sounded like a submarine hatch being closed.

"Did she just lock us in?" Kira asked.

The intrigue lessened. The confusion morphed into fear. Claustrophobia and fear of the dark increased, crawling up the steps toward her with invisible claws.

"I hope you brought snacks," Reinhardt joked.

Since he had the flashlight, he walked down first. Kira felt for his coat, keeping a hand near it should she need to clutch it. The stairs groaned. How long had it been since they'd had to withstand being stepped on? Outside, as Kira knew, the world was never truly black. But here it was. What could he possibly want to show her in a basement? But they'd walked too far for this to be a basement. They would have reached a wall by now.

"This is underground?" Kira asked.

"It is," Reinhardt answered.

An unrealistic fear crept along her arms like insects. But even if we know our fears are irrational, they still induce terror. What if Reinhardt knew she was a Soviet soldier? And he was leading her toward more *Schadenfreudes*?

No, he could have come up with something far less time-consuming and complex.

Yet, for some, the hunt was the most exciting part.

"Do you know where you're going?" Kira asked.

"Sort of."

What choice did she have but to continue to follow him? Trust that he could find his way to the surface again. Kira tried to recall all the turns and winding curves. But her memory held no vivid details, as it normally did. Just darkness. Her sense of smell took over. It was musty, but occasionally, she got a whiff of Reinhardt's cologne—a scent of anise, fennel, tarragon, and leather. Intoxicating enough to make her softly moan.

Reinhardt let out a satisfied sigh. "Ahh, here we go."

They'd come to a stairwell, a long descension of over 130 steps. Kira had already felt uneasy. The thought of going further underground nearly made her tremble. It was dark, the air stagnant. Reinhardt looked at Kira, not asking if she wanted to continue with words, but with his eyes. Was he challenging her?

"After you," Kira said.

The temperature seemed to decrease a degree every ten steps they descended, and by the time they had reached the bottom, the temperature difference was drastic. How deep below ground were they? Kira forced the thought from her mind or else she'd panic. A stone doorway with black lettering above it lay ahead. *Arrête, c'est ici l'empire de la mort.* Kira recognized the last word. It sent an icy shiver crawling along her back.

Reinhardt translated. "Stop, this is death's empire."

"Seems like a warning to heed," Kira said.

Reinhardt stepped through, then offered his hand. Kira took it and stepped through that invisible barrier. She withdrew her hand and gasped. Intricately formed into the walls like bricks were human skulls and bones. The skulls with hollow, deep eye sockets. Most were missing the jawbone. Hundreds of them. But as they wandered through, that number was far too few. It was hundreds of thousands. Maybe millions. In the middle was what looked like a giant pottery vase made of human skeletons.

"Over 6,000,000 people were laid to rest here," Reinhardt said.

"Why would the French mock them in such a macabre way?" Kira asked.

Reinhardt's face contorted in confusion. "Mock? Their intent was not to mock the dead. It was to honor them."

The skulls absorbed the golden light of the flashlight. Kira wanted to look away, but her eyes were locked in place. It was a disturbing, yet beautiful, image.

Reinhardt explained, "Back in the 18th century, *Les Innocents*, the largest cemetery in Paris, collapsed after a torrential rain. The dead avalanched. Corpses cocooned in sludge washed upon the city. Those living said that the air was so vile that milk spoiled, meat went rancid. A putridness that stayed like a thick fog. The public demanded something be done. The most brilliant Parisians gathered, brainstorming how to fix the problem." He spread his arms to point where they stood. "Their solution was to bring them here."

"6,000,000 bodies? How long did it take?" Kira asked, her eyes filled with horror.

"Two years."

"No names, no dates of birth or death …" Kira said, gazing up at the hundreds of skulls in front of her.

"The stories of 6,000,000 people have been lost. This skull indecipherable from this skull. We'll never know their stories."

His words were delivered with great reverence, a sadness taking shape in his throat. Without commanding it, Kira's gaze went to him. Moved by his sadness that the stories of millions would go unknown. Every ivory-colored skull they saw had once held a brain that had experienced every spectrum of emotion a human being was capable of. Someday, 100 or 500 years from now, the battlefields of the two world wars would be exhumed, a mass grave of warring soldiers unearthed. Soldiers who had killed one another for the very patch of earth they both now rested under. Their earthly remains forever linked. No one would know which side they had fought on.

174

She stared into the hollow eyes of a skull. No idea if it had belonged to a man or woman. Kira couldn't help but think of her parents and sisters. Gazing upon the indistinguishable skulls, she knew she had made the right decision to burn them. They were ashes free to travel with the wind's breath. But now they were truly gone. No remnants of their existence would ever be found. History would not remember them. Only Kira would. Emotion threatened to suffocate her. She wiped away the tears clinging to her eyes. Reinhardt stood silently, granting Kira her privacy.

"What other facts do you have?" she asked Reinhardt, after she had composed herself.

"Do you want to hear something gory?"

"We just walked a kilometer's worth of skeletons. What could be gorier than that?"

Reinhardt smirked in a 'you have no idea' way. "The wax off the bodies was collected and used in soaps and candles. Rumor is they're still in use today."

Gory? Yes. Disgusting? Absolutely. Fascinating? Undoubtedly so.

"So, next time you drop a bar of soap, show some damn respect," Reinhardt said.

Kira hated that she laughed, but she did. It echoed in the hollow labyrinth. They headed back to the surface. Once at the stairwell, she rejoiced in the increased temperature with every step they climbed. Her first breath of fresh winter air calmed her soul. She gulped it in, not like she had been underground, but underwater. The air was fresh. No more musty smell and the permanent aroma of death.

"Are you warm enough?" he asked.

"I'm fine," Kira answered.

Would he have offered to wrap his coat around her? To think of him wrapping his coat around her disgusted her. Like being draped in human flesh. She would never allow that symbol to touch her body. The wind was mild for the most part; only occasionally did it send a big gust.

"What is this?" Kira asked, when they had stopped walking.

"The Père Lachaise Cemetery."

"Cemetery? Do you have a fascination with the dead?"

"I do," he replied. "Do you know the limitless stories they possess?"

Kira loved reading and watching films, so how had she never considered that before? Romance, horror, adventure, drama. Worthy stories every single perished person had experienced.

"There is one man whom you must meet," Reinhardt said.

"Meet?"

The word seemed wrong considering the setting. Meet suggested an interaction. Meet was an active verb. A *living* verb. Reinhardt led her through the cemetery. Ahead, a man lay passed out on a stone tomb. Kira silently condemned him for passing out in such a place. Reinhardt headed toward him. Was this the man she was to meet? But as they drew nearer, his chest didn't rise and fall as his lungs filled with breath. It didn't rise at all. But he wasn't dead, either. **Because** it wasn't a man at all, but a copper sculpture that looked terrifyingly realistic in the blue-tinted darkness. The copper had warped green, the same shade as America's Statue of Liberty, except for his nose, lips, chin, the tips of his boots, and comically, the seam of his pants. Those bits remained copper and gave the illusion he had an impressive bronze penis.

"Who is this?" Kira asked.

"Victor Noir. He was a French journalist shot dead by Napoleon Bonaparte's cousin, Prince Pierre Bonaparte, in 1870."

Reinhardt was filled with fascinating tidbits of information. A walking encyclopedia.

"And this warranted a statue?" Kira asked.

She hoped it didn't sound demeaning. Everyone thinks the people they love deserve to be immortalized in bronze.

"He was viewed as a symbol of opposition to the Imperial regime," Reinhardt said.

A symbol. Kira lowered her head. Did this man know the symbol he became?

"Do you know why certain areas haven't oxidized?" Reinhardt asked.

Of course she didn't, and he knew that, but it was the tool of a storyteller. Something Gerasim would have done.

"It is said that if you wish to find a lover, you kiss his lips. If you want to get pregnant, touch his right foot."

Out of precaution, Kira stepped back with her right foot; Reinhardt laughed.

"If you wish to get pregnant with twins, touch his left."

Kira dragged her left foot back. "And his crotch? That has seen considerable … fondling."

Reinhardt's smile was uncontainable. "That you rub for the best sex of your life, or at the very least, to find love within a year."

"Does not say much about the French men, if the women rely on a statue," Kira said.

Reinhardt snickered.

"Shall I test it?" Kira asked facetiously.

"Tread with caution."

Kira thought the whole thing ridiculous, but that didn't mean she was prepared to test fate.

"So, your plan was to take me to a fertility statue?" she asked.

Reinhardt took her jab in stride and with a smile. Kira turned to leave and slipped on a bit of ice. Had she been wearing functional shoes, it never would have happened. Her hands stopped her fall, her fingers feeling the cool copper. She checked where her hand was. She squeezed her eyes shut. Her hand was directly on Noir's crotch. Reinhardt hoisted her to her feet, biting back his grin.

"Not a word," Kira said.

"I wouldn't dare," Reinhardt said.

Kira bit the inside of her cheek, flushed with embarrassment yet fully aware of how comical it was. They walked to the cemetery entrance with Kira more mindful of her steps. Reinhardt did his best to stifle his laughter by biting his lip. Kira tried to keep a straight face, but when they caught a glimpse of each other, they burst into laughter. At the entrance, a horse-drawn carriage waited for them.

"Is that for us?" Kira asked.

"Of course. Do you think the dead need it?"

Kira pushed him playfully, feeling the firmness of his chest. But the moment her hand grazed his uniform, who he was came back to her. A German. A German soldier. A possible *Schadenfreude*.

He offered his hand and helped her into the carriage. Where the touch of his uniform only brought dark feelings and thoughts, the touch of his hand brought elation. Sensations she wasn't accustomed to. Some she had never felt before. And how good his hands felt in the cold. Like holding a hot cup of coffee.

"What about curfew?" Kira asked.

Reinhardt waved the worry away. Snow fell lightly. The white horses proudly shook their heads at it. Kira found the clicking of their hooves relaxing. The entire setting was romantic. The singular clichéd word lacked originality, but, sometimes, a single word fits best.

"So, now you have seen Paris and those who once called it home," Reinhardt said.

Visiting the catacombs and a cemetery had not been expected. She could have theorized a hundred scenarios and they wouldn't have even been thought of.

"Do you know why I showed you these places?" Reinhardt asked.

She hadn't the faintest idea, but she had found it fascinating. Equally macabre and moving. Kira shook her head in reply. She still didn't even know why she had agreed to come.

"You have fierce eyes, Kira. I suppose that is because you are a fierce woman. But there is something else hidden behind that fierceness," Reinhardt said.

He had no problem looking into her eyes. She tried to mirror that fearlessness.

"And what lies behind them?" Kira asked.

She expected a line, a come on. She waited to smile, waited to laugh.

"Sadness," he said, then paused. "I do not think I am going out on a limb by saying you have lost much in this war. I wanted to remind you that the dead are never truly gone. But unlike the millions in the catacombs, those we have lost will not fade into the obscurity of history, so long as we tell their stories. Whoever it is you have lost ... their stories are gifts you can always open."

Those fierce eyes filled with unexpected tears. Kira scrunched her toes, dug her pointer finger into the cuticle of her thumb, grinded the inside of her cheek. Anything to cause pain elsewhere than in her chest. That horrible blunt pain pulsating with each heartbeat. She wouldn't let those tears fall, not here, not in front of him. But the faces of her father, mother, and sisters flashed before her. Memories replayed. Hearing their laughs, the smell of the smoke from the fireplace, its heat on her skin, the crackle of the wood. Her father dosed off in his chair, her mother seated on the floor in front of him, hugging his leg. Nousha and Lina doing each other's hair, and Kira on the couch reading.

Kira couldn't stop the tears from flowing down her face. She'd held them in for so long. They ran down her cheeks like a freed river. She'd always been told that time heals all wounds. That isn't true. Some wounds we live with so long we forget what it felt like before. Reinhardt peered into her eyes. There was no doubt. He saw her. He understood her in a way no one else had. He saw through the defenses she had erected and saw her pain. Reinhardt softly wiped her tears with his thumb. He stroked the side of her face. His eyes showed so much understanding. A level of compassion she had never expected to see, least of all from a German. He removed his hand and let her grieve. He sensed Kira didn't want him to witness what she would call a 'moment of weakness.' He let her experience that hurricane of emotion. Only the click-clack of the horses' hooves broke the silence.

"I will need to drop you off at your place. Otherwise, I fear you may be detained for being out past curfew," Reinhardt said a few minutes later.

Kira gave the address, instantly wondering if she shouldn't have. A German now knew where she was staying. That fact presented its own long list of potential problems. If she was aware of all the problems she was creating in the moment, how many would she find alone in her apartment, free from his intoxicating presence?

A few blocks later, the carriage stopped. Reinhardt stepped down and offered his hand to Kira to help her down. He held her hand as he escorted her to the apartment building's front door.

They stood there, nervousness radiating from them.

"Thank you, Reinhardt."

"My pleasure."

A tear trickled down her face. She wiped it away, laughing to make light of it. "So much for me being fierce, huh?"

Reinhardt shook his head, his eyes never leaving hers. "Showing emotion doesn't make you weak."

Their eyes locked.

"Well, Kira, I hope you have a good night."

179

Kira unlocked the door and turned the handle. She paused. Indecisiveness gripped her. She turned back to Reinhardt and called his name. He stopped and turned his head to look back at her.

"*Je vous verrai plus tard*," she said.

He smiled. "See you tomorrow." Then he showed off with a colorful French phrase Kira was unable to decipher any words of. "Keep reading." Even being annoying he was charming.

The horses lifted their heads and trotted away, the bells around their necks jingling. Reinhardt stood on the foot rails, staring at Kira as the horses trotted away. Kira watched him go, the snow falling beautifully around him.

How cruel that our own bodies can betray us. Red ears and quickened breath reveal anger. Blushed cheeks and diverted eyes reveal a crush within our midst. Direct eye contact and a flirty touch reveal lust. All the while, Reinhardt had gazed deeply into her eyes; she had assumed it was sex he thought about. Not because she was vain, but because she had been told it was what men thought about. But he had read her like one of his books … like one of *her* books. Read through all the defenses and lies into the deep center of a complex truth. He had understood her at a level no one else had, and it hadn't required a single spoken word. How powerful was that? And how horrifying?

Kira was torn. Her thoughts were tumultuous and volatile. Reinhardt was a German. Like the man who had killed her father and sisters. He seemed so different, yet he wore the same swastika. If she were back in Stalingrad, she wouldn't have given a second's thought to shooting him.

She sat on her bed, staring out at the city, but not seeing it. Too many thoughts played on her mind. If Reinhardt could read through her so effortlessly, what if he could sense why she was here? The true reason, not the lie that she was a music student visiting. He was impossible to ignore. His charming smile replayed in her mind. When she took a deep breath, the smell of his cologne caressed her nose.

Sleep was a struggle. She was awake long enough to remember every design in the apartment's stucco ceiling. Stared at it for so long she started to see art in it. The night was a month long; the brief sleep granted was as temporary as a sneeze.

As she dressed the following morning, she reminded herself who she was and why she was in Paris, speaking the words out loud in front of the mirror. Certainly clichéd, but sometimes you have to talk to yourself eye to eye.

Afraid that complacency would lead to dangerous thoughts, she went for a walk, going beyond her normal checkpoints. By the time Kira returned, it was the longest walk she'd gone on since arriving in Paris. Her empty stomach gurgled, pleading for food. The exact translation: I want an apple strudel. But she couldn't go there, for there may be a certain tall, handsome, wavy dark-haired, blue-eyed man sipping coffee and reading. So, much to her annoyance, she steered clear of the Givre Strudel. The restaurant she chose instead disappointed her. Restrictions and rations impacted French restaurants. Some couldn't adapt to making things taste good with less than normal amounts. But Josephine had found the secret. If Josephine had managed to make an apple strudel taste that good on reduced rations, the non-rationed variety must have been downright sinful. Maybe the Germans who loved it equally had arranged that the Givre Strudel be exempt from rationing.

The meat this restaurant served was beyond questionable. Kira had been blessed with the meat she normally ate. From grass-grazing to dinner-table in the same day. Her body had adapted to eating Soviet army rations, but it had gotten addicted even quicker to the high sugar and fat content of the strudel. If this is what people meant by expressing the need to experience culture, Kira agreed. But even more addictive than the food was Reinhardt.

Several things scared her about last night. She had given him her address, and no matter what her gut told her about him, he was still an enemy. *The* enemy. He could stop by at any time. But what scared her the most was herself. Her own thoughts, her own body. As she struggled to sleep, she contemplated how she had wanted that night to end. Even though she told herself it had ended exactly as she wanted it to, she knew the truth. She had wanted him to kiss her. To feel his body pressed against hers, his long hands pressed along her sacrum, his lips delicately pressed against hers and then more forcefully. She couldn't trust herself. She was a passenger in her own body.

She spent the day reviewing Wolff's files, assembling and disassembling her Mosin–Nagant, practicing her double bass, and reading either her dictionary or her novel. After eating the rest of a subpar sandwich for supper, she practiced her double bass again, playing "Ode to Joy." She could hear the beat in her mind, smiling to herself when her mind and fingers merged. She was far removed from being ready to play in an orchestra, but to the average ear, she thought it was passable. Near dusk, she went on another walk. Each silhouette and shadow she passed, she wished it wasn't him. But also prayed that it was.

Lingering Thoughts

He'd forgotten all about the war. Ever since he had left Günter and the others behind in Russia to receive his Oak Leaves, Reinhardt had only thought of returning to the fight. To get back in his Messerschmitt and embrace the ultimate adrenaline rush of aerial combat. Yet, now, these thoughts were secondary. He'd felt her stare. Powerful enough to make him lower his book. Her beauty was unpolished, natural. Her body was desirable. He wouldn't pretend to act like he hadn't noticed it. Studied its curves. She was tall and lean, with buxom breasts and an ample ass, and thin, kissable lips. The way she went from appearing proud as a lion, that nothing in the world could affect her, to being unfathomably sad in a flash. The way the sadness came and went like a sudden rain cloud. But her eyes … those emerald-green eyes issuing a stay back warning. His whole body had told him not to heed that warning. There were no specks of brown or blue to dilute their vividness. The strength that radiated off her was an inducing gravity he couldn't deny. He needed to be in her orbit. He couldn't pay attention to the world around them when he was with her. He only wanted to see her and her reaction to it.

She was guarded. To use a military term, well-fortified. He'd been too ecstatic after he dropped her off to return to his hotel room to sleep. He needed to share this news, the discovery of Kira. He wrote to Mathias, detailing everything about her, but knew his words wouldn't do her justice. A person can tell you how breathtaking mountains are, but you don't truly know until it's your breath taken from seeing them. At the end of his letter, he redrew their chess match. He advanced his queen to a position of threat. Only fitting a letter about an enchantingly powerful woman ended with a move from the board's most powerful piece.

He woke early the following morning, excited at the prospect of seeing her again. The thought of seeing her striking eyes was caffeine. There was an unsettledness in his stomach that would only go away when he was by her. It was the only antidote to the dope-sick feeling.

He stopped at a bookstore for his next read, then went to the Givre Strudel with that nervous, excited feeling that sets in at the possibility of seeing someone you pine for. It was a feeling he'd had loads of times before. Yet this time was different. Her strength. That was what attracted him to her most of all. It was quiet, yet undeniable. He had to see her again. She was a magnet; he was a slab of steel.

Hope swelled in his chest like a balloon as he stepped into the Givre Strudel and popped like one when he glanced about the café. No Kira. He forced a smile at Josephine and sat in his usual spot. He tried reading, but Kira had taken the enjoyment away. He didn't want to read about romance; he wanted to experience it. He enjoyed his coffee and strudel, thanked Josephine, and left. He spent his day walking, reading, and playing chess in a park with some other German soldiers and officers. His opponents knew nothing of strategy and Reinhardt disposed of them in less than ten moves, even with Kira on his mind. An elderly French man then destroyed Reinhardt. Even if Kira hadn't been on his mind, the elder man had been playing the game for decades.

The following day, he repeated yesterday's activities, and like the previous day, there was no Kira. He debated on visiting her at her building but decided against it. He had truly only dropped her off so she wouldn't get arrested for violating curfew. Kira appeared to be a reserved person, and a reserved person wasn't the type to enjoy somebody randomly showing up at their door. Kira knew where to find him if she chose.

The high of Kira subsided to the point where it was no longer only Kira he thought about as he lay in bed. It was the war. Günter and Uwe. His sisters Evonne, Griselde, and Lonita, his parents, Mathias, and everyone back home. He reminisced about his life before the war started. Yet he couldn't deny the itch to get back in the air was spreading across his body like a rash. An itch only scratched when he was in the cockpit of his Messerschmitt, the roaring-lion sound of the engine filling the sky.

But then those emerald green eyes would come back to him ...

A Glimpse of Heaven

Kira maintained her same cautious routines over the next couple of days. And it was pure hell. Yet Reinhardt knew where she was staying. If he truly wanted to see her, he knew how, and more importantly, where. Complacency was torture. The irony that as a sniper she could stay motionless for hours on end wasn't lost on her. In sniping, there was an end goal, a mission. She tried tricking herself into thinking she had a mission now, too.

Avoid Reinhardt.

Was it arrogant to think she needed to avoid him? He hadn't even tried to kiss her. He may not even be attracted to her. But could she truly believe that? The way he gazed at her ... fiercely, longingly. Kira had to clear her head. It seemed entirely within the realm of possibility she would try to assassinate Wolff with her double bass and try to play "Ode to Joy" with her three-line.

She went to her fridge and cursed the empty shelves. She had eaten the last of her food earlier. The clock on the wall warned her it was late, but she grabbed her coat anyway. She hadn't decided on what she wanted to eat but damn it all to hell if her legs didn't take her to the Givre Strudel. She stepped inside. Josephine sat at a table with the dark-haired, mustachioed man Kira had seen before. They chatted in French. He nodded cordially at Kira, sipping his espresso, grimacing at the weakness of it. Kira nodded back.

No Germans were in the café. Good.

Josephine rose from her seat to take Kira's order.

"It's been a couple of days. I thought maybe you had left," Josephine said.

Kira smiled, not sure what to say and if Josephine truly wanted to hear it.

"Are you still serving?" Kira asked.

"I can see what's left. What do you want?"

"Apple strudel." The words came out like a reflex. "If you have it …" she added.

Josephine smirked. "I have other items on the menu, you know."

True. But if you panned gold every time, you don't go further down river hoping it was better.

"Then I'll try a coffee, too, please," Kira said.

"Aren't you adventurous?" Josephine teased. "Fair warning, what I have to serve is hardly true coffee."

The dark-haired man with the thin mustache rose from the table, leaving a considerable tip for a simple espresso.

"*Bonne Nuit*, Josephine," he said.

Kira was proud she had translated 'good night' with little effort.

"*Bonne Nuit*, Durand," Josephine replied.

He had a distinct limp—his knee looked incapable of bending the way it should. The bustle of the supper rush had long ended. When Durand left, Kira was the only customer. The coffee came first. It took merely a sip for Kira to know Josephine had been right. It tasted more like a small bit of coffee had been left in the cup and refilled with water than legitimate coffee. But the strudel did not disappoint. It never would.

The door opened once more. Kira turned out of instinct. Her heart leapt into her throat, pushing bits of strudel out of her mouth and onto her lip.

Reinhardt.

He found her instantly, lips curling into a smirk on that lean face of his. He greeted Josephine and asked if coffee was available. He sat in the corner where Kira had first met him. Josephine disappeared into the kitchen, leaving Kira and Reinhardt as the only two in the café. Neither spoke. Both stared. The distance between them filled with an indelible force. A magnetism. She had to look at him. He had to look at her. Bold and brilliant blue into effulgent and enigmatic emerald.

Josephine set his coffee down. Reinhardt asked for a strudel. Josephine informed him that she had served the last one. Reinhardt looked at Kira, lips curled. She tried to hide the satisfaction it brought. Reinhardt took his coffee and sat at her table.

"Seeing as you robbed me of my strudel, would you at least indulge me by letting me watch you eat it?" he asked.

Kira scrunched her eyebrows. "Because that wouldn't be weird." She slid the plate near him. "Split it."

Reinhardt grabbed a fork. They shared a nod then cut into the strudel. Forkful by forkful getting closer to each other. It should hardly be erotic, but the closer their hands got, the hotter the air grew. They both paused at the last forkful. Reinhardt glanced up; Kira, too. Neither said anything, only taking the silence as an opportunity to admire the other.

"I suppose I should be a gentleman and allow a lady the last bite," Reinhardt said.

"I suppose you should."

"Though, I don't think you want to be treated in such a way." He stabbed his fork into the strudel and shoved it into his mouth.

Kira's eyes widened in surprise. Reinhardt put his hand to his mouth as he chewed, suppressing his laugh.

"I should slap you!" Kira said.

"Don't threaten me with a good time."

Kira tried with great effort for her lips to comply and form a frown, but that smile on her face was unyielding. She held it so long, the tops of her cheeks started to cramp.

Strudel gone and coffee empty, they rose from their seats. Both left a generous amount of money. Outside, cold air and sleet greeted them. They strolled in the same direction (Kira didn't know if it was intentional or not) in silence.

"So, what brought you out for such a late coffee?" Kira asked.

"My mind is restless. I cannot sleep, so I'd rather not even try."

"How come?"

"I find myself ... missing."

"Missing? Someone? A woman?"

Reinhardt shook his head. "Friends back on the front. My sisters. My parents. My best friend back home."

"Your best friend is not fighting?"

Reinhardt shook his head. "He can't."

He explained Mathias's failing heart. Neither had a destination in mind. They'd walk straight until one turned.

"Ironic," Kira said.

"How so?" Reinhardt asked.

"Some people would do anything to get out of fighting, but so many, like your friend, would give anything to fight."

"He loves Germany, as I do."

Germany. Home of the *Schadenfreude*.

"Mostly, I miss my life. How it was before the war," Reinhardt said.

His words resonated with her. More than he knew. More than she could tell him. Kira asked for the time. Curfew would begin shortly. She needed to course correct back to her apartment and pick up her pace. The last thing she needed was to be detained for breaking curfew.

"I'll walk you," Reinhardt said.

"You don't have to," Kira assured.

Reinhardt dismissed it. "Please. It gives me a reason to walk this magical city."

Kira didn't object. He made her feel safe from *Schadenfreudes*. The silence that fell between them should have been uncomfortable. But it wasn't. It seemed natural. Nothing forced. Kira glanced at him. He wanted to say something, he just wasn't sure when or how to say it. When he caught her looking, he had no choice but to speak.

"I wanted to apologize, Kira, for the other night."

"For what?"

"What I said about you having lost ... I don't presume to know you—"

Kira put her hand on his forearm. "You were right."

She didn't say anything more. She couldn't. Because of her cover story to a degree, but mostly because to voice the truth would hurt too much.

"Tell me about Mathias. What did the two of you do?" she asked.

"He's been my best friend since we were boys. His father was a crop duster. I fell in love with flying the first time he took us up."

"So, you always wanted to be a pilot?"

Reinhardt shook his head. "No. I didn't want to fight."

"You were conscripted?"

Maybe there was hope he wasn't a *Schadenfreude*. Just another poor schmuck forced to fight.

But Reinhardt shook his head. "No, I enlisted. I signed up for him. To fight in his stead."

He hadn't told anybody the reason. Not his parents or his sisters. Not Günter or Uwe. Maybe a part of the reason he told Kira was that there was no chance she could betray Mathias's secret to him. But mostly, he found himself wanting to tell her everything because he wanted to know everything about her.

"You're in the *Luftwaffe*?" Kira asked.

He nodded. That explained why she hadn't recognized his patches. She'd studied *Wehrmacht* and *SS* ranks. Though her hatred of his uniform remained, she couldn't deny how honorable his actions were.

"Mathias would have been a superb fighter pilot," Reinhardt said.

He focused his praise on his friend; the admiration he had for him was obvious.

"When we were thirteen, we took his father's plane up," Reinhardt said. "Bounced on the runway. Landed rough. Busted the wheels off. Spent the rest of the summer picking rocks from a field for twelve hours a day to earn the money to fix it."

Kira smiled at his memory. "And now you are a bomber or fighter pilot?"

"Fighter pilot."

The next logical question would have been to ask how many kills he had. But Kira didn't want to know. She would judge him for it. His answer would tarnish the way she felt about him. Exactly how she felt about him, she couldn't decide. Her emotions were volatile.

"And you're a good pilot?" she asked.

"The best."

She looked for a smirk. But Reinhardt had delivered it as nothing more than a fact. It seemed impossible that someone could state that and not sound arrogant, but he had. It wasn't something he was boastful about, more like it was a curse that others viewed as a gift.

"Will you come with me?" Reinhardt asked.

"To where?"

"Surprise."

"Not fond of those."

"No, I imagine you're not. You like order. To be in control of your environment."

"Did my eyes tell you that, too?" she asked lightheartedly.

He shook his head. "No, your body language did."

Kira hated how her own body betrayed her. Even though it was true, she still rolled her eyes.

"Well, will you come with me?" Reinhardt asked.

No. The answer was no. It had to be no. She was here to complete a mission. She had to go back to her apartment. He smiled. Why was he smiling? She'd said no.

Only she hadn't. She had nodded. She was *still* nodding.

Reinhardt led her toward a German patrol jeep. He gave the driver his name and rank. He opened the back door and gestured for her to enter. Getting into the back of a German vehicle was beyond stupid. She studied his face, that handsome face. It was kind. He couldn't possibly be cruel, could he? He offered his hand. Trusting him and not his uniform, Kira met his gaze, then took his hand. She sat, feeling the chill of the crisp leather seat. The jeep drove through the Arc de Triomphe and out of the city.

"Please tell me where we are going," Kira said.

Knowing she hated surprises, he answered quickly. "To an airbase a few minutes away."

"Airbase?"

He nodded. "Are you afraid of flying?"

"I had a bad experience."

To put it vaguely.

"I want to show you the plane I fly," he said. "If you're not comfortable, we don't have to go up."

Go up. As in, go up in the air. Defy gravity. Her stomach curdled like spoiled milk.

They came to an airfield, housing fighter planes, bombers, and dive bombers. The jeep squealed to a stop in front of a chain-link fence. A guard stepped out. Reinhardt rolled his window down and announced his name and rank. The guard snapped into the Nazi salute, then took Reinhardt's identification. A second guard dragged the gate open, and the jeep drove for less than a hundred yards.

Reinhardt stepped out and offered his hand to Kira. He rushed toward a plane as if it were his dog, petting the belly of the plane with his palm. He told Kira it was a Messerschmitt Bf 109F. Reinhardt flew its predecessor, the 109E. F as in Friedrich. E as in Emil. The 109F offered a vast improvement in aerodynamics, the front more streamlined and smoother, a redesigned wing with new leading-edge slats and tail section. Reinhardt also said it possessed greater fuel efficiency. Throughout his detailing of the specs of the plane, he spoke with excitement and reverence. Like a tiger trainer who loved the tiger but understood it was an animal that could never truly be tamed.

"Did Mathias's father's crop duster have these?" Kira asked, tapping the MG-42 in the wing.

Reinhardt chuckled. "Not his model, no."

"So, your plan was to take me up?" Kira asked.

"Only if you want to."

Kira looked at the plane. It was far smaller than the Yak she'd flown in from Russia, and that plane had crashed.

"You're the best pilot in the *Luftwaffe*, huh?" Kira asked, half-joking, half-serious.

"In the world," Reinhardt said.

Kira stared at the plane, then Reinhardt. How could she be exhilarated and terrified in equal amounts? Reinhardt was passionate about flying, and there's something about being around a passionate person that makes you passionate. Kira clenched her eyes and exhaled a deep breath. Her fight-or-flight response was in full gear. The winner was flight apparently. Literally and figuratively. She nodded. Where before it had been her body betraying her mind, this time her mind betrayed her body. Revenge. She felt as if she had declared a moral victory until she realized that body and mind were tethered together. If either lost, both lost.

Reinhardt examined the plane, completely ignoring Kira as he did. A pilot's safety inspection was of the utmost importance. Once completed, he climbed the ladder, opened the canopy, and climbed inside. Kira climbed up and discovered one major problem.

"There's only one seat ..."

"Oh, we won't let that stop us."

Reinhardt offered his hand and helped her onto his lap. His hands went around her waist, so he could get at the controls. There was no way this could be anything but intimate. His head nestled into the cup of her shoulder; she sat on his lap. If he got aroused, she'd know the same time he did. The plane's vibrations only heightened the arousal. She could feel his exhale on her neck, his fingers on her stomach. Was he caressing her or was it the plane's vibrations that did that? He breathed in the smell of her hair, sighing softly at the appealing aroma.

The plane surged ahead. Her body jerked back. She squeezed the seat. Only realizing it was Reinhardt's legs when he grimaced. The plane shuddered. The engine roared. And then it was calm. The plane's engine quieted to a hum. The sky was crisp and clear. They were above the clouds, flying amongst the stars. The experience could not have been any more different from her flight from Sweden to what was supposed to have been Spain. That had been nerve-wracking terror. This was awesome. A freeing experience. A complete liberation of everything. She was a bird flying through the sky. Intrinsically, she knew she could be at peace, release her worry. Reinhardt held too much reverence for the sky, too much respect to attempt any barrel rolls or loops. This was her moment, an experience she'd never forget, and he would do nothing to tarnish it.

"The night ... it's so gorgeous," Kira said.

"You've never truly seen the stars until you've seen them from up here," Reinhardt said.

Kira arched her head toward him. Even through the powerful odor of oil and fuel, she could smell his cologne. Even through the vibrations of the plane, she could feel his body. And even through the cold, she could feel his heat. An overpowering compulsion to kiss him spread from one body part to another, all traveling to her lips.

She bit her lip, running her tongue over her the bottom lip. But he had a plane to fly. The way he held himself seemed to say, *Don't waste your time staring at me, take in every star you can.*

Kira heeded his unspoken advice. Taking in every view, fighting the urge to reach out to touch the stars. She turned to face Reinhardt. He met her gaze.

A million reasons to break the gaze. A single reason to hold it.

The short distance between their lips was a road that needed to be traveled. A distance that needed to be eliminated. He closed the gap. She, too. But mere millimeters apart, both stopped. Reinhardt wouldn't advance any further. It was up to Kira to decide if she wanted it to happen. She closed her eyes, forgetting about the complexities of it all, ridding everything but the basic summation that she was a woman, he was a man, she wanted him, and he wanted her. She embraced her basic instincts and kissed him. And he kissed her right back.

Nighttime Stroll

The plane had landed. Kira had not. She still soared in the clouds. Complicated. Everything was complicated. Colonel Volkov had trusted her to complete the mission of killing Wolff. Many had had trepidation about sending a woman. *Women are too emotional. Don't send a woman to do a man's job.* But that was bullshit. Kira didn't believe a man wouldn't have succumbed to the same desires she had. They'd spend their nights in brothels. If she failed her mission, could she plead sabotage? Leave out the detail that the sabotage was orchestrated by her own hands ... and lips. She had to stop thinking that way. She hadn't failed her mission. She could return to the Soviet Union with everyone none the wiser. Reinhardt Friedel could be a secret, a memory she returned to when she pleased.

Paris was gorgeous, but large cities weren't where Kira belonged. Before the war, it was the bluff she went to clear her head. Kira needed a recharge. Everywhere she went, there were people. And not a few, but hundreds. So, Kira boarded a bus heading south of the city. She'd asked Josephine for a place out in nature. A little over an hour later, Kira stepped off a bus in Nemours. She'd bought shoes and pants from a thrift store and filled a canteen with water. The sight of forests relaxed her. The fresh air and bright snow recharged her body and mind.

The trail was easy enough, so she made it harder, climbing atop stones, ducking under branches, and leaping overturned trees. She reached out to touch everything she could. Cold stone. Textured bark. Disintegrating leaves. It was only when she was out of breath that she truly breathed. She came to a steep hill, and then to a long rock ledge that spanned her peripheral. This wasn't the bluff upon which she'd sat and read hundreds of books, but it was the closest place to it she'd find. She was so far from home. Home. It wasn't that anymore. Now, it was just the place she was from.

She drew a book from her small bag, sat, and read. The cold was mitigated by a high sun. She read page after page, chapter after chapter. As she got lost in the realm of fiction, an engrained thought popped into her unconscious: *I have to get home.*

It was a thought she had had a thousand times. It had been planted so deep in her self-conscious. Muscle memory. My God, how she wished she could go home. But she couldn't. Her life was not written words in the pages of fiction. When she closed her book and stood from this rock, her family would still be gone and her house would still be rubble. There was no home. Not anymore.

Her excursion into nature healed her, but it had brought its own side effects of homesickness and nostalgia. Both overwhelmingly powerful. She napped on the hour-long bus ride back to Paris. The fresh air had tired her out, so much so that she remained groggy on her walk to her apartment. She took a bath, letting the hot water massage her body. Deciding she would stay in the bath until she fell asleep, or the water went cold. The result was a tie. Kira forced herself from the tub and dried off. The floor was cool, drawing her body's heat out through her feet. She quickly dressed, then opened her fridge. Empty. She cursed. She had forgotten to pick up her rations. Could she make it to morning? Her stomach rumbled at the offensive thought. The clock showed it was a few minutes past 7:30. If she made up her mind and hurried, she may get to the Givre Strudel before it closed.

She rushed out of her door and raced down the steps. The only things stopping her from running were her damn Oxford shoes and that it would look suspicious to any German soldiers patrolling the streets. She nearly fell inside the Givre Strudel, startling Josephine and Durand.

"Are you alright?" Josephine asked.

Kira nodded, out of breath and flushed with color.

"Do you have any leftovers I can buy? I need to be home before the curfew," Kira explained.

Josephine rose and said she would look. Durand studied Kira as he sipped his coffee.

"Are you not worried about the curfew?" Kira asked in her best French.

Either her French was off, or Durand didn't feel like speaking, because he simply shrugged. Josephine returned with a white bag with the top rolled down.

"There are a few croissants and some berries, and a couple of macaroons."

"*Merci*," Kira said, fishing out *Francs* from her pocket.

But Josephine paid no attention to her. Her eyes soared beyond her and through the glass of the front door. Kira turned to see what had captivated her. Leather-clad

SS officers stumbled across the street, smoking and passing a flask amongst themselves. The *SS* were cruel enough without the influence of alcohol.

"You should go out the back," Josephine said.

Durand struggled to his feet, grimacing at the pain his leg caused him. He peaked out the window.

"Will you be okay?" Kira asked her.

"She'll be fine," Durand said.

"Walk like you have somewhere to be, not like you are fleeing," Josephine added.

Before Kira could even comment what a fine line that was, Josephine led her to the back door and cracked it open enough for Kira to slip out. Kira's body responded with goosebumps and a heightened awareness. She inhaled deeply through her nose and let it out through her mouth, fighting her body's plea to run. She dashed, a woman chilled from the wind and late to get home. The drunk *SS* officers stopped and fell silent, trying to center their drunken vision to see Kira shuffle across the street. Kira kept her eyes ahead, pulling her collar up to conceal her face, hoping it passed as a woman protecting herself from the bitter cold. She quickened her pace. One of the men called out to her. Kira continued on, trying to sell that the howling wind was too loud for her to hear him. The white bag in her hand was dead weight. Hunger had foolishly led her out. Now, she couldn't possibly fathom eating. Killed over a croissant, berries, and macaroons. Not even a damn strudel.

She reached into her purse and brandished her keys. The German shouted. Their elongated shadows warped across the street, lumbering toward her. She bounded up her stoop, steadying her hand to insert the key on the first attempt. The wind caught the door. Kira fought to close it, then locked it. She yanked her shoes off so she could sprint up the steps.

Glass shattered. They were inside. Shouting. Sprinting. Tripping up the stairs in their drunken state. Kira glanced below her. The three *SS* officers gained on her. Kira thrusted her apartment key into the hole. The lock turned. She rushed inside, but before she could close the door, one of them rammed it with his shoulder, knocking Kira to the floor and the door against the wall.

"When I say stop, you stop!" the wavy blond-haired German shouted, spittle flinging from his mouth. His breath reeked of liquor and smoke. He could have been handsome if not for the rage in his drunken, bloodshot eyes. The other two laughed; one of them shut the door. He appeared to be the max weight any army would tolerate. The other was gangly, the type you'd give leftover food to because you thought he was malnourished. Kira studied their uniforms, deducing their ranks. The wavy blond-haired man standing over her shouting was the highest ranked among them. An *SS-Sturmscharführer*.

"Why did you run?! What are you hiding?!" he yelled, his voice getting progressively louder.

"I'm not hiding anything. You frightened me," Kira said.

Her German surprised him, but even in his inebriated state, he caught her accent. Only, he was too drunk to place it. He bent down, almost losing his balance, and retrieved the white folded paper bag.

"And what is this?"

"Supper ..." Kira uttered.

He tore open the bag. The food inside clattered to the ground. He kicked at it with his shoe, then tossed the bag. It fell slowly, like a small parachute.

"Why are you in Paris?" he asked.

"I am a student, studying music," Kira said.

The *SS-Sturmscharführer* laughed derisively. "Is that so?"

He yanked her to her feet, then shoved her toward her bed. He drew his flask and took a hearty swig, then grinned at the burning sensation it caused in his chest.

"Do you know what my favorite music is?" the *SS-Sturmscharführer* asked.

Kira knew she didn't want to know the answer. He struggled to get his coat off, then flung it at the table. He unbuttoned his shirt. They were going to rape her, take turns, maybe even go for seconds. Her TT-30 pistol was in her bathroom, the distance blocked by two men. She could take the skinny one, but the heavier one had at least fifty pounds on her. Her three-line was uselessly disassembled in her double bass case. She could assemble it in a measly ninety seconds. But she didn't have ninety seconds. All three men had Lugers on their hips. Rape was inevitable. But they would have to beat her unconscious. She'd punch and kick. Once they pinned her, she'd tear into their flesh with her teeth.

"My favorite music is a woman moaning in my ear," the *SS-Sturmscharführer* said.

196

He licked his lips, then lunged forward. His weight knocked her onto the bed. Something that had felt so soft now felt like she had been thrown from a two-story building and landed on pavement. Sheer terror paralyzed her body. Kira wouldn't lie here as he violated her. She squirmed, snapping her teeth near his neck.

He drew back, laughing with his friends at this feral creature. Nousha and Lina had experienced this horror. And now she would, too. The thought of that *Schadenfreude* raping them removed the terror and morphed it into rage. She'd let him climb atop her, and when he thought she had given up resisting, she'd tear a chunk of his throat out with her teeth. When his hands rushed to his gushing wound, she'd dig her fingers into his eyes and smash them like grapes. But a different thought took hold. Now, she would truly understand what her sisters had experienced. The fate her father had made her promise to prevent. She deserved to feel this.

The drunken *SS-Sturmscharführer* drew a knife. "Hush, hush, little bird," he whispered.

This was it.

But then the front door blasted open. A booming voice shouted. Goosebumps spread across her skin from the power behind it. The *SS-Sturmscharführer* didn't even have time to turn to see who spoke. He was dragged off the bed and thrown to the ground. Kira looked to see her savior.

Tall. Dark, wavy hair. Star-blue eyes. Reinhardt Friedel. His sly, playful demeanor was gone. For the first time, he showed rage and power. The veins in his neck bulged, his ears were peppermint red, his knuckles white from his clenched fists. His eyes looked like an ice storm on Saturn.

"What the hell do you think you're doing?!" he shouted.

She'd never seen him like this. Never imagined he was capable of this level of rage. The *SS-Sturmscharführer* struggled to his feet. The other two had sobered up in the last few seconds. Fear has a way of doing that.

"I asked for her papers. She ran," the *SS-Sturmscharführer* said, straightening his uniform.

"You never asked me for my papers!" Kira said.

"Shut up, whore!"

Reinhardt took a threatening step at him. The *SS-Sturmscharführer* took a step back.

"She can speak whenever she'd like! If she decides to recite Shakespeare, you'll stand here silent as a corpse or you'll be one!"

The other two looked like they might dive headfirst out of Kira's window.

"Three drunken men charge a woman at night," Reinhardt said.

"She is not French. She is not German," the *SS-Sturmscharführer* said.

"And what nationality would she have to be to make it okay?" Reinhardt asked.

"Spoils. Of. War." Each word was a snarl.

"You represent Germany! My Germany! You disgust me!"

Reinhardt's rank of major outranked them all, but it wouldn't have mattered. With the rage surging through him, he would have cursed Hitler himself.

"I have been tasked with additional security for *Oberst-Gruppenführer* Wolff's arrival. I vet whom I deem necessary," the *SS-Sturmscharführer* said.

"Is that so?"

"Yes, that is so."

"I'm sure *Oberst-Gruppenführer* Wolff will understand when he finds out the safety of he and his family was in the hands of drunken imbeciles." Reinhardt stared them all down. "Now leave before I have you disciplined!"

The other two rushed to the door, but the *SS-Sturmscharführer* lingered behind.

"She says she is a music student," the *SS-Sturmscharführer* said.

"And ..." Reinhardt said.

His posture reminded Kira of a wolf ready to fight.

"Prove it. Play your instrument," the *SS-Sturmscharführer* said, his eyes moving from Reinhardt to Kira, a serpent's smirk curving on his lips.

"You expect her to play after you tried to rape her? She's terrified."

The *SS-Sturmscharführer* nodded in mock understanding. "Then I shall return tomorrow with *Oberstleutant* Heis, *Major*," he said, emphasizing the two ranks.

Reinhardt had been trumped. He had stopped tonight, but tomorrow this *Schadenfreude* would return.

"I'll play," Kira said.

Reinhardt turned to her. His eyes went from glacial and glaring, to warm and compassionate.

"You don't have to," he said.

Kira smirked at his naivety. Yes, she did. Her legs were wobbly, her hands shaking as she grabbed the double bass case and heaved it onto her bed. A tsunami of panic washed over her. Had she put everything away properly? Was the false bottom flush, so that Reinhardt and the others couldn't tell it was there? She cut her deep breath short, worried it would be a sign of guilt. She flicked the locks and opened the case. She lifted the instrument out, and closed the case and slid it under the bed. She couldn't risk it falling off her bed and having a disassembled three-line rifle scatter across the floor.

She took position, her eyes closed, so she could visualize how Wesley's fingers had moved along the strings and the stroke of the bow across them.

"We are waiting," the *SS-Sturmscharführer* said.

Kira ignored his jest, keeping her eyes closed. In her mind, she was nearly through the final movement of Beethoven's "Ode to Joy." This was no different from prepping for a sniper shot. Kira's eyes snapped open. Confident and calm. She played. The first notes were off-pitch. The *SS-Sturmscharführer* licked his lips, a lion who had found its sickly gazelle. Kira adjusted the strings, then played again. She had no idea what the notes were called, but she didn't need to. The muscle memory she had developed over the last week kicked in. Her fingers bent, arched, and curled. It was music she created. Not just any music. One of the most famous musical compositions ever created—Beethoven's "Ode to Joy."

Right now, this was her sniper rifle. She couldn't kill the *SS-Sturmscharführer*, but she could kill that drunken smirk. Her quality was impressive enough that not even he could make a spiteful comment. Dare she say it was beautiful.

"Satisfied?" Reinhardt asked.

He stepped toward the *SS-Sturmscharführer*, close enough that the tips of their boots almost touched. Reinhardt had half a foot on him. He glared down.

"I suggest you sober up," Reinhardt said. "You have wasted a great deal of time. It would be a shame if anyone found out instead of verifying the safety of *Oberst-Gruppenführer* Wolff and his family, you'd gotten drunk and demanded a private concert from a frightened woman."

The other two finally intervened. They both put a hand on the *SS-Sturmscharführer*'s shoulder, telling him it was time to go. He followed them out of the room. Reinhardt locked the door behind them. He crouched, so that he was eye level with Kira.

"Are you alright?" he asked.

Kira nodded. It was all she could do. She wasn't aware she still had the bow in her hand until Reinhardt gently took it from her and set it on the windowsill. He went to the kitchen and filled a glass with water and told her to sip it. Every vile act they would have committed to her played in her mind. Had Reinhardt not shown up ...

"I could use something stronger," Kira said, hiccupping a laugh.

"Me, too."

Kira sipped the water. Her mouth absorbed it like a cotton ball. "What were you doing here?"

Reinhardt avoided her gaze, his cheeks reddening slightly. "I wish it were as innocent as right place, right time. But the truth is I've been walking this street all night. I had to see you. An aching in my bones."

Another sip of her water because it was all she could think to do. Her mouth was desert dry, but drinking water seemed as fruitful as watering sand.

"You play beautifully," Reinhardt said.

Maybe, but it was all a lie.

"Who taught you?" he asked.

She didn't want to lie to him, but she couldn't tell him an English man had taught her days ago to help her cover as a music student to disguise her mission to assassinate a high-ranking Nazi. But perhaps she could reveal a bit of truth in the lie she needed to tell. He didn't deserve lies, not after what he'd done. He had proven unequivocally that he was no *Schadenfreude*. To the contrary. He was one of the most honorable men she'd ever known.

"My father taught me. He was a proud man. Not all of him came home from the war. But he taught me everything."

"Did your mother play?"

Kira shook her head. "No, my sisters neither. It was something my father and I shared."

Reinhardt showed his appreciation for her vulnerability with a smile. He deserved more. The secret weighed heavily, tethered to an anchor and tossed overboard. She had to let go of it or she'd drown. Everything in this apartment was a lie or a secret. He was sitting on classified documents detailing the pending murder of the very man who the *SS-Sturmscharführer* was assigned to protect. There was a disassembled Mosin–Nagant rifle in the double bass case and a pistol in the toilet water tank. If she were caught in her assassination attempt, Reinhardt could be killed. By drunken luck, the *SS-Sturmscharführer* had found someone who meant Wolff harm. Reinhardt had stopped him. Had defended her. What she wanted to tell him she knew she shouldn't.

"You said to me that I have lost much during the war," Kira said. She paused to meet his eyes. She needed the look of reassurance from him to continue. And he gave it. Those brilliant eyes now looked like a lake on a sunny day—inviting and warm.

"Germany invaded my town. My father was killed … my two sisters Nousha and Lina …" Her throat closed. The words broke off. Her body's way of trying to protect her from the immense pain those audible words would cause. "They were … raped and murdered."

Once again, Reinhardt's eyes filled with an unfathomable sadness. He gently took her hands in his.

"I'm so sorry, Kira."

Kira broke his gaze and finished her water. Speaking it aloud was a strange sensation. In some ways, it was freeing, and in others, it imprisoned her in that reality. Speaking those words to Reinhardt had bonded him to her, whether he knew it or not. He sat there stroking her back until Kira composed herself.

"Does this place have a roof?" Reinhardt asked.

Kira looked at him, dumbfounded. She couldn't help but make a snarky comment. "Do you see stars above your head?"

Reinhardt flashed a smile in response to her sarcastic jest. "*Touché.*"

He left the room, telling Kira to grab a blanket as he did. Kira gathered a spare blanket from her bed and waited in the empty apartment. Reinhardt told her to follow him. He reached for her hand and led her down the hall to a custodial closet. Inside it, a ladder led to the roof. They climbed it. Reinhardt opened the hatch.

The frigid air swirled around them. Reinhardt took the blanket and wrapped it around his shoulders, then stood behind Kira and covered her with it. She rested her hands on his crossed arms.

"Close your eyes," he whispered.

Kira did. He put his hand on her hips, prompting her to walk ahead. She took slow, tentative steps, unaware of where the roof ledge was. He signaled for her to stop by squeezing her hips.

"Open your eyes," he whispered.

She opened them. A faint gasp followed. The Eiffel Tower stretched before them, lit by a backdrop of stars and a full moon.

"It's extraordinary ..." Kira gasped.

Paris had been more beautiful than any words in any novel. And this image might just be the one she remembered first.

"It truly is. I'm thankful she was undamaged during the invasion."

They gazed in silence at the golden tower lit by the moon's ethereal glow.

"That solider spoke of an *Oberst-Gruppenführer* coming ..." Kira said.

"Yes, Wolff. Most of the high-ranking leaders of the Reich are in a constant state of paranoia. Especially since Heydrich's death."

Kira recognized the name. Heydrich was the Chief of the Reich Security, Main Office. He'd been murdered in Prague in June of that year.

"Don't worry. That vile worm was only using *Oberst-Gruppenführer* Wolff to justify his actions," Reinhardt said.

"And this Wolff, is he a *Schadenfreude*, like all Germans?" Kira asked.

Reinhardt looked at her—offended, hurt even. "Like all Germans? Is that what you think of me?"

"No." Kira let him see the truth in her eyes.

Finally, a hundred percent truthful answer. She thought she knew before, but after what had happened, she knew for certain. Reinhardt Friedel was the antithesis of everything she considered Germans to be. And it changed everything she thought she knew about why she had joined the fight.

"And Wolff?" she asked.

"I only met him once. On my train ride to Paris. He is devout, but he loves his family."

"You don't agree with Hitler, with Wolff, yet you fight with them. *For* them."

Reinhardt shook his head. "I fight for Germany. For its lakes, its mountains, its grassy fields. It is my home. I fight for my parents, my grandparents, my sisters, Mathias. Germany is not defined by the men who rule it. It existed before the *Führer*, and it will exist long after."

Kira frowned. It was her first glimpse at his naivety.

"There may not be a Germany if this war continues," she said.

Reinhardt's face warped with sadness at the thought that his beloved Germany could fade into history like Rome before it.

"Stalin is not free of sin either," Reinhardt said. "Do you know the travesties he's committed against his own people?"

"Germany broke the pact, not the Soviet Union," Kira said, bringing her gaze back to the Eiffel Tower.

"That isn't an answer."

"Then tell me what is."

"Leningrad has been under siege since '41. Stalin did not allow its citizens to evacuate, and now, they are starving without even a fool's hope of supplies coming in. Do you know the reports coming out of the city? People have dug up dead cattle, carving around rotten flesh. They catch rats loaded with disease to eat them, and the most desperate have resorted to cannibalism. All because Stalin was too proud, too narrow-minded to accept defeat. He has forsaken millions to die in his labor camps, executed military commanders because he feared they would threaten his rule. Kira, we're both ruled by unjust men."

"I would not fight for Stalin. I would fight for the Soviet Union. For my family."

"As do I."

National pride warmed their bodies. A German and a Russian willing to die for neither a German nor a Russian leader. Hitler was Austrian, Stalin Georgian.

The snow fell harder, the winds swirling and blowing it at them. The temperature dropped. Kira and Reinhardt hurried downstairs to Kira's room, stomping the snow off their shoes. The hour was late, a new day minutes away.

"I can't in good conscience leave you here alone tonight," Reinhardt said.

"I'll be okay," Kira said.

"Oh, of that I have no doubt. But you must forgive my stubbornness."

Kira allowed Reinhardt to stay. She changed into her pajamas in her bathroom. When she stepped out, Reinhardt had stripped down to his T-shirt and pants. He stretched over the couch, his feet hanging over the edge. Kira shut the light off, then crawled into her bed. She stared at the ceiling. Reinhardt, too.

"Are you awake?" Kira asked.

"I am," Reinhardt answered.

"Can I tell you something?"

"Tell me everything."

She wished she could, but there were things she could never tell him. And for the first time, it truly felt like she wasn't lying only to others but lying to herself.

"Ever since my sisters were raped and murdered, I've contemplated the horror of what they experienced. But it was always a guess. A true answer I could never know. Earlier … when I thought I was going to be raped … I wanted it to happen … needed it to happen. So that I knew the pain they experienced. Knew what my failure had caused them."

Reinhardt was intuitive enough to know not to interrupt her. She knew she shouldn't feel that way. The best thing he could do for her was listen. And he did.

"I should have been there … I was reading at a bluff. I was too late. Before my father died … he asked me to save them."

Reinhardt got up from the couch and crouched beside her.

"Look at me," he said, his tone sympathetic. He gazed deeply into her eyes. "Listen to me, Kira. What happened to your sisters was horrible, inexplicable. But it didn't happen because you weren't there. You mustn't blame yourself."

But Kira *did* blame herself, and she always would. Time would never lessen that. She had her shot at the *Schadenfreude* who had raped them. God had penalized her. Kira had been willing to allow another woman to be raped to save her own sisters. And the cruel irony was that it was her sisters she had watched being raped.

"You are fierce, so I know you loved them fiercely," Reinhardt said. He squeezed her hand and started to return to the couch. But she stopped him, reaching an outstretched hand to him. She pulled him near, prompting him to crawl into bed next to her. Nothing more would happen. Not after she'd nearly been raped. Reinhardt wouldn't press for it, either. Lying next to her was all he craved. Face to face. Kira balled his shirt into her hand. Even when she fell asleep, she'd have a lock on him so he couldn't leave her. He stroked her hair, tracing the waves in it, his eyes locked in on hers, reading her like one of his books.

For Reinhardt, it was what he had been searching for. The feeling he could see in Günter's eyes when he stared into Klara's. Kira was the strongest woman he'd ever met. She intimidated and inspired in equal measure. She was a flame that he couldn't help but be mesmerized by the way it danced in the darkness, oblivious to the damage it could unleash. The sun he needed to revolve around.

Jürgen Wolff

Reinhardt left as the sun rose. Kira was still asleep. Had it all been a strange mix of a nightmare and a dream? But when she took her first deep breath, she was hit with the lingering scent of his cologne on her pillow. It had been real. All of it. The good and the bad. Kira bathed, dressed, then walked to the Givre Strudel. Reinhardt had beaten her there, already in his spot and an open book in front of his face. She greeted Josephine.

"Everything fine last night?" Josephine asked.

"Yes," Kira said, and left it at that. The truth was too long to tell.

Kira sat near Reinhardt's table. He glanced at her, unable to stop his smile from spreading. The café was packed as usual, a mix of elderly Parisians, young French women, and German soldiers. Some Kira had grown accustomed to seeing, others were new. Kira and Reinhardt alternated between who stared at whom, neither wanting to get caught. The distance between them felt electric, dangerous, as if anyone who walked between them would get shocked.

The front door opened; the bell atop it rang. A man Kira knew but had never met stepped in. A man whose face she'd studied long enough to memorize it. Long, oval-shaped face. Narrow, sapphire eyes with a smug expression. Jürgen Wolff had arrived in Paris. He held the door for his wife, a woman who looked at least a decade younger. Her blonde hair was styled in pin curls. She was striking. Two children skipped in between them. A girl, twelve and a boy, eight. Exact ages she knew only because it was listed in Wolff's file. Every German in the café, including Reinhardt, rose to their feet and saluted Wolff, shouting "*Seig Heil!*"

The world could be cruelly and comically small. Paris was home to millions and a temporary home to thousands more. The one man she had been targeted to assassinate had come to the café she frequented. Kira tried to wipe every thought from her mind, as if they would otherwise be heard.

Eight-year-old Manfred Wolff spotted Reinhardt first. His eyes lit up. He sprinted to Reinhardt, all clumsy feet, calling his name. He bumped into Kira's table. Christiania Wolff disciplined him and apologized to Kira, who could only force an underdeveloped smile. Was she really going to have to eat breakfast alongside them?

"Major Friedel," Wolff called, opening his arms like a father figure.

Reinhardt embraced him. "Welcome to Paris, *Oberst-Gruppenführer.*"

Wolff asked how Reinhardt's vacation had been so far, then snapped his fingers to no one in particular to join the two tables. An awkward number of soldiers responded and pulled the two tables together. Wolff saw the medal and its ribbon being used as a bookmark. He grabbed the medal and tossed the book aside, not giving a damn what page Reinhardt had been on.

"This does not belong concealed in some book, Reinhardt," Wolff said. He fastened it on Reinhardt's chest. "For how else will everyone here know they are in the presence of a Hero of the Reich?"

Reinhardt looked as if he'd rather be anywhere than where he stood, being shown off as if he were a prized racehorse.

Wolff addressed the entire café. "You gaze upon The War Eagle. The greatest fighter pilot in the war."

Kira studied the reactions of everyone in the room. Jürgen Wolff looked at him like a proud father; Christiania did not gaze upon him like a son, but more like a woman studying a plaything; Susanne flushed red—Reinhardt was her first crush; Manfred gazed upon his hero; the German soldiers beamed proudly; the young Parisian women knew he was the enemy, but couldn't deny how handsome he was; and the elderly Parisian men and women scowled at Reinhardt. Hatred in their eyes and hearts.

And how was Kira reacting? What was her expression, her body language, telling them? She brought her hand to her mouth to help conceal whatever expressions her face made. Reinhardt, sweet, protective, and kind, was a vigilant pilot. Victor of hundreds of dogfights. Where had he fought? Over the English Channel? Had he been in the sky the night Yuri and Semyon had died? Had he fought in the East? In Russia? Her home? How many of her countrymen had he slain? Did she know any of them personally?

Kira left as discreetly and fast as she was able. A black Mercedes was parked directly in front of the Givre Strudel. Wolff's car. She knew where Wolff would stay.

The same place Hermann Göring, head of the *Luftwaffe*, had set up headquarters in 1940: the Ritz—one of the world's most famous hotels. Seeing Wolff had re-centered her focus. Things had grown blurry, murky, lines distorted. Reinhardt Friedel was a dangerous distraction. He wasn't a *Schadenfreude*. He didn't get enjoyment from his kills. But he served the Reich. And right now, he was eating a late breakfast with the man whom in a few days' time she would kill.

Kira wandered Paris. She had to keep moving. If she stayed still, her thoughts would swamp her. She turned the corner of the street that her apartment building was on. Reinhardt was on the stoop, reading. She'd been gone hours. How long had he been waiting? She wanted to both flee and rush toward him. The result was nearly tripping over her feet.

"Do I need to bow in front of the hero?" Kira asked.

Reinhardt stood. Up on the stoop, he looked gigantic. "It is customary. I could take your hand if you do not."

"That seems the Nazi way," Kira said. She nodded at the Knight's Cross. "Why did you keep it hidden?"

Reinhardt didn't even glance down to acknowledge it. "A medal for bravery? Every person who fights is brave. Every person who lives during this war is brave."

"Will you tell me why you received it?" Kira asked.

Reinhardt hesitated. It was personal. But not any more so than what Kira had revealed.

"Tonight. I will cook supper for you, we will imbibe drinks, and I will answer anything you ask me."

Kira couldn't form the words to agree, but she did nod. The affirmation Kira had had at the Givre Strudel left with Reinhardt. The dangerous distraction would be returning to her apartment that evening. Wolff was in Paris, and Kira had introduced a variable into the mix. An extremely handsome variable. That's the power of addiction. We know it's wrong, but we can't stop. The high is worth all of the possible destruction.

Reinhardt returned that evening, carrying a bag of groceries, a bottle of whiskey, and a box of chocolates. Kira refrained from commenting on the lack of rationing. Reich heroes were given special privileges. And she certainly wasn't going to complain about it—she could use the reprieve from ration food.

"What are you making?" Kira asked.

"Correction. What are *we* making?"

"I believe you said *you* would cook supper for *me*."

He shrugged. "I lied."

The answer to what *they* were cooking was fried sausage, sauerkraut, and cucumber salad. Reinhardt hadn't been able to acquire the sour cream needed to make it a creamy salad, so it was simply oil, vinegar, and a sparring amount of sugar and dill. He filled the dinner detailing some of his favorite foods from back home. For Kira, they didn't have large grocery stores to buy food from all around the world. They ate what they hunted and grew. Eating had never been a pleasurable activity. It'd been fuel. But Paris had changed that.

"You promised to tell me about how you earned that," Kira said, nodding at the Knight's Cross with Oak Leaves.

Reinhardt sipped his whiskey, enjoying the burning sensation it caused in his chest. He knew he would have to tell the story. He had put it off for as long as he could. She had confided in him about something far more painful.

"We'd flown into an ambush …"

He told her about Klaus's death and about Günter. How he'd saved him and six others by flying them out on the wings of his plane. It was incredibly impressive. Kira imagined having to hang onto an airplane wing and shuddered. He added no embellishments. No hint of arrogance in his voice. He spoke as if he were reading a manual, not detailing a heroic rescue.

"May I?" Kira asked, gesturing to the Knight's Cross. Reinhardt nodded. She felt the cold cross in her fingertips, feeling the differences in the emboss.

"The Nazis chose a cross?" she asked.

"The Iron Cross predates the Third Reich," Reinhardt said. "It is the symbol of absolute bravery. Germany was not allowed to have any medals after the Great War. The *Führer* brought it back."

Brought it back with a swastika, Kira noticed. But bravery was a trait that could be commendable even to the enemy. Kira respected the soldier he was. She asked about Günter, and he told her about him and his wife Klara, their reprieve in Italy, and the chess matches they played, which was the perfect segue to his last surprise in the bag he'd brought: a chessboard.

"Do you play?" he asked.

"Not very well," Kira replied.

"Good," Reinhardt said, flashing that unbelievable smirk of his.

They cleaned the dishes and cleared the table. As they played, they munched on the chocolates. Rich, creamy, delicious, and making them crave the next one before they had even swallowed the ones in their mouths. How would he treat the game? Would he let her win? Would he be uber competitive? The answer was the latter. He viciously took her rook, then queen and, two moves later, it was checkmate.

"I like you, Kira, but not enough to disgrace the game and let you win."

Kira asked questions as they played, liking the strategy involved. It wasn't much different from her strategy when sniping. Make the enemy focus on where they thought the attack would come from and strike them from somewhere else. Seeing the hesitation as Reinhardt realized what had happened made her smirk. He'd taken the pieces she wanted him to take, all the while weakening his back line and trapping his king. Reinhardt nodded, impressed, a sly smile spreading on his face. It was a novice mistake, but one he hadn't expected her to capitalize on.

After three more games—ruthless Reinhardt wins—Reinhardt requested she play "Ode to Joy." Kira obliged. The instrument had been a surprising gift. The Soviets could have come up with a different cover story, and Kira would have missed out on discovering a love of music. And they could have sent someone else, and she'd have missed out on discovering another love. She still hadn't decided, and wasn't sure she'd ever decide, if meeting Reinhardt was fortunate or unfortunate. He was fire. He could heat the house or burn it down. Fire is always dangerous.

Then something happened she didn't think happened on dates … if this was a date. They both read their own books in silence. After they both reached the point of diminishing returns because their eyes weighed heavy, Reinhardt snapped his book shut.

He kissed her goodnight, telling her he had to wake early for breakfast with Wolff and his family.

Christmas was only a few days away and the weather responded accordingly, dropping ten degrees. But as of now, if it did snow, it didn't stick. For Kira, it felt wrong. There needed to be snow on Christmas.

She assembled her rifle, practicing working the bolt. She didn't need to study Wolff's pictures anymore. She knew what he looked like, she'd seen him at the Givre Strudel on a handful of occasions. She knew how he walked—shoulders pressed back, feet slightly pointed outward, and his hands crossed behind his back. She knew how he smelt—cigarette and coffee with a failing hint of cologne and the waning smell of his wife's perfume on his cheek from where she had kissed him.

Kira tossed the files into her bathroom garbage bin and lit them aflame. Burning all the evidence until it was black ash, emptying the charred pieces into the toilet, and then flushing. Her holiday was over. It was time to complete her mission.

Christmas Eve

Christmas Eve had always been a day wrapped in tradition. But those traditions had died with her family. Kira would always feel lonelier on the holidays. This Christmas Eve would see not a new tradition, as tradition implies something routinely done. What she had to do could not be repeated. Kira would kill Wolff. She'd scouted the Ritz and the Place Vendôme surrounding it. Afternoon walks with Reinhardt had yielded valuable information. Wolff was on the third floor facing the Place Vendôme. Reinhardt had been in the room, young Manfred his tour guide. She didn't like that Reinhardt had inadvertently revealed information. There would be many Nazis who would accuse him of treason if she were caught. She also didn't want to hear any stories that humanized Wolff and steered the conversation elsewhere whenever Reinhardt brought him up. Wolff was a *Schadenfreude*.

Reinhardt had asked if he could take her somewhere during the evening of Christmas Eve. He gave away no information when asked, only that she should wear a dress. Kira styled her hair and makeup, remembering Veronika's advice. Advice that seemed like it had come years ago. It was all too painfully easy to imagine her sisters around her at the mirror, both futzing with her hair, combing and brushing it every which way until they both agreed on how it looked. Drilling her with questions and hypothetical situations that could arise on her date. But there were no apparitions of ghosts of Christmas past. Only Kira in the small Paris apartment. Alone.

There had been the Kira before her mother had died, and the Kira after. A Kira before her father and sisters' deaths and the Kira after. And now, another metamorphism had taken place. The Kira who left for Paris no longer existed. That Kira had hated all Germans. They were all *Schadenfreudes*. She wanted to kill every last one of them. But that bigoted point of view had been proven false by the actions of one man. A man who had awoken something deep inside her that she thought would lie dormant forever.

A knock on her door startled her, breaking her pensive thoughts. She opened the door. Reinhardt was in full dress uniform. His two medals around his neck and on his chest. Kira's dress was a deep red, a fitting color for Christmas Eve. Reinhardt marveled at her beauty, his eyes wide in amazement. The way the dress clung to her curves. Her voluptuousness. And those emerald eyes …

"You're staring," Kira said.

"Yes, I am. I cannot help it. Kira … you are stunning."

Kira blushed. "You're still staring."

Reinhardt didn't break his gaze. "I don't want to forget anything about the way you look."

Reinhardt helped her into her coat. She asked where they were going, but Reinhardt only nodded ahead, as if that helped any. A Christmas chill swept through the streets, blowing the smell of weak coffee and pine. Reinhardt entwined his hand in Kira's. It was the perfect mitten. They came to a building with Palladian entrances. One of Paris' premier theater and opera houses: the Théatre du Châtelet.

"Special Christmas performance," Reinhardt explained.

The atmosphere resembled what Kira envisioned an American Hollywood film premiere to be. Women clad in gorgeous dresses and sparkling jewelry. Men in suits or military uniforms. All gossiping as the line advanced. Inside, servers in white suits and white gloves carried trays of champagne. Nazi photographers snapped pictures. The lobby was adorned with holly, mistletoe, and bulbs of gold, silver, crimson, and evergreen. Christmas trees rose to the ceiling. And everyone inside was in their best spirits in a way people only ever are on Christmas. Inside this immaculate theater, the Second World War did not exist. And what a grand reprieve that was.

"Oh, Reinhardt, so good of you to come!" Christiania Wolff said.

She was clad in a green dress, her lipstick a striking red. Her husband was close behind, dressed in full military regalia. Reinhardt greeted him with the Nazi salute. Manfred and Susanne fought for Reinhardt's attention. Reinhardt gave them both equal amounts, asking them what they hoped to find under their Christmas tree.

"Who is this tall beauty?" Christiania asked.

"My date, Kira," Reinhardt said.

"A pleasure to meet you officially," Christiania said, offering her hand.

Kira hesitated briefly. It was wrong to shake the hand of a woman whose husband she would attempt to assassinate in a few hours. But she had no choice. She forced a nervous smile. Wolff shook her hand, too. To his credit, his eyes didn't find her cleavage once. And who else roamed the lobby looking for threats but the drunken *Sturmscharführer*. His eyes met Kira's but only for a moment. This brief introduction had reaffirmed in his mind how foolish he'd been. Reinhardt and Kira followed the Wolffs to the third floor. The interior of the theater had a large ovular opening with a domed glass ceiling and a sparkling chandelier. The walls were gold, the seats scarlet. Kira had grown up with bucolic beauty. Nature was beautiful. But this was of an elegance she'd never seen, and it took her breath away.

"Spectacular, isn't it?" Wolff commented.

Kira's lips curved into an uneasy smile. "Truly."

Wolff had a supreme confidence about him. And why shouldn't he? He had acquired a gorgeous wife and produced charming children. He had wealth and power in equal measure. Women and men leaned over from the rows ahead and behind to share a word, to shake his hand.

Reinhardt followed behind to their seats. There was anticipation in the air; the lights dimmed. The audience fell silent. The opera began. A heavyset, bearded man had a booming, deep voice, and the lead woman who sang like an angel was not even five feet tall. It didn't seem possible that someone so small in stature could have such a powerful voice. It was far more engrossing than Kira had expected it to be. In a different time, an alternate reality, maybe Alekseeva would have ended up on the stage, sharing her beautiful voice with the world. She should have been able to have that chance. Instead, she had died in a fiery inferno. The sadness of her death now had a soundtrack, and the memory and music were too much. Tears trickled down Kira's cheeks. Reinhardt squeezed her hand.

The powerful voices ended with a standing ovation. The lights powered on, signaling intermission. The audience filed out to use the restrooms, get drinks, and chat about the first half of the show. It was magical. All of it. Men and women dressed in their best, filled with Christmas spirit. The gorgeous holiday decorations. The opera. The drinks. And Reinhardt. Her time with him neared its finale, its own curtain call. The physical urge had always been there, as primitive as a tiger's need to hunt. But now there was something else. A longing for something permanent. Something she could draw back on. She was in a position of regret, no matter what she did. If she embraced that lustful feeling, she'd regret falling victim to it. If she denied it, she'd regret not experiencing it.

Oser Vivre. Dare to live.

"Merry Christmas, Kira," Reinhardt said, clinking his glass of wine against hers. His cologne contained pheromones. It had to. Every smile he shared caused a firework to go off inside her.

The crowd slowly shuffled back inside. Kira stopped Reinhardt from joining them. She took his hand, leading him to the first unlocked door. Inside were cleaning chemicals, serving napkins, glasses, silverware, and toothpicks. A lone window framed the city. Kira closed the door. Reinhardt looked amused, fighting off laughter.

"What are we doing?" he asked.

Kira gazed into his eyes, studying them, memorizing them. But they were always changing. Different stars in a different night sky. Even if she had a photograph of them, it could never do them justice. She caressed his cheek with her fingertips, and stepped onto the tips of her toes and kissed him, tasting the merlot on his lips. She unbuttoned his uniform and untucked the shirt underneath. He stopped her, stepping back so he could see her eyes, gauging if she truly wanted this to happen. That silent question was its own answer. Kira bit her lip and nodded. He smiled. All trepidation ended. They tore off each other's clothing as fast as they could. Porcelain flesh against porcelain flesh. Feeling the power his sinewy frame possessed. The strength yet gentleness of his hands. She turned her head to the side as he kissed her neck, gazing out the window at the city she'd fallen in love with. The opera drifted through the walls. Their bodies matched the rhythm of the crescendo. Lips pressed together. Hands exploring. Fingertips caressing.

Afterward, they stared into each other's eyes, trembling. For the first time, Kira didn't try to hide, deny, or protect anything her eyes revealed. Hoping they were a book Reinhardt could effortlessly read.

Reinhardt stared at her in disbelief at what an incredible woman she was. Then he dressed and offered to wait for Kira, but she told him to go ahead. Kira dressed, then paused by the door. She took a pen from a box and a thick serving napkin. She wrote on it, fanned it to dry the ink, and folded it in half. Reinhardt waited outside the theater door, a smile spreading the moment he saw her. She straightened his collar and then stroked his smooth cheek, slipping the folded napkin into his pocket. They returned to their seats midway through a song, but it didn't take long to be coaxed into the drama on stage. So much of her wanted to stay, but she couldn't. Was there a reality where she could stay in Paris with Reinhardt, eating apple strudel every morning and gazing at the stars every night? The man a row ahead of them, clad in the Nazi uniform, silently answered that foolish question for her. No, there was not. The world was at war. And she and Reinhardt were enemies.

The song ended. Thunderous applause broke out.

Kira leaned into Reinhardt. "I'm going to use the toilet."

"I can wait for you outside," he said, motioning to stand.

Kira stopped him, putting her hand on his forearm. "I'll be fine."

He smirked. "Of that I have no doubt."

She wanted to take in his handsome face as long as she could, memorize every line, every curve the way she had Wolff's. But she had to cut it short, or he would become suspicious. Kira shimmied through the row, pausing at the exit to gaze at Reinhardt lit only by shadow. It would be the last time she ever saw him.

Lone Gunman

Even though her absence wouldn't be noticed for several minutes, Kira rushed out of the theater. Eyes misty, heart thumping. Most of the staff looked at her as a woman whose heart had just been broken. And in a way, it had. Though no one had broken it. She'd severed the vital organ herself. Her mind usurped control over her body, ignoring all the chemical reactions pleading for her to return to Reinhardt. To rest her head against his broad shoulder, entwine her icy hand in his warm one. It was a self-betrayal she didn't know if she would ever forgive herself for. Reinhardt represented everything she had thought she'd never find. He represented a life away from war. But it was a mirage. Something that could never be.

Kira hurried to her apartment, cursing her impractical shoes once again. Once inside the apartment entryway, she dusted off the snow clinging to her coat. She retrieved her TT-30 pistol from the toilet's water tank, unloading and inspecting it. Then she dragged her heavy double bass case and suitcase from under the bed. Her hand rose to the light switch but paused before she flicked it off. This unnoteworthy apartment had become a home of sorts. It had been free of smells and scents when she had moved in. Had she added any? Would her perfume linger? The scent of her soap in the bathtub? Would the smell of the foods she cooked stay in the kitchen? She breathed in the air once more, then flipped the light switch off. She subdued her emotions. There would be time to process her stay in Paris but not right now. She needed to focus, to be totally vigilant.

Kira stuck to the shadows, struggling with the cumbersome luggage. The Ritz Hotel overlooked the Place Vendôme, the octagonal square she had toured with Reinhardt. The bricks were gray, and in the middle of the square was the Vendôme Column, the same shade of green as Victor Noir's statue. The column had been made from enemy cannon fire and its construction was ordered by the famed Napoleon. She liked the idea of using what the enemy had used to destroy to rebuild. This had been one of her favorite parts of Paris. Across from the Ritz was a building with half its upper floors under construction. Kira stepped inside it. A German guard in his mid-twenties dressed in black with a red armband rose. The radio on the desk softly played Christmas songs.

"You cannot be in here, Miss," he said in French.

"I am sorry," she answered in German. "I just arrived and am heading to my hotel to see my fiancé, but I was hoping to use the toilet first."

She played the role of a frail debutante struggling with her luggage. The guard's demeanor shifted with her German reply. Less skeptical, more willing to help.

"The toilet is down the hall and to the left. You may leave your luggage there," he said.

Kira didn't feel like lugging the luggage down the hall and to the left, and had it been normal luggage, she wouldn't have. She had a rifle in there, she didn't want to leave it. But would it strike him as odd if she refused? Take it with her and there was a zero percent chance he'd be able to snoop inside. But it may strike him as suspicious, and he could ask to see what was inside. She couldn't debate her decision anymore, or the guard may make that decision for her.

"Oh, thank God," Kira said, sighing with relief when she set it down in front of the desk.

Kira hurried down the hall and to the left. She pushed the door for the women's bathroom open, so if the young guard was listening for that familiar sound, he'd hear it. But instead of going in, she continued ahead to an exit. She opened it just enough, so that the wind couldn't whistle as it squeezed through. She grabbed her golden lipstick case and jammed it between the door and the door frame. Certain it would hold, she hurried into the bathroom, flushed the toilet, and washed her hands, so that the guard would be able to smell the soap and see the drops of water on her hands. She returned to the front desk. The guard worked on the radio, trying to get "Silent Night" to come in clearer.

"I should have learned the violin," Kira said, heaving the double bass case off the floor.

The guard smiled. "Or you should have become a singer. No case required."

Kira returned his smile and thanked him. "Merry Christmas."

"You, too."

Kira stepped out and walked the length of the building, then turned to walk along its side, searching for the door. She tested a door, but it was securely locked. The next

218

one, too. A panic crept in, spreading with the chilly wind. Had the lipstick tube rolled out of place? Had the German guard been overly cautious and searched and found it?

But the next door opened. She picked up the lipstick tube and listened for any movement. Satisfied there was none, she rushed inside and to the stairwell. She crept up each stair cautiously—stairwells are notoriously loud. She paused occasionally to hear if anyone ascended or descended. Once on the third floor, she set her suitcase by the door. The room was covered in boxes and pallets and smelled of fresh coats of paint. She moved boxes in front of the door; if someone would try to enter, the boxes would slide and topple over and warn her. She opened the double bass case and removed the instrument and the false bottom. She pieced her rifle together. The lighting was poor, most of the room cloaked in shadow. But it didn't matter. Kira had practiced assembling it with her eyes closed, going by touch alone. She finished and brought the rifle to shooting position, testing the feel against her shoulder. She worked the bolt and gazed through the scope. Satisfied everything was in working order and in alignment, she loaded the rifle with five 7.62x54mmR rounds. She set her TT-30 pistol close by. No emergency whistles or flares. This was her backup plan, her saving grace. Her final act.

She had nothing to do but wait. She scanned the Ritz, looking for any oddities. The opera had to be over. Wolff would arrive here soon; his children would be tired. A black Mercedes pulled up to the hotel entrance. This was it. Any tiredness, any complacency she had vanished. She steadied her breathing. Wolff stepped out of the car. Kira moved her finger closer to the trigger. Before she could settle on the shot, Wolff bent down into the car and stood once more with sleeping Manfred in his arms, his small head resting on his father's shoulder. She could still take the shot, but it meant splattering Wolff's brains all over his son. If the situation were reversed, a *Schadenfreude* wouldn't have hesitated. It would have only excited him more, like the man who had raped and murdered her sisters. The memory caused her finger to twitch, ordering it to squeeze the trigger. But Jürgen Wolff's sins were his own. Not his son's. If she shot Wolff now, she may as well shoot the boy to save him from the horror, guilt, and grief he'd struggle with for the rest of his life.

The moment passed. Wolff and his family were inside. Had she just failed her mission? She pushed the cancerous thought from her head, and instead, focused her gaze on the third floor and the window of the room Wolff was staying in. A light came on, but only shadows were visible. After tucking their children into bed, Wolff and his wife loaded an extravagant number of presents under their Christmas tree. Each wrapped and covered in curled ribbon and bows. Wolff passed in and out of view too quickly to risk a shot. The dread that she had missed her moment crept in, buzzing around like a housefly with a death wish. It was impossible not to think of the

219

Schadenfreude who had raped and murdered her sisters. The same way he came in and out of frame just as Wolff did now.

She squeezed her eyes shut, then opened them. Focusing on Wolff, waiting for her moment. Wolff stood at the window, smoking a cigarette. Kira held her breath for the shot, but then exhaled it when *Frau* Wolff stood in front of her husband, his arms draped over her shoulders. Shooting a father with his son in his arms had been too much. But what about shooting a husband in front of his wife? A month ago, she would have fired without hesitation. But Reinhardt crept into her thoughts. If someone had planned to assassinate her, she'd hope Reinhardt was nowhere nearby. The guilt and grief would be unbelievable. She moved her trigger finger in front and to the side.

Christiania Wolff leaned in and kissed her husband goodnight. He stayed, half a cigarette remaining to be smoked. Kira's moment had finally come. She knew what would happen when she squeezed the trigger. Under pressure of the action spring, the striker would move forward sharply. The ending point would penetrate the ignition capsule at the bullet's base, the power charge in it would explode, and the bullet, fastened in a brass casing by a ring, would propel forward. Violently, the bullet would spiral through *Oberst-Gruppenführer* Jürgen Wolff's head and end his life.

Wolff gazed out at the Place Vendôme, his fingers massaging his cigarette. His last view would be a beautiful one, his wife's taste still on his lips, his children safely sleeping in the other room. Far better than the last moments afforded to millions of people. He didn't have to face sheer terror and horror. For all he knew, he would get to see the ultimate joy on his children's faces on Christmas morning. Far better last moments than Lina and Nousha experienced.

She curled her index finger forward toward the trigger, applying enough pressure for the bullet to fire. The recoil thrust into her shoulder; her body absorbed it. Unseeable to the human eye, the bullet pierced the window so cleanly that the glass didn't even spiderweb. Her target's head snapped back. His body buckled like an accordion. Jürgen Wolff was dead.

On the Run

Kira pulled the rifle away from the window and crawled out of sight. She calmed her nerves, ignoring her body's pleas to sprint away. She focused on disassembling the rifle. It wouldn't take long after *Frau* Wolff's screams for the guards to rush into the room. And it wouldn't take long for them to deduce where the shot had come from. Time was the enemy. She disassembled the rifle as fast as she could, ignoring the nerves flaring inside her.

Something moved at the entrance. No, not something. Someone. Kira reached for her TT-30, listening. The sound of fingernails on cardboard. The young guard must have heard the shot. Kira crept toward the door. If she fired again, it would remove any question of where the shots were coming from. But she would have no choice. She would have to shoot her way out.

The famous poem read, "Twas the Night Before Christmas, when all through the house; not a creature was stirring, not even a mouse." The first part of that poem was true. It was the night before Christmas, by mere minutes. But the second part of the poem was not true because two mice were stirring, gnawing on the cardboard flaps of the boxes she had stacked by the entrance. She sighed in relief, then rushed back to retrieve her suitcase and double bass case. The mice had cost her precious seconds. She opened the stairwell door and listened for the sounds of thundering footsteps. When none came, she risked making noise by jogging down the steps. The building would be under lockdown soon. She was in no position to remove risk entirely. Having a lone German guard investigate amplified footsteps on a stairwell was greatly preferred to having two dozen angry Nazis demanding blood. She snuck out the back door and broke into a run until she came upon other pedestrians. Once she did, Kira moved at the pace of someone running uncomfortably late for a train. Curfew was in effect, and the only people out were the homeless, who filled every crevice they could find to stay out of the cruel wind. The Germans would look for anomalies. And right now, that was the woman running as fast as those impractical shoes would allow.

Whistles and shouts ripped through the wind. The Nazis were on the hunt. Kira wouldn't be able to outrun them. She bit her lip, weighing her options. Deciding, Kira approached a homeless woman. How she had come to such a sad condition, Kira did not have the time to ask. She offered the frizzled-haired woman her coat and a handful of *Francs* for the woman's battered brown blanket. The woman accepted. Kira wrapped the blanket around herself like a cloak. The motion unleashed the blanket's fetidness, a disgusting blend of mold, body odor, urine, and feces. Kira gagged. She wiped the makeup from her face and ran her fingers through her hair to give it a disheveled look.

She approached a burning barrel filled with dying embers. Smoke wafted out. Kira reached inside and grabbed a handful of soot. Running it in her hands like a bar of soap. Hands covered, she rubbed it on her face. There was one more thing she needed to do. She had too many possessions for a homeless person. She opened her suitcase and stuffed all the lovely dresses into the burning barrel. The double bass had saved her life, given her a new passion, but it was too cumbersome. It had to go. She took the instrument and tossed it in. She clutched the case close to her chest. Lugging the double bass around had been vexatious, but now it felt like she was missing. She watched the fire. The last piece of music the instrument produced was the crackle of its own flesh.

She left the funeral pyre and rushed to the Arc de Triomphe. Trees lined the street. The night was quiet and calm, the dual result of curfew and Christmas Eve. Engines warned of approach. Flashlights and headlights broke through the crisp night. Kira joined the homeless gathered under the trees, sleeping. They'd covered themselves with papers, tarps—anything they could get their hands on to keep warm. To these people, despair hadn't started on 10 May 1940 when the Germans had conquered Paris. To them, it didn't matter who ruled. Life had been grim, it was grim, and it would always be grim regardless of who ruled.

Kira laid down amongst them, curling around her double bass case hidden beneath the blanket that had been used as toilet paper. Car doors slammed. Boots clacked against the street. German words broke the silence. One a familiar voice: the *SS-Sturmscharführer* who had tried to rape her.

"Search them all," he ordered.

German soldiers dragged people to their feet, gazing at the scared, shocked, and, in some cases, drunk eyes of the homeless. Even with alcohol heavily rationed, drunks find a way. The air smelled of unbathed flesh. The *SS-Sturmscharführer* scanned his flashlight indiscriminately, not caring if it was aimed directly in someone's eyes. A soldier stopped to speak with him. The *SS-Sturmscharführer* turned his attention, but his flashlight beam came to rest on Kira. She buried her face in the disgusting blanket. She clenched her eyes, praying she'd go unnoticed.

"You," the *SS-Sturmscharführer* beckoned.

Kira couldn't see him, but her body knew it was her he beckoned. An arctic chill crept on her skin. Her strength fled her body.

"Reveal your face," he ordered in French.

Kira steadied her breath. Would he recognize her? Men had the benefit of growing or shaving a beard. Such a drastic change that people could not recognize two pictures side by side as being the same person. Kira didn't have that advantage. She had to rely on disheveled hair, a soot-covered face, and a plague-covered blanket. She lowered the blanket and squinted at the blinding beam of light. The *SS-Sturmscharführer* glared at her. His face revealed nothing. She expected a smirk to spread as the recognition set in. But instead, his lips curled downward into a scowl. To him, Kira was simply another disgusting rodent rotting away in public.

"Mostly women and old men, *Sturmscharführer*," a soldier said. "The few young men are drunk."

"Continue the search. He couldn't have gotten far. Return tomorrow and arrest the drunks," the *SS-Sturmscharführer* said.

The soldier's face contorted in confusion. "Pardon me, *Sturmscharführer*, but they won't be drunk tomorrow. How will we know?"

"Then assume they all were drunk and arrest them all."

The soldier looked around, counting the number of homeless silently. "We may not have the room. There are so many."

The *SS-Sturmscharführer* drew his Luger and fired, emptying the clip at the homeless closest to him. The spared homeless shrieked and screamed.

"How about now, *Schütze*? Is there enough room, or shall I reload?"

"No, sir … there is enough room …"

"Wonderful." He turned to direct all his men. "Continue searching. I want men at every train station and bus station. All modes of transit have been stopped, but this coward will look to leave Paris as soon as possible. Do not shoot to kill. We will skin this coward alive."

The *SS* soldiers marched along, leaving the dead homeless where they lay. Kira rose and grabbed the double bass case. The *Schadenfreude SS-Sturmscharführer* hadn't recognized her, but in conjunction with the case, he may have. Her mind raced. The bus and train stations had been halted sooner than expected. She had to find a way out of the city. Who could help her? Reinhardt? What would he think of her if he found out what she'd done? He was loyal to Germany. Even if he was willing, helping her would make him betray his beloved homeland. She wouldn't put him in that position. Who else did she know? The old woman who rented her apartment?

Josephine.

She may help. There had been that look in her eyes the first day they met that told Kira she had held no love for the Germans. But the Givre Strudel was closed. She'd given details of her building and the street she lived on once before. It was her only card to play. All in. Win the pot or lose it all.

Kira entered the apartment building. Doors were everywhere, and glancing up the stairwell, there were more floors and more doors. Kira had no clue which was Josephine's. She'd have to knock on strangers' doors early Christmas Day and ask for Josephine Moreau. The first three doors were no answers. Either they were gone or extremely deep sleepers. The fourth door was open and shut once the woman saw it wasn't someone she knew banging on it. It took until the second floor before an elderly man provided an answer. Kira thanked him, then rushed to the designated door before she forgot which number it was. Josephine answered on the third round of knocks, cloaked in a black nightgown. Her eyes were strained red from what appeared to be crying.

"Kira … what are you doing here?" Josephine asked.

There was another question Josephine wanted to ask regarding Kira's appearance, but she waited. Even woken from sleep, Josephine's natural beauty shone through.

"I need your help to get out of Paris. The less you know, the safer it is for you," Kira said.

It was the last news Josephine wanted to hear early Christmas morning. She wanted nothing more than to return to sleep or return to whatever thoughts had made her cry.

"Are you in danger?" Josephine asked.

"Yes …"

Josephine sighed then nodded, motioning to the apartment behind her. "Come inside."

Kira stepped in. Josephine closed the door behind her and locked it.

"Wash up. I have to make a call," Josephine said.

Kira followed Josephine's pointing finger to the bathroom. Kira's appearance in the mirror startled her. She knew she smelled worse than her dastardly appearance. She scrubbed her face, ran wet fingers through her hair. Far from great, but better than it had been.

"I have a ride coming, though it won't be until after curfew is lifted," Josephine said.

Kira thanked her. Josephine went into her bedroom and returned with a bottle of perfume.

"Thank me by spraying that on yourself," Josephine said.

Kira did. The citrus lavender was a saving grace for both their nostrils.

"Did you hurt somebody?" Josephine asked, her pale-green eyes piercing Kira, studying them for any hint of deception.

"Yes."

"He was German? A soldier?"

"Yes."

"Did anybody see you come here?"

"I don't think so."

Josephine studied Kira a moment longer. Kira's instinct was to look away, but to do so would only instill suspicious doubt.

"Are you hungry?" Josephine asked, breaking her piercing gaze.

Hungry? How could she be hungry with everything that had happened? Excitement. Nervousness. Fear. It didn't seem possible, but … yes, she was.

Josephine pointed to a plate of homemade bread. "Butter's been rationed, sorry," Josephine said.

Butter would have been delicious, but it wasn't needed. The bread was fluffy and moist.

"You must be exhausted," Josephine said.

Her words were like curses—Kira hadn't been hungry until it was proposed, and she hadn't been tired until it had been suggested.

"You must have many questions," Kira said.

"I do. But I know you can't and won't tell me the answers to most of them. And I wouldn't ask. I want credible deniability," Josephine said.

Kira had questions for Josephine, but since Josephine hadn't asked hers, she wouldn't ask Josephine. Their conversation was sparse and separated by strings of silence. Just being seated for an extended period on a wooden chair coaxed her to sleep.

"Rest on the couch. It will be a while yet," Josephine said.

Kira wanted to refuse, but the comfort it offered was too great to ignore. Josephine set a blanket and a spare pillow on it, then returned to her bedroom. Kira didn't even remember shifting around to find optimal comfort. Sleep came as fast as the bullet that had murdered *Oberst-Gruppenführer* Wolff. But she had perfected light sleeping and woke the moment Josephine opened her bedroom door.

"He's here," she said.

Kira rose from the couch, rubbing her eyes to free them from rheum. Josephine led Kira down the stairs. An old truck coughed out an unhealthy exhaust. The dark-haired, thin-mustachioed man Kira had seen at the Givre Strudel nodded behind the wheel.

"Kira, this is Radley Durand," Josephine reintroduced.

Durand smiled. He had an effortless suaveness to him.

"You have pissed off the Germans?" he asked in French.

Kira translated it word by word in her head, then answered yes.

"Excellent," he said. He grabbed Kira's double bass case and loaded it into the truck. He told Josephine he'd see her later and then got in his truck. Kira paused, trying to find something better to say than thank you. But it was the only thing that came to her.

"Where you are going … will you be safe?" Josephine asked.

Kira shook her head. "I return to Stalingrad."

Kira watched Josephine's olive eyes process what Kira had said. Confusion at first, then shock, then a look of approval.

"Durand can take you somewhere. Help get you to England. Maybe even America."

"You could have left, too, yes? But you stayed because France is your home. Russia is *my* home."

Josephine's reasons were her own, just like Kira's were her own. Neither woman needed to understand it any more than that. Kira got in the old truck, and it faithfully puttered ahead.

"Where will you take me?" Kira asked Durand.

"West to a train," he answered, adding a complimentary *chu, chu, chu* to help the translation.

"Train to where?"

"*Espagne.*"

"Spain?"

Durand nodded, then mimicked a plane taking off with his hand. "To Russia."

Another plane ride. One had been one of the scariest moments of her life. The other had been one of the most awesome experiences of her life, and up to that point, the most romantic.

Reinhardt.

It'd been hours since she'd fled the theater and fled him. Soon it would be a week, a month, then years. She'd never see him again … no good would come from dwelling on it. She scrunched her eyes, as if doing so could wring him from her thoughts.

The drive was quiet. Durand knew little German and Kira knew little French. The phrases she'd learned really didn't play well in deep conversations. "Where is the toilet?" wasn't really applicable at the moment.

"Papers?" Durand asked.

Kira looked through her purse for the forged identification and held them up. Durand nodded approvingly. He pulled his truck to the side of the road. He carried her double bass case inside the train station and purchased a ticket for her. Twenty minutes later, a train shrieked into the station.

"*Merci*," Kira said.

"France was defeated. The French keep fighting. Travel safe, *Madame. Au revoir* and Merry Christmas." Durand bowed his head respectfully, then left.

Christmas. She'd forgotten all about it, looked through all the decorations and the noticeable absence of people. Durand had a wedding band on his finger, more than likely had children, and he'd sacrificed his Christmas morning driving a stranger to a train station.

The war had shown her *Schadenfreudes* at every turn. But it had also shown her men and women who were kind and good. Both Josephine Moreau and Radley Durand had sacrificed part of their Christmases to help a stranger for no other reason than Kira needed help. What was Durand's story? Was there more to his words "The French keep fighting"? Were those literal words or figurative?

She stepped onto the train and sat by a window. A few moments later, the train surged forward. Paris had woven a place inside her heart. Kira was not a crier, but as Paris drifted behind her, she was filled with melancholy. She had lived a glimpse. A glimpse of the woman she could have been and the life she could have lived. Kira Kovaylova, a musician, not a sniper. A woman who enjoyed pastries and coffee, not a woman who lived off the food she provided. Wore dresses, not pants, styled her hair in victory rolls, not braids. A woman fiercely in love with a handsome, charming, sophisticated man from Germany. Simply a different country, not an enemy. By definition, a glimpse is temporary, but she had memories that would never fade. If she lived to be a wrinkly old woman, she would think back to Christmas 1942 and her time in Paris with Reinhardt Friedel. Leaving Paris was killing that glimpse. And it was the hardest kill she had ever dealt.

Return to Reality

Three songs passed before Reinhardt left his seat to check on Kira. He asked a female server to check the restroom. When she shook her head, he checked every women's restroom in the theater. With no sign of her inside, he went outside. Only the howling wind greeted him.

Kira was gone.

He dug his hands into his pockets to keep them warm. His fingers caressed something. He drew it from his pocket. It was a folded napkin with crisp calligraphic writing on it.

I wish the world was different. I love you.

Attrition and affirmation. He read the note a hundred times. Staring off into the distance. Kira was gone.

There was before Kira and after Kira. His life wouldn't be the same. Why hadn't he asked her where she was from? What city? What address? Why hadn't he told her he loved her? He'd known. There was the fear he would have come on too strong. He'd only known her a couple of weeks, but that had been enough. When you know, you know.

The plane ride east offered cruel contemplation. So much to think about. Not only Kira, but the shocking assassination of *Oberst-Gruppenführer* Wolff. Shot dead on Christmas Eve. His wife and children in the other room. Young Manfred and Susanne had been inconsolable. A level of heartbreak no child should ever experience. But mostly, Kira dominated his thoughts; every road led back to her. But the sky led back to Russia and the war. Where he belonged.

After landing, a jeep drove him to the base. The winter weather was grueling. The air was so frigid it was painful to breathe. His feet and hands quickly went numb and red. Those weeks in Paris had made him soft. He stepped out of the jeep and headed to the barracks. Defeat greeted him. Long faces, blank stares. The only sounds were sneezing and coughing. He recognized some men, but many of them were fresh faces who had replaced the familiar faces he had known.

He scanned the room for Günter and Uwe. It took a moment to recognize Günter. He was gaunter, the fervor in his face gone. He smiled, yet it was a pained smile—he'd summoned as much joy as he could. Reinhardt had felt guilty about his reprieve in Paris before, but this was unbearable. The men before him had lived a dozen hard years in those two weeks.

Günter hugged Reinhardt.

"How are you?" Reinhardt asked.

Günter shrugged. "Our army is trapped at Stalingrad."

"Trapped? How?"

"The Soviets cut off all resupplies. Our men are starving, freezing, and running out of ammo."

"How many?"

"Hundreds …"

Hundreds. Horrible for those hundreds of men. But Reinhardt had thought too fast; Günter hadn't finished the number.

"Hundreds of thousands."

Reinhardt's stomach plummeted. This was a catastrophe.

"What are we doing to get them out?" Reinhardt asked.

Günter and Uwe shared solemn looks.

"There's not much we can do," Uwe said.

"We have to get them out," Reinhardt said.

Günter shook his head, trying to remember Reinhardt had been away and didn't know this to be common knowledge. "They haven't surrendered. They won't surrender … they can't surrender," he said.

The German Sixth Army required fuel, food, and ammunition to continue fighting. A requirement of 750 tons per day was established. Later, that number was reduced to 500 tons. Göring demanded the number, but Chief of the General Staff of the

Luftwaffe, Hans Jeschonnek, had deemed only 350 tons was possible—400 tons less than what Paulus and the Third Army required. Junkers Ju-52s were used to deliver the supplies, but the airfields outside Stalingrad, an area known as the Cauldron, were under constant threat from Soviet ground and air forces. Resupplying the encircled Sixth Army was a tremendous risk to the pilots who would do so.

Reinhardt volunteered to be among those who would risk all. Günter and Uwe joined him. None were naïve; they knew many of the pilots who had braved the trip hadn't returned. The reasoning was simple. If their places were reversed, he hoped others would do the same.

The Junkers Ju-52 was a much different aircraft than the Messerschmitt Reinhardt was accustomed to flying. It was a transport aircraft. If the Messerschmitt could be compared to a cat—quick and evasive—then the Ju-52 was a cow. The goal was to deliver supplies. Survival would be a bonus.

Reinhardt, Günter, and Uwe studied the aerial photographs of the Cauldron. Pitomnik and Bassargino were the two main airfields left under German control. With constant bombardment, the airfields were far from smoothly paved. The weather was poor, the sky dark, meaning Reinhardt and the other *Luftwaffe* pilots would have to rely solely on their instrumentation. But if they couldn't see, it meant the enemy couldn't see them, either.

It felt different from all the other sorties they had flown. In his Messerschmitt, Reinhardt was supremely confident. Skill against skill, he liked his chances. But in the Ju-52, he was vulnerable. A fat and slow target. Günter and Uwe barely spoke. All three smoked an *Eckstein*, gazing into the cruel and cold winter sky, trying not to consider that the sands of their hourglass were almost up. His time in Paris seemed a mirage. A dream he'd had. Reinhardt wanted to think about her. But he couldn't be distracted.

"Good luck," Günter said.

Reinhardt shook his hand. "You, too."

Uwe tossed his cigarette and squashed it with his foot. He took a deep breath and could only muster a nod to Reinhardt and Günter. They boarded their aircraft. Reinhardt fired the engines. Even just sitting in the plane, he could feel how much heavier the Ju-52 was than his Messerschmitt.

The Ju-52 lumbered down the runway, then rose into the midnight air. Visibility was scarce. A pilot had to trust his instruments. Not being able to see out of your car windshield during a snowstorm was terrifying. Now, imagine if you were thousands of feet in the air. Reinhardt flew into a black unknown. He descended, carefully watching the altimeter needle drop. The wheels bounced off the runway. Soldiers rushed to unload the supplies. My God, they were gaunt, looking like boys wearing their fathers' clothes.

Reinhardt rushed out to help. An *Oberstrumbannführer* approached. He had an unkempt beard, sunken eyes, and looked like an insomniac corpse.

"Can you take some of our injured?" he asked.

"Of course. As many as I can," Reinhardt replied.

Soldiers hadn't even waited for his answer before they were carrying stretchers toward the plane. The wounded were frail and frostbitten. Some looked as if they had already traveled across the mythical River Styx.

"Don't fear, Major, they are the lucky ones," the *Obersturmbannführer* said.

"I'll be back with more supplies," Reinhardt said.

A bright light exploded at the end of the runway. Their presence had been discovered. Soldiers screamed and ran. Reinhardt rushed into his cockpit. The sky lit up in strobe-like explosions. The Ju-52 rocked violently. Reinhardt sped forward. The nose of the plane rose into the air, the runway beneath becoming a bombed crater. Reinhardt rose to the safety of the sky. But not every plane had reached that sanctuary.

Reinhardt fled the city of Stalingrad and returned to their airbase safely outside the Cauldron, where he waited anxiously for Günter and Uwe. Each plane that returned carried with it fellow pilots and wounded *Wehrmacht*. Though happy to see them free from the noose of Stalingrad, it was Günter and Uwe he searched for.

Finally, Günter stepped out of his plane. Reinhardt rushed to him.

"Uwe?" Reinhardt asked.

Günter shook his head. "His plane hit a crater. His wheels broke off."

Reinhardt cursed.

"We will get him," Günter said.

"They don't have much time …"

Günter nodded gravely. The Sixth Army was starving. Prior to the encirclement, the soldiers had received sixteen ounces of bread—roughly 1,200 calories' worth. The recommended caloric intake for a soldier fighting in harsh conditions was 2,500 calories. On 23 November, the bread ration was cut to eight ounces. By 26 December, the ration was cut to two ounces—two and a half slices. 150 calories. With horse meat and fat (if available), it accounted for roughly 500 calories. A 500-calorie deficit usually yields one pound of weight loss per week. The men at Stalingrad were losing twenty pounds per week. The men carried out of the planes were horrifyingly emaciated. Skeletally thin.

Reinhardt and Günter ate their rations. It was only humane they felt guilty doing so. While Reinhardt had dined on delicious apple strudel, hundreds of thousands of Germans had been starving. Even eating rations of fried vegetables and animal meat, there were more calories in a single meal than those in the Cauldron would consume all day. There was only so much weight a human being could lose. Math would give Reinhardt the answer, but he didn't have the heart to calculate it.

The Hoffmans

When Kira stepped off the plane back in Russia, the chill was so arctic it seemed unreal such a drastic change in temperature could occur on the same planet. She was to meet with Colonel Volkov but was first granted privacy to bathe and change into her military uniform. Strangely, the dresses she'd tried on weeks earlier had felt like costumes, but now, it was her military uniform that felt as if it belonged to someone else. She braided her hair and then laced her Kirza artificial leather boots. The uniform was clean, cleaner than it had been in months. As she critiqued her appearance in the mirror, the Kira from Paris was gone.

A gangly, long-armed private escorted Kira to an office. Colonel Volkov sat behind a desk. Kira saluted him.

"The bullet heard around the world," Colonel Volkov said.

He tossed a stack of international newspapers onto the desk in front of her. All with varying headlines and different photographs, but all displaying the name Jürgen Wolff. Headlines proclaimed: "Shot Dead," "Assassinated," "Murdered," or, in Germany's case, "Reich Hero Slain by Coward on Christmas."

Kira detailed the events over the English Channel and the deaths of Semyon and Yuri. They shared a moment of silence for them before she detailed her time in Paris and her assassination of Jürgen Wolff. Reinhardt Friedel was left out entirely.

"You have fulfilled your mission. The Soviet Union owes you its gratitude," Colonel Volkov said.

"I serve the Soviet Union," she said demurely.

"And you will continue to do so, but as senior sergeant."

He attached three dark ruby triangles to the tabs of her tunic. In addition to the rubies, she was entitled to a leather belt with a shoulder strap, a single pin brass buckle, and a holster with ramrod. Was this the reward for killing a man? Some rubies, brass, and leather?

"This honor is above me," Kira said.

Colonel Volkov shook his head. "This honor has been earned."

He sipped his cup of water laced with a bit of vodka and then detailed the Battle of Stalingrad. The Germans were surrounded yet refused to surrender.

"Their only hope is the supplies being flown in. You can call the Germans many things, but you cannot refute the bravery of their men."

Brave men like Reinhardt Friedel? Her thoughts flew to him. Was he still in Paris? Did he suspect her? Had she broken his heart? Or had he returned to the Eastern Front? To Stalingrad?

"Something wrong, Comrade?" Colonel Volkov asked.

Kira forced Reinhardt from her thoughts and shook her head. "No, Comrade Colonel. I am ready to continue fighting."

Colonel Volkov nodded. "Good. You shall return to Stalingrad."

Kira thanked him and headed for the door.

"One last thing I wish to mention," Colonel Volkov said.

Kira stopped and turned back to him.

"The Germans have given you a nickname." He paused. "The Winter Tiger. Though it should be The Winter Tigress." He smirked.

Kira only processed the name with a nod and left.

The room she stayed in was small, little more than a bed that nearly touched all four walls. She lay in it, trying to ignore the claustrophobic feeling the room inflicted. Christmas in Paris had been a lifetime ago. A dream. She pleaded to return to that dream world.

The following morning, the train powered south to Stalingrad. Snow covered the scorched, cratered earth. An illusion that the war didn't exist. Kira cleaned her three-line rifle. Each step soothed her. It was the only thing that made sense. And it made her think of her father. He had found solace in cleaning the rifle, too. She missed the double bass. How quickly would she forget the music she'd learned?

The Winter Tiger & The War Eagle

Operation Winter Storm had been launched by German Field Marshal Erich von Manstein on 12 December 1942. Its goal was to breach the encircled Third Army from the southwest. Starving and freezing, the Germans were reduced to their animalistic instincts. They fought tenaciously. A worthy foe. For the Germans only had two options: sit and wait to die from starvation or cold, or fight with reckless abandon and not go quietly into the night.

Kira's sniper uniform was white, camouflaging with the snow covering the streets and rooftops. Her three-line was covered in white cloth. Keeping the scope from fogging up proved difficult. Kira nested in a crater. Overturned vehicles surrounded it, and a disabled transport truck was parked over the crater. Excellent protection. Her ushanka kept her head and ears protected, but the cruelly cold winds cut through the fur like it was a paper bag. Her gloves were fingerless. She needed skin on the trigger. Nothing could diminish that contact. It was minus forty degrees Fahrenheit. So cold her skin stung like it was being bitten by snakes. Kira could do nothing to warm herself. You didn't have to go to sniper school to know that fire and smoke were not great camouflages. She thought briefly about the hot, steamy supply closet inside the Théâtre du Châtelet. But daydreaming wasn't an option for a sniper. She had to be present.

Kira chewed on tea leaves and sugar to satiate her hunger. She didn't even need to manually chew. Her chattering teeth did it for her.

A fellow soldier crawled into the hole from behind. The bits of skin not covered by his bushy beard were painfully red.

"I bring gifts." He tossed a few rocks beside her. "Fresh out of the oven. Made with love."

Kira thanked him and picked up the rock. It was hot to the touch, something that seemed impossible considering how brutally cold it was. They'd heated the rocks in a fire. She massaged the hot rock into her icy fingers and face. The dexterity in her fingers returned; the arthritis the cold induced went away, too. Kira sipped from her canteen, then settled back into position. Glancing through the scope, scanning. With the sun nothing but a memory, the temperature dropped in the night. The rocks had gone cold. She steadied her breathing as she scanned through her scope.

Two Germans lumbered forward. Neither held a weapon. Through the four-fold magnification of the scope, they appeared less than ten meters away. The shorter of the two had his arms at his sides, his chest heaving in and out. Tears strolled down his frostbitten face. The second man had his arms wrapped around the other, encouraging him to continue ahead. There were no tears in his eyes, only a sorrowful pain. There was no mistaking, these two men were brothers. The older brother hugged the younger one, stroking his hair. He tossed his helmet. His face was dangerously red. Black frostbite spread on his nose, cheeks, and ears. Their breaths rose into the air like smoke. The older brother wiped his brother's tears away. Kira read his lips.

Ich liebe dich, mein Bruder.

"I love you, my brother." Repeating it over and over as he rubbed his brother's blond head.

Then he stepped forward and spread his arms. A chill spread across Kira's body. One that temperature cannot cause. He knew there were snipers nesting about. He wanted to die.

283. The total number of men Kira had killed. 283 men with different names, different ages, and varying appearances. But no matter how different they were, they shared one thing: none of them wanted to die. They screamed for help, dove for cover. One single thought repeating in their minds: God, I don't want to die. Yet, on this arctic-cold winter night, these two Germans didn't fear death. They embraced it like warriors of old. Vikings striving for Valhalla, Samurai dying with honor, gladiators waiting for the Roman emperor to give a thumbs down. The human body is capable of extraordinary deeds, the human mind even more so. It is one of the greatest tragedies when a person has lost all will to live.

Kira watched. Transfixed. Frozen. Who were these brothers? What were their names? What was their story? Were they *Schadenfreudes*? Or were they just men who had been forced to fight? Or men like Reinhardt who fought for Germany, not the Reich? There were cruel snipers on both sides. Those who aimed to kill painfully and slowly. Kira reserved that torturous death for the leather-laden *SS*. But these German brothers deserved swift, merciful deaths, like the deer she used to hunt with Gerasim. The wind was violent, whipping snow around the ground. Kira calculated the distance, the target angle, and the wind speed and direction. She would kill the scared younger brother first. Spare him from having to watch his older brother die. Then, as quickly as she could, she'd kill the older brother. So fast that he wouldn't be able to react to the pain of his brother's death. She practiced moving her rifle from the younger brother to the older brother.

Nousha and Lina. Kira couldn't help but see them. They hadn't had merciful deaths. Nousha would have consoled Lina like this brother consoled his. Tears blurred her eyes. She wiped them. Her vision needed to be clear. She wouldn't risk it. The Germans had nicknamed her The Winter Tiger. Tigers hunted. They didn't feast on carcasses like hyenas did. They hunted, and so did Kira. But if they were wronged, they killed slowly and painfully. She took pride in her ability to kill enemy soldiers and snipers who thought they were well hidden. And if she were honest, maybe even a little joy. But there was no joy to be had here. Only mercy.

Kira aimed at the younger brother's head. A shot echoed in the frosty night, sounding as if the bullet shivered on its lethal trajectory. The younger brother's head snapped back. His knees buckled. Before the older brother could process what had happened, a bullet ripped through his own head. The immaculate white snow spritzed in sinful red blood. Mercy granted. Pain relieved.

But only for them.

At daybreak, the Soviets pushed forward to loot the dead. Weapons and ammo were taken first, then trinkets. There was no food to be found on the German dead. Photographs were sometimes kept if they were of young women. But those of children or parents were burned along with letters—received or yet to be sent.

Kira stood over the two brothers. A cocoon of snow covered their bodies. They looked as if they were coated in ice. She used her sapper's spade to dig them free from the frozen snow. Their bodies were as cold and hard as steel. She searched their pockets. In the breast pocket of the older brother was a photograph of himself, his brother, and their parents. Their uniforms were new and freshly pressed, contouring nicely around the muscles in their shoulders and chest. Stalingrad's starvation had withered their physiques to skeletal. Their father was taller than both, bald, and unostentatiously proud of his sons. Their mother was portly, barely five feet tall, and even in the black-and-white photo, her love for her sons was unmistakable. Kira pocketed the photo and continued searching. In his pants pocket was a letter. The unsealed envelope was addressed to Conrad and Winifred Hoffman. A secondary note had been taped atop it. The same message written twice. One in German. One in Russian.

If you find my body, please send this letter.

Kira unfolded the letter. The letter had no doubt started white and pristine, but as he added further transcripts, dirt and blood speckled the pages. His penmanship on the last page was shaky, nearly unreadable. Not surprising considering how hard it must be to write when you can't stop shaking and you cannot feel your own hand, let alone the pencil in it.

"My dearest parents,

Hope is lost. Augustus and I, along with our brave fellow soldiers in the 3rd Army, have fought hard. A valiancy that I pray sends no shame back home to Germany. We are starving and have no food. We are freezing and have nothing to warm ourselves. We are fearful and have no hope. We are damned with no absolution. Father, I hope we have made you proud and you view our service to Germany with distinction and pride. Mother, no sons ever had a better mother. We love you both. It was an honor being your sons. It will all be over soon. I pray this letter finds you and provides you with peace.

Your loving sons forever,

Mikel & Augustus"

The signatures at the end were smeared. Kira had no doubt Mikel had been crying when he signed it. Kira pocketed the letter and photograph, and continued through the frozen ground littered with dead. The weight of the letter far heavier than any paper she'd carried before.

The Cauldron

The circle continued to close, a tightening noose. Reinhardt viewed it as a hanging. It would have been merciful if their necks had snapped. Instead, they cruelly dangled, legs kicking, veins bulging. Powerless to stop it.

Reinhardt and Günter volunteered to resupply the Cauldron, and when they weren't in borrowed Ju-52s, they were in their Messerschmitts fighting over the rubble city. It'd been weeks since Reinhardt had faced aerial combat. He was rusty, but it would be unfair to say the Soviet pilots hadn't improved. At the end of each night, sheer exhaustion overwhelmed him. But Reinhardt knew whatever exhaustion he felt paled in comparison to those in the Cauldron. Reinhardt had food and water. He had on a warm jacket and gloves. That truth was caffeine to his body. If he were in the Cauldron, he hoped someone would work tirelessly to get him out. But no matter how dire the situation rapidly grew, Hitler would not approve a surrender. Reinhardt asked for volunteers to fly out as many wounded soldiers as he could. There remained a single airstrip, Gumrak, under German control. The risk was never higher, never more dangerous.

Oberst Hans Speckenridge was a stern man with piercing brown eyes, so powerful he could stare men into submission. He stood tall with his hands folded behind his back.

"Help me understand this clearly," he said to Reinhardt after hearing his suggestion. "You wish to lead a squadron of planes into Stalingrad, when, by all reports, collapse of the Gumrak Airfield is imminent. Knowing the peril you'll put yourself in. And recognizing that the *Führer* has not approved any evacuation of those fighting. You are asking to break the command given by the most powerful man in Germany. You are asking *me* to break the command given by the most powerful man in Germany."

"Yes, sir," Reinhardt said, standing behind his convictions.

"You may face the *Reichskriegsgericht*."

Court martial. Reinhardt knew the risk and nodded. "I wish to save as many of Germany's sons as we are able."

Oberst Speckenridge studied Reinhardt as he wafted his decision. "I cannot sanction your request, Major Friedel. I do not wish to be shot for high treason. Nor can I risk our aircraft for what may be a fruitless mission."

Reinhardt scrunched his toes and ground the inside of his cheek to stop his frustration from showing.

"However," *Oberst* Speckenridge continued. "I shall not take inventory of our aircraft for twelve hours. Should any aircraft disappear during this time, it would go unnoticed. It would be a pity if someone were to take them."

Reinhardt smirked. "A great travesty, *Oberst* Speckenridge."

Reinhardt saluted, then left the field tent. Günter rushed toward him, demanding answers. Reinhardt told him what *Oberst* Speckenridge had said before he addressed the fifty brave pilots who had volunteered. The Junker Ju-52 required two pilots, meaning Reinhardt had enough men for twenty-five planes. Each of the planes could carry roughly seventeen men, but that number could change drastically. If the wounded could stand, Reinhardt would have his pilots push that number to reach the aircraft's max weight of 9,500 kg. The wounded men they would transport also weren't at healthy weights, further increasing the number of potential rescues. But if the wounded were on stretchers, that number could fall short of seventeen.

"I have spoken with *Oberst* Speckenridge," Reinhardt said. "Our request has not been sanctioned." The pilots looked at each other or the ground, dejected. "But he will not stop us. We have twelve hours. This choice is for each man to make. If we are caught, we risk facing the *Reichskriegsgericht*. I do not blame any man who stays here. If the *Reichskriegsgericht* isn't reason enough to stay, consider that many of us will die in this attempt. The airfield could fall at any moment. You will fly directly into the Cauldron. By trying to save the damned, we may damn ourselves."

Ernst Ziebel, all of twenty and looking younger than that, raised his hand. Reinhardt called on him.

"You are willing to risk this?" he asked.

"The men trapped at Stalingrad have braved blood and battle through vicious cold and hellacious hunger. They continue to fight with little ammo and no hope for victory. They fight for Germany. Our Fatherland. For our homes, for our families, our friends. Right now, they feel as if Germany has forsaken them. I want them to know that while they fight for Germany, Germany fights for them."

Silence stung the air. Men looked at each other as if they could somehow tell which of them would perish if they volunteered.

"I will fight for Germany. I would be honored to fly alongside you, Major Friedel," Günter said.

One by one, the pilots declared their pledge to fight for Germany, for those forsaken in the Cauldron.

The Junkers Ju-52 swarmed the sky, an angry colony of wasps charging from their hive. The sky was dark. Each pilot had to rely on their instrumentation. Reinhardt led the descent onto the battered runway. An anxious feeling roiled in his stomach. Like he was exploring a cave riddled with bones, hoping the bear wasn't inside.

The moment the wheels locked onto the runway, Reinhardt rushed out of his plane and spoke with the first person he encountered, telling him to bring every wounded man to the runway and fit as many as they could into the planes. Those wounded who could stand lumbered out of the frozen night like the undead. Their feet dragged; frostbite had killed all feeling. A man Reinhardt's height came toward him. His face was obscured by a few days of unshaven growth. His long coat was tightened at the waist with a belt, so much so it made the bottom portion billow out like a dress. Friedrich Paulus. The man tasked with the impossible.

"I thank you for your courage. You must hurry. We cannot hold this airstrip," Paulus said.

He wore the look of a man who needed not days or even weeks of sleep, but years. A heavier burden than to lead a hundred thousand men to certain death Reinhardt could not think of. He reached into his pocket and handed a pack of crackers to Paulus. A minuscule gesture, but the only one he could offer.

"Thank you. I shall see that they are given to my men," Paulus said.

"We are full, Reinhardt!" Günter shouted.

"I can get you out," Reinhardt said.

Paulus nodded appreciatively, a fondness in his eyes, but there was the unmistakable look of pain. He was a captain and would go down with his ship. "Thank you, Major, but I will stay with my men."

Paulus shook Reinhardt's hand and left the runway—bent but unbroken.

"Uwe?" Reinhardt asked Günter.

Günter shook his head. "I couldn't find him."

They boarded their Ju-52s and flew up and out of the Cauldron. When they landed, Reinhardt ordered the planes refueled. The injured were unloaded and carried and carted off to the medical tents. Those cognizant wept, reaching out to anyone, crying their gratitude for being saved.

"The runway won't hold out much longer," Günter said.

Reinhardt nodded gravely. "Pray we have one more trip."

They drank from their canteens as the planes were refueled. Every minute counted. Reinhardt, Günter, and the other pilots boarded their planes and waited as the ground crew moved out of the way. Once given the clear, they powered their engines, and the planes surged forward back into the collapsing Cauldron.

Gunfire peppered the sky, shaking the planes. The combat pilot in Reinhardt reacted by wanting to switch to evasive maneuvers. But he couldn't. He needed to get down to the runway as fast as possible. The plane whined as it descended. Flak exploded mere feet from the cockpit, whiplashing Reinhardt and Günter against their seats. Reinhardt steadied the plane, the throttle in his hand shaking violently. The wheels bounced on the runway. Firefights flashed on the ground. The Soviets had begun their final push to overtake the airstrip. Those inside took one final breath.

A terrific flash of flame shot through the black sky like a comet. One of Reinhardt's brave volunteers crashed into a building. There was no time for the injured on stretchers. Their die had been cast. Men who had been in varying states of freezing tried to force their legs to work. They tripped and stumbled, then crawled toward the planes. Sheer panic bulging from their eyes. This was it. Their final chance at survival. The Cauldron was closing.

"Hurry!" Reinhardt shouted.

Gunfire dotted airplanes, pierced flesh. A horrible realization dawned. There wasn't enough time for all the aircraft to take off. Günter had calculated and came to the same answer. Reinhardt shouted into his radio for all planes to leave at once. The first plane that took off barely ascended over the skeletal skyscrapers before it exploded. Others never even left the runway. The injured on the runway had exhausted all strength trying to get to the planes. They had none left to escape. Some sobbed, pleading for help. Reaching out with gangly limps and frozen fingers. Others accepted their fates and rolled onto their backs to die gazing up at the stars, relieved it would all be over soon.

Reinhardt's plane was destroyed, sinking into a massive crater. He helped Günter to his feet. Reinhardt sprinted away from the runway, glimpsing a He 111 taking off. It would be the last plane to do so. Gumrak had fallen. The Cauldron was closed.

Günter and Reinhardt, relatively warm and fed, sprinted faster than any of the others. But maybe it wasn't only the cold and starvation that slowed the others. Maybe it was also because they knew where Reinhardt and Günter ran to. To their own damnation and straight into the heart of the Cauldron.

The Enemy Sniper

The letter in her breast pocket weighed heavily, like some ancient artifact that housed the Hoffman brothers' souls. And it was impossible to think of them and not transition those thoughts to her sisters. And ultimately, her mother and father. Would it have been easier had they left a letter for her? Saying all the things unsaid, reaffirming those that had been said?

Kira left the battleground and reported to a command center. What type of building it had been before the battle was impossible to tell. The sign, if there had been one, was gone, and anything inside that might reveal what the building had been used for was gone, too. A lieutenant by the name of Artyom Borodin greeted her. His ushanka and eyebrows looked like they were made from the same fur.

"Comrade Senior Sergeant Kovalyova, I am told you are my best rifle."

Claiming such a boast wasn't in Kira's nature. Reinhardt had declared he was the best pilot. But when he said it, it didn't come across as arrogant, only factual. Kira doubted she could deliver it in such a way even if she wanted to.

"How many enemy kills, Comrade?" he asked.

"285." Mikel and Augustus Hoffman were numbers 284 and 285. The letter in her pocket beat like a heart.

"How many of those were snipers?"

"Forty-three."

285 had received little attention from Borodin. But at forty-three, his eyebrows perked. The Germans had high-quality snipers. The number of deer a tiger killed was irrelevant to him. It was the number of other tigers it killed that mattered. He nodded to show his respect. He pointed to a map of the city.

The Winter Tiger & The War Eagle

"The Germans have put up a strong resistance here. Among them is a sniper. His exact position remains unknown. He has killed seventeen of our men in six days. I want you to eliminate him."

"I serve the Soviet Union," Kira said.

Even though she normally didn't need one, Kira asked for a spotter. When the Germans marched through bottlenecks like pigs for slaughter, there hadn't been a need for a second set of eyes (other than to confirm kills). But against a skilled sniper, having another person was imperative. She had been impressed with a private by the name of Morozov. Lieutenant Borodin summoned him and explained the situation. Morozov was a burly man who was surprisingly nimble. His ash-brown hair was long enough that it covered his ears and looked like it had been cut with a knife. Upon closer inspection, it looked that way because it had been. Morozov had improvised the best he could.

"Kovalyova? You are The Winter Tiger?"

"You may call me Comrade Kovalyova," Kira said.

Morozov nodded, though it was obvious he wished to call her by her nickname. He stated he had been standing next to a man killed by the sniper they were tasked with eliminating. The assumed location was along a small line of ditch that had filled with water from busted piping. Steel and concrete rubble covered the south end of the flooded and frozen ditch. On the Soviet north side was an identical set-up. Kira and Morozov scouted from a distance using binoculars.

"Excellent cover," Kira told Morozov.

The steel and concrete cocoon would protect the sniper from gunfire and artillery. He would have dug a hole so that if the canopy collapsed, it wouldn't crush him. And it had the advantage that advancing Soviets would have to move up toward him, meaning he could shoot down.

"We go at dark," Kira said.

Once darkness fell, they moved. Traversing through the debris required stealth and silence. Each step must be meticulous out of fear the haphazard structure would collapse atop them or they would sink beneath its metallic depths. They trudged toward the front, then, with the help of six men, dug a trench.

"Get a mannequin, a hand mirror, and some fishing line," Kira ordered Morozov.

"What the fuck?" he asked, forgetting Kira's rank.

She explained why, and Morozov smiled. "You are sneaky, Kovalyova. The day has finally come when Russia has run out of men. We now resort to dolls."

Morozov left to fulfill his command. Kira crawled through the trench to the front. She propped her rifle on a long piece of broken pipe, then scanned through her scope. No movement. Nothing caught her eye. This sniper was fully immersed in his environment. Morozov returned. When his hands weren't holding a pair of binoculars, they were tucked into his armpits. The Soviet winter uniform comprised of warm underwear, a tunic, pleated padded sleeves, vests and pants, and an overcoat covered in a white smock, yet the cruel chill cut through every layer. Their nostrils froze. Kira made fists with her hands to try to keep feeling in them. The cold was painful. At times, so much so that it caused them to grunt in discomfort.

There had been no sign of the enemy sniper across the ditch, some 115 meters away. Day broke with no sign.

"Do you think he has left?" Morozov asked.

Kira had considered it. She herself rarely used a sniper hideout more than twice. Each shot allowed the enemy to home in on your location. It was beyond risky to stay for multiple days in one spot in which you had engaged the enemy. But then again, where was this German sniper to go? Perhaps this warrior had chosen the ground on which he would die. No matter the hideout type—open, closed, base, reserve, or decoy—there were a hundred places he could be hiding. The building behind the rubble had over forty windows. Maybe he changed floors? Then there was the building beside it. More windows. More possible hideouts. Yet, to Kira, the rubble directly across from them was the best hideout to be had. But would the enemy sniper know she would think that? Had he chosen an inferior position in an attempt to outthink her?

The day drifted to dusk. Still no sign of their sniper. Kira had napped briefly while Morozov kept lookout. But the forty-minute nap did little to assuage her tiredness. Morozov fought his own battle with tiredness, dozing off for seconds at a time. Kira let him catnap. When he woke, he reached into his pocket and pulled out a chocolate bar. He turned it over in his hands, examining it like it was a priceless relic.

"Took this from a dead German back in June," he said.

"Hard as rock, I'm sure," Kira said.

Morozov tapped it against a concrete brick. Frozen solid.

"Yes, but I will put it between my thighs. Warm it with my loins. Then we can eat it."

"Then I won't want to eat it."

Morozov smiled, aware enough to stop himself from laughing. He massaged the chocolate, pressed on it, and after twenty minutes, he peeled it open. He snapped it in half; it sounded like bone breaking. Kira took the offered piece and chomped down on it. It was too hard to chew. The threat of breaking a tooth or the German sniper hearing the gunshot-level crack seemed too real a risk, so she let her hot breath and saliva dissolve the chocolate. The cocoa and sugar exploded her taste buds. They'd been dormant since the apple strudel at the Givre Strudel weeks ago.

"Are you married, Comrade Kovalyova?" Morozov asked.

Kira told him to call her by her first name, then answered his question. "Are you?"

"I think so."

Kira shot a confused look his way.

"My wife was pregnant with our fifth child. We had a baby, then another and another, you get the idea. She raises them all alone. I am sure she has some built-up animosity toward me."

Kira smirked. "Yes, I imagine she does."

He told her about his sons, Boris, Ilya, Leonid, Maksim, and Mikhail. How they all looked different from one another. Boris looked like Morozov; Ilya looked like Morozov's wife, Alyona; Leonid looked like Morozov's father; Maksim like his maternal grandfather; and Mikhail, Morozov had never met. He had moments of sadness about that fact but kept himself in good spirits.

"You left your wife with five boys? She's left you for sure," Kira joked.

Morozov smiled, then made himself more comfortable to enjoy his time to nap. "Don't fret, Kira. Perhaps you and the mannequin can start a family. Produce little dolls."

Kira kicked his leg. Morozov smirked, keeping his eyes closed. For a moment, the thought of Reinhardt crept in. If they had had children, what would they have looked like? Blue eyes? Green? Or dominant brown? They both had dark hair, but would their child have been a brown-eyed, blonde-haired anomaly? She squeezed her eyes shut, a physical way of ending the thought. Morozov was out, soft snores escaping his open mouth. Kira's eyes grew heavy, the chocolate acting like a sedative. But then something ahead caught her eye. A subtle movement.

The German sniper. He'd adjusted his helmet ever so slightly. But it was enough. Kira looked through her scope. The German had disappeared back into his nest, concealed by the tangle of steel and rubble of concrete. She tapped Morozov with her foot. He opened his eyes, silent. She held a finger to her mouth, then pointed across from them. Morozov grabbed his binoculars. Kira only knew where to look because she had seen the subtle movement. The German wielded a Karabiner 98k. Only the top of his helmet was visible.

"Time to wake up our friend," Kira said.

Morozov grabbed the piece of broken pipe to which he had tied the fishing line. Kira readied herself behind her Mosin–Nagant. She tapped her finger against the rifle to signal she was ready. Morozov yanked the pipe. The fishing line went taut. Thirty yards to the left of them, the mannequin sprung up, a mirror fastened to its face to mimic the blinding reflection of a scope. The German sniper caught the movement. He'd easily see it was a decoy, but he would have to move in order to see that. He did, opening the side of his head and neck for a shot.

Kira squeezed the trigger. The bullet traveled cleanly through the sniper's neck. A mist of blood followed as the sniper fell out of sight.

"You got him ..."

Morozov had heard the stories about The Winter Tiger. But to see her shooting in person left him speechless. He lowered the binoculars and gawked at Kira. They waited close to an hour to see if he was truly alone.

"Cover me," Kira said.

Morozov put a hand on hers. "I feel much better about The Winter Tiger covering *me* than me covering *you*."

He grabbed his PPSh-41 submachine gun and climbed out of the rubble. Kira kept her rifle trained on the sniper hideout, looking for any signs of movement. She scanned the surrounding area to see if there was a second sniper waiting to capitalize. Morozov crept forward, scanning ahead to see if the gunshot had sprung any Germans into action. When he got to the flooded ditch, he stopped. The water was only shin deep and most likely frozen solid. But the temperature was minus forty degrees. The last thing he wanted was to break through and get his feet soaked. If he did, frostbite would be inevitable. Kira scanned the hideout once more, then followed

Morozov's footsteps, her eyes trained on the buildings for a possible second sniper. Further down the ditch, a German amtrak was on its side. Kira nodded toward it. Morozov set off for it first. Confident that if there had been a second sniper, he would have shot at them already, Kira shouldered her rifle and carried her TT-30 pistol and followed Morozov. She climbed onto the amtrak, and Morozov helped her down. He insisted he advance first. Once he gave the okay, Kira rushed ahead into the sniper hideout. The Karabiner 98k was on its side. A clip of five rounds stood vertically nearby. Empty cans of sardines and herring littered the ground. A canteen stuffed with snow. And on the ground, in a pool of blood, lay the skilled sniper. Morozov lifted the sniper's head by grabbing his hair and stared into the sniper's pale-green eyes.

"Dead," he said, releasing the sniper. The body hit the frozen ground with a thud.

The sniper's face was gaunt and gray. Morozov stripped the sniper's jacket from his body. The insignia on his uniform told Kira his rank was *Hauptsturmführer*. Inside his breast pocket was an index-sized moleskin journal. Kira fanned through the pages. It was a sniper's log. He had meticulously written Soviet movements and at what times, wind direction, target angles, sunrise and sunset times, had even drawn maps of his surroundings, designating possible hideouts with an X. Near the end, he chronicled his kill count. Each logged with a date and time. Orlov would have admired the enemy's prowess. Johan Betzer had been a prolific killer of men. He'd joined the war in Poland, then fought in Belgium and France. His kills on the Western Front were few. Unsurprising, considering how effective the German *blitzkrieg* had been. It wasn't until the stalemate at Stalingrad where he had thrived. 289 kills. Fifty-three enemy sniper kills. Betzer was an expert sniper.

"Shit, no chocolate," Morozov said.

He used his Finnish knife to cut a leather pouch free from Betzer's belt. Inside were medals taken from his Polish, Belgian, French, and Soviet victims. But it was the Knight's Cross Kira focused on. It was like the one Reinhardt had worn. *Hauptsturmführer* Johan Betzer had been awarded it for continuous bravery before the enemy. He had been a true warrior, and Kira had given him a warrior's death.

Morozov reached for the Knight's Cross.

"No," Kira said.

"It is valuable," Morozov said.

"Keep the medals he stole. Let him keep the one he has earned."

Morozov didn't like her decision, but he respected her order. She pinned the medal on Betzer's chest, knowing that's where Reinhardt had worn his. Kira had no idea if Johan Betzer had been a *Schadenfreude*. But he was a skilled and worthy opponent. Kira would prefer to see Johan Betzer's body burned, but she had nothing to burn him with. Nor could she bury him. The ground was frozen; it'd be like trying to shovel stone. He would stay in this tangled mess of steel and concrete. What would become of his body after the battle ended? What would become of his Knight's Cross? And where was the blue-eyed German who had been awarded the Oak Leaves?

Escaping Execution

On 22 January 1943, Gumrak Airfield fell. Those trapped in Stalingrad would stay trapped. Reinhardt and his brave volunteer pilots, those who had survived the Soviet onslaught, were now among the damned. Reinhardt clasped his bomber jacket, covering as much of his exposed neck as possible. The air was frozen, and the cold attacked indiscriminately. As he and Günter lumbered through the camp, it was horrifying to see how truly dire the situation was. The dead littering the streets weren't just broken and bloody, they were frozen. Blasted-off limbs hard as rock. Men with no gloves or hats, piecing together whatever they could to stay warm. Frost clung from their eyebrows. Wounds that in normal temperatures would have continued to bleed were cauterized, not from heat, but from cold. The entire line was a chorus of coughs. Reinhardt had never seen men so frail.

But a familiar person limped to them. Uwe. Roughly fifteen pounds lighter than when they last saw him. After hugging, Reinhardt explained the events that had stranded him and Günter.

"What about fires?" Günter asked.

Uwe shook his head. It was one of those questions that needed to be asked but was almost offensive to ask. "There's nothing to burn."

Günter spoke, but Uwe cut him off.

"You don't understand!" Uwe shouted, the frustration overwhelming. "These men have done everything they can to stay alive."

"I know, but we have to think—"

"They've eaten the dead …"

The guttural horror that took hold in Reinhardt following those words was one he'd never experienced before. To fathom that choice was something no one could unless thrusted into the bowels of hell. Günter was silent the rest of the night;

Reinhardt, too. They crawled into a corner, nestled into the rubble to escape the vicious wind that slashed at exposed flesh like knives. Reinhardt, Günter, and Uwe lay closer to each other than any of them were comfortable with, but survival dictated they did so. Reinhardt's hands and feet were numb, and that numbness spread up his arms and legs. Almost a month ago, he had made love to Kira in the warmth of a janitorial closet. Heat blasting from the radiator and off their skin. That was a world away and a lifetime ago. If she hadn't taken off, what would he have done? Would he have returned? Was there a life for them? As he pondered never returning to the fight, he couldn't imagine abandoning Günter and the others like that. Kira had removed that choice for him. Though her fleeing had torn him apart and left so many questions in her wake, maybe that was a gift. He didn't have to make that choice. She'd made it for him. But then the cold harsh reality of his predicament returned to him.

When the wintry air woke them from their sleep, they moved around—body squats, arm circles, and pushups—just enough to get their blood moving. They couldn't spend calories, yet they had to in order not to freeze to death—the quintessential double-edge sword. Günter had a pack of cigarettes and a can of red herring he shared with Reinhardt and Uwe. They ate it in secret, knowing hunger was enough to drive any man to murder. It may have been the last speck of food inside the Cauldron. Reinhardt thought of the crackers he'd given Paulus.

The days were grueling, the nights even more so. A constant state of hunger and cold that only worsened. On 30 January, Hitler appointed Paulus *Generalfeldmarschall*. Its sole purpose was to remind Paulus that no German commander of that rank had ever surrendered. Paulus was to commit suicide rather than disgrace Germany's great military history. In response, Paulus told his generals, "I have no intention of shooting myself for this Bohemian corporal."

Reinhardt gazed upon the hundreds of people near him. It was difficult to decipher those who were alive, and those who were dead. Sometimes, it was only a weak cough that gave it away. The camp was divided into three groups: the dead, the dying, and the damned. Reinhardt, Günter, and Uwe counted themselves among the damned. Not ideal, but it was better than the dead and dying. It became clear what they needed to do to not fall into one of the other camps. But abandoning the fight went against everything the Iron Cross stood for. Forget what Hitler and the Nazis considered the Iron Cross to symbolize. It went against what Reinhardt believed it to represent. But it was Günter who first spoke the words on Reinhardt's mind.

"We have to get out of here," he said.

"I think everyone is aware of that," Uwe said.

"No, now, while we still have strength. Each day we grow weaker."

"Flee?" Uwe asked.

"We're not in the Sixth Army. If you want to get technical, our orders are to engage the enemy in the sky. By staying here, we're breaking those orders," Günter said.

Reinhardt had made it known he sided with Günter with his eyes. Uwe argued against them, not just the principle of fleeing, but asking the question of where they would go. The burden of choice vanished when there was an unmissable buzz in the air. Soldiers who had been lethargic now moved with a speed Reinhardt had not seen.

"What is going on?" Günter asked no one in particular.

"Paulus is surrendering. The battle is over!" someone answered.

Reinhardt looked to Günter and Uwe, an adamant resolve forming in his nod. "We have to go now."

"It's dangerous," Uwe said.

"No shit," Günter chimed.

"Being a Soviet prisoner is not in my best interests. I'd rather die than work to death," Reinhardt said.

"It's the whole goddamn Red Army out there!" Uwe said.

Reinhardt nodded, for Uwe's point was completely valid. "I know. This is a choice we each must make."

"I'm getting out of here," Günter said.

Uwe looked at the ground, defeat dominating his demeanor. "I'm done fighting. My time in the war is over."

There wasn't time for Reinhardt to convince him otherwise. Time to convince him that Reinhardt didn't think the war would ever end for those taken prisoner by the Soviets. He wished Uwe well and embraced him in a hug. Günter did the same. Uwe handed Reinhardt his sidearm and his extra clip of ammo. Reinhardt and Günter followed those risking escape. But both knew too many people would draw attention. They split away from them, traveling through alleyways.

Footsteps clattered against the street. Friend or foe unknown—German boots sound the same as Soviet boots. Reinhardt raised his pistol, but then the whispered words of his native language bent around the corner. Reinhardt whispered back. Three men stepped into the alleyway, relieved to see other Germans. Ten-second introductions were made. Gruber was roughly thirty and much shorter than Reinhardt, with a round, stubble-covered face. Baumbauer was the youngest with a youthful face, the kind that made you want to protect him. Hochzeit was in his mid-twenties, had wavy, light brown hair, and a permanent 'you-got-to-be-shitting-me' look on his face.

"So, what's the plan?" Gruber asked.

"We are pilots," Günter said with a nod at Reinhardt. "So, find a plane and leave this fucking forsaken city behind."

Gruber smiled. "Good fucking plan."

Hochzeit grimaced. "Yes, good plan, except for the fact every airfield is under Soviet control."

"But there were some pilots landing outside the city, trying to smuggle supplies inside. Their planes may still be there," Baumbauer said.

"No matter what, we must get out of the Cauldron *now*. 90,000 men are surrendering, which means all Soviet eyes will be on them," Reinhardt said.

"Right, we must take advantage of the distraction," Günter said.

Keep moving—the sole goal now. Gruber had an MG-42, a cumbersome weapon to hold but powerful. He estimated he had seventy rounds left. He led while Baumbauer took up the rear with his MP-41. They dashed across streets one by one, scouted intersections, and listened for any sounds. The wind howled—a blessing and a curse. It masked their movements, but it also silenced the Soviets'. It was painful to take a deep breath, feeling as if their lungs would freeze. Exposure was an unfightable enemy. And if they didn't get to cover soon, it would defeat them.

Ahead in the middle of the street was an abandoned Soviet jeep.

"That's our move," Reinhardt said.

"Cover me. I'm the fastest," Günter said.

Gruber and Baumbauer rushed out with him to provide cover. Günter opened the jeep door and leaned in. The key had been left in the ignition, not surprising considering removing a key was risky. Keys get lost. And the driver could get killed or separated and strand his passengers. Günter turned the ignition, but the engine only made a feeble sound in response. He cursed, then ran back to Reinhardt.

"I think the gas line is frozen," he said.

"It may be out. There could be more gas around," Reinhardt said.

The five separated but stayed within sight of each other as they searched abandoned and destroyed vehicles for gas canisters.

"Found something," Baumbauer said when he got to Reinhardt. He jiggled a German-designed jerrycan in his hands. There was little gas inside, but some was better than none. The five of them piled into the jeep after Baumbauer poured the gasoline into the tank. Reinhardt was behind the wheel, turning the ignition. The beaten jeep groaned like a dragon woken from its slumber. The other four cheered it on like it was a horse in a tight race. The jeep started, a black cloud of exhaust shooting out like cannon fire. The windshield was frozen. They'd run out of gas before it defrosted. Reinhardt cranked the window down and drove with his head out of it. The sleet cut his face like shards of glass. The wind was so powerful, he had to dip his head back inside to breathe. Leaving the city was like trying to escape a booby-trapped maze. They crossed a street only to find it was blocked off by a broken tank or a fifteen-meter-wide crater. The potholes were deep enough to break the suspension. But after turning and turning back because of obstacles and finally moving ahead, the mighty Volga River lay before them—Mother Russia's natural fence to keep them trapped inside.

"We're heading east ..." Hochzeit said.

Further into Russia. That was a future issue to overcome. Right now, they had to escape Stalingrad. Reinhardt drove along the river's edge, looking for a way to cross it. Soviet troops marched nearby; unbeknownst to them, the Soviet jeep that sped by them contained five Germans. Up ahead, salvation presented itself in the form of insanity. A small airfield that housed only ten planes. Günter saw it, too, then looked into Reinhardt's eyes.

"Bold strategy. Like attacking their queen with your king," he said.

"You are shitting me," Hochzeit said, leaning forward from the back seat.

They rolled their windows up; the windows and windshield were frosted over, giving the illusion of stained glass. Reinhardt stopped the jeep.

"We'll have to be quick," he said.

"Can you fly those?" Baumbauer asked.

"Of course," Reinhardt said, though truthfully, he had no idea what "those" were exactly. Hopefully, something with room for five. But he didn't think so.

"If these are fighter planes or bombers, you'll have to lie on the wings," Reinhardt said.

Hochzeit's face matched his comment of, "You are shitting me."

"They'll be no time to decide once we're there. Choose now," Reinhardt said.

"Stay here and die or leave and die from falling from a plane? Great fucking choices," Gruber said.

"He's done this before. Received the Oak Leaves," Günter said.

"Really?" Baumbauer asked.

"Really. I was on the wings," Günter said.

Reinhardt unzipped his bomber jacket and showed them the medal adorned around his neck, only to give them confidence and speed the conversation along.

Gruber exhaled deeply. "Let's go."

Reinhardt rolled his window down, stuck his head out, then floored the gas pedal. The jeep hummed, fishtailing on the snow. He drove through the barricade. A Soviet guard waved his hands to get them to stop. Reinhardt sped toward the planes on the runway. Both Reinhardt and Günter recognized the planes as Bell P-39s. They had fought this aircraft, knew its capabilities, and knew it did not hold room for five.

Reinhardt slammed the brakes. The jeep skidded to a stop. The five dashed out. Soviet troops sprinted toward them. Gruber unloaded the last rounds of his MG-42. Reinhardt climbed into the cockpit. The instrumentation was in Russian, but it didn't matter. Flying was its own universal language and Reinhardt was fluent. He powered the engine. The needles on the instrumentation panel sprung to life. Reinhardt had expected the altimeter needle not to move. But the fuel level needle not rising was a disappointing sight.

"Have to go, now!" he shouted.

Gruber dropped his empty MG-42. Günter climbed onto the wing. The other three hesitated, most likely to say a quick prayer, then clambered on. Reinhardt sped down the short runway. He took off, keeping the plane as level as he could. Bullets whizzed past. The plane rose, but then the propeller sputtered and died. The fuel had run out. Reinhardt opened the flaps to slow the plane and increase wind resistance.

The mighty Volga disappeared in the white fog. Reinhardt coasted further east. The city of Stalingrad faded behind the white veil of winter. The ground beneath nothing but a white blanket of snow with snow-dusted evergreens.

The plane was out of control, with no way to stop it. The distance to the ground decreased with violent velocity. The color white filled the windshield. The altimeter dropped wildly. Impact was seconds away. Reinhardt closed his eyes, so he could see those emerald-green eyes one more time.

A Lost Friend

Kira and Morozov returned to the command center to meet with Lieutenant Borodin. With him was a man with a thick gray beard. Borodin introduced him as Major General Vyatkin. Kira and Morozov saluted him.

He thrust his bear-paw-sized hand out to Morozov. "Congratulations, Comrade, on killing the enemy sniper."

"The congratulations do not belong to me," Morozov said, then nodded at Kira.

Vyatkin followed Morozov's nod, but he looked as though he had made a wrong turn when his eyes landed on Kira. He had assumed the tall, burly man had killed the enemy, not the woman. But he rectified his errored preconceived notions.

"Apologies, Comrade," he said, offering his hand.

"Comrade Major General, this is the sniper our troops have named the Angel of Death," Borodin said.

Vyatkin's thin eyes widened. "And the Germans have given the moniker of The Winter Tiger."

"Winter Tigress, but when have those shits gotten anything right?" Morozov said.

Vyatkin couldn't take his eyes off Kira. It wasn't lustful, but more like somebody finding out they had been conversing with a celebrity.

"I have been told the Germans have offered you a high rank and chocolate if you turn coat," Vyatkin said.

"Their chocolate is not that good," Kira said.

Vyatkin chuckled. Morozov looked at her with skepticism. They both knew how damn good their chocolate was. Kira handed Betzer's sniper log to Vyatkin, who scanned through it.

"289 kills … fifty-three enemy snipers …" He looked up. "You bested a master marksman, Comrade Kovalyova."

Kira didn't react. Praise should never be sung solo, but by a chorus.

"And how does your kill count compare?" Vyatkin asked.

"He has bested me. 286 kills," Kira answered.

"I trust your resolve and the fact that the fascists will present ample opportunity that your tally will grow."

Yes, it would. By at least one. There was a *Schadenfreude*, a *Hauptsturmführer* who deserved death.

"Well, Comrades, I cannot offer you chocolate, but I can offer you rank," Vyatkin said. "Comrade Morozov, I promote you to sergeant. Comrade Kovalyova, you are now second lieutenant."

Kira and Morozov saluted and declared, "I serve the Soviet Union!"

Lieutenant Borodin and Major General Vyatkin nodded, then continued on.

"There was someone else worthy of a promotion. An unsung hero," Morozov said.

"Who?" Kira asked.

"Someone who stared into a sniper's scope and did not flinch … the mannequin."

The Germans had fought on until finally, on 2 February 1943, Field Marshal Paulus surrendered. The bloodiest battle in the history of mankind was over.

Only it wasn't. Not entirely at least.

Kira and Morozov met with Lieutenant Borodin and Major General Vyatkin once more on the first floor of a former grocery store. Produce crates were stacked on top of one another for improvised tables. Sadly, the produce had been consumed long ago. Kira couldn't even remember the taste of carrots or okra. She wouldn't even dare try to remember the last time she had had fresh fruit.

"There are as many as 10,000 Germans who have not surrendered," Vyatkin said. "Most hide in the city. But there are some who have made it across the Volga into the forest. You will join our troops there and eliminate them. I cannot stress the importance that our armies continue west. There is no time to look for rats, but I do not want to leave our brave civilians at the mercy of rogue Germans."

260

Nor would Kira. No *Schadenfreudes* would be left behind to rape and murder innocent people. Thinking of Reinhardt could do her no good, but it was impossible not to wonder if he was amongst the 90,000 who had surrendered or if he was among those who still fought. Or was he still in Paris? Or visiting home? Or soaring over them right now?

With the official battle ending, Soviet troops who had hunkered down in buildings and basements came out like a massive colony of ants. To count the dead was impossible; to count the injured or missing even more so. Troops lumbered past. There were some who looked ecstatic at victory, but most looked relieved the fighting was finally over. But that relief would be short-lived. They had to push the Germans all the way back to Germany. The fight was far from finished. Exhaustion few people in the history of mankind could fathom had aged them. Among them was a man with a smile Kira had not seen since before a *Schadenfreude* had changed her life. A ghost from a different life.

Gerasim.

Bearded, depressingly gaunt, but the war hadn't taken his trademark horse-like smile. Kira hugged him and could feel his spine and shoulder blades through his uniform. He squeezed her, repeating her name. She held him like he was a mirage that could be blown away with the faintest breeze.

"I can't believe you are here," Kira said.

Gerasim studied her, beaming with pride. "I heard your name many times during the fighting. Kovalyov. He is an excellent sniper. He is the Angel of Death. He is The Winter Tiger. He this and he that. I tell them all *Kovalyova* is a woman. The best sniper in the war. I'm going to marry this girl one day. They laugh at me. I tell them all she will shoot you all from a great distance."

Kira smiled, her first genuine smile since her embrace with Reinhardt at the Théatre du Châtelet.

"I'm so happy you're okay," she said.

"So am I. Though I have garnered no nicknames," Gerasim said.

Kira chuckled. His smile shifted. She knew what he was going to say. He pulled her into a deep hug.

"I heard about your father and Nousha and Lina. I'm so sorry, Kira. I wish I could have been there for you."

Gerasim was part of a past she thought she had lost entirely. But he stood proof it had all been real. Her pain had been real. And it stung once more. Gerasim squeezed her hand, knowing what was going through her mind. But with the pain, he had also brought joy. Things had always been better with him around. The world always felt lighter with him. He told her about his time in the war. How they had faced defeat after defeat before making their stand at Stalingrad.

Kira introduced Gerasim to Morozov and explained what she had been ordered to do.

"I go with you," Gerasim said.

He got his request approved. These Germans were desperate men who would do anything to stay alive but die before they surrendered. Kira and Gerasim had grown up in a setting like the one they would venture into. But sniping was drastically different from hunting. Deer didn't shoot back. And sniping in a metropolitan versus winter wilderness environment was drastically different, too. She needed to become one with an environment in which man did not belong.

Her three-man team joined five other teams. Kira spent the first two days studying the forest through her binoculars. Studying how the wind moved and from which direction. Studying how the snow drifted. The snow was two feet deep. Deep enough that an unexpected charge would take minutes, not seconds.

With the cover of night, they advanced, dug a trench, and hid inside it. Far enough from the tree line that Kira was confident it would take an equally skilled sniper to have any shot at them. Gerasim and Morozov catnapped while Kira stayed on alert. She respected the Germans' resolve. She was not meant to be a prisoner. And if she'd had their word that they would harm no person and sustain themselves off the land, she'd let them be. But she couldn't guarantee that. She couldn't guarantee every last one of them out here wasn't a *Schadenfreude*. And for that reason, every last one of them would be captured. And if they wouldn't be captured, then every last one of them would die.

Stranded

The plane torpedoed toward the ground. Reinhardt tugged on the throttle, fighting the tremendous vibrations. The plane plowed through the fluffy snow, covering Günter, Gruber, Baumbauer, and Hochzeit with it, before grinding to a stop. Reinhardt used his pistol to break the glass cockpit. Snow cascaded atop him. If winter had its way, it'd bury him in the cockpit like dirt on a casket.

"Everyone okay?" Reinhardt asked.

The four dusted the snow off, and after examining their bodies, stated they were. The color in Baumbauer's face was gone as he realized what had just happened.

"They'll have seen us crash. We need to take cover," Günter said.

The snow dragged them down, grabbing hold of their legs like invisible hands, sucking them into its depths. The wind knocked them over as they stumbled toward the tree line, then screamed at them through the trees, like ghosts warning to stay out.

"We need a shelter," Reinhardt said, after gazing at their surroundings.

"Water, too. We'll look," Hochzeit said, nodding at Baumbauer to assist.

Reinhardt, Günter, and Gruber started on a shelter. Gruber had a decent dagger that he used to cut through the broken branches that Reinhardt and Günter snapped. The design was a simple A-frame shelter. They covered the frame and the floor in pine. It would be a tight fit for five men, but that was the point—to trap as much body heat as they could.

Halfway through completing the shelter, Hochzeit and Baumbauer returned, beaming.

"There's a creek!" Baumbauer said, holding up two full canteens.

With water seemingly in unlimited supply, they downed the canteens and then Baumbauer and Hochzeit left to refill them. When they returned, they took inventory of everything they had. Both Reinhardt and Günter had Walther PP pistols. Fifteen shots between them. Baumbauer had his MP-41 with twenty-seven rounds. Gruber had his dagger, and Hochzeit had nothing but his fists. Not exactly enough supplies to defend the Alamo.

"Guess I'll find a sharp stick," Hochzeit remarked.

"Relax. We'll rest for a few hours. Solve more problems then," Reinhardt said.

They crawled inside the shelter. The forest had greatly negated the wind, and with the shelter packed, it was bearable inside. Far from warm or comfortable, but better than those days in the Cauldron had been. It didn't take long for them to fall asleep. Their bodies needed food and water, but they also needed copious amounts of rest.

At dawn, Reinhardt woke. He did his best to not wake the others when he left the shelter. Reinhardt went to the bathroom and noted the dark yellow color of his urine. He was severely dehydrated. The first order of business was to have each of them drink a canteen of water. The creek was moving enough that he felt comfortable it was safe to continue drinking. It was a risk they had to take. Dysentery in three days was better than death today. They hadn't been able to get anything to burn to boil water. After each man drank a canteen's worth of water, the direst need was brought up.

"What about food?" Hochzeit asked.

"Seen nothing but pinecones," Baumbauer said.

"We can eat those," Günter said. "They're edible."

"Pinecones?" Hochzeit asked, with his signature look.

"I said they were edible, not delicious." He shrugged. "It's something."

"Damn right it is," Reinhardt said.

They rubbed pinecones against a rock and licked the powder that flaked off. The taste was neither good nor offensive. It was simply calories. It'd been over three days since they had eaten. Calories equaled more time. More sand in the hourglass.

They ventured to the tree line to see if any Soviet troops advanced on their position. Their own footprints were long buried by fresh snow. Even the plane was hard to spot. Reinhardt wasn't sure he would have seen it if he hadn't known it was there.

There were a million things that needed to happen to get them out of Russia. To contemplate that would only cause panic. Survival had to be broken down to one goal at a time. One hour at a time. And at times, it was surviving one minute to the next.

They hadn't seen any wildlife, and though meat sounded heavenly, the idea of Hochzeit unloading his MP-41 was nerve-wracking, not only because he could waste all his ammo, but the gunshots could be heard and investigated. And if they couldn't get a fire started, they'd have to eat it raw, which presented an array of potential problems.

Calories had to be saved, so they spent most of the day catnapping. Gruber, Hochzeit, and Baumbauer went to bed early. Reinhardt and Günter sat in front of the shelter on a bed of pine needles.

"Could use a pillow," Reinhardt said.

Günter sighed. "Could use a lot of things." He stared up, deep in thought, at the canopy and the opening to the night sky. A quality of thought that was cancerous and cannibalistic.

"What is it?" Reinhardt asked.

"I don't want Klara to wonder what happened to me. I want her to find out definitively, so she can move on without wondering. I don't want her to think I'm dead and not move on. Or worse, move on while I'm still alive."

"Don't talk like that. We're not ready to quit yet."

"I know. I'm not. Got a dusting of pinecones in my stomach. What the hell is there to complain about?"

They shared a brief laugh. It wasn't worth the effort and calories to fake laugh for long.

"You have a photograph of Klara. That's your compass. Your due north. You're lucky to have it," Reinhardt said. He hesitated. "I met someone in Paris." He paused. "Truly met someone. Incredible. Fierce. Smart. Cunning. Beautiful. Kira Kovalyova."

"Kovalyova? She's Russian?"

Reinhardt nodded, his eyes distant as he pictured her fierce eyes. "There is a life out there, beyond this war."

"You're talking like you want to be done."

Reinhardt exhaled. "I think I do. I wanted to fight for Germany, Günter. But what I saw at Stalingrad was a betrayal."

"We can't lose this war, Reinhardt. The Great War nearly destroyed Germany. It won't survive another defeat."

"It may not survive a victory."

Reinhardt had never had a strong opinion about Hitler and the Third Reich. Hitler had been fanatically pro-German, but forsaking a hundred thousand men to die of hypothermia or starvation was counter-intuitive to that claim. And then there was Kira. He'd seen a glimpse of the life he hadn't known he wanted.

"Kind of wish we would have stolen a boat instead of a plane," Günter said.

"Or a plane with some fucking fuel," Reinhardt said.

Their smirks changed to fully fledged smiles. Even laughter. And how great that laughter felt. Not food for the body, but food for the soul. However, their bodies didn't give a shit about food for the soul. If they didn't find food soon, they'd starve to death.

"Well, I may not have any food or a pillow, but I do have this." Günter reached into the deep pocket of his bomber jacket and drew out the chessboard Klara had given him. He opened it and laid the pieces out. They played the game, silently moving pieces across the board. They both made mistakes you only make when you play chess without a clear mind. Bishops and knights taken by pawns. Early checks. Reinhardt pinned Günter's king with a pawn and his queen. Günter toppled his king and said goodnight. Reinhardt sat a while longer. Closing his eyes subjected him to the dream world where he could see her again. Maybe in Paris or perhaps home in Germany. The escape was a drug but waking from it was a cruel sobriety Reinhardt couldn't stand.

As expected, pinecones did not assuage their hunger. And it wasn't buying them days of life, but hours. Maybe not even that long. They ventured deeper into the woods to see what bounty it could provide. Having a water source was vital, so they followed the creek. The sound of trickling water was tranquil and soothed the spirit. No gunfire, no hum of plane engines, no deafening blasts. And though it did nothing to satiate that literal hunger, the quest for something better, the hope that it existed had been affirmed. Maybe it is something engrained in our DNA. That the sound of trickling water means survival. Means salvation. It was a soothing balm. It appeared the others shared Reinhardt's zen-like experience. They stood at the water's edge. For how long, none of them knew.

Then they carried on, the creek growing wider and deeper. The thick canopy had prevented the forest floor from getting covered in snow, therefore reducing the amount of energy expended to walk.

A brown shape lay ahead. Gruber recognized it as a deer. Its neck had been bitten into. Blood surrounded it.

"Fresh," Gruber said.

Reinhardt hadn't been a hunter, so he took Gruber's word for it.

"But that means something killed it," Hochzeit said.

"No shit," Gruber jested.

"Meaning it's something's dinner, asshole," Hochzeit said.

"Yeah, our dinner," Gruber said.

"Could be a wolf kill," Baumbauer said in a skeptical tone.

"I haven't had meat in weeks. Fuck, months. I'm taking this," Gruber said, pointing at the deer with his knife.

"This is all pointless unless you can cook that," Günter said.

"I'll eat it raw. It's that or die," Gruber said.

"You'll still die if you eat that raw. You'll just have a pleasant case of the shits before you do," Günter said.

Reinhardt weighed the options. The others were waiting for his feedback. He wasn't going to eat raw meat. Besides, what did fresh truly mean? Minutes ago? This morning? Yesterday? Cooking it was not a choice but a necessity. But what had killed this deer? Something with sharp fucking teeth. The thought made him scan around. Risk. Reward. He had to weigh them up. This was food. To pass it up for a supper of pinecone flour was treasonous. And thinking something else would present itself was damn foolish.

"I say we eat it," Reinhardt said. "But we be smart. We clean it. Wash all the blood off our hands. Leave the carcass. And we have to cook it."

Günter settled into the idea after Reinhardt had given this phantom predator some thought. Gruber skinned the deer while Reinhardt and Günter looked for wood dry enough to burn. They returned to their shelter and stocked the driest wood they could find for burning. Günter used his lighter to set a couple of pages from Reinhardt's novel aflame. The searing paper ignited the branches. Günter breathed life into the fire. Heat they hadn't felt in days. But for Hochzeit, Baumbauer, and Gruber, it may well have been heat they had not felt since before winter. Sometimes, it was hard for Reinhardt to remember the three of them had been in the Cauldron far longer than he and Günter had been. Their desperation was at a level that far exceeded his own.

The cuts of meat were covered in pine. They skewered sticks through the meat and held them over the fire. The controlled crackling fire was peaceful. Not like the fires of war that swooshed and roared and were sometimes followed by the screaming of men. Reinhardt and the others feasted on the meat. Delicious and tender, with a subtle hint of pine. After finishing eating, they threw more pine needles into the flame to help mask the smell of meat. Somewhere in these woods was an angry predator missing part of its meal.

The deep snow had hindered Soviet troops from traveling into the woods. But winter wouldn't last indefinitely. And Reinhardt didn't plan on living here the rest of his life. He was gathering strength and energy. They had to make a move and soon.

Gunfire broke the early morning quietness. Reinhardt and the others stumbled out of their shelter, listening for where it came from. They breathed a sigh of relief after confirming the shots weren't directed at them. For the moment, at least. Reinhardt scouted ahead, staying hidden behind the trees. Soviet troops fired into the trees west of them. The woods were so large that Reinhardt and the others hadn't even realized not too far from them were more German troops avoiding capture. They'd seen nothing, heard nothing. How easy it was to become disorientated in the woods.

He returned to the others and provided an update.

"What do we do?" Baumbauer asked, scratching at his beard. Something that was both an actual itch and a nervous tick.

"Stay hidden," Gruber said.

"Leave them?" Hochzeit asked. He didn't like the idea of not giving aid to fellow Germans.

"I don't even have a gun. Neither do you. What should we do? Cheer them on?" Gruber said.

"The Soviets will keep searching," Günter said. "It'll be the five of us versus who knows how many of them."

"We hide. Go further into the woods," Gruber said.

Further into Russia. Further away from home.

Reinhardt shook his head. "No. I won't do that. My goal isn't to go deeper into Russia. If that's your plan, you are free to do so."

"What's your plan?" Günter asked.

"The plane we took is facing the Soviets," Reinhardt said.

"Buried in the snow and out of fuel," Hochzeit reminded him.

"Yes, but it has two .50 cals," Reinhardt said.

He had flown into the boiling Cauldron to help the entrapped Germans. The battle may have officially ended, but these Germans still needed help. He held no ill will to Gruber, Hochzeit, and Baumbauer. Gruber and Baumbauer had been quick no's. Hochzeit had been persuaded to say no, too. They had been in the Cauldron since the beginning. They were three of the men Reinhardt had come to save. Günter was undecided.

"Stay with them," Reinhardt said, removing the burden of choice. "Only one of us can fit in the cockpit, anyway."

Günter told him he'd wait by the tree line. Reinhardt crept out, powering through the sludge-like snow. A lone colored figure among a veil of white. A nice target for an enemy sniper. He climbed into the cockpit of the plane. The Soviets closed the distance between themselves and the German resistance. Reinhardt fired. The .50 caliber rounds sounded different from other rounds—more fearsome. They blasted the snow away from the plane and put golf ball-sized holes in the advancing Soviet troops. It didn't take long for them to decipher where the shots were coming from, and they fired a volley of their own. Most bullets punctured the snow in front of the plane while some flew above and beyond. But a few pierced the plane's wings, close enough to make Reinhardt's skin tingle. The .50 cal ran dry. Reinhardt turned to crawl out. But his foot slipped between the seat and wedged between it. Günter looked on, beckoning him to hurry. Reinhardt tugged on his foot, cursing. Günter dashed out to help. Finally, Reinhardt's foot released. He turned.

"I'm com—"

A searing pain ripped through his back and out of his chest, knocking him out of the plane. He fell into the cold snow and didn't move. Günter slid to the ground, recognizing that Reinhardt had been shot by a sniper. Soviet troops charged toward the plane. They were closer to Reinhardt than he was. And he had only the Walther PP. It was useless from this distance. Reinhardt showed no signs of movement. To go to him, Günter had to risk his own life. Any sign of life from Reinhardt and he would have.

But there was none. His good friend had left this world. Günter held his gaze and then fled back into the woods.

Savior in the Snow

The Germans made a stand. Firing from cover of the tree line, the Soviets overwhelmed them. From 400 meters, Kira sniped at those who stayed out from cover for longer than a few seconds. Gerasim and Morozov were among the Soviets who advanced. But out of nowhere, large caliber rounds blasted through the chilled air. Obliterating her fellow Soviets. Morozov was in her scope and then he wasn't. His head had been shot clean off—magnified in gruesome detail. Kira swung her rifle toward where those shots had come from. A crashed plane obscured by snow. She hadn't missed it; she'd studied it when they had first arrived. It was empty and snow-covered. Somebody had returned to the plane.

Kira focused her gaze, ignoring the reality that five children had just lost their father in the most horrific way. The German in the plane had his back to her, trying to flee after he had exhausted his ammunition. She squeezed the trigger. The German shifted. For the first time she could remember, she didn't know the outcome of her shot. The German had been knocked out of the plane by the force of the bullet, but it was far from a guaranteed kill shot. She left her trench and advanced toward the plane. She didn't use the scope but was ready to shoot should the German move. The deep snow made it cumbersome; she stumbled twice.

When she got within ten meters, she shouldered her Mosin and drew her TT-30. Eyes darting from the German on the ground to the tree line. She tapped the German with her foot. No movement. Pistol trained on the back of his head, she rolled him over. Her eyes widened in horror. She stumbled backward.

It wasn't him. It couldn't be him. Reinhardt dead in the snow. Dead by her own hands. Her world spun violently. She checked his pulse and was ungodly relieved there was one. His eyes strobed open and closed. Somehow, bleeding and freezing, seeing Kira brought a smile to his face.

"Are you real?" he asked.

Her eyes darted to the advancing Soviets struggling through the snow.

"We have to move," she replied.

She helped Reinhardt to his feet. He had been confused before, but after seeing the rifle slung on her shoulder and the uniform she wore, he'd never been more confused in his life. But there wasn't time to ask anything. She lifted him to his feet, draping his arm over her shoulders. They headed away from the plane, following the tree line west toward the Volga. Reinhardt grimaced, his groans growing louder, more severe.

"Wh-Where ... taking ... me?" he asked.

His weight grew limper; too heavy for Kira to talk. If Reinhardt was seen, he'd either be killed or taken prisoner. But since he was injured, she didn't have a hope that they'd let him live—they'd get no work out of him. Kira struggled under his weight, collapsing in the snow. Reinhardt drifted in and out of consciousness. His sinewy frame shifted from being a blessing that helped power them through the snow to a curse as it went completely limp. Survival dictated they get to cover inside the trees. She called his name, encouraging him, begging him to continue. Sweat dampened her skin.

Once she was roughly 400 meters inside the forest, she eased him to the ground as best as she could. His wound had bled out onto the snow. It wouldn't take a skilled tracker to deduce where they'd gone. Kira grabbed a pine branch and used it to sweep snow over their tracks and brush fresh snow over the blood. Fortunately, the fiercely falling snow helped with her objective.

Kira returned to Reinhardt. She needed to treat his wound, get a fire started, and build a shelter. And do all of them quickly. One mission at a time. Reinhardt's health was critical, and she had to start with that. A shelter and fire would do him no good if he bled out. She stripped off his jacket and shirt. The bullet had gone through his back and exited away from his heart. Had he not turned, she would have sent that bullet straight through his heart. She cleaned the wound and covered it with gauze from her own supply kit. Goosebumps spread across his flesh. Kira had to work fast. They wouldn't last long out here without a shelter, let alone now that she had stripped him of his jacket and shirt. She taped the gauze onto his skin and then covered him with his jacket. Using her knife, she cut pine branches and covered him with them. Not a wool blanket, but it was something. The wind corkscrewed through the trees, nipping at them like chained guard dogs. Reinhardt was unconscious, and if she didn't get a shelter in place fast, he'd never come to.

Kira had grown up making shelters in this type of setting. Talked her parents into allowing her to spend the night in what she had made. In the summer, she and

Gerasim would spend a week in them. She piled a stack of wood, curling small twigs for kindling. Holding them under the flame of her lighter, the fire engulfed the wood. Now, there was time to build—Reinhardt was safe. She held her hands close to the fire, making fists to regain needed feeling in them.

Once the dexterity returned, she cut two sticks into Y-shapes and placed a long ridge pole between them. She covered the area underneath with pine branches. The ribcage framework was next. Her sweating increased, so she removed her jacket—sweating was not something someone wanted to do in this environment. She dragged Reinhardt inside and finished covering the shelter with pine. The fire was dying, and she wanted nothing more than to rest, but she couldn't. Not yet. Through great exertion, the shelter had been completed in less than forty minutes, and between that and dragging Reinhardt, exhaustion overwhelmed her. But she willed herself to gather more wood for the fire. The wintry winds knew it had seconds before she disappeared back into the safety of her shelter. It shoved her, howled into her ear. The white-out conditions tried to trick her into losing track of where her shelter was. And she almost did. If the fading fire had gone out, she wouldn't have found her way back to it. She dropped the wood beside the fire and fell to a knee. Weakly, she tossed the wood onto the fire, careful not to suffocate it. She was both freezing and sweating. She crawled into the shelter.

"Ki-Kira ..." Reinhardt stuttered weakly.

She tilted her canteen to his mouth, wiping away the water that dribbled down his chin.

"It was you ... you killed Wolff ..." he said.

His piercing eyes locked onto her, not only looking like two stars but having the power of them, too. Kira didn't look away, but Reinhardt was powerless to resist exhaustion and drifted to sleep. The snow continued to fall thick and heavy. Good for Kira and Reinhardt, as it meant that the Soviets wouldn't advance in this weather. But for what Mother Nature gifted, it also demanded payment. After the blizzard had dumped twelve inches, the temperature plummeted. It extinguished their fire, and all the branches were wet or frozen, essentially making them flame-retardant. Kira stashed more pine branches in front of the opening. Her blanket was the only thing they had to keep them warm. Pressed together, praying their shelter would hold and that it proved warm enough. As she fought off exhaustion, a macabre thought took hold. If she fell asleep, would she ever wake up?

Even at night, there were no sounds. Wildlife was nestled away from the extreme cold. If the wind hadn't died down, it would have blown away the pine covering their shelter. But as it was, it was so freezing that even the wind had fallen dormant. She had insulated the shelter as best as she could. Now, it was nothing more than a waiting game.

At daybreak, Kira checked Reinhardt's wound again. She had to reuse the gauze. The wound didn't look infected, but it had to be sealed. It also didn't appear to be a sucking chest wound—one where air was sucked into the wound, threatening to collapse the lung. Reinhardt was in and out of consciousness, too weak to speak, which was okay with Kira for now. She didn't know what to say to him. His eyes had shown so much the previous night. Confusion. Bewilderment. And betrayal. Would the Reinhardt she knew in Paris no longer exist? Had she created a *Schadenfreude*?

Kira had only a few rations left. She added sugar cubes and tea leaves to her canteen to add calories for Reinhardt, who was still too weak to do anything but sip water. His wound wasn't leaking blood around the gauze, a great sign, but the longer it stayed open, the more problematic it could and would become. There was only one option. She stripped his shirt and jacket, and then ran her knife under her lighter long enough for the blade to glow orange. She placed her sniper log in Reinhardt's mouth, waking him. His eyes darted from Kira to the glowing knife in her hand. With his bare chest and the journal in his mouth to bite down on, he deduced what was about to happen. He squeezed his eyes shut and bit down on the journal. Kira pressed the blade against his flesh. Reinhardt squirmed from the sound of his skin sizzling, grabbing a branch and snapping it in his hands. He rolled onto his side, waiting for Kira to cauterize the entrance wound. She held the blade to the flame, then pressed it against his flesh. Reinhardt groaned, his legs kicking. Kira splashed what Reinhardt had thought was water. But it stung way too much to be that lifesaving substance. He took the small flask and took a swig. Vodka. It burned in his chest, but the burn was its own soothing balm.

"You are a sniper?" he asked, when the pulsating pain subsided.

Kira nodded as she helped put his shirt and jacket back on.

"How?" he asked.

Answering how would also require answering why. He knew a partial truth. Kira gave him the full truth and explained everything. Her work at a munitions factory and her shooting exhibition that had been seen by Colonel Volkov. She detailed her rank and the number of kills she had tallied. There was a moment where Reinhardt was impressed, but then the reality hit that each of those nearly 300 people were his fellow countrymen.

"And your victories … they came against my countrymen," Kira said.

Reinhardt nodded solemnly. Both now self-conscious of their numbers. Kira studied him, noting the differences to how he had looked in Paris. There, his hair was wavy and combed, his face lean and cleanly shaven. His shoulders were broad, his chest muscular. Stalingrad had weighed heavily upon his good looks. Killed his vibrancy. His beard was dark and thick, but it couldn't hide how gaunt his face looked. Even those blue eyes weren't as bright as they had been in Paris.

"Are you the one who shot me?" Reinhardt asked.

Kira met his eyes and nodded shamefully. "But I didn't know it was you."

"Guess I'm lucky to be alive."

Kira reached into her pocket and shared her rations with him. Not much, but something. Kira would look to hunt tomorrow.

"How is it that you're here?" Kira asked.

"I couldn't sit idly by while my countrymen froze to death."

"You shouldn't be here. You shouldn't have come."

Reinhardt flashed a smirk like those in Paris that had enchanted her, sending a wave of heat washing over her.

"Yes, I can think of hundreds of places I'd rather be than Stalingrad," he said. Kira asked how his pain was. He shrugged in response. "Everything is numb."

Both a lighthearted joke and the truth. He asked how she knew how to build shelters like the one they were in and said it was far better than the one he, Günter, and the others had built. She explained she had built them her whole life. Kira grabbed her three-line and told Reinhardt she was going to hunt. He offered to go with her, but he got as far as sitting up before the pain overtook him. It was far safer for Kira to wander than Reinhardt.

She was gone less than ninety minutes. The shot had been true. A painless death. Judging by the stag's thin frame, she'd spared it from dying a slow death. Cleaning and carrying it had always been a two-person job. Gerasim had always been there. Where was he now? Had he survived the shooting? Morozov was dead, killed by the man she cared for. Would he understand why she did? Or look at her actions as treasonous? Kira worked on a fire, a troublesome task that took an hour. She skewered the venison and cooked it over the flame. Reinhardt shook his head, frustrated at his own shortcomings. Five men had struggled to survive. Kira looked as though she could live out here indefinitely.

"I had heard rumblings of a sniper named Kovalyov," Reinhardt said.

Kira shook her head. "The Germans got my name wrong. Kovalyov is a masculine ending."

Kira had to explain that in Russia, women take on a different ending to their last names from their fathers. Her father was Igor Kovalyov. Russian middle names were patronymic. Kira's middle name was derived from her father's first name with a feminine ending. Usually ending in either *avna* or *ovna*. Female surnames end in A.

"Kira Igoravna Kovalyova," Kira said.

So, not only was it preconceived notions on gender that made the Germans think one of Stalingrad's deadliest snipers was a male, but they had also gotten the last name wrong.

"Reinhardt Casper Friedel." He smiled. "So, you are the one they call The Winter Tiger?"

"And you are the one they call The War Eagle."

"I am more than a nickname."

"So am I."

"Yes, you are."

The next day, Reinhardt's strength had doubled. He could stand and even joined Kira to look for water.

"This is where you belong, isn't it?" Reinhardt asked.

"It is. It's peaceful." She breathed in the fresh air; it felt like it massaged her soul.

Reinhardt agreed with her statement. "You would love Germany. Its mountains, its lakes. It is so magnificent."

The longing to return home filled every word.

"And what about the summer? What would Kira Kovalyova be doing?"

Nostalgia fondly came to her. "I hiked. There was a bluff near my house, close, but far enough away that I was the only one willing to hike to it. I'd sit there for hours and read, basking in the sun. When it got really hot, I'd swim."

"As would I. There was a vacation spot close to my hometown. Near Jade Bight. Mathias and I swam there hundreds of times."

They stayed by the creek, listening to its tranquil sounds. With having a fire, they didn't have to risk drinking the water. They could boil it first. They filled their canteens with snow and set them beside the fire. And because of how frigid the temperatures were, it didn't take long for the water to go from scalding to ice cold. When dusk died, they sat inside their shelter.

"Now, I may not have food, but I do have something," Reinhardt said.

He drew a book from his jacket pocket. It was bent; the pages curled.

"Had to burn some," Reinhardt said, explaining the missing pages. "I hope it was useless exposition."

He read the book out loud. His voice was soothing even without a storyteller's flair, like Gerasim. After each chapter, they switched. They read deep into the night until the only thing keeping them awake was the sound of their own voices. The fire outside blazed. The interior of their shelter provided a warmth greater than either had experienced in days.

"Can I ask you something? And I want the honest truth," Reinhardt said. Her silence was taken as a yes. "Was it real for you?"

Kira didn't need any explanation or any time to answer it. "Yes."

Reinhardt reached for her hand. With the other, he stroked her face. Both had a million thoughts to toil over. Reinhardt was deep in enemy territory. Somewhere, hopefully, Günter, Gruber, Baumbauer, and Hochzeit were alive. Somewhere in woods like this. Kira was caring for an enemy soldier, ignoring reporting for duty. Treason carrying with it the punishment of possible death. But as they fell into each other's eyes, there was an acceptance that all those worries could be set aside. Without warning or planning, both had eliminated the distance between them. Chapped lips against chapped lips, savoring their sapid taste. Wrapped up in a blanket, their body heat defying physiological logic. There was no one to hear them. Out in the Russian wilderness, they were the only two people in the world. Overcome with a frenzied passion to explore every inch of flesh, to gaze into each other's eyes and never break it. Body temperatures rising to the point it seemed the snow around the shelter would melt to pools of water. Bodies moving in rhythmic tandem, reaching a crescendo of mutual pleasure.

"I'll have to find a way to replace those spent calories," Reinhardt said.

Kira's head rested on his stomach, her long hair covering his chest like a scarf. He stroked her hair with the tips of his fingers as she ran her hands softly along his torso.

Dawn greeted them through the shelter opening. The fire was slowly dying. Kira and Reinhardt spent the early hours scavenging for food. She pointed out the plants to avoid eating and those a person could eat. She told him how to find nuts, where to look for potential food sources, and how to make quick shelters. She pointed out pine needles. Reinhardt had known they were edible, but he didn't know they were high in vitamin C and helped combat scurvy.

"How is it you know all this? I know you said you built shelters as a child, but someone must have shown you how," Reinhardt said.

"My father for a while. But when my mother died … there wasn't much that brought him joy," Kira said.

Reinhardt absorbed her wilderness knowledge like a sponge. Listening and asking for clarification when he didn't understand. They had to be careful gazing into each other's eyes. His blue and her green inspired desires. Once those fires were lit, any willpower was immolated. The weather over the last few days had been as moderate as a person could hope for with Soviet winters. But Kira looked to the distance with worry. The winds of winter were about to shift. A storm loomed.

"What is it?" Reinhardt asked.

"A blizzard's coming," she said.

The Blizzard

Reinhardt didn't waste time questioning how she could know that. Kira had grown up in Russia; you learn to recognize the warning signs of winter storms.

They had to work fast. Reinhardt had fished out an empty jerrycan from the creek. He cleaned it out and filled it with water they could boil later. They had plenty of venison left, so Kira gathered cattails growing by the creek. She said after they were cooked, they took on a potato-like taste. But Reinhardt had severe reservations that it could mimic a nice baked potato. She dug through the snow by an oak tree and harvested the few acorns she found. Snow fell, slowly at first—a final warning of the ferocity Mother Nature was about to unleash. Food and supplies stocked in their shelter, the next task was to find a safe way to move their fire inside. Smoke inhalation would be fatal, and even if they couldn't see smoke, there was still the risk of carbon monoxide. They stacked rocks in a hearth formation to protect the fire from the wind. They expanded their shelter so that they had to walk around a short barricade to get in or out. This would prevent snow from building up inside the shelter. They stocked the entrance with interlocking sticks as a further deterrent from snow piling inside. Still, it was going to get brutally cold with winds straight from the Ice Age.

Kira and Reinhardt barricaded themselves inside. They had added extra pine for insulation and had a pile of rocks they had stashed in the fire that they could lie next to for warmth. They had doubled the foliage covering the shelter, but it did little to muffle the wind's deafening howl. Kira and Reinhardt had nothing to do but stay cuddled against each other under the blanket.

"Did you get in trouble for Wolff? Was I suspected?" Kira asked.

Reinhardt shook his head. "No, you were simply the woman who broke my heart on Christmas Eve."

Kira lifted her head from his chest to gaze into his eyes. "It wasn't like I could tell you the truth."

"No, I suppose not. Why Wolff? Did you know his family was in the room?"

"I did. I waited until it was only him. As to why, you know the answer. Wolff was fanatical and competent. A dangerous combination."

Reinhardt hesitated, then nodded; he knew she was right. Stalingrad had weighed heavily on his soul. Changed his thinking. Hitler forsaking his countrymen was something he could never forgive.

"Your kills. Do you remember them all?" he asked.

She didn't need to think about it. The answer was no. So many of those kills had been fueled by grief and rage, and those were blinding emotions. But two of those now 293 kills hadn't been fueled by rage or revenge. They'd been merciful. She told Reinhardt about the Hoffman brothers. She drew the letter from her pocket. Reinhardt took it and read it. He wiped his eyes after. Kira placed it back in her pocket. She asked if he recognized the names—Augustus and Mikel Hoffman. He shook his head. But though he didn't know these exact brothers, he knew men like them. The war was full of millions of Augustus and Mikel Hoffmans.

It was impossible to know what time of day it was. They sipped water and once they were hungry, they ate strips of venison and cooked cattails.

"Not exactly apple strudels, huh?" Reinhardt said.

Kira sighed. She couldn't even remember what they had tasted like, only that it was the most incredible thing she'd ever eaten. It was comparable to viewing the Sistine Chapel and then only seeing children's art the rest of your life. Yet for Reinhardt, the venison and cattails were sustenance. That week without food had tested him. He appreciated the food, no matter how untasteful it was.

Reinhardt added wood to the fire, then returned inside. He commented on how vicious the weather was. A white out. He'd been unable to see a single tree. Ice clung from his beard and from his eyebrows. His cheeks were an angry red. They shared a sip of Kira's vodka. During Stalingrad, a ration of 100 grams had been issued, revoked, and reissued because its allotment was heavily disputed. Many leaders thought vodka gave their men courage, while others thought it simply made them drunk. Both were probably true.

Kira and Reinhardt read his book, made love, read the book, and made love again. She taught him Russian words and phrases. They talked, baring their souls by disclosing fears, dreams, losses, and moments of embarrassment. He talked about his sisters, and she described Nousha and Lina in the detail they deserved.

Reinhardt's blue eyes were even more striking with his thick, black beard, and she couldn't help but stare at them and admire them. His fingers ran her curves, squeezed her breasts, and grabbed fistfuls of her dark hair. She guided him inside her, then placed her hands on his hips.

After, they held each other close—both out of want and need. The war had taken everything from Kira. Her father. Her sisters. Her home. Alekseeva. Morozov. Galina and her family. Maybe even Gerasim. But it had given her Reinhardt. The greatest unexpected gift. A man who made her feel everything she had never felt before. And because of the blizzard, there was no worry about being caught. This was their own patch of earth. They were Adam and Eve, and it was too damn cold for any snakes to tempt them with forbidden fruit.

Reinhardt gazed at her. "Would you run away with me if I asked?"

She couldn't tell if the question was playful or real. "Where would we run off to?"

"Wisconsin."

"Wisconsin? This is in Germany?"

Reinhardt shook his head. "No, no. America."

He explained there were many people of German heritage there. People who were good, honest, and hardworking. But before they settled down, they'd travel from New York to Los Angeles. See a play on Broadway, visit Chicago. Ride horses in Texas. See the ancient sequoias in California.

"After our adventures, we'll grow cherries and sell them. Pies, wines, and everything in between," he said.

"Cherry strudels."

His eyes lit up. "What a splendid future this will be!"

She asked what he knew about growing cherries. He stated he heard that some German prisoners of war had been sent to Door County, Wisconsin, famous for their cherries, where they helped on farms. Many of them stated they were treated kindly and enjoyed their work. Kira and Reinhardt pondered what could have been their greatest mistake: Did the Givre Strudel have a cherry strudel, and they'd missed the chance to try it?

They detailed dreams of a future for hours. But it was a future neither was naïve enough to believe as certain. War never asks its soldiers what their plans are. It doesn't care. Over those three days, when they weren't embracing each other fully in the present, they dared to dream of a future. But as the storm lifted and skies cleared, a suffocating reality came with it.

"What is your plan, Kira?" Reinhardt asked.

They were lying down, trying to sleep. She knew what he meant, but she didn't want to face that harsh reality right now. She wanted to pretend it was about their scripted future.

"Live in Wisconsin. Figure out how to make the perfect cherry strudel."

His smile was the saddest smile she'd ever seen. Filled with melancholy. "You can't stay here."

Another truth she knew, but she wanted to scream, *Why not?!* In a month or so, the harsh winter would be behind them. Spring would bring an endless bounty. There was no reason they couldn't stay in these woods.

"I won't surrender, Kira. I have no desire to be a Soviet prisoner."

"It may not be that long. Your invasion of Russia failed. Soon, the Americans and British will get a foothold in Europe. Germany's die will be cast."

Reinhardt wore the smile of a parent listening to a child's youthful naivety. "Hitler will fight until every one of Germany's men, women, and children have fallen. It will be years."

"Then I will speak on your behalf. I will tell them you only flew into Stalingrad to evacuate the injured."

Reinhardt gently placed a strand of her wavy hair that had fallen over her face behind her ear. "I'm the *Luftwaffe*'s best pilot. They'll demand I renounce Germany. I won't do that. They'll never release me. And if you request it, you'll be demoted. Or worse, accused of treason. Everything you have worked for will be gone. Just another weak woman fooled by a man. All the respect you have garnered … I won't let you lose all you have earned for me." He squeezed her hand, a sad smile on his tired face. Those eyes that could burn so bright looked as if they would never burn again. "You have to let me go."

Never had words crushed her like they did then. *You have to let me go.*

Kira had lost too much to believe in false hopes. Once the storm lifted, more Soviets would sweep the area. If she was discovered with Reinhardt, it'd be treated as treason. He was right. All the respect she'd earned, so much harder so being a woman, would end. *Just another weak woman fooled by a man.*

"I don't want to lose you," she said.

Reinhardt kissed her forehead. "Which is what gives me strength to do what we both know has to be done."

"Where do you expect to go?" Kira asked.

"Home."

Home? How? If he had any sort of plan, it remained unspoken. Maybe because there was no plan except to stay alive and uncaptured. It was incredibly unlikely he could make it home. But that didn't need to be said out loud. She knew it, and he knew it. Some things are too fragile to even whisper.

As they tried to sleep, Kira prayed for another blizzard. Let some monumental event escalate the end of the war, so that they could walk out of this forest not as a German fighter pilot and a Soviet sniper, but as a man and woman in love and ready to begin the rest of their lives together. Reinhardt stroked her hair, eyes open, deep in thought. After verifying she was deeply asleep, he freed himself from her embrace. She had stored strips of venison, acorns, and cattails. He hoped she'd understand he needed it. She could replenish far easier than he could. At the entrance, he turned to gaze upon her once more. Her jet-black hair and ivory skin. The faint line of her lips. Her eyes were closed. How he wished to see those fierce emerald eyes one more time. He had no doubts Kira could keep them alive. That she could build them a log cabin. But there were too many dangers. Not just for him, but more importantly, for her. He wouldn't let her. He couldn't. This winter mirage could last no longer.

Reinhardt Friedel took a final look at Kira Kovaylova, then stepped out into the orange-washed dawn and the endless expanse of white.

Return to Command

She knew he was gone before she even opened her eyes. The void beside her felt like a phantom limb. Kira stepped out of the shelter, scanning for him. His tracks had disappeared, covered by the blowing snow. He'd been gone for a while. Too long that even if she wanted to run after him, she wouldn't catch him. The reality she hadn't wanted to accept was thrust upon her. That's the thing about reality. We can breathe it in slowly or let it suffocate us. She placed her hands in her pockets. One hand grazed paper. She'd read hundreds of books and knew the feel of cream-colored paper from a novel. She withdrew it and unfolded it. In the blank space at the bottom page was handwritten text: *I wish the world was different. I love you.*

She gathered her possessions and her Mosin. She stopped to gaze upon this crude shelter that had been a home. No bed. No electricity. No plumbing. No running water. But it had been home because of Reinhardt.

Kira's trek out of the woods exhausted her. Some spots were as deep as her hips, forcing her to use her three-line as a walking stick. Near the Volga, a Soviet patrol picked her up and brought her back inside the skeletal remains of Stalingrad. She met with Borodin and told the lie of how she had tracked Germans into the woods and had gotten trapped by the blizzard.

"I am happy you are alive and well, Comrade," he said.

"The Germans … have they all been captured?" she asked.

"The resistance has been quashed. Mother Nature will finish off any we may have missed."

Kira bit the inside of her lip to prevent any emotion from showing. There was a possibility Reinhardt had avoided Soviet troops. But there was no avoiding the Russian winter. She couldn't ask any more questions. Reinhardt had removed her from having to make a choice. She wouldn't offset his sacrifice by asking stupid questions.

She was granted some rest and recovery. She ate her allotted daily rations in a single serving. The nurse said her vitals were good, and that she had no frostbite. After being cleared, Kira searched for Gerasim, asking everyone she saw. Just as doubt crept further inward in her mind, a thin-faced soldier pointed with his lit cigarette. She followed the invisible line to Gerasim. She rushed to him and threw her arms around him, squeezing him in a tight hug.

"I thought you had died!" he said.

Though it pained her to tell the lie, she did. She told her best friend she had gone into the woods to track down Germans. She trusted him with her secret, but to tell him the truth would break his heart.

"Just like when we were kids. Building shelters," he said, grinning like a horse.

"Morozov ..." Kira said.

His smile vanished. "His body was collected. I wrote to his wife. I hope he would not mind."

Kira thanked him for doing it. She owed Morozov's wife a letter, too. He was a good soldier and a friend. Never once had he tried to force himself on her in those small quarters. Sadly, that was a noteworthy achievement. There were plenty of men who would not have kept their hands to themselves.

They spent the day together, wandering the corpse city. Its residents picked up bricks, one at a time. It seemed inconsequential considering the whole city had been destroyed. But the cleanup had to start somewhere. Many of the 90,000 German prisoners worked to clean up the city they had destroyed.

When night gathered, Kira and Gerasim sat on a rooftop to watch the stars.

"I saw you up there, you know," Gerasim said.

Kira waited for him to explain.

"During night and breaks in fighting, I would gaze up at the stars like we used to. When I saw a shooting star, I knew it was a bullet fired from your rifle."

"I'm not a Greek goddess—"

"I disagree."

Kira smiled. "I missed this."

"Me, too. You know you are always the brightest star in the sky. The one I always look for."

Silence set. Each staring at the stars, some orbs of bright light, others as small as pinpricks.

"Have you heard from home?" Kira asked. The word didn't fit anymore for her, but it did for Gerasim.

"My sisters are well. Ekaterina married."

"She did? I thought you gave her specific instructions that you must approve?"

Gerasim smiled. "When has Ekaterina ever listened to me. Papa says he is a good man. Respectful. Treats her well."

"And Semyon?"

"Still fighting. Near Leningrad."

Kira was happy no bad news had come his way yet. The Petrovs were the closest thing to family she had left.

"It's been so long, Kira. I think about our last night a lot. I knew things would change." He shook his head. "But I could never imagine just how much. Especially for you. I wish I could have been there for you. You had to go through it alone. I'm so sorry."

Kira took his hand and squeezed it. "I know you do. But there was nothing you could have done. Nothing could have diminished that pain." Kira released his hand and they stared at the stars again. "They haven't changed. Everything that happens down here ... they are the same as the night you left."

And that was so refreshing. That among chaos there was a constant. For that night they pretended, silently, that the years had turned back. It was like any other night that they had stargazed. Tomorrow, they would hunt and bring the harvested animal to the butcher shop. Gerasim would ask her to marry him. They'd stargaze. But too much had happened for either of them to truly fall into the realm of make-believe.

Gerasim would head west the following day. The Germans had retreated, but the Soviets needed to keep them in constant retreat. Kira had been ordered to instruct new snipers, something she had no interest in doing. She belonged in the field. Doing, not saying.

Would this be the last time she saw her friend? They stayed out there all night until the stars gave way to dawn. And then, the following morning, she said goodbye to Gerasim again.

"Marry me," he said. He flashed that great smile of his.

Kira chuckled. "Maybe tomorrow."

His beard looked good on him. The war had warped the boyish features he had had, molded them into a man's. Yet Kira felt no attraction to him. Her time with Reinhardt had only affirmed it. Her love for Gerasim could never be anything more than brotherly. But she did love him. The war hadn't taken his kindness, his humor, or his positivity. Gerasim would always be loyal to her. And she would always love him in her own way.

He wrapped her in a hug. "You stay safe," he whispered.

"You, too." She didn't release him from her hug. She whispered into his ear. "I do love you. You know that, right?"

He pulled back to gaze into her eyes and nodded. "Goodbye, Kira."

The days that followed bored her soul. How had Orlov taught at a sniping school for as long as he had? There were some competent shooters in her group, and they were all willing to learn. But after a month, she requested a meeting with Colonel Volkov.

"What is on your mind, Comrade?" Colonel Volkov asked, gesturing to the open seat in front of his desk.

"I live to serve the—"

"Yes, I know, and you have done so with distinction. Speak candidly."

"I fucking hate teaching."

Volkov smiled, nearly coughing on his cigarette smoke. He hadn't expected that level of candor.

"I belong out in the field. Making a difference," Kira said.

Volkov studied her. "You have more to say. Say it."

"When I first started fighting, I thought every German soldier was a *Schadenfreude*. I have realized that many of the men I have killed were just following orders. They fought for their own survival. Killing a hundred of them didn't have the same effect as

287

killing Wolff. This war ends by killing the fascists ordering these men to fight, not the men who fight."

Volkov was silent, looking like a worried and proud parent. "Men like the man who killed your family."

Kira nodded. She didn't look away. Instead, she let Colonel Volkov stare into her eyes, so that he could see the steely resolve in them. The murder of her family had been the driving force behind everything she had done.

"I will see what I can do. You must accept the risk of any mission you are sent on," Volkov said.

"I do."

"You may be stranded with no one to help you …"

Kira tapped her TT-30. "Seven for them. One for me."

"Is that your goal, Kira? An assisted suicide?"

He had matched her candor with his own. She should say no right away. But the word wouldn't form. The idea had been presented to her, and she honestly couldn't answer. "I'm not sure. I am not afraid to die. But do I seek it? I don't know … I don't think so. Not anymore."

It was a truth Volkov weighed. A better answer than yes, but not as good as no. But certainly, more truthful.

"I have no desire to help you with that. I will see what mission I may find. But rest assured, whatever I do find, your mission will only be a success if you return. Understood?"

Kira saluted and left. She had nothing to do but stroll the city. How long would it take to rebuild? How many families had been displaced? Lost every possession they owned? And how many families' loss had extended beyond the materialistic? Lost loved ones? Her thoughts went back to Galina and her family. Generations gone.

As mid-April came, the harsh winter finally lifted. The snows melted, and the temperature crept toward freezing. While a temperature of thirty-five degrees Fahrenheit was still cold, for Kira and those who had been at Stalingrad during the grueling winter, it was a sixty-degree swing. For the first time since she had joined the war, boredom beleaguered her.

At last, Colonel Volkov summoned her. Kira had a new mission and a new target.

Survival Dictates

He had wanted to watch her longer. Because every second he did, the more vivid his memory would be. The lighting. The shadows. The contour of her body. The coloring. It was all Reinhardt had. No photograph. No drawing. But she was there every time he closed his eyes. The way she'd looked at the Givre Strudel, seated tall and proud. Stoic with those unbelievable eyes, both strong and sad.

The snow had proven cumbersome, but once the temperatures dropped, it froze, becoming easier to walk on. Easier, but not easy. Even twenty pounds lighter than his normal weight was heavy enough that he sunk through in spots. When he started sweating, he stopped and drank water. It was a struggle to accept he wouldn't get home to Germany in a day. His goal was to keep moving until dusk descended. When it did, he'd work on a shelter. Nothing as elaborate as what Kira had made, just something that would get him out of the cold and wind. He napped until the cold woke him in a shiver. When it did, he exercised to pump blood back into his arms and legs. He left at dawn, continuing along a creek further south. His venison was gone, the acorns and cattails, too. He pushed on, ignoring the tremendous gurgle in his stomach. If it became extreme enough, he'd grind up a few pinecones.

His mind tortured him, making him recall every time he hadn't finished his food. Every time he had turned down seconds. Regrets. And as he sat in his impromptu shelter with his arms crossed, fighting the shivering, he thought of the events that had brought him here. Why had he flown back into the Cauldron? He'd been warned. Hell, he had broken official command to do it. Who had he saved the last time? No one. And he'd led several other pilots to their deaths. Those that hadn't been shot down and killed were either taken prisoner or dead now, too. Or lost in the brutal wilderness.

But that choice had given him Kira. And no matter what happened, those days in the shelter had been some of the greatest of his life. The kind that bring a man peace.

He could feel his body weaken. His feet felt heavier, his shoulders dipped inward, no longer possessing the strength to keep them pressed back to stand tall and proud. His mind wandered, a defense mechanism to disappear into the sanctuary of hallucination. A way out. He could simply sit down and fade away. But something sobered him up—the sight of footprints. Several of them. Not animal tracks. Human footprints. Boot tread marks. Reinhardt sighed; he had no energy left to be demonstratively on edge. He raised his pistol and followed the footprints. He could try to run, but he knew he didn't have the strength. His legs were too weak. He felt like an aged racehorse. His only hope was that he could sneak behind them and shoot them before they even knew he was there. The tracks led to an old cabin, one that had been built well over a hundred years earlier. A body lay on the frozen ground. Stripped of any clothing except for his underwear. The body was blue, like an alien from a science-fiction book. When he got closer, he recognized him. It was Gruber. There were no gunshot or knife wounds on the body. Nothing to show that his death had been in combat. He had frozen to death. Somebody had taken his clothes. Reinhardt listened for any sounds coming from inside the dilapidated shack. It was unlikely there were any Soviet troops inside. After all, why would they be stationed this deep in the woods? Coughing was the only thing he could make out. If he announced his presence and there were Soviet troops inside, he would get shot. But if they were Germans in there and he didn't announce his presence, he may get shot.

Sometimes survival isn't about one good choice and one bad choice. It's the better of two shitty choices.

"Hello, I am coming in. Don't shoot!" he announced.

He took a deep, powering breath as he opened the door. Three men lay on the floor next to a meek fire. Hochzeit, Baumbauer, and Günter. Each had easily lost fifteen pounds since Reinhardt had last seen them.

"Reinhardt …" Günter said, his voice weak and gravelly. "How …"

Reinhardt gave a quick recap of how he was alive but left Kira out of the story for now. Günter and the others were in terrible shape. Baumbauer's cough was guttural, sounding as if a demon was escaping his lungs. Their canteens were empty, but they were too weak to fill them. Reinhardt first restocked the fire, then packed their canteens with snow, sprinkled pine needles in them, and set them beside the fire so they would melt. He forced them all to drink the pine-needle tea.

Now, Reinhardt needed to find food. Thanks to Kira, he knew which mushrooms were safe to eat. He picked until his pockets were full and ate his share before heading back to the cabin. Keeping the three of them awake proved difficult. They barely had the energy to chew. The mushrooms didn't offer many calories, but again, it was better than nothing. What he had to find were acorns. They were high in fat, making them more calorie dense than carbs and proteins. Reinhardt scoured beneath oak trees. After close to forty minutes, he'd found twenty-one. He wrapped them in his scarf and used Gruber's knife to smash them open. He divided the nuts amongst them, one at a time, to verify no one would fall asleep in the middle of chewing and choke. Baumbauer had fallen asleep twice.

The area around the cabin offered little subsistence. The gap between floor and door was larger than desired, and the wind never missed an opportunity to sneak in and remind them it was waiting for them whenever they stepped outside. But it was better than any shelter they'd be able to make.

Günter was more coherent after two days; Hochzeit marginally, but Baumbauer hadn't shown any improvement. In another day, Günter would be able to move. Not twelve hours' worth of walking, but at least a few. Baumbauer couldn't even make it outside to piss. Horrible thoughts consumed Reinhardt. How much better would it be if Baumbauer died and died soon? He hated himself for thinking that. But every one of them battled time. Baumbauer wouldn't be able to travel, and they couldn't carry, drag, or pull him. Reinhardt hadn't chanced escaping Stalingrad to end up in his own self-induced Cauldron in a cabin in the wilderness. His goal was to get home. And every hour wasted, that goal grew further away and more unlikely. They may as well plan on going to Mars.

The following morning, Günter helped Reinhardt pack snow into the canteens. Hochzeit could sit up and his coughing had improved. Staying put at this shack for five days fought against Reinhardt's mantra of, *Move. Just keeping moving.* He did his best to hide that inner conflict from Günter, but he didn't want to waste the effort to do so. For all he knew, forcing a look of content on his face burned calories, and he wouldn't waste a single one.

"What is it?" Günter asked.

"We have to keep moving," Reinhardt said. "Every day, we grow weaker. The distance I can travel today will be less tomorrow. And less the day after. Maybe exponentially so."

"Baumbauer can't."

"I know ..."

Günter shot a nervous, quizzical look at Reinhardt. "What are you suggesting?"

Reinhardt sighed as if he'd been asked how to calculate an obscure physics equation, and he was just as frustrated. "He's not going to make it …"

"So, we just leave him?"

Reinhardt didn't answer right away, which sickened Günter.

"Time isn't going to help him or us," Reinhardt said. "He's dying, Günter. Tomorrow, a few days from now, a week. And that whole while, we what? Sit here? Get weaker? Thinner? Get discovered by Soviet patrols?"

Günter rubbed his forehead, thinking it through, not liking where his thoughts took him. "I don't know … I was going to go after you when you were in the plane."

"I know. But you didn't. And I hold no blame for that. You thought I was dead. You did what you had to do. Your goal is to return home to Klara. It's up to you to decide if you're moving toward that goal."

Günter struggled with the idea, yet the choice needed to be made. He removed Klara's picture from his pocket. Reinhardt was silent, letting Günter gaze upon his wife. Reinhardt knew that the inanimate picture of her would convince him, persuade him, talk reason into Günter better than he ever could. And he meant what he'd said. Günter needed to make his own choice because he'd have to live with it forever.

"I need to get home to her …" Günter said. "But we can't leave Baumbauer to die that way."

"Then we end his suffering."

Reinhardt couldn't believe the words he'd just spoken. He'd flown into the Cauldron to save men like Baumbauer. Now, he was going to abandon him. Günter looked sick. Reinhardt felt the same way, the urge to vomit creeping into his throat.

"We have to tell Hochzeit," Günter said.

They had him come outside. His breathing was slightly wheezy, but the fresh air did his lungs good.

"What is it?" he asked.

"We have to keep moving," Reinhardt said.

"Baumbauer isn't ready yet," Hochzeit said.

"He isn't going to be ready," Günter said. "Ever."

Reinhardt nodded to Günter, overcome with appreciation that Günter had stepped in without being asked. Günter knew these men better than he did. A week or so more, but conditions such as these bond people exponentially quicker.

Hochzeit scoffed at them. "What are you going to do? Just leave him?"

"No, that'd be cruel," Reinhardt said.

"Well, then what—" Hochzeit's facial expression changed as the horrible realization dawned on him. "You're going to kill him ..."

"We're going to end his suffering. But if you can look us in the eye and tell us you think he'll get better, we'll listen," Günter said.

"We are all racing time, Hochzeit. And time is winning," Reinhardt said.

"... I was with him all winter. Do you have any idea what we survived?" Hochzeit asked.

Reinhardt stayed silent. They had survived things he didn't know about, but he also had survived things they didn't know about. He wasn't going to get into a pissing contest.

"Tanks, fucking guns, flamethrowers, grenades, bombs. This is how he goes?" Hochzeit said. "You two don't have any idea what it was like on the streets. Fighting building to building ..."

"We defied orders flying into Stalingrad to save people like you, like Baumbauer. And we have done all we can," Günter said.

Survival isn't civilized. It's primitive. Its tools were schemes and manipulation. And they sometimes needed to be used.

"You can stay with him, but we're leaving," Reinhardt said.

Reinhardt left him. Günter followed. They had to prepare for the long journey. Leaving Hochzeit to consider what Reinhardt had said. Run through the scenario of taking care of Baumbauer alone. Gathering supplies, foraging for food, and collecting water. And if Baumbauer died, Hochzeit would be all alone.

All alone. Not a friend to be found for thousands of miles.

"Okay ... okay," he said louder the second time.

Baumbauer didn't even wake as the others readied themselves for travel. The old cabin had wooden forks, spoons, bowls, and a metal spatula. They stashed them in

293

their bags. They crafted snowshoes using pine branches and shoelaces from Gruber's boots. The design compliments of Kira. The whole while hoping for a miracle. That Baumbauer would stand up and be ready to march. But once the supplies were packed and the snowshoes fashioned, there was only one thing left to do. Hochzeit bent down and squeezed Baumbauer's ice-cold hand.

"I'm sorry … forgive me … I'm sorry," he whispered.

He went outside, thick tears strolling down his face. Günter and Reinhardt stood behind Baumbauer. The pistol in Reinhardt's hand shook. Günter put his hand on Reinhardt's gun hand and raised it. Baumbauer's breathing was a faint, raspy gurgle.

"We do it together," Günter said.

Reinhardt's breathing raced; his stomach churned like an ocean storm. The room was silent except for the faint sound of Baumbauer's gravelly breathing. A foul odor escaped his lips. There was some sort of nasty infection inside. The phlegm in his chest could be heard with each breath he took. Reinhardt made sure the barrel of his Walther PP was aimed at the back of Baumbauer's head. He squeezed his eyes shut, then pulled the trigger.

Spy Master

The Allies followed up the monumental victory at Stalingrad with taking control of Libya on 5 February and the bloody Guadalcanal on the 9th. Yet these victories were not what Stalin had demanded. The Soviets needed a second front. It was now June; the vicious Soviet winter had gone. In its place were vibrant green grass, blooming flowers of all colors, and an azure sky with clouds looking like swabs of cotton. But none of that bucolic beauty could lessen the bloodshed.

The Kremlin summoned Kira to Moscow. Two soldiers stood guard by a set of twin doors. Without a word, they opened it, and Kira stepped in. At a long table were high-ranking Soviet generals, chiefly General Georgy Zhukov—the defender of Moscow, Leningrad, and Stalingrad. Colonel Volkov was there, too, giving her an encouraging nod. There was an empty seat in the middle. Kira saluted. The men stayed silent. The doors opened, and they leapt to attention. Josef Stalin stepped inside; his mustache as thick as advertised. He nodded at the salutes and sat in the vacant middle seat.

Colonel Volkov addressed the room. "Comrade Second Lieutenant Kovalyova, you have been summoned here because of your mastery in sniping and your competency in espionage. The Motherland asks for your help."

"I live to serve the Soviet Union," Kira said.

Stalin inclined his head ever so slightly. Volkov sat. A young private turned on a projector, and those at the table turned to see an image projected on the wall. A balding man with rimless glasses stood. He was Lavrentiy Pavlovich Beria, head of the NKVD—The People's Commissariat for Internal Affairs. History also remembered him for his assistance in Stalin's great purges.

The projector cast a voyeur's photo of a man in his mid-fifties, unshaven, with hair that shot out in different directions like plucked cotton.

Beria spoke. "This is Randall Von Bluthund. A German physicist. Hitler still believes victory can be achieved on the ground, but there are many who believe Germany's only hope for victory is with the creation of a nuclear bomb. Von Bluthund is a member of what is called the *Uranverein*—Germany's atomic project. He conducts his research in Berlin."

Was this the man she would be tasked with assassinating? Assassinating a high-ranking Nazi in Paris had been extremely dangerous. If not for Josephine and Durand, Kira would not have made it out. But to assassinate a vitally important Nazi in the Lion's Den—the heart of the Nazi regime—seemed impossible. To leave the city alive would require divine intervention. But Kira had witnessed what a *Schadenfreude* with a gun could do. To fathom what they could do with a nuclear bomb was beyond the scope of horror.

Beria continued, "Randall Von Bluthund was born in 1891 in Salzburg, Austria. He studied Theoretical Physics at the University of Berlin. He pursued a graduate study in physics under Max Born. Upon completion, he moved to the United States in 1923. When the war started in '39, he was sent to Norway to oversee the production of heavy water. But our surveillance shows he was summoned back to Germany to help create the nuclear bomb. This cannot happen. Your mission: Operation Vinegar. Kill Randall Von Bluthund."

Colonel Volkov chimed in. "For perspective, if the Nazis hit Moscow with an atomic bomb, hundreds of thousands of people would die instantly. Tens of thousands more would die of acute radiation."

Beria placed a silver briefcase on the table and clicked it open. "To help with your mission."

He held up forged German identification papers. The left-hand side listed name, birthdate, place of birth, profession, and current address.

"You are Johanna Eisenhardt. Born 4 May 1916. You are a radio operator. Born in Kissing, Bavaria," Beria said.

Kira repeated the facts silently in her head a half-dozen times. Inside the briefcase was a small purse, currently empty. The contents that would go in it were in the pad foaming of the briefcase. Each item was labeled. Photographs of the fictional Johanna Eisenhardt's mother and father and a handful of brothers. A lipstick tube, a pack of cigarettes, a makeup mirror, blush, and duster. But these were not simply as they appeared. Not only would the lipstick coat her lips in a deep red shade, it could also shoot a single bullet from the base of the tube. The cigarette pack had a small camera inside. The blush brush was also a spring-activated knife. The last item was a hundred-page document. A detailed fictionalized biography of Johanna Eisenhardt. Compelling lies were in the details. Ninety-five percent of what was in the biography would never be used, but it was imperative she know it. At a hundred pages, it wasn't something Stalin, or the others, had time to sit and listen to being read.

The slide changed to a map of Northern Germany. Beria used a pointing stick and slapped it against an estuary.

"As for getting you into Germany ..." Beria began.

Whatever it was, Kira hoped it would go more smoothly than the flight with Yuri and Semyon. Beria stated that the area he had smacked was Am Stettiner Haff. Located in Northern Germany, it was separated from the Pomeranian Bay of the Baltic Sea by the islands Usedom and Wolin. The name of each island was accompanied by a slap from the stick.

"You shall parachute into this estuary and head inland to Ueckermünde." Another smack with the stick.

The projector operator handed a dictionary to Kira.

Beria continued, "This is no ordinary dictionary. These are covert words. There are only two copies. The one in your hand and the one on my desk. Set the words to memory and burn your copy before you depart."

Stalin put his cigarette out in the ashtray in front of him, its crystal etched with a Soviet star. A gesture that told Beria to wrap the meeting up. Kira knew not to ask questions, even if she had them. And had them, she did. Stalin rose, the others, too.

"The Soviet Union is grateful for all you have done to aid the war effort, Comrade Kovalyova. I expect this mission to be a success," Stalin said.

"I serve the Soviet Union!" Kira said.

Stalin headed to the door, placing his cap back on his head. He paused and turned back to Kira. "If by chance you see Hitler and the moment presents itself, tear out his throat."

"Yes, *Vozhd* Stalin!"

Colonel Volkov lingered behind and waited until the others had left to speak. Beria had a reputation with women. A powerful man with powerful urges. Volkov wouldn't leave him alone with Kira. Realizing he wouldn't get his coveted moment alone, Beria sighed and left.

"Are you comfortable with this mission?" Volkov asked.

"How will I get my rifle?" she asked.

"No rifle this time."

Kira had even more questions than for her mission to Paris. There had been nothing about how she returned home. And the pragmatist in her knew why. There wouldn't likely be a return home. This mission, even if successful, would end in her arrest or her death. The Mosin–Nagant was her safety blanket. She would have to kill Von Bluthund differently. Exactly how would have to present itself.

And had she heard the word 'parachute'?!

Kira had training the following morning, meeting with a soldier of the *Vozdushno-desantnye voyska SSSR* or VDV (Soviet Airborne Forces). Nikita Moshkovsky was in his late forties, with large droopy ears and a nose that looked like it had been broken a dozen times. He had been one of the Soviet Union's first paratroopers during the experiment on 2 August 1930. Later in his long, distinguished career, he was part of the Vyazma Operation of February/March 1942 that helped troops at the Kalmin Front and Western Front encircle the German Army Group Centre. He was a brazen individual, and fearlessness exuded off him like a musk. It made sense to Kira, since the man had made a career out of jumping out planes.

Moshkovsky strapped Kira into the parachute, pulling the straps so tight it felt like a vise. He grabbed her right hand and placed it on the draw cord. He explained that when she pulled the chute with her right hand, her left hand should rise across her face.

"Stops you from turning," he explained.

Right now, none of this was scary because she had her feet firmly planted on the ground. The real thing wouldn't be so mundanely calm.

"What height will I be jumping from?" Kira asked.

She had discovered she wasn't a fan of airplanes, a fear shared by many. But who wouldn't have a fear of jumping out of a plane thousands of feet up in the air?

"500 feet or below to avoid radar," Moshkovsky answered.

It was elation she felt first. 500 feet was better than 3,000 feet ... but was it? 500 feet gave little time to react and even less time to react to any problems that may occur. She didn't know how fast a human being fell from the sky. A hundred miles per hour seemed like a fair guess. Kira didn't like that math. In fact, she hated it.

"Is there a reserve parachute?" Kira asked.

Moshkovsky smirked and shook his head. "Just added weight."

Meaning, if the first parachute didn't deploy, there'd be no time for a second one, anyway. What a comforting thought. Moshkovsky had her pull the string and showed her how to escape the giant jellyfish-type parachute before it dragged her under water. He was dire with his warning about it, telling her he'd seen men drown by being wrapped up by their own parachutes. If the parachute clung to you, stay calm. Kicking and flailing would only further twist the chute. Instead, stay calm and grab handfuls of the chute until you find the opening. If the chute wrapped around her face, she was to use her knife.

At night, she studied the hundred-page backstory of Johanna Eisenhardt, discovering her mother was Evelyn and her father was Johan. She had a fear of caves thanks to a field trip that found her lost in one. Her favorite teacher, *Frau* Thielke, found her an hour later. She studied her dictionary of covert words. Studying until she read the same line over and over, as her brain couldn't retain the information because she was too tired. At midnight, she woke in her chair, her neck and back aching. She crawled into bed and even in her somnolence she appreciated having a warm bed to crawl into.

The following day, she was trained on how to operate a switchboard by a robust woman named Mila. The woman had been at Stalingrad, fearlessly keeping communications up. Other women had served as paramedics, medical assistants, and doctors. General Vasily Ivanovich Chuikov had praised the courage of women like Mila. She trained Kira as if her life would depend on it—as she should. Communication between Stalingrad and Moscow was vital. Stalingrad had demanded, and Moscow supplied. Food, clothing, men, armaments, and ammo. Kira appreciated the importance of people like Mila—the unsung heroes of war. She studied Mila's movements, treating it the same way she had sniping. The afternoon saw another lesson with Moshkovsky. This lesson was hands on. A plane took them up. She was linked with him; he would pull the cord. Her insides were a volcano. She wanted to scream out that she couldn't do it. Find someone else for the mission. Her hands shook; her body felt as though her soul had gotten a head start to heaven.

"Ready?" Moshkovsky asked.

There was no way in hell Kira could make the audible sound of 'yes.' She couldn't even get her head to nod. The swallowing back of her vomit would have to suffice. The plane door opened. The wind was louder than she'd ever heard it. It whipped her face, sucked her breath away as if she sucked on a vacuum hose. Moshkovsky was behind her. He shuffled forward, forcing her closer and closer to the edge. Instinctively, she tried to dig her nails into the side of the plane to stop herself from falling out, but before she could reach it, Moshkovsky shoved her out. Her body traveled too fast for her soul to keep up. Her stomach bridged the distance between them. She couldn't breathe, only able to keep her eyes open because of the goggles she wore. Moshkovsky pulled the cord, and they were thrusted upward so hard and fast, Kira grunted. The descent was best described as a controlled crash. Kira bent her legs to cushion the landing.

She skipped supper, still waiting for her stomach to land. It was somewhere in those Sirius-stratus clouds. At night, an agent from the NKVB showed her how to operate her arsenal of spy equipment. After that, she crammed an hour's worth of studying in. During Stalingrad, Kira and thousands of others had gone as many as four days without sleep. War was physically exhausting and mentally challenging. But the week of learning how to parachute, how to operate a switchboard, using her spy equipment, and learning a fictional backstory and coded language was a different level of exhaustion. A mental complexity she hadn't experienced since sniper school. She slept in late. Her flight was to leave at ten that night. She spent the day studying, then met with Colonel Volkov for dinner inside the Kremlin. There was a small table just for them, but large enough that it wasn't intimate.

"I know how important it is for you to know that men like Wolff and Von Bluthund are evil. *Schadenfreudes*," Volkov said.

He handed a file to Kira. Inside it were typed reports, photographs, and newspaper clippings. Colonel Volkov took a long drag from his cigarette before speaking.

"When the Nazis rose to power in 1933, many Jews had the foresight to evacuate Germany. They sold their businesses, and Germans—including Von Bluthund— bought them for next to nothing. He made hundreds of thousands from their plight. In America, he was accused of raping a student at the University of Chicago. His anti-Semitic rhetoric was taken straight from the pages of *Mein Kampf*." He took another drag, breathing the smoke out through his nostrils. "If Von Bluthund helps create an atomic bomb, it won't just be the Jews the Nazis will use it against. There is no place for Soviets in a German-ruled world. They'll bomb Moscow, Leningrad, Stalingrad, and every metropolis in between."

They ate their bland supper of soup. Surely Volkov could have arranged for something better, but he was never one to eat or drink better than his men. Kira respected him for that.

"There is something else asked of you," Volkov said.

Kira waited for him to continue.

"If you find any documents that could help the Soviet Union's development of a nuclear weapon, you are to photograph them and bring them back."

"Yes, Comrade Colonel," Kira said.

"And above all, you are to return. Understood?"

Kira nodded, though she couldn't tell if it was something he truly felt was attainable.

After supper, a car dropped Kira off. She gathered her supplies. Nerves wreaked havoc. No suitcase this time. She'd have to buy outfits. She changed into her jumpsuit, flipped through her covert dictionary once more, then tossed it into her garbage can and lit it on fire. Impossible not to think how easy it'd been to start a fire and how unimportant it was here. But in the forest, survival had depended on getting one started and keeping it lit. She stopped her train of thought, knowing who those tracks would lead to. Her clothes were kept in a waterproof bag tied around her waist. A Soviet AR-NAT1, a jeep-like vehicle, waited outside, and took her to an airfield. It was a breezy spring night; mosquitos buzzed around, looking for flesh to feast on. A pilot greeted her. He smiled like he was chewing on gum. Alexi Vaschenko.

"Smooth sailing to Germany," he said.

She could only hope and hope she certainly did. The sky was calm, but Kira knew the *Luftwaffe* brought their own storms. Even if the flight went smoothly, she still had to jump out of the plane. Vaschenko's shorter and stockier co-pilot, Bohdan Skilar, checked off items on a clipboard.

"So, you'll be parachuting out?" Vaschenko asked, impressed.

That was the plan if she could get her body to comply. The first time she climbed a tree, she went all the way to the top, some forty feet. She had stayed up there, clutched to the trunk until her mother had come. Self-preservation had glued her to that tree, and she feared a similar situation may happen on the plane. Was it better to know she had to jump? Jumping out of the plane over England had been a split-second decision. It'd been like being oblivious that there was a bomb under the table, then *bang!* But this plane ride would be like knowing for hours there was a bomb under the table, and she was powerless to do anything because she was tied to the chair.

Pilot, co-pilot, and passenger all seated, Vaschenko and Skilar prepared for takeoff. At the thrumming of the engines, Kira disappeared into the memory of her flight with Reinhardt. Those nerves had been different. Excitement. The feel of his muscular chest, the smell of his cologne, and the vividness of those blue eyes even in twilight. Should she have tried harder to persuade him to stay? She never thought about where he was or if he was still alive. There were too many questions. She preferred to be blissfully ignorant. *Reinhardt is alive.* But she could barely finish that thought before doubt crept in. She had shown him as much as she could to help him survive.

They flew north toward Finland and then over the Baltic Sea. All around her were gradients of black, pinpricked with starlight. All the while, flying at below 500 feet to avoid radar detection. Vaschenko and Skilar relied on their instrumentation. Kira couldn't imagine sniping and not being able to see. Relying only on distance, wind direction, and target angle. It was impossible to not feel as if at any moment they would crash into the water. Then came those three words she had dreaded since she had found out how she would arrive in Germany.

"Prepare for jump."

Kira swallowed the rock in her throat, feeling it sink into her stomach with a plunk. She strapped herself into the parachute, then stretched and did arm circles because of a sudden fear she'd cramp if she didn't. Two dark masses loomed through the cockpit glass: the islands of Usedom and Wolin. Beyond them, the lagoon she had to land in. A max depth of twenty-eight feet. She'd be traveling a hundred miles per hour. Only enough distance to reach the bottom of ... almost 19,000 lagoons ... Math can be so damn cruel. Kira opened the door. A cacophony of whistling wind and grumbling engines deafened her. The light on the door would flash green when it was time to jump. She stared at the light; her breathing rushed. The light lit, casting the plane in its green hue.

Kira's hands dug into the door frame—a defense mechanism. She overrode it and leapt from the plane to the black abyss below. Plummeting. Spiraling. Unable to breathe, the wind feeling like her face had been covered in plastic wrap. She reached for the cord with her right hand; her left hand crossed her face. The parachute billowed out, thrusting her up in the air, slowing her speed enough that her legs didn't break on impact. She speared into the water. Five feet. Ten. Fifteen feet below. Her parachute floated atop the water but started to fill. Kira swam for the surface as the giant jellyfish-like parachute descended toward her. It clung to her mouth and nose, contouring around her shoulders and torso. Its weight increased exponentially, dragging Kira to the bottom like a cast anchor.

Stolen Meal

There'd been little talking as they trekked onward. That bullet still resounded in Reinhardt's ears. Had he done the right thing? Was there a right or wrong thing when it came to survival? He was certain he'd ponder that question for the rest of his life.

The snowshoes had worked well, but after hours of use, they broke apart. As good a sign as any to stop for the day. A rock ledge provided a great natural windbreak. Reinhardt and Günter used it and sandwiched a long branch between the stone and the tree across from it. They piled sticks vertically and interlaced pine branches in between. It was crude, but quick. Reinhardt planned to be here for mere hours. Hochzeit sat, his gaze distant. His thoughts most likely were on Baumbauer, and Reinhardt let him grieve. Günter worked at starting a fire. Reinhardt packed their canteens with snow and pine needles. After the fire ignited and the snow melted, they drank. The bed of pine insulated them from the frozen ground they'd shoveled away. Reinhardt was cognizant of calories. Calories consumed. Calories burned. He never stood when he could sit, never sat when he could lie down. And he wasted no time now, trying to fall asleep. Except *trying* was too active. He simply lay there, letting his eyes drift deeply into the recesses of sleep.

He and Günter woke on a handful of occasions, each time because the fire was a few embers away from being extinguished. Hochzeit didn't wake on his own. He stayed asleep while Reinhardt and Günter made new snowshoes. They were a necessity. They'd doubled the distance covered because of them. Reinhardt let Hochzeit sleep until his patience ran out. The weather was calm, the sun high. It wouldn't get any better. And he'd found out first-hand how quickly a blizzard could set in. The thought of not covering a single mile was too awful to consider.

"We're leaving," Reinhardt told Günter.

Günter woke Hochzeit. But if Günter was an alarm, Hochzeit simply hit snooze. He rolled over away from them. Reinhardt grabbed him and sat him up. Hochzeit cursed at him, colorfully asking what his issue was.

"We're in Russia. That's my issue," Reinhardt said.

"You'll be in Russia tonight, Russia tomorrow, and Russia the day after tomorrow, and Russia the day after that," Hochzeit said.

"You want to stay, your choice. I'm leaving."

"Going to shoot me?"

Günter spoke before Reinhardt had to. His hat covered his ears, so their reddening was concealed, but his cheeks flushed with heat. "Bullshit thing to say, Hochzeit! You could have stayed with him! You left because you wanted to live. We all made the decision!"

Tension, hostility, friction were all roadblocks to Reinhardt's goal of getting home. They needed each other to survive. In peace times, they'd get in a fist fight and get a beer afterward or they'd hold this grudge for months. They didn't have months, and they sure as hell didn't have beer. So, instead, Reinhardt made a simple gesture to show Hochzeit no hard feelings would leave the shelter. He offered his hand and helped him to his feet.

Snowshoes on their feet and walking sticks in hand, they set off. Heading further south, envisioning they followed the mighty Volga. Russia was a cruelly giant country, the Soviet Union even larger. The best they could do was conquer it step by step.

They came to an overturned tree covered in moss and fungus. Reinhardt examined the mushrooms; Hochzeit and Günter reached for them.

"Wait," Reinhardt said.

The mushrooms had white caps. Many edible mushrooms looked like this, but Kira had warned him about these death-cap mushrooms. He told Günter and Hochzeit he thought they were poisonous.

"How poisonous? Like hallucinations?" Hochzeit asked.

"No, like kill you poisonous," Reinhardt said.

Hochzeit had that 'you-got-to-be-shitting-me' look on his face again. Mouth salivating, body trembling, food in hand. Such a simple last step: raise hand to mouth. But he sighed and tossed them far away, wiping any residue on his fingers onto his pants.

"Is there anything in this god-awful fucking country that doesn't want to kill us?" Hochzeit asked.

"Nope. Every last thing wants us dead," Günter said.

"If those had been strawberries, I'd have eaten them," Hochzeit said.

They continued on, finding nothing on their trek that caught their eye as far as easily accessible food went. Once they stopped for the day, they could search. They came to a gap in the trees. Nothing but snow in front except for a field of barren trees that looked as though red Christmas bulbs hung from them. Why wouldn't whoever lived here celebrate Christmas all year round? It was almost March and winter showed no signs of ending. But as they got closer, they weren't Christmas bulbs. They were crab apples.

"Is anyone else seeing apples?" Günter asked.

Reinhardt had thought he was seeing a mirage. What were the odds of all three of them seeing the same illusion? This was real. Frost covered the pruning crab apples. Kira had told him about these, too, saying winter was the best time to pick them.

"If you're about to say these are poisonous, keep it to yourself. I don't care," Hochzeit said.

"No, I was going to say dig in," Reinhardt said.

They bit into the fruit, feeling its sugary syrup light up their taste buds like an American sky on the Fourth of July. The crunch of the apple was one of the greatest sounds in the world. There were six trees with over fifty apples. Each one delicious. Reinhardt tossed the core into his canteen, letting his water take on the faint taste of apple juice. They ate six apples each, then plucked every apple from the trees. They needed to ration, but my God, what a find! Not only impacting them physically, but psychologically, too. They could smile, laugh, enjoy the sun above them. They had food in their stomachs, and they had food for later.

Their path led them back into the woods. Reinhardt gauged they had about an hour of daylight left, so they stopped. Hochzeit worked on a fire, Günter on the shelter, and Reinhardt scoured for food. He secured a few acorns, enough for each of them to have four. He ventured deeper to find cattails growing by a creek. He cut at them with Gruber's knife. He thought back to what Kira had told him. He had tried so hard not to get lost in her green eyes. She'd had to repeat much, and even in his memory, her eyes still distracted him. They tasted like potatoes. That's what she'd said. Clearly, Kira had never eaten a potato.

The creek didn't have any fish that he could see, and it was getting dark. He didn't want to waste any more time or energy, so he returned to the camp. Günter had shoveled out the base of an evergreen and laid down pine. The snow wall around them was three feet high and an excellent wind shield. The fire was small and wouldn't last long. Hochzeit had had a hell of a time finding anything dry enough to burn. They cooked the cattails and roasted the acorns, and each ate a crab apple. After, they rested against the trunk of the evergreen. The wind whipped and whistled overhead. With no fire, it was the coldest they'd been in days. After this winter, summer could last years. Decades. Reinhardt never wanted to be cold again.

"Well, that night sucked," Hochzeit said, as they prepared for a new day.

The snowshoes only lasted a day at a time, so they'd all gotten adept at making them. Günter demanded he be recognized by the Reich as not only an *Experten Jagdflieger* but also a stellar shoemaker. Hochzeit took the lead hiking, but also with the conversation as well.

"Imagine in a few months when we are out of this frozen shit pile. Back home in Germany. It's summer. The sun is so hot you can cook on the sidewalks. Girls in swimsuits, bodies glistening with sweat. Bratwurst sizzles on a grill, and you've got a nice mug of dark beer with a frothy head ..." he finished with a sigh.

"That's the most beautiful poetry I have ever heard," Günter said. "But instead, the sun barely makes it to us. The icy, vicious winds chase the sunlight away. There are no women for hundreds of miles. Maybe even thousands. And we have a few pinecones and crab apples."

"Don't forget pine needles," Reinhardt said.

"How dare I forget!"

The snow was no longer hard but melting into slush. The crab apples were gone; only their cores remained stuffed inside their canteens for added flavor. But with the snow melting, the forest floor's treasures would reveal themselves. Hochzeit stopped and pointed at a mass ahead. The massive six-foot-wide rack was instantly recognizable as a moose. The body had been feasted on to where only its bloody ribs and antlers were visible. All three scouted and scanned. The moose was a giant. A bear or a pack of wolves must have taken it down. They drew their weapons and advanced on the moose. There was no foul smell emitting from it, and the meat didn't look green or questionable. Hochzeit carved at the remaining flesh. The discarded parts of the organs lay in a pile. Too cold for flies to feast on them. He cut and carved strips, wrapping them in his pack. Reinhardt and Günter kept an eye out, the whole while telling Hochzeit to hurry. The air had an unsettlingly quiet eeriness to it. And that moose had been gigantic. Whatever had killed it was a caliber predator that far exceeded their own prowess.

A loud huffing noise came from the top of the hill. A behemoth brown bear raised its nose, sniffing the now human-tainted air. It locked eyes with Reinhardt, then saw Hochzeit stealing its meal. The bear protruded its mouth, clacked its teeth, and let out a bone-quivering roar. And then, with speed unfair for something so heavy to have, the behemoth bear stormed down the hill right at them.

Emma Kuhn

Her legs thrashed. Her hands tried to tear the fabric free. But even when she separated it, there was only water. No air to be had. The parachute clung back to her face. Kira reached for her knife and stabbed the canvas, dragging the blade as far as she could reach. The parachute floated past her to the sandy bottom of the lagoon. Her chest felt like it would explode. Her head throbbed. At Stalingrad, she had been hungry and thirsty, but the human body was remarkably adaptive. Human beings could go days without food and water. But it could only go a few measly minutes without air. And when in a panic, even less. Kira kicked and reached for the surface. She broke through; her gasp of breath sounded like a crashing tide. She gathered her breath and waited for her coughing to subside. There were no lights ashore, and had it not been for the tide pushing to shore, she wouldn't have been able to tell in which direction to swim. She stayed in the shallows, scouting like a crocodile would. She crouched ashore and hid behind an old wooden fishing shack. Scanning around to make sure she was alone, she unclasped the waterproof bag from her waist and then stripped out of her jumpsuit. After burying it in the sand, she dried her hair with a small towel and stepped into her Johanna Eisenhardt costume—a lovely spring dress that was a wash of mandarin orange and pink. Her hair and makeup would have to be done later. Once on the street, Kira used the towel to swat the sand off her feet, and then slipped into cumbersome white heels.

She was in Germany. Reinhardt's home. She had expected to see Nazi flags, swastikas, and anti-Semite propaganda. But as she walked by the closed shops, businesses, and taverns, she didn't see any. Only German crests of proud families. Kira found an open bathroom near the bus station and locked the door. In front of the mirror, she applied makeup, remembering what Veronika had shown her. It'd been months since she had applied any. Subtlety was key. German women would have little makeup available to them.

It'd be hours before the first bus, so Kira sat in the stall and rested her head against the wall. Again, the marvel of the human body and its ability to sleep anywhere. Kira only woke hours later because of the sound of relentless knocking. She unlocked the door and almost apologized in Russian. The waiting woman's nose was raised with an arrogant air, so that she had to always look down at who she was speaking to. Most likely, some *Schadenfreude*'s wife. Kira elected not to apologize at all, stepped past her, and walked across the street to the bus station bench. The sun was bright, a brilliant warm day already under way at such an early hour.

When the bus stopped, Kira and the handful of strangers waited to get on. Women in their twenties and thirties stepped off, makeup smeared by day-old tears. They returned from seeing their husbands or boyfriends before their deployment, visiting them in the hospitals, or collecting their remains. Kira stepped onto the bus and sat in the middle on the left side. The driver was an older man with a gray walrus mustache. A mother with two children claimed seats behind the driver, an elderly couple took the first seats available, and two men younger than twenty claimed seats all the way at the back. Kira had wanted to stay awake and view Germany through her window. But if she had fallen asleep on a hard, porcelain toilet, she would certainly fall asleep on a padded bus seat. A large bump made it sound like the wheels had fallen off the bus and woke her. She was glad it did, for up ahead was the beautiful Brandenburg Gate, inspired by Ancient Greece's Acropolis with the *Quadriga*—a symbol of victory. Napoleon famously had it sent to Paris. The Brandenburg Gate represented hundreds of years of history. But the five red Nazi flags had only been there less than ten years, albeit ten years too long.

The bus passed through and stopped at a bus stop. The doors opened, the hydraulics sighed, and a leather-clad *Rottenführer* stepped onto the bus. He was young, and Kira's first and only thought about him was that he was fanatical. Fanatical eyes, fanatical gaze, and fanatical purpose. He ordered everyone to have their identification papers ready. He showed no favor to the elderly couple. To him, they were remnants of an era that never raised Germany to the glory it deserved. The mother and two children were next. His eyes studied the mother's body, liking how well it had responded to childbearing. Kira was next. She held out the ID of Johanna Eisenhardt. The *Rottenführer* didn't try to pass his gaze upon her breasts as an inconspicuous glance. Kira rehearsed the information in her head. Birthday? 4 May 1916. Hometown? Kissing, Bavaria. The *Rottenführer* nodded and slapped her ID against her breasts—a cheap, perverted way to cop a feel.

"Bavaria, huh? I am from Bavaria," he said.

"What city?"

"Würzburg."

A city with a population of over a hundred thousand. She could add to her lie.

"I have family that lives there," Kira said.

"Lots of Jews lived there."

"Not anymore."

The *Rottenführer* smirked. "No, not anymore."

Kira forced a smile and continued on her way. She couldn't admit this to anyone except for Reinhardt, but she was in awe of the city. It was ravishing. The architecture, the people. All of it. Directly in front of the Brandenburg Gate was the Hotel Adlon Kempinski. Though the Nazis preferred the Hotel Kaiserhof, which was mere blocks south across the Propaganda Ministry and Reich Chancellery, the Hotel Adlon Kempinski was still a social center and where Kira would be staying. She checked into room 214, then took her *Reichsmarks* and set off to expand Johanna Eisenhardt's costume. She bought a pair of black Oxford pumps and black heels, and two dresses—a black Manhattan dress and a blue dress with floral designs—should any social situations arise. The Third Reich liked their parties. She dropped the clothing off at her hotel room, then found a restaurant for a late lunch. Rationing had hit the capital city, and Kira had a baked potato with a small spoonful of sour cream and some grated cheese for some added panache. It was a far cry from an apple strudel.

Back in her room, she paged through her ration book. It contained color-coded stamps for sugar, meat, fruit and nuts, eggs, dairy products, cooking oils, breads, grains, margarine, jams, and jelly. Every possible thing a person could eat had been rationed. Still, rationed food was better than no food. The entrapped people at Leningrad would have given anything to eat the potato she had just eaten.

In the afternoon, she smoked a cigarette across the Reich Chancellery. Kira hated the Nazis, but she couldn't deny they had an impeccable eye for opulence. The Reich Chancellery was a marvel. The Third Reich was the third successor to the First Reich—the Holy Roman Empire—and the Second Reich—the German Empire (1871–1918). But it had crafted architecture that trumped both. Albert Speer's crews had worked round the clock to complete the Chancellery. At the entrance was an eagle with its wings spread above four columns. Two soldiers stood guard. To her left, rows upon rows of Nazi flags in the courtyard fluttered in the summer breeze. Military police and soldiers surrounded the Chancellery. To attack here would be like trying to kill Hades in the Underworld. But Kira could think of only one person. Somewhere in this building was the world's most notorious man: Adolf Hitler. Though he had committed atrocities, Hitler was merely a failed artist. Not a brilliant physicist capable of creating a weapon that could kill hundreds of thousands in seconds. Von Bluthund was the objective. The mission.

Even at dusk, the temperature was still warm. What little breeze there was only brought a wave of humidity. Kira walked the city enjoying every step, but knew she had to get back to her room before her curfew. She waited to cross a street when a soft voice said, "Excuse me." Kira turned to see if anyone else was around that the comment may have been directed at. There wasn't. The girl who'd spoken appeared nervous, a few years younger than Kira. And, without a doubt, the most gorgeous woman Kira had ever seen. Blonde hair styled in waves to her shoulders, cornflower blue eyes, and kissable red lips. The smell of fresh flowers softly wafted off her. What the hell did this woman have to be uncertain of? She was the Aryan dream.

"Sorry, I'm new to the city," the woman said. "I'm looking for the Hotel Adlon Kempinski."

"I'm going there. You can follow me," Kira said.

The woman's eyes crinkled, relieved. "Thank you so much. I'm Emma Kuhn."

"Johanna Eisenhardt."

Emma commented on Kira's beauty and her wardrobe. Kira reciprocated it, then offered to take one of Emma's bags.

"What brings you to Berlin?" Kira asked.

Emma bit her lip nervously. Whatever she was going to say wouldn't be the standard 'visiting family and friends' or 'vacationing.'

"My brother Torben was at Stalingrad. I have not heard what has happened to him. I came here hoping somebody can give me answers. Fruitless, I know. But better than doing nothing, right?"

Kira offered a smile in return, but inside she could only think of the hundreds of thousands of frozen bodies lining the streets, and the frail and frozen faces of some 90,000 Germans who had been taken prisoner.

"There's a celebration at the Chancellery on Saturday. I'm hoping to get work there and get answers about my brother. Is that why you have come? For the work?" Emma asked.

The best lie was the one given to you. Why search for one?

"Yes, it is," Kira said.

Even Emma's gait exuded sex appeal. It wouldn't take much for Emma to find a powerful, lustful Nazi that would find the exact coordinates of Torben Kuhn in hopes of sleeping with her. Her brother had been at Stalingrad. Had he been one of the men Kira had killed? One of the dead men littering the streets? Or had he made it to the forest? Was he taken prisoner?

Kira waited at the front desk as Emma checked in. Emma's room was only seven doors down from her own.

"Say, I'm not overly tired," Emma commented. "Care to have a drink?"

Kira wasn't sure why she said yes. Maybe because Emma was nice and too good-looking for her own good in a city of monsters. There was a resemblance to Nousha, and the thought of Emma being raped made Kira protective. But Emma had that unsure look in her eye, a longing that dimmed when she talked. Kira could pretend that accepting the offer was research. After all, Emma knew of a big Nazi party she hadn't. But most of all, she felt inclined to protect her.

The hotel room was quaint, the bed neatly made, with a spectacular view of the Brandenburg Gate outside the window. Emma poured them a glass of Riesling. Emma was a naturally anxious person, but after a couple of glasses, she lowered her defenses. Her brother Torben had been in the doomed Sixth Army. There were only three possibilities: he was dead; he was a prisoner of war; or he was lost in the Russian wilderness. With the battle having been over for four months, there hadn't been any information about bands of resistance. Mother Nature would have taken care of any Germans the Soviets had not. Kira kept that information to herself. Hope was the most fragile thing in the world. And in the current state of the world, the rarest commodity. Emma had it. That was to be nurtured, not destroyed. Yet that didn't mean Kira was envious of Emma's hope. She knew her father and sisters were dead. That knowledge had allowed her to grieve. Emma's grief would have to be postponed. For how long remained to be seen. Perhaps she'd never get the closure she sought. Kira had seen piles upon piles upon piles of dead Germans tossed into mass graves or burned. The Soviets didn't take the time to collect dog tags or collect records of who they were. They wouldn't even be able to offer that level of closure to their own people.

Emma described her life and asked Kira about hers, listening to her answers. Torben was her only sibling, and they were best friends. She had a love of acting and envisioned herself the next Ingrid Bergman. Another truth Kira had thought she had known shattered. Like Reinhardt, Emma wasn't a *Schadenfreude*. Kira had expected every German she encountered to be fanatical, marching up and down the streets in Hitler salutes. Those people certainly existed, and in droves, but there were also people like Emma who were simply trying to find answers and bring their loved ones home. By the time Kira left Emma's room, they had had enough wine that they were giggly. But the giggling ended for Kira once she climbed into bed. A nagging worry had tightened in her chest ever since Emma mentioned her brother.

What if she had killed him? For the first time, she tried to recall every man she had killed. But there were too many. She only remembered Barys Lukashevich, the *Hauptsturmführer* she had let run, and the Hoffman brothers. But as always, the last face she thought of before drifting off to sleep was Reinhardt. Being in Berlin, she felt closer to him than she had since he had left that blustery winter morning. Yet never so far away.

The Bear

The roar raised every hair on Reinhardt's body. He knew of spiders and frogs whose venom could paralyze their prey. The bear's roar had the same effect. Reinhardt was rooted in place, mouth drooping, eyes bulging. Non-reaction is a psychological response. We expect things to be normal. Abnormal events like a territorial bear charging at you couldn't be real. The universe would right itself. We just have to stay put. *This can't be happening.* But those who survived combat had learned that that universal truth wasn't a truth at all. Horrible things happened. And in war, they happened every minute of every day.

The bear could only be described as a fur-covered tank. It knocked Hochzeit to the ground, raising its paw and those knife-like claws, ready to slash open Hochzeit's back and rip out his organs. Reinhardt raised his Walther and fired into the bear's side. The first two shots did nothing but annoy it. It turned its attention to Reinhardt. It defeated the distance between them in mere seconds. Reinhardt fled, weaving between trees. The bear followed, snapping off thick branches like they were twigs. Günter fired, but his three shots only hit bark. Hochzeit struggled to his feet, his arm bleeding from where the bear's massive paw had clubbed him. He could only hold and raise his submachine gun with his left hand. The unnatural hold and the gun's power caused the bullets to fire errantly high. The bear gave up chasing Reinhardt and went back to bleeding, injured Hochzeit. It rose onto its hind legs, stretching to over eight feet, snarling, hot saliva dripping from its fangs. Reinhardt tackled Hochzeit out of the way. Günter fired, striking the bear in its exposed stomach. Reinhardt crawled to the SMG and unloaded every round into the bear's exposed belly. It collapsed to the ground with a death moan. Reinhardt struggled to catch his breath. The adrenaline rush was a level he'd never experienced, even with all his sorties. They'd taken on a bear. A bear!

Günter helped him to his feet. Hochzeit clutched his arm, grinding his teeth because of the pain. He had five slashes of varying depth that covered shoulder to elbow. If the bear had struck cleanly, it would have mauled his arm completely off.

"We have to seal this up," Günter said.

Yes, they did. They needed to clean it, sew it shut, and wrap it in gauze. The only problem was they had nothing to do that with. Reinhardt drizzled water onto the wound. Günter reached into his pack and took out Gruber's shirt. He cut a strip and tied it around Hochzeit's wound. He fashioned a sling. It would do until they found a way to properly seal it. Hochzeit sat against a tree, taking deep breaths. Günter and Reinhardt carved into the animal. A bounty of fatty meat, thick fur, and sharp claws. It took hours and considerable effort, but it was worth every evaporated minute and expended calorie. The bear was well over 800 pounds and there was no way they could take as much food as they wanted. They'd camp here for the night, eat their fill of bear, wake, eat as much as they could, then continue south. A somewhat cruel predicament to be in. Bear and moose meat in abundance. Too much food. It was so cruelly ironic that they couldn't help but laugh.

"What type of medal do I get for being injured by a Russian bear?" Hochzeit asked.

"Oh, the Knight's Cross with Oak Leaves and Swords. Without question," Günter said.

Reinhardt held a spatula that Günter had taken from the cabin into the flame. When the spatula glowed orange, he rose and grabbed the nub of a thick branch. He handed it to Hochzeit.

"You want me to throw it?" Hochzeit's joke didn't land with either Reinhardt or Günter. "What's going on?"

"We have to seal the wound," Reinhardt said.

There it was—that 'you-got-to-be-shitting-me' look. Reinhardt ordered Hochzeit to bite down on the stick. Günter removed the blood-soaked rag and then entwined his hand with Hochzeit's. Reinhardt grabbed the spatula. It looked otherworldly in the dusk. Hochzeit's eyes widened to the size of ping-pong balls. He tried resisting, but Günter grabbed his hands and told him to hold still. It would be over quickly. If they didn't do it, he could bleed out. Hochzeit bit down on the stick, his teeth indenting the wood. The spatula sealed skin and sizzled. The stick stifled his screams. His eyes rolled back, and Hochzeit passed out.

They let Hochzeit sleep late, knowing he needed the rest. Günter used the last of their shoelaces to fashion necklaces, with the bear's claws dangling from it. They'd left the bear hide sprawled out, fur side down, and scrubbed away all the bits of skin and membrane. Neither knew how to tan a hide, but this was good enough. Now, they had a big fur blanket to wrap themselves in. Once Hochzeit woke, they ate more bear and moose, drank a canteen's worth of water, and set off.

Hochzeit's arm throbbed, but the cauterization had done the trick. He had a hell of a scar to talk about at dinner parties. They pressed through the woods and came to a large clearing. The sunlight sparkled against the snow like gems. Reinhardt's walking stick hit bottom. But it felt different. Not like the frozen ground they'd traveled on for miles. This was ice. He was confident of each step before he took it. The sun beat down a little too powerfully for his comfort, though. Surviving had been overcoming one obstacle after another. They had wanted sun. Now, walking on temperamental ice, they didn't want any. They had no food then too much food. Mother Nature was amused at flipping the script. Much to their delight, the ice held.

An icy chill swept through them. Wind speed soared, shoving them backward. Another blizzard was on the precipice. The Russian winter had one last storm to unleash. This one came without warning, or at least none Reinhardt could spot. Kira would have.

Snow fell so fast and thick, they couldn't see. There was no chance of a fire. No ability to craft a decent shelter. They stopped in the woods. The shelter they had concocted nights before by digging around the trunk of a giant evergreen wouldn't work. They'd be covered in a foot of snow by morning. With his good hand, Hochzeit used their spade to clear a space. The wind was so loud they had to scream to be heard. Günter and Reinhardt snapped branches and smacked them against the tree trunks to get the snow off. A veil of white clouds blocked the sun. There would be no warm embrace from it. They struggled to complete the shelter. Fingers and toes numb, cheeks and noses red. It wasn't their finest shelter, and with no fire, it wasn't the warmest. It was strong, though. Reinhardt had recalled how Kira had woven and linked branches for added durability. They unraveled the bear hide and wrapped it over themselves. Breathing into their hands between munching on strips of bear meat.

"Nothing else to do but sleep," Reinhardt said.

Each man tried to steady their shivering. Reinhardt tried to disappear into the memory of how the sun felt in July. Hot and relentless. But it didn't work. He was only aware of how brutally cold it was in the here and now. There was no escaping the deafening sound of the wind, either. Loud and powerful enough to make three grown men quiver with fear. Snow weighed heavily on the branches above them. The tree groaned under the weight. Sagging lower and lower until *snap!* A bough stretching twelve feet sped like a meteor to the shelter beneath it.

The Wolf Den

The broken bough sped to the ground, ripping away pine leaves and branches. The shelter imploded in pine needles and branches. The crashing branch barely missed them. What the hell had happened? Artillery? Mortar fire? Reinhardt brushed the pine needles off and asked the others if they were okay. Hochzeit looked at the size of the branch that had torpedoed through their shelter. Had it hit any of them, it would have obliterated bone. A hit to the head would have killed them. He wore that 'you-got-to-be-shitting-me' look. Literally everything in Russia was trying to kill them.

Though it would be a couple of hours until the sun rose, they couldn't go back to sleep like this. There was the fear that at any moment, another branch could snap and speed toward them like a wooden stake. But mostly, it was the snow falling through the opening. They had to fix it, or they wouldn't make the night. Günter examined the broken shelter and then threw a broken branch to the ground.

"It'll take all night to fix this!" he yelled over the howling wind.

"We don't have all night! We'll be dead in twenty minutes!" Hochzeit shouted.

Reinhardt squeezed his eyes shut. The desire to give up was overwhelming. Just disappear back into that supply closet in the Théatre du Châtelet with Kira. Let that memory take hold and let the Russian winter finish him off. He was nearly there. Sound and images came to him. The guests laughing during intermission, clinking glasses, the way the Christmas bulbs sparkled. The way Kira looked. Her eyes, that impossible blend of fierceness and vulnerability. The way that dress hugged her curves. The feeling of her fingertips on his chest. But the sound of his name broke that merciful reprieve.

"Reinhardt!" Günter yelled. Reinhardt looked at him. "I said, what do we do?"

Reinhardt had no answer. His hands, feet, and face had lost feeling. His thighs were so cold they burned. It even hurt to breathe. Embracing death was too easy. He had to fight. They had to move because if they sat, the way Reinhardt felt, aching and freezing, he'd never get back on his feet.

"We must move! Find something to block the wind!" Reinhardt shouted.

Reinhardt had them stand in a single-file line, each man clutching the back of the man ahead of him. It was dark and the swirling snow made it hard to see. It'd be too easy for someone to get separated. Hochzeit was the lucky one in the middle. Reinhardt led, taking frozen pellets of ice and snow to his face. Hypothermia would set in soon. He couldn't hear himself cough, but he could feel how deep it was. He spit out phlegm. Each step was harder than the last. His legs felt like two cinder blocks. A massive gust of wind knocked him to the ground. Reinhardt was too weak to stand back up. Hochzeit and Günter lifted him up. The only thing that wasn't frozen was time. It ticked away with cruel indifference.

Reinhardt struggled forward. His eyes had adjusted to the dark enough that he could see they had come to a precipice. It was a frozen waterfall of no more than ten feet. Reinhardt led them down and behind the frozen waterfall to a small ledge just wide enough that they could sit on it. The volume of the howling wind lessened; the impact of the freezing winds diminished, too. The three of them huddled together, wrapped tightly in the bear-fur blanket. They wouldn't be able to sleep; they could only hope they could wait out the storm. Reinhardt focused on his breathing. Anything that wasn't numb throbbed. If he were to die this night, it'd be a hell of a way to die. He'd rather have died in combat. The pain was so extreme that during his diminished thinking, he thought he was on fire. For the next three hours, they stayed huddled together, squeezing each other's hands to make sure they were still alive.

When the sun rose, drops of water dripped from the frozen waterfall. It took a few minutes for them to comprehend they had survived. They had made it. Reinhardt couldn't stop tears from streaming. And when he glanced at Günter and Hochzeit, they were crying, too. They hadn't said it, but none of them had expected to live. Mother Nature had reminded them that it could destroy the entire human race if it wanted to.

They ate strips of bear and drank a canteen's worth of water before setting out after that orange horizon. They pressed further south, coming to a creek with cattails taller than them. They cut them and stored them in their packs.

"Any trees in Russia grow bratwurst?" Hochzeit asked.

"Yes, they grow near beer creeks," Günter said.

"If you come to the chocolate fields, you've gone too far," Reinhardt added.

The joking banter kept their morale up, and with the fatty bear meat, they had the energy needed to cover serious ground. It was hard to estimate how much distance they had created from Stalingrad, but Reinhardt had to believe it was enough that the Soviets wouldn't have expected them to have made it this far. Were there other Germans still alive and free somewhere in the Russian wilderness?

They came to the base of a large hill. It'd grant them the ability to scout ahead a great distance. It was a steep climb, one in which they had to use their hands to help them crawl up it. After reaching the top, they were rewarded with a view of a frozen lake, and further in the distance, more forest. Forest stretching as far as they could see. It was slightly disappointing, but what had they hoped to find? A major Russian metropolis? The Red Army? Would that have been better? Gazing ahead only reiterated a question they had put off. How would they get out of Russia? Hochzeit and Günter enjoyed the view. A sparkling frozen lake, snow-dusted giant evergreens, and a baby blue sky with a bright sun limning it all. It should be captured in a landscape painting. But something had caught Reinhardt's attention—the lone tree atop the hill. The base had been dug into. There was no snow around it. He sniffed the air. It smelt musty. Reinhardt approached the tree. Piles of scat, covered with fur, were scattered about. He squatted and grabbed what appeared to be a femur bone. Turning it over in his hands. Two indentations that could only be punctures caused by fangs.

"Oh my God ..." He dropped the femur bone and jerked up.

"What's wrong?" Günter asked. The gravity of Reinhardt's delivery had broken his fixation on the Monet-worthy landscape.

"This is a wolf den ..." Reinhardt gasped.

The elevated position gave wolves sight to see potential enemies. The musty smell, the scat, the bones. There was no snow near the tree. Most likely because their prey's hot blood had melted it. Three city fools. What would Kira have said? "*Run, you idiots!*"

"Are you sure?" Hochzeit asked.

"You feel like finding out?" Reinhardt countered.

There was no time for stupid questions.

"Go! Now!" Reinhardt shouted.

They stormed down the hill, struggling to stay on their feet, slipping on the slick snow. Günter fell, somersaulting down. Then Hochzeit and Reinhardt. Their bodies smacked the ground, each hit feeling like a blow from a hammer.

319

Reinhardt was first to his feet and helped Hochzeit. Physically, they were gone from the den. But their scent clung to everything. The wolves would pick it up. From the top of the hill, the lake looked as small as a pond. Now, from the ground, it looked like an ocean. That bright sun had faded behind gloomy gray clouds. There wasn't a single bone in their bodies that didn't ache.

Maybe they were safe, could breathe a sigh of relief.

Ooooooowhoooo!

One howl after another until the whole pack howled. Coming from the hill. The wolves knew. Strangers had been in their home. Reinhardt, Günter, and Hochzeit stared up at the hill, unable to move. The wolves loomed, and even in his fear, Reinhardt was mesmerized by their mythical majesty. The wolves' howling changed to growling. They stormed down the hill much more gracefully than their human trespassers had. Reinhardt, Günter, and Hochzeit sprinted across the frozen lake so fast they risked falling head over heels. The ice was clear enough to see the frigid water beneath. Thundering footsteps were unwise, but they had no choice. They glanced behind as they sprinted.

Nothing. Nothing.

The wolves broke through the tree line. But they didn't follow them onto the ice. They broke off into two groups and ran alongside the shore of the frozen lake. Snow that gave humans fits was nothing to them. They surrounded the lake. It was a relief they hadn't chased behind them, but that also meant they didn't trust the integrity of the ice. Reinhardt, Günter, and Hochzeit stopped. Breathing racing, their exhales rising into the air like smoke. Twelve wolves. Even from this distance they appeared huge, like extinct dire wolves, ranging in color from gray to rustic brown to black. The alpha wolf looked like Fenrir from Norse mythology. It waited at the end of the lake, blocking their escape. Shoulders hunched, it bared its bone-puncturing fangs, hot saliva dripping off, melting the snow beneath it. Reinhardt and Günter drew their pistols. Hochzeit wielded Gruber's knife.

"How many shots?" Reinhardt asked Günter.

He checked. "Three. You?"

"Two."

Hochzeit cursed. Even five kill shots left seven wolves. More than enough to eat them alive. Russian wolves were some of the largest in the world. These wolves probably weighed roughly sixty kilograms and were all muscle. Given the shape he was in, Reinhardt was lucky if he had ten kilos on them. It wouldn't be a fight.

"What are they waiting for?" Hochzeit asked.

"They don't trust the ice," Günter said.

A terrifying reality. A species that not only survived in winter but thrived knew the ice wasn't safe. Reinhardt took a step forward. The wolves growled and snapped their jaws. The lake groaned as if some aquatic beast beneath the ice had been disturbed. The ice crackled, spiderwebbing around them. Reinhardt ordered them to lie down and spread their arms to disperse their weight. Even with all their clothing, it felt like the ice was on bare skin. But it worked; the ice stopped cracking. They crawled forward, then cautiously rose to their feet once on sturdier ice.

"We can't stay here, Reinhardt. We'll freeze to death," Hochzeit said.

Reinhardt ignored the comment. He was well aware of that fact. He knew once the sun fell and darkness descended, death would come with it. If the temperature didn't drop, the ice would continue to crack and break. They could plummet into the paralyzingly cold water at any second. Trapped under the ice to drown in freezing panic. If the temperatures did drop, the ice would stabilize. A useless victory, as they would either die a painful death of hypothermia or the wolves would trapeze across the ice and maul them to death. Ripping bits of their flesh away so they could get to their insides. Each one of them a horrible way to die. The wolves were in no rush. They'd wait them out. Reinhardt chuckled to himself. The breaking ice stranded them, but it also saved them. Saved and screwed over at the same time by the same thing. Cruel irony.

Every minute that passed felt like an hour and felt like a second. Time was both ally and foe.

"What do we do?" Hochzeit asked.

Reinhardt listed their choices of death, at the end of which Hochzeit cursed, sounding as if he were ready to cry. Günter stared at his photograph of Klara. Reinhardt thought of Kira, letting his mind draw her face. Those fierce emerald eyes, as fierce as the glowing eyes of the wolves. God, he wanted to know every thought she'd ever had. But being with a woman like that brings a man peace.

"There is a fourth option," Günter said.

There was, but Reinhardt wasn't ready to contemplate it. Not yet.

"We have five total shots. We decide our own fate. I didn't survive all the shit we've been through to get eaten by wolves or fall into a frozen lake or sit here and freeze to death," Günter said.

"What are you saying?" Hochzeit asked.

"We end it on our terms," Reinhardt said, holding up his pistol.

'Sho—!'"

The ice under Hochzeit snapped. His weight caused his end to dip and the other end to rise out of the water. He gasped. Bubbles shot to the surface, and then the water went calm.

Reinhardt and Günter searched for him, scraping away at the fresh snow that covered the ice. Hochzeit banged his fists against the ice. Ice that had been as brittle as glass on top was thick as steel underneath. Reinhardt and Günter stomped, punched, and bludgeoned the ice, but it wouldn't break. Günter fired three shots into it near Hochzeit. The ice shattered. They reached in, the freezing water jolting them like electricity, and dragged Hochzeit out. He gasped for air. His fingers were bent awkwardly, as if they had frozen as he tried to make a fist. He spasmed violently. Reinhardt wrapped him in the bear fur and hugged him, trying to get the fur to soak up the water. Günter and Reinhardt shared a look of solemn severity. Any hope of a miracle surviving the night had ended. Hochzeit needed a fire. And now, instead of five shots, they had only two. Their fourth and final option wasn't an option for all three of them. If that was the route they chose, then one of them would be left to face the savagery of the wolf pack alone.

The Reich Chancellery

Kira woke with a pounding headache. Too much wine. Her sips of water under the faucet were a lazy attempt to remedy it and, to no surprise, didn't work. Someone knocked on her door; it sounded like a gun had been fired right next to her head. She lumbered to the door and opened it. Emma held a cup of coffee for her. Kira thanked her, and together, they walked to the Reich Chancellery. The streets were full of traffic and the sidewalks filled with people heading to work. The exercise and fresh air helped fight the hangover, and by the time they arrived, Kira's pounding headache had subsided. Kira glanced up at the Chancellery. What she wouldn't give to have a sniping location and her three-line rifle. Kill Hitler, Goebbels, Bormann, and Göring. Eliminate the Third Reich. But she had only a single bullet, and it fired out of a tube of lipstick.

Kira and Emma crossed the street. Emma flashed a silver-screen-worthy smile at the guard. But if there was one thing a fascist enjoyed more than an attractive woman, it was being a Nazi. This guard took his duty seriously. He was cold and calculating.

"What is your business?" he asked.

"We are here for work," Emma said.

The guard checked their identifications, cross-referencing the pictures with their faces. He waved them through. Emma lingered behind.

"Excuse me, but my brother was at Stalingrad. In the Sixth Army. Torben Kuhn. Do you know of him?" she asked.

"No, but if he performed his duty, he died fighting," he said dismissively.

Emma's face collapsed. Kira ushered her forward, tempted to use that single shot on this *Schadenfreude*.

"Easy for him to say those things. He wasn't one of the brave men who fought," Kira told Emma. "He doesn't know anything."

She was surprised finding herself defending the Germans who fought at Stalingrad. They were worthy of respect. They had fought through truly horrible conditions. Emma showed her appreciation with a soft smile.

A low-ranking *Schütze* led them inside the Chancellery. The majesty of it took Kira by surprise. The flooring was granite. The walls looked like an opulent hotel. On this floor alone, there seemed to be a never-ending number of rooms. The hallway was longer than a racetrack. Art adorned the walls, but they walked too briskly for them to give anything more than a passing glance.

The silent *Schütze* spoke for the first time not to Kira or Emma, but to a woman with silky, silver hair tied into a tight bun. She was old-school German based on the way she sat straight, shoulders pressed back. *Frau* Schmitt thanked the *Schütze*, then studied Emma and Kira's appearance through her black horn-rimmed glasses that sat on the edge of her nose.

"You are here to inquire about working the party this Saturday, yes?" she asked.

Emma answered yes; Kira nodded.

Frau Schmitt stared at them over her glasses. "You both have experience, do you?"

Both Kira and Emma confirmed.

"You will not speak to any of the Reich leaders unless you are spoken to. Is that understood?"

Both nodded. If Emma was caught asking about her brother, she'd be fired. To her credit, Emma kept her true reasoning to herself. *Frau* Schmitt ordered them to follow her. She gave the abridged tour. Hitler and Reich leadership were not shown. The kitchen was filled with state-of-the-art stoves, counters, fry tops, sinks, and cupboards. Silverware so clean it sparkled. Connected to the kitchen was the dining hall. French doors lined the wall. Sunlight limned the bouquets of roses, carnations, chrysanthemums, sunflower lilies, and tulips on the white cloth-covered tables, their petals basking in the sun. But edelweiss was the most predominantly featured flower. *Frau* Schmitt informed it was the *Führer*'s favorite flower. The room was empty, but Kira could easily envision it packed with prominent people. Music, conversation, the finest food and drinks.

Frau Schmitt had two identification badges created, one for Johanna and one for Emma. They stayed to dry dishes without being asked. Kira couldn't help but think that Hitler could have used the very spoon she dried. He was here. Somewhere in this immaculately designed megaplex. Closer to him than any Soviet or any Ally.

From what she had seen of the Chancellery, Kira's favorite locations had been the *Ehrenhoff* (the Courtyard of Honor) and the Mosaic Hall. The Courtyard of Honor was sixty-eight meters long of open sky. Roman columns loomed at the entrance with two bronze statues of nude men designed by Arno Breker. They represented the Party and the Armed Forces. One held a torch, the other a sword. A gold Nazi war eagle hung above the door. The Mosaic Hall had floor and walls of red marble, swirls of gold washed in. Opulent extravagance. Not to mention the art that hung throughout the Chancellery. Some was so exquisite that even Kira had to stop and stare at the lifelike paintings.

Kira and Emma continued to find odd jobs about the Chancellery, sweeping and vacuuming—and then left at three. The Nazi flags on the courtyard across the street flapped like the sails of a great ship. Emma pointed to a window. Even from the distance, Kira could make out the fierce face with fierce eyes, the combed-over hair, and the toothbrush mustache. Adolf Hitler was out on his balcony, enjoying the summer air. Pedestrians Nazi-saluted him, screamed their praise as if Jesus Christ had walked out of the tomb on the third day. And in that moment, Kira realized something. Hitler was more than a leader. He represented an ideal, a way of thinking. He was more than a man. Killing him would only make him a martyr. Immortalize his cause. And the Third Reich would continue. Goebbels or Bormann would resume command. The only way to defeat an idea was to show the flaw in it. The defeat at Stalingrad had shown the world, devout Nazis included, that the German war machine was not invincible. The war had waged for four years. The German people grew more and more tired of it. Let Hitler transform back from myth to man. His greatest strength was his ability to inspire, to manipulate. He was an incompetent military strategist. There were far more brilliant battle technicians to fret over. Men like Rommel, Guderian, Von Manstein, Doenitz.

Kira studied Emma's reaction to Hitler. There wasn't joy or spite, excitement or boredom. Her reaction was much more nuanced than that. He had boasted grand abilities and had been forced to perform. For her sake, her missing brother's sake, and her country's sake, Emma hoped he did.

They'd eaten a hodgepodge of food at the Chancellery, so with a full (as full as anyone got these days) stomach, they set off to explore Berlin: the Tiergarten; the Spree; the Berlin Victory Column. Locals called it *Goldelse* or Golden Lizzy. The golden statue of Victoria stood out like a beacon. Hours of wandering, talking about their favorite foods and drinks. Emma talked about Torben and their parents. Kira asked if there was a man in Emma's life. Emma shook her head, partly dejected, partly embarrassed.

"I do not mean this to be conceited," Emma said, "but men want my body more than they wish to get to know me. It happens so often. I have stopped looking."

Kira could relate to the part about having stopped looking even though she had never tried to look. Unaware of everything she missed out on. But she was testament that even if you didn't look, it didn't mean you wouldn't find it.

"Sometimes when you stop actively trying to find something is when you find it," Kira said.

After a couple of hours of walking, they returned to the Hotel Adlon Kempinski.

"I have something I have to do," Kira said.

Emma looked somewhat hurt for not being invited, but Kira couldn't have her along. She'd have too many questions. Kira confirmed the address on the envelope, then lumbered to it. Her body didn't agree with the decision she'd made. A sign dangled from a chain in front of the modest home: the Hoffmans. Silhouettes moved behind the white drawn curtains. One tall and bald, the other short and stumpy. In her hands, Kira stared at the letter from Augustus and Mikel. The news in this letter would shatter the Hoffmans' world. In time, they would try to glue it back together, but it would never be like it had been. The cracks would always be there.

Kira didn't expect emotion to affect her, but she felt it in her throat, in her eyes, and in the form of a strange tingle on her skin. She held the envelope in her hand, a metaphorical heart, then slid it under the door frame. She knocked once, then rushed away. Of all the sights she'd seen, the horrible and vile, watching a mother and father react to discovering their sons had died was something Kira couldn't handle. That unfettered grief she herself had experienced with her sisters. Even if some motherly instinct had told her that her sons were dead, there was no way the mother could possibly know that the person who had killed them stood outside her door. Kira could only hope that the letter would provide some level of comfort and closure unafforded to millions of parents. Kira walked away as fast as she could without running. But as she strode away, wiping at those damn tears threatening to streak down her cheeks, a heart-wrenching scream rang out into the calm summer night.

Forsaken

His hands were painfully cold. He was unable to even make a fist. So, Reinhardt couldn't imagine the pain Hochzeit was in being drenched to the bone. So cold, the pain would be indistinguishable from fire. He would freeze to death in minutes. A decision had to be made.

"We have two shots," Reinhardt said.

Günter squeezed his eyes shut, contemplating the horrible choice they had to make. Hochzeit was unable to make that 'you-got-to-be-shitting-me' face. He could only shiver. His face was white, his lips blue. The wolves had scurried back into the trees at the sound of gunfire but were back on the edge of the ice. Acting as if they knew how many bullets Reinhardt had. The snowflakes in their hourglass were approaching their end. If they were going to fight to live, the fight needed to happen now.

"You two choose," Reinhardt said.

"Leave you to the wolves? No, I fired those shots," Günter said.

"To save Hochzeit. I'd have done it if you hadn't."

Hochzeit, wrapped in the bear fur, struggled to speak. "I'll ... I'll ... b-b-be d-dead s-soon."

Reinhardt was no Kira Kovalyova with a gun. He'd have to wait for the wolves to charge. He couldn't afford to miss a single shot. The yellow-eyed alpha wolf stepped onto the ice, testing its strength. It took another step. And another.

Rock solid.

The other wolves followed its lead.

Reinhardt cursed.

"This is it," Günter said.

He held his gun like a club in one hand, Gruber's knife in the other. Hochzeit trembled too much and had no dexterity in his hands to even form a fist. Reinhardt steadied his pistol, waiting for which wolf would charge first. In his other hand, he had the bear's claws secured between his fingers. They wouldn't have the force of 800 pounds behind them, but they were sure as hell a lot better than his own fingernails. He knew a warning shot would only scatter the wolves temporarily. After Günter had shot the ice, they had waited in the trees for only a few moments. Wolves aren't intimidated easily.

"Do you want the bullet?" Reinhardt asked Günter.

"Ask me in thirty seconds," Günter said.

Reinhardt had only one idea: kill the alpha. He didn't know if it would scare the others away or give them a greater reason to attack. He had to hope it was the former. The alpha blocked their route south. The lake was surrounded. Survival is about overcoming obstacles. Sometimes, those obstacles are literal wolves.

"Can you run?" Reinhardt asked Hochzeit.

He shook his head, spasming from the cold. "I-I c-c-can't f-feel my l-l-legs."

It would be like trying to run with two cement blocks for legs.

"We'll carry you. Do your best to keep your legs from dragging," Reinhardt said.

The wolves snarled and growled as they closed the distance, waiting for the best moment to strike. Soon, they would all charge at once. And that would be the end. Reinhardt would die on a moonless, cloud-covered night as wolves ate him alive.

The time was now. He and Günter secured their hands under Hochzeit's armpits.

"We charge the alpha. Shoot it. Hope the others flee," Reinhardt said.

He was glad neither asked what would happen if he was wrong. Most likely, no matter what they did to stay alive, the outcome would result in them being feasted on. Maybe they didn't ask because they knew that. This was the ultimate act of desperate men. They were no different from any other prey except considerably weaker and slower. Reinhardt wouldn't die trying to avoid dying. He'd die trying to live. And to him, that was a powerful distinction.

Adrenaline surged through their blood. The hairs on their arms stood, chills spreading across their backs. A feeling coined the fight-or-flight response. Well, Reinhardt and the others experienced both. Fight while taking flight.

"Run!" Reinhardt shouted.

Hochzeit's feet dragged limply along the ice, and he did his best to lift them to prevent added resistance. The ice groaned under the concentration of weight.

The wolves sprinted behind and at them, gaining on them from all sides. But a sixth sense made them stop as the ice broke behind Reinhardt, Günter, and Hochzeit. The wolves simply adjusted course. That massive alpha was less than ten meters away, looming larger and larger with every step they ran. It arched its back, securing its paws into the snow. Reinhardt raised the Walther PP. The wolf leapt. Reinhardt fired. The bullets ripped through the wolf's side. It yelped as it collapsed atop them. It snapped its jaws, trying to bite anything it could. Even through his thick jacket, the wolf's teeth pierced flesh.

Reinhardt and Günter heaved it off and lifted Hochzeit to his feet. They were close to the edge of the lake now. The other wolves howled to or for their wounded leader. Reinhardt had no idea why he thought getting to the tree line would offer any form of salvation. The wolves would only continue the chase. They were mere feet from the edge of the lake. A wolf leapt onto Hochzeit's back, tearing into his shoulder and knocking them all to the ground. It tossed the bear fur aside like a dog with a blanket. It bit into Hochzeit's ribs, crunching through the bone. His scream ripped through the night.

The other wolves were close behind. Even the alpha limped toward them. It was a horrifying moment, deciding to stay and fight or save themselves. Hochzeit's eyes were the size of an owl's, filled with a feral fear only known to those poor souls who have been eaten alive. He punched at the wolf's snout, his terrifying screams echoing across the wilderness. Two more tore into and tugged at his legs. Reinhardt charged to help, but Günter grabbed his arm.

"We can't save him!" he screamed.

Hochzeit looked back at them with sheer desperation. But there was also a pleading in those terrified eyes. Reinhardt raised the pistol not at the wolf, but at Hochzeit. His agonizing screams gave Reinhardt the strength to fire. A better death than being eaten alive.

But the gun clicked; it was empty.

Günter tugged at Reinhardt, yelling they had to move as Hochzeit's guttural screams rang out. They stumbled into the trees. Some wolves stayed to feast on Hochzeit while others continued the chase. The black shadows of the trees moved when the wolves bulldozed through. Even if they had an 800-meter start, the wolves would catch them. But an 800-meter start to where? More trees? Another frozen lake? They couldn't outrun them to anywhere.

"Up the tree!" Reinhardt said.

They climbed an evergreen, ignoring the sticks poking their chests and backs and slicing their faces. The wolves scratched at the trunk, claws tearing away strips of bark. Reinhardt didn't know what sort of climbing skills wolves had. If it had been a tiger, it would have beaten them to the top. The pack circled the tree, howling like witches spewing curses around a cauldron. Reinhardt and Günter climbed as far up as they could get—some fifty feet. Both breathed deeply and were sweating profusely. How long would the wolves wait? All night? A few days? Maybe a moose or deer would distract them. After all, if they had been defending their territory, mission accomplished. Or had the attack on the alpha made it personal? Did wolves carry grudges? Their location was cruel, granting them a view of the frozen lake. Hochzeit's ravaged body was sprawled on the ice, surrounded by a pool of blood. The alpha and the betas returned to the body and tore into it. The omega stayed behind, responsible for warning the pack of danger. The wolves tossed aside Hochzeit's stomach. The alpha feasted on his liver. Reinhardt and Günter wanted to look away but couldn't. It was a moment neither of them would ever forget for as long as they lived. Whether that was daybreak or decades. Hochzeit's screams had lasted far longer than they had hoped. War offered hellacious views, but it was sounds that would stick with them. They'd seen and heard much, but witnessing the savagery of a man eaten alive trumped them all. Hochzeit's screams had been different, and they replayed cruelly in their minds.

The evergreen's thick branches protected them from the cold, but neither Reinhardt nor Günter slept. Adrenaline was too high. As was their worry about falling out of the tree or discovering that wolves could, in fact, climb trees. When day broke, the only parts of Hochzeit that remained were bones and boots; the wolves had taken the rest. The wolves had slept at the base of the tree, taking turns sleeping and looking more like loyal dogs than savage beasts. Sitting on a branch for ten hours was as comfortable as it sounded. Perhaps stupidly, but Reinhardt and Günter had held their pee the entire time, fearing that urinating may suggest they were marking territory. The pungent smell of urine stung their nostrils, telling them the wolves had claimed it. Reinhardt and Günter also weren't willing to entice them by eating their bear meat. They didn't speak as they watched the sun rise against the magnificent landscape. Both knew they couldn't stay in this tree. Reinhardt had no desire to be a prisoner of Soviets or wolves. Freedom had to be fought for. There was no hope of outrunning the wolves on the ground. Reinhardt scouted the surrounding trees. Branches draped and crossed over.

"Like monkeys," Günter said, after hearing Reinhardt's plan of climbing from tree to tree.

Though monkeys had hand-like feet, and tails.

Reinhardt led, his hands grasping the branch above him as he trapezed to the end of the branch he stood on. The branch drooped from his weight. He lunged for the next one. Günter followed his steps. They shimmied, scooted, and crawled from tree to tree. The sound of swooshing water grew louder until it was deafening. Rapids. The water foamed where it crashed against rock. A massive fallen tree bridged the river.

"We get down and cross. You go first," Reinhardt said.

Günter knew it was pointless to argue that it was his turn to go first; it would only waste time. He climbed down the tree as fast but as carefully as he could.

Snap! Günter crashed to the ground, rolling his ankle and jamming his knee. He writhed in pain. Howling echoed from the close distance. Reinhardt had a choice to make. Stay in the tree, safely away from the wolves, a choice that meant forsaking Günter to a horrible death. Or he could jump down and try to save Günter, and perhaps also die in the act. His feet were on the ground before the thought had even been completed. He hoisted Günter to his feet. They limped toward the log, the wolves' howling growing louder. They were mere feet behind them. A few more seconds and he'd feel those fangs tear into his leg or back. The log was slick. Günter sat on it, one leg on each side, and shimmied forward. Reinhardt sat right behind him like they were a two-man bobsled. They moved as fast as they could.

The wolves stopped at the edge of the water, growling, deciding whether to risk continuing. Freezing water washed over the log, trying to push Reinhardt and Günter off. They leaned forward, chests flat against the log as the bone-chilling water crashed over them. The wolves decided the human intruders fleeing across the river was good enough for them and retreated into the woods. All except the omega, who was tasked with making sure the humans continued their retreat.

Once off the log, Reinhardt examined Günter's ankle. It was swollen with shades of purple and blue. Reinhardt put the boot back on and tightened it, hoping it would mitigate how swollen the ankle got. It was like trying to squeeze a child's shoe on. They were drenched and shaking violently.

"W-we have t-to g-g-get a f-fire st-started," Reinhardt said.

Günter didn't even try to speak. He only nodded. He used his hands to shovel away snow as Reinhardt broke off branches. His boots were filled with water. His toes hurt so damn bad they felt like they would snap off like carrots. Kindling and sticks laid out, Reinhardt tried flicking his lighter. But he couldn't get his thumb to move. He cursed, then breathed onto his thumb, trying to regain feeling. A cool gust of wind made him grunt.

Günter rolled over, too weak to sit up. He stared blankly up at the gray sky. Reinhardt's eyes strobed. His head sagged, the lighter falling from his fingers. It fell and bounced off his boot. The sound jolted him awake. A flash of clarity. He had seconds to get a fire started or he would die. He flicked the lighter. The flame erupted only briefly before a gust of wind vanquished it. He turned away from the wind and flicked the lighter once more. Protecting the sprouting flame. The kindling caught fire and spread. A surge of heat washed over them.

That was all the strength Reinhardt had left. If the wolves found a way to cross, he would die without a fight. The fire would last only as long as the wood did. It would need to be replenished. This was far from an ideal place to rest. Minimal wind cover and no shelter.

The fire had saved them from freezing to death. Reinhardt and Günter regenerated enough strength to put together a shelter. Albeit a crude one. They situated the fire right in the opening and then skewered their socks and boots on sticks, so that they could dry. They munched on soggy bear meat. Neither said a word the entire night. Hochzeit's death was too fresh and too painful. They both knew the other still heard his screams.

The next few days were slow-moving. Günter's body couldn't match his determination. The weather changed in their favor, though. The snow melted. Many places became sludges of mud. But as April (Reinhardt guessed) arrived, it brought with it a bounty of options. Kira had told Reinhardt that grasshoppers were a *Kaloriebombe*. But that phrase was usually in regard to cakes or casseroles, not creepy crawlers. They collected a handful of them. Believe it or not, grasshoppers contain a whopping twenty grams of protein—almost as much as four ounces of chicken breast. They skewered them on sticks and dangled them over the fire, hoping to taste smoke rather than whatever crunch and jelly-like substance the grasshoppers contained. Reinhardt tried it first. Biting into the hard endoskeleton and feeling it crunch and then ooze made him gag instantly. He tried to pretend it was something else. Anything else. He needed to eat. So, they ate it, but by God did they not enjoy it.

Günter's ankle improved. The spring sun had a tremendous impact. It was revitalizing. They played chess every night, which was an essential distraction. And after God only knows how many miles and weeks, their one-day-at-a-time goal had brought them to a massive body of water. If Reinhardt had kept his bearings, it was the Caspian Sea—the world's largest inland body of water. Salt water. So, any thoughts of drinking it were vanquished. For so long, the goal had been to keep heading south. Reinhardt allowed himself to ponder every step from Stalingrad to the sea that brought him here. They'd been pushed to the brink. Starving. Freezing. Exhausted. Attacked by a bear. Hunted by wolves. They had started off as five. Gruber. Baumbauer. Hochzeit. They hadn't been afforded the view he and Günter gazed out upon. To feel the salty air fill their lungs, the sea mist spritzing their skin.

It was nearly fifty degrees Fahrenheit. Their uniforms were covered in dirt, sweat, and blood. No one would be able to tell what color they had been before. Nothing gave away that they were German *Luftwaffe* pilots except for their bomber jackets. Their hair was long. Reinhardt's a wavy mess; Günter's straight and shaggy. Their beards were inches long and rough as steel wool. They were frail and thin. But they were alive, and the next step in the journey was upon them.

A Discovered Party

The war had turned. On 13 May, the German Afrika Korps and Italian troops surrendered in North Africa. Over 250,000 soldiers had been taken prisoner. With North Africa under Ally control, the threat of an Allied invasion of Southern Italy wasn't likely, it was certain. The German propaganda machine was careful to limit what was revealed, and any defeats were dubbed "strategic withdrawals."

Kira and Emma worked all day and into the mid-evening hours at the Reich Chancellery. What would her countrymen think if they knew she was serving food to Nazis? Kira and Emma arrived before the High Command. fFrau Schmitt tasked them with ensuring a fresh pitcher of water and clean glasses were in each office.

Kira stood in Hitler's 400-square-meter office. Ornate and opulent. Three golden-yellow chairs sat in front of a long desk. Hitler's chair had a long back and was cardinal red. Paintings hung on the walls. The room basked in sunlight. Emma set the glass pitcher of water on a table near the middle of the room. Kira stood fixated on Hitler's desk. This was where the son of a bitch sat.

"It's something, isn't it?" Emma asked.

"Yes, it's something," Kira said.

Had Polish plunder provided the paintings? Had Jewish possessions and money built such an extravagant office? In that moment, she forgot about her revelation the night before. Hitler deserved to die. Kira may not be able to kill him, but when Emma stepped outside, she took the liberty of spitting in Hitler's pitcher of water and stirred it with her finger. *Drink up, you son of a bitch.*

The Reich Cabinet Meeting Room, like every room, was gorgeous. A long table had twenty-five chairs with black war eagles and swastikas adorned on them. Hitler's seat was at the head of the table. More paintings hung on the walls. The room was apparently seldom used, but *Frau* Schmitt insisted they place twenty-five glasses in front of each spot and six pitchers of water.

"So, what is this party?" Kira asked.

Emma shrugged. "Honoring elite soldiers …"

"Huh?" Kira asked.

"I think they are trying to boost morale. Tell us everything is well."

"Do you believe that?"

Emma looked into Kira's eyes. To tell the truth was treason. "No …" Emma said. "The Soviets push west, the Allies from the north. It's only a matter of time until they try to land in France."

Kira knew Emma was right. If every German saw that reality, perhaps they could demand a surrender. But that demand could start elsewhere and from someone else. It wasn't safe for Emma to voice such thoughts. She'd shown trust in Kira, in telling her many things. If Kira ratted on her, there'd be no proof required. Sedition took only a whisper. Emma would be fired in the best of circumstances. Killed in the worst. Kira told Emma to keep those thoughts to herself and to put on a fake smile. Emma had been candid since their first meeting. But she didn't even know Kira as Kira. To her, she was Johanna Eisenhardt. That filled Kira with shame.

Getting details on the party was tricky. In one sense, asking questions was normal. But they had to be generalized. Asking specifics was suspicious. Kira needed to get her hands on a guest list. Surely, they were mimeographed copies of it that every guard would have. But snooping was risky, and really, she only needed to know if one name would be on it: Randall Von Bluthund. Conversation with no ulterior motive had always been awkward for Kira. Speaking naturally while trying to accomplish a hidden goal was a much-needed skill in a spy's wheelhouse. She chatted with *Frau* Schmitt, who was more than willing to talk about her family. She had lost two sons during the Great War. One had been a pilot who died when his plane crashed into a field. And one had been killed at Belleau Wood. Her third son was a mechanic working now in the *Wehrmacht*. And her lone daughter, Marion, had birthed six beautiful grandchildren. Kira waited for *Frau* Schmitt to ask some questions of her own. When she did, she crafted a lie that she had wanted to study theoretical physics, stating she had seen Von Bluthund speak and had been in awe of his intelligence.

"What a pleasant treat for you, *Herr* Von Bluthund is among those being honored Saturday," *Frau* Schmitt said.

"A treat indeed."

So, the solution of when and where had been added to the answers of who and why. The only question that had to be solved was how. Randall Von Bluthund would be killed here at the Reich Chancellery on Saturday, 5 June because he may create a weapon that could destroy the world. But how would she kill him? And how in God's name would she escape?

Final Act for Escape

The water was a gorgeous blue with hints of green. Reinhardt and Günter had escaped Russia. Maybe the only two German soldiers to do so. But they were still in the Soviet Union. That hammer and sickle stretched from dusk to dawn. Their canteens were bone dry. With no snow to melt and the massive sea before them salt water, they had to hope for rain. Nature gives and nature takes. As they followed the shoreline, they came to a clothesline with clothes swaying from the sea breeze. Verifying nobody was around, they plucked clothes from it. They changed out of their uniforms and into the stolen clothes. Günter's fit decently; Reinhardt's did not. His pants barely covered his ankles and the sleeves of his shirt barely touched his wrists. Günter didn't let the opportunity to smirk at the comical look go to waste.

"Shut up," Reinhardt said.

"I didn't say anything."

Reinhardt and Günter traveled the shore, carrying their boots in their hands. The sand massaged their calloused feet. So often, Reinhardt had spent hours at the beach. It was one of those moments where he missed having Mathias beside him. God, did he miss home. But it was so much easier having a great attitude with the sun beating down. The vicious cold had wreaked havoc on their psyches. Like nothing was meant to survive in those arctic temperatures. But here, it felt like life should thrive. They filled the walk talking about the future. Now, getting home didn't seem like an impossible goal. It seemed inevitable. Reinhardt talked about summers with Mathias and his winter with Kira. Günter talked about Klara. There was excitement in his voice. They played more chess. The board was scuffed, and the pieces were chipped. The chessboard had been through a lot, and never in the history of chess had there been more battle-tested pawns.

Things went their way. It even rained long enough to fill their canteens and then stopped, so they didn't have to sleep in it. Neither took joy in stealing the rowboat they found. They had no money, nothing to trade. It could be somebody's livelihood.

But Reinhardt hoped they'd understand why they had to do it. Reinhardt had been a swimmer, not a boater. Günter hadn't grown up on the water at all. But rowing was basic, and they got the rhythm of rowing in unison quickly. The sun burned their bare skin, their necks so much that it was painful to turn their heads. They pulled the rowboat ashore and headed inland. The sun had revitalized them but also exhausted them.

It'd been two days since they'd eaten and hours since their last drop of water. Kilometer after kilometer they humped, until they came to a sight neither of them would ever forget. A memory that would always bring a smile. A fruit farm stretched out before them. Grapes. Pomegranates. Tangerines. Oranges. Survival is a complex thing, bringing and demanding an array of emotions to achieve it. Reinhardt hadn't expected to tear up seeing fruit. But he did. Günter actually sobbed. They both fell to their knees, praying to fruit deities. They plucked fruit after fruit, explosions of flavor erupting in their mouths with each bite. So sweet it tasted like sugar. They ate the rinds of the oranges and tangerines, ate the seeds of the grapes. Nothing was wasted. Juice dribbled down their chins, the citrus juices burning their cracked lips. They ate until they literally couldn't eat any more, then stocked their bags full. By far the greatest thing Reinhardt had eaten since Paris. His grandmother had called fruit nature's candy. Never had that felt more true. Their stomachs were ill-equipped to handle all the citrus, but they'd deal with the heartburn and ulcers when they came. For the first time in months, they were full. Filled with not grasshoppers and cattails (that did not taste like potatoes) but sweet, delicious fruit. Their bodies were machines that now had a full tank of gas. They created distance between themselves and the fruit farm should any farmer decide to examine his crops in the middle of the night.

Under the canvas of stars, they slept in a grassy field. Each morning, it took more and more grit to get going. Their feet were bloody and calloused; they had learned to ignore the pounding pain as best as they could, but it felt like with each step a baseball bat smacked them.

The distinct sound of a motorcycle carried into the woods. Then screeching brakes followed by the lull of an idle engine. From the trees, Reinhardt and Günter watched. A Dnepr M-22 motorcycle with a sidecar was on its side, black tire tracks swerved behind it. They guessed that an animal must have darted out in front of it. Reinhardt and Günter had no weapons, but the thought of how much distance they could cover with a motorcycle was a reward worth the risk. They cautiously descended to the road. The Soviet who had been in the sidecar was sprawled in the road; his broken leg unnaturally bent over his head. He'd been thrown from the car. The driver was pinned under the motorcycle. Blood ran out of his mouth. He died before Reinhardt and Günter had to decide what to do with him.

338

"Hurry and change into these uniforms," Reinhardt said.

Together they heaved the motorcycle right side up and dragged the bodies into the trees. The chance that the motorcycle was out on its own was slim. It either led a convoy or brought up the rear. They assumed they had led. Better to assume the worst. Quickly, they changed into the Soviet uniforms.

"Our beards will give us away," Reinhardt said.

Unwashed beards could be a breeding ground for lice, which carry typhus. Such long beards would certainly be reprimanded by a ranking officer. Of all the ways to get caught, having a beard was at the bottom of the list.

"Give us away? Expecting breakfast with the Soviets?" Günter asked.

"There must be a base ahead."

"And you're planning on driving through it?"

Hochzeit would have been proud of Günter's 'you-got-to-be-shitting-me' face. Reinhardt nodded, stating if they were found sneaking around, they'd either be shot or questioned. And once they couldn't answer the Russian questions being asked, they'd be shot. Entering the Soviet camp gave them the best place to blend in because, honestly, how mad would you have to be to do it?

"I know. Think of it as chess," Reinhardt said.

"Yeah, well, we won't be losing a piece, Reinhardt. It'll be our lives."

"It's a risk, I know. But I don't know how much more walking I can do."

Günter exhaled. He could walk even less than Reinhardt. "Could be so fucking ridiculous no one would ever suspect someone to do something so stupid ..."

Reinhardt smiled: *That's the spirit.*

They took turns carving chunks of their long hair and beards using Gruber's knife. Hardly a smooth shave, but it was passable that it was only a few days' growth, not months. Besides the uniforms, each Russian soldier had carried the Tokarev TT-33. The man who had been in the sidecar had also carried a PPSh-41 submachine gun. Günter stashed their packs in the sidecar. They shared a moment, realizing every scenario that could go wrong. They were embracing a one-in-a-thousand type moment. Reinhardt knew a few Russian words—some he had sought; others Kira had told him. All were to impress her, though he didn't plan on telling any man how amazing his eyes were.

Reinhardt started the motorcycle and brought it onto the road. He'd missed the speed, the thrill of traveling fast. They covered more ground in twenty minutes than they would have walking all day, and their feet thanked them for it.

Every curve could lead to salvation or damnation. More open road or a Soviet checkpoint. After forty minutes, they came to that Soviet checkpoint. A large chain-linked fence with a parking beam prevented access. Reinhardt slowed his approach.

"Act like your jaw is broken and you can't speak," Reinhardt whispered to Günter. "*Ебать.*"

"What does that mean?"

"Fuck."

"What's wrong?"

"No, that's what it means."

"Fitting."

Reinhardt approached the guards. Günter rubbed his jaw with his left hand. The guard surveyed them, then nodded at Günter and spoke. Reinhardt hoped whatever it was warranted an answer of yes or no.

"*Da,*" Reinhardt said.

Günter mumbled the curse word. Not flawless, but it made it more believable that his injury hindered his speaking. The next question was a single word. One Reinhardt knew. *Fritz.* Soviet slang for Germans.

Reinhardt shook his head. "No. Animal."

Reinhardt knew maybe fifty words. The single word responses may grow suspicious, so he asked a phrase most beginners learn when starting a new language, and the phrase Kira had first taught him at the Givre Strudel.

"Where is the toilet?"

The guard looked into Reinhardt's eyes, his face calculating, his lips straight. But then they curled into a wide smile. Taking Reinhardt's succinct statements and apprehensive demeanor as someone who desperately needed the toilet. He chuckled, pointed to somewhere beyond the gate, and gave detailed instructions, none of which Reinhardt understood. The parking beam lifted, and the fence opened. Reinhardt drove through. Neither he nor Günter dared speak, fearing they would be overheard.

As they drove through, they discovered this was no small base. There were hundreds of troops, dozens of vehicles and tanks and even aircraft. The nerves they felt firing like pistons were overwhelming, like being Daniel in the lion's den. Every single one of these Soviets would have no hesitation in killing them. The motorcycle was out of gas and Reinhardt had no idea how to ask to have it filled, so he parked it next to the other motorcycles and they set off on foot. Every nerve ending in their bodies wanted them to run. It was basic survival instinct: run from danger. Yet here they were having to override evolution. They found the tent serving food. Did they dare get in line? Maybe, but not yet. It was too busy. Lines always had one person ready to bare their soul to the first person they saw. They walked to the fence line. It was roughly fifteen feet high, with barbed wire atop it. Expected, so not overly dejecting. It'd be a hell of a climb, and besides, climbing over the fence meant they planned to continue on foot. Reinhardt's feet couldn't take any more walking. His boots were like corn husks peeling apart. Günter's limp still hadn't gone away, either. They wouldn't get far. And that was under the assumption they did not lacerate their bodies on the barbed wire. However they escaped, it would be something with an engine and a seat. The motorcycle had been a godsend, but Reinhardt's last choice. It left them open to the elements. Heavy rain could sideline them, or they'd risk a major accident. A jeep would be good. Enclosed. Powerful. Able to drive off-road. But Reinhardt was a pilot, and his eyes were drawn to the planes. Risky. But the plane was fastest, could cover the most distance, and was something the troops on the ground couldn't follow and could only take crack shots at.

"I have reached my end," Reinhardt said.

His body had done all it could to survive. His feet were bloody and bruised. He'd lost God only knew how much weight. He was malnourished, dehydrated, starving, achy, and exhausted. His body had given him everything it had.

Günter thought about it. His face was solemn. They'd had to contemplate death often on their escape from Stalingrad. Forced to descend into that realm of darkness. It was an exhausting state to be in. Though they understood the finality of death, it didn't hold the same weight it once had. It had become just another potential outcome.

"We flew into this hellhole. Let's fly out," Günter said.

There was far too much commotion to think about escaping now. Nighttime was when they'd have to try. Of course, there'd still be guards, but these hundreds of troops would be asleep on bunks stacked four high. Right now, they had to try and look busy. Any soldier who saw two useless bodies walking around aimlessly would complain. So, Reinhardt and Günter snuck into the food tent and washed dishes, eating the bits of food that remained in and on the bowls and plates. Something limited to slurping leftover broth. Soviet troop rations had faced cuts like everybody else's had. But transferring dirty dishes from tables to plastic bins and cleaning them was shit work no one would complain about if someone else did it. The cook raised two bowls of some sort of soup to Reinhardt and Günter. The silent universal way of saying, *Get it while it's hot.* Reinhardt had no idea what it was. Some strange cross of soup and stew, as if they had enough food to use for it to be more than soup, but not enough to be considered stew. He made out bits of okra and specks of a meat he couldn't identify. They used their chunk of bread to scrape every drop of broth from the bowl.

After, they found a vacant spot near the fence line and sat. Reinhardt's feet throbbed. He removed his boots and socks. His toenails had broken off. The lone remaining nail on his big toe had grown in, bleeding at the cuticles. The bottom of his feet were deeply calloused and consistently yellow, with streaks of blue and black where the bruising was most severe. The air attacked the cuts, causing a stinging sensation to join the pulsating pain.

Günter's eyes widened. He wanted to ask about Reinhardt's feet, but since he couldn't guarantee they were alone, he didn't dare utter any German words aloud. Planning their escape was a necessity. Complaining about ailments was not. Günter searched in the bag he'd taken from the Soviet in the sidecar. He pulled out a roll of gauze. Reinhardt wrapped his feet with it, then grimaced as he tugged his socks and boots on. They returned to the food tent to finish cleaning.

Cleaning dishes for hundreds of people took a long damn time, but it was the perfect camouflage. Whoever had been delegated the task most likely saw it was being done and sought a nap somewhere. Wearing only a white undershirt as they washed and dried also helped hide whatever rank these soldiers had been. Nobody could say washing dishes was above or beneath them.

Occasionally, Günter would utter the Russian word for fuck, adding different emphasis and connotations. Fuck to show relief, frustration, or disappointment. Fuck—the most versatile word in all language.

Reinhardt and Günter examined the aircraft, recognizing some as the make of plane they had dueled before. None of these planes could get them to Germany, though. Best-case scenario, it got them out of Soviet-occupied territory. They did not know where the lines on the map were. To the best of their knowledge, it was April or May. Had one side *blitzkrieged* the other? Or had the fighting dwindled to a standstill? Bloody fighting for mere meters of land like it had been during the Great War?

Bret Kissinger

The planes were either bombers or fighters. Fighters would be single-engine, single seat. Some bombers had two seats. Taking separate planes doubled their chances of one of them surviving, but it meant separating. Reinhardt let Günter decide.

"Stay together," Günter said.

Reinhardt's choice, too. He wouldn't have made it alone. It seemed Günter thought the same. So, they'd have to pilot one of the two-seater bombers. Guards would be at post, but their attention would be focused on threats outside, not inside. But once the plane hummed to life, all eyes would be on them. Hopefully, they'd have a few moments of confusion where Soviets looked to their commanding officers for verification that planes were taking off. Maybe other pilots would run toward their planes, thinking they had missed a command.

... Or they'd be shot dead.

Once the sun set, the movement around the camp slowed. Soldiers headed for their bunks, while officers met to plan future battle strategies. Now, the nerves and anxiousness Reinhardt and Günter had felt all day changed to excitement. The thought of flying out of here produced adrenaline and superseded any trepidation and tiredness. They had their packs and weapons. No matter the uncertainties of the next few minutes, one thing was certain: they would not be taken prisoner. They'd die in a shootout.

Reinhardt and Günter entered the barracks. Rows and rows of bunks filled the inside. Coughs and snores chimed. Climbing into empty bunks and lying there, Reinhardt knew there was no risk he'd fall asleep. You'd expect that after weeks and weeks of sleeping on the ground that lying in a bed would feel heavenly. But it only felt strange. However, he also didn't have to worry about sleep because he was too excited. This journey neared its end—one way or another.

The likelihood that everyone in this barracks was asleep was unlikely. But Reinhardt and Günter simply had to play into the realm of reality. It wasn't unlikely for men to get up and piss in the night. Just like with the bear, people want to believe everything is normal. They'll accept a lot to believe that.

An hour later, Reinhardt hopped down and tapped Günter's shoulder. Packs slung around their shoulders, they exited the barracks. The camp was dark, save for the silhouettes of guards, flashes of lit lighters, and the lit embers of puffed cigarettes. Once they reached the planes, they crouched alongside them. As a pilot, you inspected your plane in great detail. A malfunctioning car could be pulled over to the side of the road. Planes crashed. But there was no time for inspection. Reinhardt crawled onto the wing and into the cockpit. Günter into the seat beside him. Once they fired the engines, the time clock started. Günter nodded encouragingly. Translation: *Do it.* Reinhardt started the plane. The sound drowned out the shouting of the confused guards. Spotlights lit. Reinhardt pressed the throttle, and the plane sped down the short runway. Men sprinted after them but abandoned the chase quickly. An alarm sounded. The plane's nose lifted toward the sky, rising higher and higher. Once more, Reinhardt was in the air, finally speeding away from the expansive Soviet Union and to more friendly horizons. But the planes on the ground swarmed into the sky after them.

The Soviet fighter planes gave chase, but they didn't fire. Not yet. For all they knew, two Soviet pilots had gone AWOL. There was no need for shooting yet. The two planes flew behind them side by side. They'd give Reinhardt a moment to obey, then they'd shoot him down. Stalin had no sympathy for men who fled. He had infamously authorized the shooting of any soldier who fled the field of battle. The only reason Reinhardt's pursuers hadn't fired was because Reinhardt and Günter were in a highly valuable airplane. Had they been foot soldiers, they'd be dead already.

"What are we doing?" Günter asked.

"Make them think we're landing," Reinhardt said.

He lowered the plane, advancing toward the Soviet camp. The planes behind him slowed to give him space to land.

"Get those bombs ready," Reinhardt said.

Günter smiled at the audacity of it. Killing men asleep in their bunks didn't fit Reinhardt's code of honor. There was no reason for them to die. They offered zero threat. But destroying all the Soviet aircraft on the ground and preventing them from ever being used against Germany was fair game.

"Going to get exciting here," Reinhardt said.

"Thank God. This whole journey has been quite boring," Günter deadpanned.

Reinhardt didn't know what this plane's limitations were, but he would find out. Force those pilots trailing them to decide what they were willing to risk to bring Reinhardt down. He pressed the throttle, then pulled back on the yoke, climbing higher and higher into the sky. The force warped their faces. Their cheeks jiggled. Spittle flew from their mouths. The planes behind chased, and for the first time, fired at them. Reinhardt yanked the yoke forward. The plane dove violently. The twin engines hummed louder and louder, sounding as if they would soon exceed their threshold. Günter pressed his hand against the instrumentation panel to brace himself.

Faster and faster. The bullets zipping past them stopped now that they risked shooting their own soldiers on the ground. By now, they'd have radioed for more pilots to take to the sky. The ground grew wider and more defined. Günter looked nervously at Reinhardt. He was maxing out the plane's capabilities without ever having flown it before. Reinhardt leveled the plane, yelling for Günter to drop the bombs. He did. They left a trail of flames and explosions. Shrapnel hit one of the pursuing planes, causing it to spiral into the fence. The other abandoned the hunt. Maybe he recognized the superior skill of Reinhardt or maybe he understood the desperation Reinhardt was in. A desperate pilot who flirted with recklessness was not only a danger to himself, but to everyone else in the sky. Whatever the reason, Reinhardt and Günter had the skies to themselves and left the flaming destruction behind.

Looking for Answers

Kira took mental notes of the exterior and interior of the Reich Chancellery. Noting where offices were, how many guards stood vigil, and when they changed shifts. If she wandered past where she was allowed to go, she noted who stopped her and when. Russia had seen war; Paris, too. But the Reich Chancellery acted as its own centrifuge, creating its own gravity and time. Though the war's impact wasn't felt by Hitler and his cronies, it was felt across all of Germany. 100,000 restaurants and clubs had been closed. Stalingrad had been a historic defeat, but Kira had to admire the Reich's ability to keep support, and fanatical support at that. Back on 18 February 1943, weeks after the loss at Stalingrad, Joseph Goebbels, Minister of Propaganda, had given a speech in front of thousands at the *Sportpalast* asking the German people, "*Wollt Ihr den totalen Krieg?*"

Do you want total war?

His speech had stirred resolve into the German people. But did the German people truly know how dire their situation was? No, the Reich would never let on. They had promised a thousand-year Reich. They couldn't admit that it may not last eleven years. But there was a group of men, including Von Bluthund, who could save the day and destroy the world. Kira had still yet to determine how she would kill him. She was not a true spy, so she had to treat this mission like a sniper. Find the best location with the lowest risk. Camouflage herself, this time not with foliage but with clothing. She'd look like any other server. Needed to plan her shot for the most opportune moment. Lowest risk and highest reward. Yet she knew she may have to decide if she truly felt she could escape alive. She may have to choose a moment of execution that damned herself to a horrible death. If she killed Von Bluthund in the crowded dining room, she would have exhausted her one shot. Which meant she would be taken alive and forsaken to a torturous death.

There was a new energy inside the Chancellery on Friday. Almost kinetic. Esteemed guests arrived, recalled from the Italian, Eastern, and Western Fronts. Kira and Emma ensured each room had pitchers of water. Though Emma didn't voice it, it was easy to see she had a mix of excitement and worry, dread, and hope. Surely, one of these high-ranking generals knew of her brother. But Kira didn't share her optimism. She knew first-hand how war was fought. How impossible it was to catalogue the dead. And even if one of these military leaders knew Torben, odds were that it was not good news they had to share. So often in war, the worst is assured.

A short man with sad eyes was among the guests filing in. His insignia was that of field marshal. He was known as 'the Desert Fox.' Erwin Rommel. To Kira, those sad eyes belonged to someone who had seen Germany's fate in the cast die. He had suffered a great defeat in North Africa. But his prowess and his compassion were respected by not only his men but the Allies, too.

Emma bit her lip, deciding on whether to ask. Even though Kira knew the brutal truth Rommel could unleash, Kira nodded encouragingly. She wouldn't find a better person to ask, and Emma needed answers. Spending a whole life wondering was a cruel fate she didn't want her new friend to face.

"Excuse me, sir," Emma said.

Rommel was in his early fifties, but the African sun had aged him. He waited for Emma to speak.

"My brother, Torben Kuhn, serves in the *Wehrmacht*. In the Sixth Army."

Rommel's eyes gleamed even more sadness after hearing Emma's brother was in the Sixth Army.

Emma continued. "I am sorry to bother you, but I just want information. Some hope ... some closure."

Rommel took her hands in his like a father would his daughter. "I am sorry, *Fräulein*. I did not serve on the Eastern Front. I was in North Africa. But I do know the men who fought at Stalingrad fought admirably and fought bravely. I would have been honored to serve with them and your brother, Torben. I cannot provide you hope, but I also cannot take it from you, so hold on to it."

He squeezed Emma's hands supportively, then continued inside. Emma went to the bathroom; Kira covered for her, knowing Emma needed a few moments to steady her emotions. The rest of the day was overwhelmingly busy. The dining hall was packed with officers and their spouses. The chefs made potato dumplings, red cabbage, sauerkraut, soup, and grilled kielbasa. Apple cake was served for dessert. Rationing didn't exist inside the Chancellery. The spouses, ever mindful of their waistlines, left food on their plates and in their bowls. They had no idea how starved their soldiers at Stalingrad had been. Total war for all Germans except the High Command. Food was scraped off plates into garbage cans, drinks poured down drains. Kira thought of Reinhardt, and how frail he had been from starvation. What would he think if he saw this scene?

Kira recognized many of the generals from newspaper clippings. Hermit Hitler was not among them. Goebbels and his wife Magda made the rounds with their children. Magda's oldest, Harald Quandt, was from a previous marriage and wasn't present as he was serving in the *Luftwaffe*. Did he know Reinhardt? But the Goebbels' other six children were all present. Magda and Joseph apparently loved the letter H because they had named their children Helga, Hilde, Helmuth, Holde, Hedda, and Heide. All six children born in an eight-year period. And if rumors were to be believed, Hitler had a hand in that.

Kira and Emma kept the liquor and wine glasses full. Once the women got giggly and the men demonstratively loud, the patrons left the dining hall. Kira, Emma, and other servers loaded the dirty dishes and silverware into plastic bins. The tablecloths were stripped, the tables wiped, and the carpets vacuumed. More and more guards— *Wehrmacht* and *Gestapo*—filed through the hallway, and in and out of the many rooms. Somehow, Kira would have to isolate Von Bluthund. But he wouldn't arrive until tomorrow, and they had a mountain of dishes to wash and dry. Luka, the chef, first ordered them to eat a slice of the apple cake. Not as good as the apple strudel at the Givre Strudel, but it was the best thing she'd eaten since then. He offered them leftovers. The Reich hierarchy wouldn't touch leftovers, and they couldn't give them away because the Reich didn't want vagabonds begging for handouts. The fermented cabbage and sauerkraut was an acquired taste, but Kira grew to like that sour flavor.

It was after five by the time everything was cleaned up, put away, and restocked. Emma and Kira wished *Frau* Schmitt a good night and then walked off their meal. Both were preoccupied with their own thoughts. Emma thought about Torben. Kira thought of the coming day. This could be her last night alive. Even her senses were aware of that possibility. The sights were crisper, the sounds more vivid. Kira found it best to focus on Emma rather than her own dire destiny.

"Are you alright?" Kira asked her.

Emma shrugged. "Can I trust you?"

Yes, of course she could. Only she couldn't trust Kira's name, where she was from, her heritage, her career, and why she was here. But Kira nodded. She had no intention of betraying her trust. She wished she could tell Emma the truth. Truth can be such a burden when carried alone.

"How can they act like that?" Emma asked.

Kira didn't need an explanation. The decadence and lavishness of the High Command. Rationing across Germany. Soldiers who had starved to death. Emma spoke at length about Goebbel's demand for total war, about making sacrifices. And none of those demanded sacrifices were being done by the men demanding them.

"Do you know what is happening to the Jews?" Emma asked.

"They're being sent elsewhere. *Lebensraum*," Kira said.

Emma shook her head, eyes glossed with emotion. "I have heard terrible things, Johanna."

Kira's heart sank at hearing her fake name. Emma revealed a vulnerable truth to a liar. Kira had known about *Kristallnacht* and the destruction of Jewish property, how Jews were treated as less than human. She recognized the pain and confusion, a sense of loss in Emma's bewitching eyes. Emma was lost. Not physically, but emotionally. Overwhelmed by the stresses of war. Kira reached for her hand and squeezed.

"What have you heard?" Kira asked.

"They're killing them …"

Kira considered what she had said. Could that be true? Wouldn't the world know? But there was a feeling in her gut that knew it was true. Stalin had forsaken his own people to die. Was it so much of a stretch of the imagination for Hitler to kill who he perceived as the ultimate enemy to the prosperity of Germany?

"Do you ever wish you could go back in time?" Emma asked.

She never sounded so young.

"All the time," Kira said.

"Me too …"

Did Reinhardt know what was happening to the Jews and others deemed non-desirables? How had these German people allowed such a vile group to rise to power?

Back at the Hotel Adlon Kempinski, Kira struggled to fall asleep. She sat by her window, gazing at the Brandenburg Gate. The smoke from her cigarette drifted to the ceiling. Sleeping seemed like a waste of someone's final night on earth. She wanted to spend it with Reinhardt. She hadn't allowed herself to think of him for more than a fleeting thought. Those thoughts weren't a road, they were a staircase that descended to a dark, damp, and desolate cellar. There were only questions there that she couldn't answer. She pressed the thoughts from her mind. Yet, if this was the last night of her life, why shouldn't she allow herself to think of Reinhardt? Disappear into the steamy memory of the two of them inside the Théatre du Châtelet. Where Reinhardt was healthy and strong. Before the harshness of Stalingrad. She found his striking blue eyes, his charming smile, and she held onto them for as long as she was able.

The *Schadenfreude*

The Reich were sticklers for details. Every decoration had been carefully chosen. The dining room looked extravagant. The swastika and Nazi war eagle adorned plates, silverware, and glasses. The flowers were fresh, the napkins crisply folded. The room was peaceful and, at the moment, vacant. But inside the kitchen, it was the polar opposite. Chefs baked, boiled, broasted, and broiled. Kira and Emma, along with other servers, enjoyed cups of coffee outside in the garden. The servers would need the caffeine to get through the night. Guests were trickling in now, going through the rigorous checkpoints. The mission ahead filled Kira's thoughts. What would Emma think of her after? Would she feel betrayed? Or worse, would she be linked to the assassination plot? Could Kira weigh Emma's life with Von Bluthund's? Would the collateral damage be worth it?

Frau Schmitt was on edge, wanting the party to be perfect for the *Führer*. Kira and Emma headed inside and to the kitchen to do whatever they could to keep her calm. The heat swarmed them. Smells wafted at them from the ovens and stove tops. Savory and sweet. The smell of cooking meat and the smell of vinegar-based dishes. Vinegar. Her mission was Operation Vinegar. It was only fitting it was a staple in many of the night's courses.

Frau Schmitt had Kira and Emma take bottles of *Spätburgunder* (Pinot Noir) and offer it to the guests inside the dining room. Men dressed in military uniforms and tailored tuxes greeted each other. Women in stunning dresses laughed and complimented one another. Kira and Emma refilled their glasses. Their mission was to be little more than statues who refilled drinks and cleared plates. The women laughed at jokes; men discussed war until their wives ordered a change of topic. None of the principal players were here yet. No Von Bluthund. No Hitler. No Göring. No Bormann. Rommel was present, looking out of place and not minding that he did. Each time Kira and Emma went back to the kitchen to get more wine, more guests arrived. Purse-lipped Goebbels and his wife Magada, wearing a black dress with a pink collar and cuffs, entered. Then Bormann, in military uniform and with his beautiful wife Gerda. Everybody stood, blocking Kira's view of who had entered. The fanatical greeting of "*Seig Heil*" was shouted, arms snapping into salute.

"*Heil, mein Führer!*"

Kira had to play along to avoid contempt. The act felt sinful. Grotesque. Immoral. Hitler waved to the crowd. The most infamous man in the world. He nervously flattened his comb-over with his hand. Randall Von Bluthund was close by, wearing glasses that Himmler had made famous. He was in a dark suit, his hair uncombed. It seemed scientists never had the time to comb their hair. He appeared uncomfortable. Nervous even. Maybe it was the torture of having such a high-functioning brain that could never shut off. But nothing could have prepared her for who else had entered the room.

It couldn't be. He had to be a mirage. The *Hauptsturmführer* who had killed her father and raped and murdered her sisters. Only now, his rank was *Obersturmbannführer*. His hair had grayed even more. Sweat beaded on her lower back. Her own body didn't know how to process it all. Seeing him brought the memory of her sisters' cold bodies back to her. Her failed promise to her father. Anger flooded her cheeks and ears, turning them red. Her eyes fiercely pierced the *Obersturmbannführer*.

Emma gazed at her, saying something Kira couldn't hear. All her senses had dulled, so that her eyesight was pristine.

"Johanna … Johanna," Emma repeated.

Hearing her fake name broke her trance. Kira turned to her.

"Are you alright?" Emma asked.

Before she could even lie or nod, a hush took over the room. Hitler stood, his eyes scanning the room and finding Kira's.

Oak Leaves, Swords, and Diamonds

The music stopped. The chatter ended. Hitler stood. The first two seats on each side of him were unoccupied. At the end of the rectangular table, on each side, Goebbels and Bormann sat.

"On this glorious night, we share food and drink, and honor heroes of the Reich. Valiant sons of Germany!" Hitler said in full oratory mode.

Kira had never experienced someone control a room like Hitler could. Yet it didn't matter what he said. The people gathered in this room would cling to every word, even if he talked about his favorite colors.

"*Rottenführer* Hans Schwarzbaum fought against the British and Americans in North Africa. A mine exploded, taking his left eye and his left arm. But *Rottenführer* Schwarzbaum continued fighting. Dismissing medics who tried to drag him from battle. He shouted, 'I still have an eye! I still have an arm! I can still fight!' Stand and greet this hero!"

The band started up, playing "Der Königgrätzer Marsch." The room stood and applauded as *Rottenführer* Schwarzbaum, cane in his right arm, limped inside. He dismissed the cheers and applause with a nod.

"*Rottenführer* Schwarzbaum, I thank you, the Reich thanks you, and Germany thanks you."

The man raised his lone arm in the Nazi salute. "Send me back, my *Führer*! I still have an eye and an arm to give to Germany!"

Whistles and cheers erupted. Hitler smiled, then went back to his notes. Had he taken the time to write them himself, or had someone prepared them for him? The music stopped. Hitler continued.

The Winter Tiger & The War Eagle

"The attacks against Germany and its soldiers continue to evolve. Every day, the British, Americans, and Soviets try to create weapons that can eliminate the German people from this world. They know they cannot compete with the skill and bravery of German soldiers, so they look elsewhere. But they are elementary in their knowledge compared to us. We continue to lead developments thanks to men like Randall Von Bluthund, one of Germany's most brilliant sons."

The music started again. Von Bluthund stepped in, nodding bashfully at the crowd. His demeanor was not what Kira had expected. There was no arrogance or violent gleam in his eyes. He appeared uncomfortable, like he'd rather be anywhere else than here. This wasn't Kira's moment. She'd have to wait. She'd never get close enough to him. Von Bluthund sat next to Goebbels, leaving the seats opposite the *Führer* empty. The music cut out.

"Our strategic withdrawal from Stalingrad came with sacrifice. Many gave their lives. Though most of our troops escaped the city, there were some who were trapped inside. Some fought gloriously to the death, few were taken prisoner."

Kira bit the inside of her cheek. Most had escaped? Damn near a hundred thousand Germans had been taken prisoner. Emma looked on, sadness radiating off of her. To her, this statement wasn't a general statistic. To her, her brother's fate lay somewhere in that statement. He was either in the "many," the "most," the "some," or the "few."

"But two men refused to surrender and vowed to return to Germany. They are the *Luftwaffe's* most lethal *Rotte,* combining for over 350 confirmed kills. These two *Experten* pilots traded their Messerschmitt Bf 109s for Junkers and risked their lives to fly into Stalingrad. Once we confirmed our strategic withdrawal, they escaped into the wilderness. The Russian winter first tried to freeze them to death. But they created fire and built a shelter. The Russian winter had failed. Then it tried to starve them. But these two men were resourceful, finding the food it had tried to hide. The Russian winter had failed once more. Then it sent a massive bear to attack them. To which they thanked the Russian winter for the bountiful feast and fur blanket!"

Generous laughter from the crowd. Was this true? Kira knew Hitler to embellish.

"The Russian winter had failed a third time. These two men had proven themselves too cunning and resourceful, so it tried to kill them in their sleep. Launching a massive broken branch that sped to the earth as if it had been blasted out of a cannon. Like most Russians, its aim was poor. It crashed next to them. To which they thanked the Russian winter for the wake-up call!"

More laughter and whistling cheers.

354

Bret Kissinger

"The Russian winter had failed four times. It conceived its last play. To send the cunning predatorial wolf to finish the resilient Germans off. But these men outsmarted the wolves and escaped by climbing the trees, but not before they injured the alpha wolf. A truly remarkable escape that hadn't yet ended. These incredible Reich heroes infiltrated a Soviet camp. Ate amongst them! Napped beside them! Then, by cover of night, they commandeered a Soviet aircraft and out flew their Soviet counterparts. They bombed the airfield so that their aircraft could never be used against Germany, then flew to the Crimean Peninsula and back to the Fatherland's stern embrace. No two soldiers have shown greater resolve! Ladies and gentlemen, *Hauptmann* Günter Mueller and Major Reinhardt Friedel!"

Reinhardt Friedel. The sound of his name paralyzed Kira. "Der Königgrätzer Marsch" started again. The two pilots entered the room to a standing ovation of whistles and cheers. Men looked on in admiration. The women either wished to have sons like them or make sons *with* them. Reinhardt had regained the weight he had lost at Stalingrad. His hair was cut, and his face shaven. But his eyes had lost some of that vividness. That distant matte gleam her father had had, the look of someone who had witnessed something horrid. Kira slid behind Emma, trying to shield herself from being seen. Reinhardt and Günter shook hands with Hitler, who then gestured for the crowd to quieten down. But even he had trouble getting the applause to end. A story of sheer will and incredibility was Nazi fodder. After four minutes, they finally obeyed their *Führer*.

"It is this dedication to victory that we must all embrace. Soldier and seamstress. Farmers and factory workers. For this steadfast dedication, I award *Hauptmann* Mueller the Knight's Cross with Oak Leaves and Swords."

He placed the medal and ribbon around Günter's neck. Applause and whistles broke out. Hitler waited for them to fall silent.

"The highest honor a German can be bestowed is the Knight's Cross with Oak Leaves, Swords, and Diamonds. An honor only five have received. I have read and heard about Major Friedel often during this war. The War Eagle. A moniker feared in the West and the East. No soldier has better represented Germany. Therefore, I award Major Reinhardt Friedel the Knight's Cross with Oak Leaves, Swords, and Diamonds."

The cheers and claps were so loud that silverware and plates clanged. Kira clapped along with the others, unsure if her action was that of a Soviet spy or a loved one beaming with pride. She was proud of his heroism but conflicted at the same time. Reinhardt was by all definitions the enemy. But he was an enemy she loved with every fiber of her being.

With the accolades bestowed, Emma set about refilling glasses, leaving Kira alone. Reinhardt's eyes found her. A magnetism had drawn them together. Delighted yet horrified to see her. It was too much. Hitler. Von Bluthund. The *Hauptsturmführer* now *Obersturmbannführer* who had murdered her father and sisters. And Reinhardt. She couldn't process it all. It was too overwhelming. She struggled to breathe. She stormed to the door, then thundered down the hallway. She needed fresh air. It was as if all the oxygen inside the Chancellery was gone. Nothing but the hallucinogenic fumes of Nazi ideology. She got as far as the Mosaic Hall until her hyperventilating forced her to stop.

The door opened. Kira tried to act like her world hadn't imploded. She wiped her eyes, pretending she had something in them. It had to be Emma coming to check on her. Kira would have to tell her more lies. But when she turned to tell her she was okay, it wasn't Emma coming toward her. It was Reinhardt, looking both fearful and furious.

"What the hell are you doing here?" His tone was aggressive, but he gingerly took her hands in his.

Kira stared at him as if he was a ghost. She'd never expected to see him again. Never thought he'd make it out of those woods. It was a truth she never allowed herself to think of. Why she diverted every road of thought that led to him.

"Why are you here, Kira?"

Kira was silent.

Reinhardt's fierce eyes changed. The light in them dulled. "No ... these men are cruel, but they are cunning. You will be killed before you can even attempt whatever it is you are here to do."

Kira gazed into his eyes, stroking his cleanly shaven face. He had been lean before, but he'd lost every ounce of fat his body had once had. How thin had he been when he first returned home?

"Please, Kira." He leaned closer and whispered into her ear. His lips were so close to hers it sent chills on her arms and neck. "To kill Hitler here ... it's insane."

"The *Obersturmbannführer* in the front. Who is he?"

Reinhardt looked confused and annoyed at the question, taking it as an attempt to change the subject. "Herman Ludensdorf, why?"

"It's him."

Reinhardt studied her eyes, her thin lips. Realization brightened his eyes.

"Oh, Kira … he's the man who killed your family."

His eyes flashed sadness, two twinkling stars alone in the night sky. Kira admired his eyes, his face.

"It's wonderful to see you." She kissed him and smiled through the tears blurring her eyes, unaware that she was still stroking his cheek. She broke her gaze and his soft grip on her hand, and then returned to the dining room.

"Are you alright?" Emma asked when Kira returned.

Kira forced a nod. It was all she could do. She couldn't explain the truth to Emma, it was too dangerous. But she also wasn't sure she could process it all.

Kira and Emma returned to the kitchen to help serve the food. *Frau* Schmitt served the head table while Kira and Emma were relegated to the back. Fine with Kira; she couldn't imagine having to serve those vile creatures. The course consisted of Hitler's favorite dish—*Leberknödel* (liver dumplings)—served along with *Himmel und Erde* ('Heaven and Earth')—a combination of black pudding, fried onions, and mashed potatoes with apple sauce—and *Spargel*—white asparagus—steamed and served with olive oil. And for dessert, decadent *Schwarzwälder Kirschtorte*.

Emma braved advancing toward those up front, trying to gather any information she could about her brother. No matter how hard Kira tried not to look at Reinhardt, she failed. Her eyes found him in the crowded room with no effort. She almost over-poured because she had been gazing at him and not the cup. But then her eyes found Emma. She was bashfully chatting with Ludensdorf. Maybe he wouldn't rape a German, but a man like that would certainly lie to get her into bed. That salacious smile, that gleam in his eyes. He hadn't thought about Nousha and Lina since the moment he had killed them. How could Kira stand here and do nothing? This was the *Schadenfreude* who had set her on her path. She only had one shot with the lipstick. Fine. She'd save that for Von Bluthund. Kira slid a knife from a dirty plate and hid it against her side. The blade wasn't serrated, but it didn't matter. She'd thrust it into his throat and twist. She'd fire the lipstick at Von Bluthund and spit at Hitler. A legendary way to die. And if she was lucky, she'd be able to gaze at Reinhardt as she was riddled with lead. She'd be reunited with her family soon. She took a deep breath to steady her nerves then bounded forward, the knife in her dominant left hand and the tube of lipstick in the other. Ludensdorf was too engaged looking at Emma's breasts to notice Kira. Emma saw her, though. She had a quizzical look on her face in response to Kira's aggressive march. Kira raised her arm, but a hand grabbed her wrist before she could even lift the knife.

Reinhardt. His eyes held a warning, his lips a smile. He brought their hands to his side, concealing the knife between them. Ludensdorf looked at them both in a 'what-the-fuck-do-you-want?' way.

Another man, standing like a suit of armor, approached them. He had thin, slicked-back hair and an appearance that reminded Kira of a pale-skinned Dracula who hadn't fed in months. She knew him by reputation. Heinrich Müller. He shared his name with another prolific Nazi, so this one was known as '*Gestapo* Müller.' He said nothing, only watched intently.

"Wonderful to see you again," Reinhardt said, leaning in and kissing Kira's cheek.

She'd missed the smell of his cologne and the texture of his lips. Reinhardt didn't know the name she was using. If he called her Kira, it wouldn't line up with the forged ID and she'd have a hell of a time talking her way out of it.

"You know Major Friedel, Johanna?" Emma asked.

Bless you, Emma!

"Sort of. We met in Jade Bight," Kira said.

Reinhardt took the fake name in stride.

"Johanna was a vision on that beach. Things had been serious, for me at least, before I left for war," Reinhardt said.

Günter joined them, drinking his glass of wine, a woman clinging to his arm. Reinhardt introduced him and his wife, Klara.

"Reinhardt is a fine man, Johanna. My husband wouldn't be here if it weren't for him," Klara said.

"Nor would I be here without Günter. But the men who deserve the acknowledgment never made it home," Reinhardt said.

He and Günter fell silent. Gruber, Baumbauer, and Hochzeit weren't names the *Führer* had called out. Kira could feel Emma deflate.

"Emma's brother served at Stalingrad. He was a *Soldat* in the Sixth Army. Torben Kuhn," Kira said.

"*Obersturmbannführer* Ludensdorf said he may have some information in his office," Emma said, a hopefulness in her voice.

Kira scowled, her hand tightening around the knife. Reinhardt tightened his grip in response.

"Apologies, *Obersturmbannführer*," Reinhardt said, "but you weren't at the Battle of Stalingrad, were you? Is it common to have information about soldiers on other fronts? Seems unlikely."

Günter buried his face in his wine. Reinhardt had just called an *Obersturmbannführer* a liar. Emma looked at Ludensdorf for an explanation.

Ludensdorf smirked. "Just trying to provide hope to a hopeless cause. If you will excuse me, there are many who I must speak with."

Kira scowled at Ludensdorf, hoping if she stared hard enough and long enough he'd burst into flames. After he was gone, she turned to Reinhardt and tried to show her appreciation with only her eyes. Reinhardt didn't release his grip on her.

"I am afraid I do not know your brother, Emma," Reinhardt said softly.

"Nor do I," Günter said.

Reinhardt closed their circle, his voice only a bit louder than a whisper. "Don't give up hope. Nearly a hundred thousand men were taken prisoner. He'll send word when he is able."

Emma smiled, thanked him, and then returned to the kitchen. Günter and Klara told 'Johanna' it was great to meet her, then continued making rounds. Reinhardt had his arm securely wrapped around Kira's elbow. His strength annoyed her and aroused her all the same. He was silent as he led her out of the dining hall and down the hallway to the *Ehrenhoff*.

"What the hell were you going to do with this?" Reinhardt whisper-shouted, brandishing the knife he had yanked out of her hand.

"Kill the man who raped and murdered my sisters. Killed my father," Kira said.

Reinhardt's anger faded. "And die in the attempt?"

"If it is fated."

"Is that why you're here? For Ludensdorf?"

She shook her head.

"You need to leave … Please …" Reinhardt took her hands in his. Even in the muggy summer, her fingertips were cold.

"I have a mission."

"Who?"

"It is best you don't know."

Reinhardt pointed back inside the building. "Those men run Germany, Kira. They're dangerous."

Kira slid the knife from his hands and into hers. The doors of the *Ehrenhoff* opened. Ludensdorf strutted out, lighting a cigarette, flanked by *Gestapo* Müller and two armed guards. Reinhardt pinned Kira to the wall and kissed her. His hands locked with hers, imprisoning them like shackles. Ludensdorf and the others stormed past and outside. Her body had ached for his kiss, but her soul yearned to break free from it and kill Ludensdorf. But Reinhardt was too strong. His large hands completely covered her own. The strength in his torso was impossible to move. Once they were gone, Reinhardt released her. Kira dashed after them, but Ludensdorf was long gone. She stormed back to Reinhardt and shoved him.

"He got away! How could you? You know what he did ..."

"I won't stand by and watch you throw your life away."

"Stay away from me."

"Your country sent you to die, Kira."

"And your country left you to die."

Kira wanted to storm away from him, but she couldn't. Why, she couldn't say. If a person is mind, body, and soul, then Kira's mind demanded she leave. But her body and soul wouldn't let her. Reinhardt was who she had been searching for since she had woken up in that shelter and found out he had gone. Reinhardt was what she had spent her whole life searching for, even if she hadn't known it.

"Please, Kira," Reinhardt pleaded. "Don't do it. Don't give up your life for Hitler."

"It's not Hitler."

"Who? ... Göring? Goebbels? ..." He thought through the names and faces of those in the room. "Von Bluthund?" He nodded to himself as if the answer had become clear. "Because of his work."

"If Hitler had a nuclear weapon, do you think he'd hesitate to use it?"

"… No." Reinhardt bit his lip and shook his head. "You told me you wanted to kill *Schadenfreudes.*"

"Von Bluthund is." She detailed his rape in America, how he had basically robbed the Jewish and stolen their businesses.

Reinhardt adamantly shook his head. "Von Bluthund is a good man. He doesn't own any businesses. He left Germany because of who rose to power."

"He had no trouble accepting their praise."

"And what choice do you think he had?"

"There is always a choice."

Reinhardt looked at her earnestly, holding her hands in his. "Your government lied to you. When you're caught, they'll kill you, Kira. Slowly. Painfully."

Kira studied him, taking in his handsome face. She kissed him goodbye. He grabbed her by the waist and spun her back to him. He rested his forehead on hers.

"You were why I persevered, Kira. So many times, I wanted to give up … but seeing you … feeling you …"

Kira kissed his forehead and returned to the dining hall, leaving Reinhardt with nothing to do but watch her go.

The Plea

Ugh, Reinhardt! He's complicated everything. Forget the emotional turmoil. There was an entire room of people who'd seen him talk with her. Any action here inside the Chancellery would bring him under suspicion. If they caught her, Reinhardt would be arrested because of her. And the *Schadenfreude* who put the rifle in her hand had strutted right past her.

Inside the dining room, men boasted about the war. The keys to victory were simple. Easy to say from the sidelines. Von Bluthund sat at the head table nursing a glass of water. Kira refilled it. *Gestapo* Müller, returned to his post, was too close by for her to try anything. And even if he hadn't been, Reinhardt had planted a seed of doubt and it had grown far faster than she had hoped. He wouldn't lie to her. He believed what he said.

Von Bluthund took another sip of his water, then rose and excused himself.

Emma approached and asked if everything was alright.

"It's complicated," was all Kira could give her.

"What a small world that you should be here when Major Friedel was honored."

"Small world indeed."

And it made a complicated mess of things.

Von Bluthund left the room. Kira needed to follow, but first she had to speak with Emma.

"Don't go into any rooms alone with these men, Emma. They'll promise you information to sleep with you. But none of them have the answers you're looking for."

"How do you know that?"

Because she'd been at Stalingrad. The streets were littered with bodies. Frozen corpses with indistinguishable faces. Bodies so badly shot and blown up there were no faces left to see. Millions of dead men. A hundred thousand prisoners. There was no mathematical way to catalogue every one of them. But Kira Kovalyova knew that. Johanna Eisenhardt did not.

"Trust me, Emma. I must go."

Reinhardt was back in the dining room. Wives shamelessly felt his chest, passing it off as wanting to see the Knight's Cross with Oak Leaves, Swords, and Diamonds better. Kira didn't meet his gaze, and even closed her eyes, knowing they would betray her and find him, her wishes be damned. She walked as fast as she thought she could without arousing suspicion and rushed outside. If Von Bluthund had taken a car, he was gone. She'd missed her shot. Failed her mission. Should she go back inside and attempt to assassinate Hitler? As she pondered her shortcomings, she glanced down the street. A figure with scrunched shoulders lumbered away. Kira rushed after him. Should she shoot him in the back of the head? Maybe she wouldn't even have to break her stride. But curse Reinhardt and that blossoming doubt. Had the file been forged? Doctored? Concocted by a group of writers in a writers' room?

"Excuse me," Kira called out. Von Bluthund turned. "I need to ask you a few questions."

Von Bluthund stepped back, his eyebrows drooped with confusion, yet he was edgy, with squirrel-like movements.

"You're going to save the Reich?" she asked, trying to keep accusation from her tone.

Von Bluthund's eyes swelled with sadness. "Sure …"

He kept walking. Kira reached for his arm to stop him.

"Why do you say it like that?"

"Who are you—"

"Please. Just tell me," Kira said.

She locked in on his sad and scared brown eyes. He studied hers, intimidated by their fierceness.

"It took God six days to create the world. Man can destroy it in six seconds," Von Bluthund said.

The sentence sent shivers through Kira's body. Man usurping the power of God.

"You don't think man should have that kind of power, do you?"

Von Bluthund laughed painfully at her comment. "Do you?"

"Then why help them?"

"Because sometimes there is no choice."

He started walking again. Kira paused, then pulled out the lipstick.

"*Herr* Von Bluthund."

He turned around, annoyed. Then he took notice of the lipstick held awkwardly in her hand.

"There is always a choice," Kira said.

His face was melancholic, heavy, as if chains hung from it. Then that sad face flashed anger—not entirely directed at Kira, but the world at large.

"You're right, *Fräulein*. There is always a choice. Tell me what you would choose. You live in America because you don't like the direction your country is taking, but your sons and daughters do not want to leave. They are grown, so you cannot force them to. So, they stay. I was told that if I did not return to help create the bomb, my sons would be sent to the front lines. My daughters would be sent to officers' warm beds. I did have a choice. And I chose."

What a burden to carry. Weighing your children's lives against millions. Maybe even billions. Kira's quest for vengeance for her family had led her to killing 296 Germans. None of whom were Ludensdorf—the man responsible. Some had been *Schadenfreudes*. But most were just young men who'd been ordered to fight. Could she blame Von Bluthund for his choice? No … she couldn't. But did that mean he shouldn't die? That he didn't *need* to die? Her mission was no longer clear. It was caked with muck. In Christianity, God had sacrificed his only son. He had asked the same of Abraham, and Abraham had been prepared to do it. Was Von Bluthund expected to sacrifice all his children?

Von Bluthund watched as Kira processed it all. The way she held the tube of lipstick in her hand.

"This wasn't a random meeting, was it, *Fräulein*?" he asked. "And that is no ordinary tube of lipstick … you're here to kill me."

He didn't sound scared or worried. It had been delivered like a scientist who had come to a conclusion. Kira didn't refute it. She was torn on what was right and what was necessary.

"You must do this," he said. There was a pleading in his voice. His demeanor was like that of the Hoffman brothers she'd mercifully killed at Stalingrad. But they were trapped with no way out. A quick death was their only solace. But as she pondered, Von Bluthund was trapped, too. Live and create a weapon capable of ending the world. Flee and forsake his children to die. The world wasn't as black and white as Kira had thought, and she was smack-dab in the middle of the gray. The morality of it had been so much simpler when it had been good versus evil.

Von Bluthund cautiously reached for Kira's hands. Slowly enough to show he was no threat. He raised her hands, so that the lipstick tube was mere inches from his chest.

"I beg you. You can't let me work on the bomb. I won't abandon my children. Murder is the loophole. I don't create a bomb and I don't flee. I haven't broken my vow to the Reich. My family is safe."

Kira studied his face. His dark eyes at one time had glistened with joy. But now, there was only sadness.

"Please. You are the answer to my prayers. Do not fret about taking my life. I will beg God to abstain you from this sin."

Her eyes stayed locked on his. Time felt infinite.

Kira twisted the knurled end of the lipstick. The faint pop that followed surprised Von Bluthund. A circle of red appeared on his tux. He slid onto the sidewalk.

It was over quickly; Von Bluthund was dead. His only crime was being too smart for his own good. Kira felt the shadow advancing behind her before he spoke. A *Gestapo* officer dashed across the street. He'd been outside the Reich Chancellery. Had he been ordered to follow Von Bluthund or her? Kira didn't wait to ask. She sprinted away. The *Gestapo* officer chased after her, blowing his whistle.

"We are going to skin you alive!" he shouted.

He drew his pistol. Across the street, a second patrolman hearing the whistle, drew his pistol, too. Kira stopped, deciding where to run. Her Oxford pumps were better than heels, but they weren't designed for running. Crack shots struck the brick beside her and the asphalt in front of her. She turned down an alleyway barely wide enough for her to fit through. The men chasing her would have to shimmy through sideways.

365

Kira emerged through the opening. The first guard tripped, but the second hurdled over him, following Kira through the next alleyway. He was tall, quick-footed, with long strides. He dove atop Kira as she ran into another alleyway. The silver blade in his hand wasn't shiny but dull, but it penetrated flesh all the same. A sharp pain throbbed in her side where the knife plunged. He punched and kneed her.

"Squirm little sheep," he said.

The first *Gestapo* officer was out of breath but on his feet. The second sat atop her, pinning her arms to the ground.

"I say we have a little fun before she isn't so pretty anymore," he said.

He looked down at her, face filled with salacious savagery. His lips curled into a smirk. He pressed his lips against hers, his breath foul. Kira bit his bottom lip as hard as she could and tore at it like it was a rough piece of meat. The taste of his blood coated her lips. He howled in pain, his hands instinctively darting up to his torn lip. She reached for his holster, and with the gun still in it, turned and fired into his chin before he could stop her. Bits of blood, skull, and brain rained down on her. She yanked the pistol from the holster and fired at the first guard struggling to decide whether to attack or flee. He fell in the street, the notes of his blowing whistle growing weaker and weaker until falling silent.

Kira struggled to stand. She made it only a few steps before she collapsed. Time and place warped. The alleyways of Berlin changed to the grassy fields and pine forests of her home in Russia. She was trying to run there, too. Whistling echoed from somewhere. Nousha? Lina? Her mother telling her it was time to come home for supper? Kira smiled at the thought. Everything had been a horrible nightmare. Her family was alive and well. Shortly, they'd become annoyed at her for making them wait. The whistle shrieked again.

No … the whistle wasn't from here. It was from the other world. The real world. Berlin took shape again. Dark and foreboding. No lit streetlights. Berlin was in a blackout, so there were no unintentional beacons for enemy bombers to home in on. Kira labored to her feet. Voices carried from both directions out of the alleyway. She reached for the fire escape. A searing pain pulsated where she had been stabbed. The ladder sped down with a resounding crash. She scaled it, keeping her hands low as she climbed. If she didn't raise her arms, the pain from the knife wound was manageable. In fact, her throbbing head hurt more. Her feet were heavy, clanging against the wrought iron. Once on the roof, she toppled over. Below, the bodies of the two guards were discovered. At least five different voices made their way to the roof. She listened to hear if the fire escape ladder had been pulled. But she couldn't trust her own senses. It was too dark to see how badly she was bleeding. But she knew it was a lot because her hands were saturated.

The roof had a lone access door, industrial blue in color. She had the pistol, but she had to check how many bullets she had left. She needed to know she had one left for herself. Being a *Gestapo* guinea pig was not a fate she would forsake herself to. Their torture techniques were infamous. Four rounds. Three for them. One for her. Her mind wanted to protect her from the pain by transporting her back home. Telling her she wasn't lying on hard concrete, but on a comfortable bed of grass with a summer sun warming her body, easing every morsel of pain. Thundering footsteps resounded up the stairwell. Kira steadied her focus. She propped her arm on her knee, gun trained at the door. This was it.

The door opened. Reinhardt dashed to her.

"Damn you, Kira," he said, checking her over. But his words didn't sound angry, only filled with pain.

Her face was bruised, swollen, and bloody. Her dress was torn, her bra exposed.

"We have to move," he said.

"How did you find me?"

"Blood on the fire escape. They missed it the first time. They won't miss it again."

Reinhardt looked down at the street. There were at least ten figures covering the building scouting for clues. On top of the roof were scaffolding boards and cans of paint and epoxy. Reinhardt slid two boards across the gap separating their roof and the one opposite. Double stacking them for added support. He lifted Kira. Her head fell onto his shoulder. He had her securely in his arms. Kira's job was to simply move her feet, so that they weren't dead weight. The boards were much springier than hoped for. They'd have to hurry. Reinhardt glanced to make sure no one was looking up at them. Coast clear, they rushed across. The boards reverberated like a spring once they stepped off. Reinhardt grabbed the boards and repeated the process with the next roof. The last crossing was all Reinhardt. Kira had no strength to help him. Her feet dragged limply. He scooped her into his arms; she could feel his muscles tighten. The roof access door was locked. Reinhardt drove his boot into it until the door burst open. Kira hated being the damsel in distress and how the roof mirrored being trapped in a tower. But she also needed to be close to him. Like somewhere inside them were two magnetic forces.

Reinhardt carried her down the steps until they came to another door. It was locked from the other side. Reinhardt rammed his shoulder into the wood to break it free. The unlit sign in the window said, "*Apotheke.*" Shelves were half-filled with gauze, bandages, aspirins, and other medicines. Behind the counter were prescription drugs. Reinhardt set her behind the counter, then gathered supplies. A flashlight beam peered through the glass. A guard raised his hand and peeked through, then continued on his way. Reinhardt slid across the counter, tossing the gauze, peroxide, and bandages beside her.

"Pill or liquid?" he asked, holding a bottle of pain medication and a bottle of vodka.

Kira nodded to the vodka.

Reinhardt smirked. "How stereotypically Russian of you."

He tore away her dress to examine the wound. A striking contrast of cardinal red against ivory skin. He dabbed at the wound with a towel. Without warning, he poured peroxide on it. It felt like acid. Kira took a swig of vodka, a big enough one that the burning in her chest mirrored the burning on her flesh. He put sulfa powder onto the wound to help stop the bleeding. He took a deep breath. A nervous breath.

"What?" Kira asked.

"I've never sewn before, let alone stitched."

"I've never sewn a day in my life, either."

That was all Nousha and Lina. Reinhardt's hands were always steady. His body was impervious to showing nervousness. He threaded the needle and sewed it through her wound, apologizing every time the needle pierced flesh. When he was finished, he took a swig of vodka. All the bloody towels and wrappers were tossed into the garbage. Reinhardt plucked a suit dress from the clothing rack and a drooping hat. He helped her out of her torn and bloodstained dress. As a gentleman, he knew he should look away. But he couldn't. His eyes took in her body, losing their need to blink. Kira found his eyes. For a moment, nothing but the wanting of him, the needing of him, mattered. Forget about the *Gestapo* searching for her, or the knife wound in her stomach. The pleasure would outweigh the pain. Their fingertips rose to meet, powered by that unexplainable magnetism.

For Reinhardt, there was only one thing that could overpower his prurient desire: her safety.

"We have to go," he said.

Her face shifted lugubriously. He was right, but her body and heart didn't care. Only her mind saw the rationality of it.

"What is the plan?" she asked.

"We walk out of here as if we're on a nighttime stroll."

"You're serious?"

He smirked, oozing that confident glimmer from his eyes. "Did you not listen to Hitler? I infiltrated a Soviet camp. These are Germans. It'll be a walk in the moonlight. Literally."

Kira shook her head at his audacity but nodded for him to go ahead. They looked for any signs of flashlights before unlocking the door. Her hands wrapped around his arm looked like a common display of affection, which it was, but it also steadied her. Her hunched-over stature looked like a woman who wanted to be as close to her man as possible.

There wasn't a soul for the first two blocks. But as they crossed the next intersection, a half-dozen guards aimed their flashlights at them. Reinhardt whispered to her to trust him. Kira's hat dipped over her swollen left eye. The mirage would only hold if they didn't command her to remove her hat.

Reinhardt held out his hand to block the blinding light. The *Gestapo* ordered them to stop. A man tossed his dying cigarette toward them and then smiled at them. It was *Obersturmbannführer* Ludensdorf. The most unnerving smile she had ever seen. Like a predator who'd been told smiles were disarming, but he'd never learned how to do one. His eyes were too fanatical for it to ever be taken as a friendly gesture.

"Good evening once more, Major Friedel," he said.

"Good evening, *Obersturmbannführer*. What is this all about?" Reinhardt asked.

"Surely you heard the whistles?"

"Certainly. But I'm not a trained dog."

Ludensdorf may have smiled and had a lighthearted tone to his voice, but internally, he was critiquing them. Testing them.

"Did you just leave the Chancellery?" he asked.

Reinhardt could feel Kira's fingertips tightening around his arm. If she made a scene here, there was nothing he could do. There were five men within fifteen feet who could shoot a hundred rounds at them in seconds. As for Ludensdorf's question, Reinhardt knew if he was involved, news of Von Bluthund's murder had made its way to the Reich Chancellery. It would have been put on lockdown. No one in. No one out.

"No," Kira answered first, having had the same thought process.

Ludensdorf leaned down to smile at her. "*Fräulein* Eisenhardt, yes?"

"Yes."

"You've changed your clothes."

"Yes."

"Did you spill something on them?"

"I'm afraid I tore her dress," Reinhardt said, with a devilish smile.

Ludensdorf smirked. "Understandable, Major Friedel. We are men of passion. But where did you acquire these clothes? There are no shops open. They certainly did not fit in a purse even if you had one?"

"My hotel room," Kira said.

"The Kaiserhof?"

She shook her head, regretting the gesture immediately because the pain amplified. "Adlon Kempinski."

Ludensdorf sighed overdramatically as if everything had explained itself. But then, just as dramatically, confusion morphed on his face. "But excuse me, *Fräulein*. You were working at the Chancellery. The staff looked incredibly busy. How is it you are here and not there?"

"That is my doing," Reinhardt said. "Being a so-called 'Hero of the Reich' has its advantages."

"And disadvantages."

Reinhardt waited for him to explain. Ludensdorf ate the silence, then his playful manner ended. The transition was as quick as a dog that had suddenly spotted the mailman.

"*Herr* Von Bluthund was shot and killed tonight. Within the hour."

"That explains the whistling, then?" Reinhardt asked.

Kira wasn't an actress and thought if she tried to convey shock, it would only come across as disingenuous.

"Dangerous night for heroes of the Reich to be wandering around," Ludensdorf said.

"Have you caught him?" Reinhardt asked.

"Him?"

"The man who killed Von Bluthund."

"No, we have not caught the *person* responsible."

Even in the darkness, the whites of Ludensdorf's eyes were nearly fluorescent. The blood vessels in them looked like the tentacles of a jellyfish. If Kira didn't have so much hatred for him, she would have been horrified. And if Reinhardt wasn't here, she would have lunged at Ludensdorf and choked him.

"Then I guess I should get *Fräulein* Eisenhardt back to her hotel," Reinhardt said, gesturing for Kira to walk. But Ludensdorf put a hand on his chest.

"Nonsense. After all, your heroics are in the air. On the ground, you're a walking bag of bones and blood like the rest of us. You will be driven."

He snapped his fingers. Whether the soldier had overheard Ludensdorf or Ludensdorf had trained him like a dog, he knew the command. A black car pulled up. Reinhardt helped Kira first, then sat. Ludensdorf closed the door and leaned in through the open window.

"A tragedy for the Reich. Reminds me of *Oberst-Gruppenführer* Wolff's death in Paris." He cocked his head. "You were also present for his death, correct?"

"I was in Paris, yes," Reinhardt said. "I shared a train ride with him and his family. My heart broke for their loss."

Ludensdorf nodded, then sighed. "So much travesty follows you like a curse. Perhaps it's best you stay far away from the *Führer* and Reich leaders." He paused, breathing in the summer air. "Stay safe, Hero of the Reich. I need to question those inside the Chancellery. I may start with the blonde servant. The one with the dead brother. See what she can … reveal."

371

He smacked the top of the car to signal to the driver to leave. Reinhardt squeezed Kira's hands, so she couldn't lash out at Ludensdorf. The car pulled away.

"Take us to the Kaiserhof," Reinhardt ordered.

"Sir, my orders are to take the *Fräulein* to the Hotel Adlon Kempinski."

"The lady will stay with me. Take us to the Kaiserhof. Now."

The driver did as commanded and parked alongside the Kaiserhof. Reinhardt helped Kira out of the car and into the hotel. The stairwell loomed ahead. Reinhardt helped her up. She felt like a limp puppet. Once inside, he carried her onto his bed. He asked Kira how she felt. Kira shook her head, hoping it looked like she was fine and not in the tremendous pain she was in.

"What does your friend Emma know about you?" Reinhardt asked.

"Nothing ..."

The phrase caused a different pain. Kira had given Emma only lies. Emma had been so transparent with Kira. Nobody ever feels sympathy for a gorgeous woman. Women want to be them; men want to sleep with them. But being blessed with remarkable looks was not a choice. Emma probably had trouble finding girlfriends because most women would be intimidated by her looks. Always second fiddle. It'd take a woman like Kira who didn't care about the traditionally feminine. And men had probably been nothing but predators. Emma was a pretty flower everybody wanted to pluck. Kira was just another added to a long list of disappointments.

Reinhardt told her to rest and said he had to make a telephone call. Kira tried to speak Emma's name, but her mouth couldn't form the words. Her body needed her asleep so it could heal, and it trumped whatever pledge she made, and she drifted into the blackness of a dreamless sleep.

Fernweh

He shook her for over half a minute before she woke. When her eyes opened, the pain returned. Reinhardt was still in uniform and hadn't slept. Kira had expected him to tell her it was nearly noon the following day. Instead, it was shortly before 1 a.m. She'd only been sleeping for a little over an hour. A fact that seemed impossible. How could she be this groggy, this thirsty, and have to go to the bathroom this bad after only an hour? Reinhardt made her sit up, so she wouldn't fall back asleep. He brought a glass of water to her lips. Her mouth absorbed it like a dry plant.

"We have to go," Reinhardt said.

He'd tried to remove any worry from his voice, but Kira picked up on the remnants. Ludensdorf had worried him. Reinhardt helped her up and into the bathroom. After, she checked her gauze. It was stained a deep red, but the blood was dry and contained.

She couldn't stand straight. Every time she tried, it felt like the stitches would tear. Out front, Günter and Klara waited, both looking concerned. After all, it was the time of day where only bad things drew you from bed. Reinhardt thanked them for the car and said 'Johanna' had to get home. But while Kira settled into the passenger seat, Günter pulled Reinhardt aside.

"Reinhardt … be honest. That's not Johanna, is it? The dark hair, the green eyes …"

"It's Kira. I must get her out of here. The less you know, the better."

Günter only sighed. There was no time to discuss anything. He owed Reinhardt his life several times over.

"Risk. Reward," Reinhardt said.

It was all he had to say. Just like it had been during their escape from Stalingrad. Reinhardt had weighed the risk. But love is blinding. The scales weighed down with risk; Reinhardt simply chose to ignore it. He hugged Klara and told her he'd pilot her car expertly.

"Emma," Kira said, when Reinhardt sat in the driver's seat.

"What about her?"

"We have to get her out of here. If they suspect me, they'll come for her. I can't forsake her. I won't."

"You make it damn difficult to save you, you know that?"

Reinhardt drove to the Hotel Adlon Kempinski. Kira told him to wait in the car. She refuted his offers of help. She wouldn't baby herself. The elevator took her to their floor, and she stopped first in her room to claim her own luggage. She knocked on Emma's door. Visions of Emma bent over an office desk as Ludensdorf tightened a belt around her throat flashed in her mind. A flurry of knocks went unanswered. On the fourth flurry, the door finally opened.

"Johanna!" Emma gasped. "I was so worried! What happened?"

"Emma, you must listen to me. You must leave Berlin."

"What? Why?" Then Emma took in the bruising on Kira's face and her pained posture. "Oh, my goodness, are you hurt?"

Kira grabbed Emma's hands, staring into her eyes. How much time they had was unknown. For all Kira knew, Ludensdorf was on his way here right now.

"You missed all the excitement. The Chancellery was on lockdown. *Herr* Von—"

Kira cut her off. "Von Bluthund was murdered. I know, Emma. I did it ..."

"What?"

"I'll explain it. I promise. But if they find out I did, it won't be safe for you. They'll think you were involved."

Emma drew her hands away. Betrayal warped her beautiful face.

"I'm sorry, Emma. But I know what type of men these are. They'll torture you. Rape you. You need to come with me now."

"Or I could scream. Turn you in."

"You could."

But Kira had no worries about that. Rational people did that. Emma was naively kind. And no one threatened to scream. They just screamed.

Kira reached for her hands again. "I'll explain everything. I promise."

Emma didn't move. Those big cornflower-blue eyes were locked on Kira's emerald-green. Emma snapped into action and grabbed her suitcase. Even in her confusion and warranted anger, she helped Kira down the steps. Kira had insisted on taking them. Elevators didn't allow for reaction. If the doors opened and Nazis were there, there was nowhere to run. Nowhere to hide. Kira sat in the back of the car with Emma. She stayed silent, focusing on Berlin. It'd be the last time she'd see it. As the war progressed, the city would be bombed. Tanks and artillery would roll and blast through. Soon, all of this could be destroyed. Hundreds, thousands of years of history vanished.

After the city was replaced with a rural backdrop, Kira turned to Emma and revealed everything. Starting with her true name. She told Emma how Ludensdorf had raped and murdered her sisters and killed her father. How she had become a sniper in the Red Army, her mission in Paris, and meeting Reinhardt. So much information, so much truth, that no one could process so much so quickly. But the first words Emma spoke were, "I'm sorry about your family." Then she asked about Stalingrad. Kira told her the truth about the battle as kindly as she could. She had reiterated what Rommel had said. She had no hope to provide, but she couldn't take it from her, either. And then Kira explained to Emma and Reinhardt about Von Bluthund's murder. About the truth he had shared. The awful predicament he had been in. Neither accused her of lying. They knew Kira too well and even if they hadn't, they both knew what the Reich was capable of. Knew the lies they passed as fact. Truth in Nazi Germany was a mineral deep in the earth that had to be mined.

"Why did you befriend me?" Emma asked, after a long string of silence processing her thoughts.

"I didn't want to. You reminded me of my sisters." Kira paused. Emma wanted more, and Kira owed her much more.

"I know how desperate you were for information about your brother, and I knew the *Schadenfreudes* you would come across. I didn't want you to face the same fate as Nousha and Lina."

Emma squeezed Kira's hand, then asked Reinhardt where they were going.

"My best friend will fly us out of Germany."

"Mathias?" Kira asked.

Reinhardt looked in the rearview mirror and nodded. Shortly after, Emma fell asleep. Kira tried to fight it, but she was in and out, too. It was only when the smooth roads of the *Autobahn* transitioned to a vibrating gravel road that she woke.

Reinhardt parked. A long field of corn stretched as far as they could see. The stalks rose above knee height. It went far beyond what they could see in the dark, and in front of the field was a strip of dying grass and a plane. It was an old plane, something from the Twenties. Far older than anything any country used in the war today. But Kira knew this was the plane Reinhardt had learned how to fly in. A short, shy man greeted them. Next to Reinhardt, he looked ten years younger. His eyes found Emma, then Kira, then drifted back to Emma. Reinhardt made quick introductions, then helped Mathias inspect the plane. Emma asked Kira where they would go. Kira didn't have an answer.

She pulled Reinhardt aside. "Where are we going?"

"Mathias will fly you out of Germany. Help get you back to Russia."

"And what about the rest of you?"

"Mathias will return home. It's best Emma does, too."

"And you?"

Reinhardt didn't answer, nor did he meet her eyes. She forced him to by steering his face toward hers.

"I'm fighting on the wrong side, Kira. History will prove it."

The words gutted him. He loved Germany, as Kira loved Russia. But she could understand on a smaller scale what he felt. But as she thought about it, maybe it wasn't on such a smaller scale. Stalin was willing to send millions to die rather than abandon his namesake city. He'd purged hundreds, maybe thousands, of military officers who he thought could threaten his power. No different from what Hitler had done. Stalin forbid civilians from evacuating war zones, and scorched the earth, destroying the crops his own people depended on. Stalin had ordered his own soldiers to be shot if they turned back. Kira had said countless times that she lived to serve the Soviet Union. What was true for her with that statement was she lived to serve Russia. The land. The people. Not Stalin and the Socialist Republics. For Reinhardt, it was the same. He served Germany, not the Reich.

"Then we leave together," Kira said.

Reinhardt smiled fondly. "And go where? The whole of Europe is at war."

"America."

"They may not be keen on a Hero of the Reich immigrating."

"They won't know."

But even Kira knew that was a lie. Of course they would. Cameramen had photographed Hitler pinning the Knight's Cross with Oak Leaves, Swords, and Diamonds to his chest. It would be in every German newspaper. He was The War Eagle. The most famous, skilled pilot in the war.

"Chance it with me ..." Kira said, staring at their entwined hands. "Wisconsin. You and me. Growing cherries and making pies and strudels, remember?"

Reinhardt guided her chin up. "You sure have come a long way from banishing me from your table. Here you are, asking me to travel across the world with you."

Kira smiled and rolled her eyes. Somehow, she always smiled when with him, even when there seemed to be no reason to smile. When the war made it feel like humanity would never smile or laugh again. She traced her fingers across his smoothly shaven face. Both eliminated the distance between them and kissed. The type of kiss that made the world stop and speed up at the same time.

But no matter how close their bodies pressed up against one another, it wasn't close enough. She rested her head on his chest. He stroked her long dark hair, traced his fingers along her palms. He sighed. Mathias had the plane ready. Their time together drew to a close.

"In German, there's a word called *Fernweh*," Reinhardt said. "Are you familiar with it?"

Kira shook her head. It was one of those words that had no direct translation.

"It means to have a consuming longing for someplace you've never been. I've never experienced it before, never knew I could feel it. Not until I met you. You're the place I long for, Kira. Wherever you are is where I want to be."

"We're ready," Mathias said, his eyes apologizing for interrupting their embrace.

Mathias helped Emma into the plane. His face blushed at her touch. Reinhardt helped Kira into the backseat she shared with Emma. It'd be a tight fit, but they'd make it work.

Reinhardt stopped Mathias. He removed his Knight's Cross from his breast and pinned it to Mathias. "For unwavering bravery."

There wasn't time for words, so Mathias hugged his friend, then sat in the pilot's seat and prepared for takeoff. The engine came to life. The propellers, too. There was no place for Reinhardt. Her eyes found his. He smiled morosely. Kira yelled for him, but the plane was too loud. She yelled for Mathias to stop. But Reinhardt had asked him to do this. He wouldn't stop on her account. She tried getting out of the plane, but when Mathias accelerated, it shot her back in her seat. He was going too fast for her to get a proper final look. The plane rose into the air, higher and higher. Reinhardt watched as Kira disappeared. Every time they parted, she'd taken a piece of him with her. Leaving him with a longing for the place wherever she ended up.

Fernweh.

Return to Russia

Loss trumped her fear of flying. Kira stared blankly at the ground thousands of feet below her. Emma squeezed her hand. Had Emma taken Reinhardt's spot? No ... It was never his plan to come. *Fernweh.* Finally, a word for a feeling she'd had her whole life.

The sun rose, a majestic paint brushing of orange and purple that gave Mathias visibility of the ground. He descended for landing. Emma's soft clutch tightened. It was Kira's turn to comfort her. Since she hadn't had to jump out of the plane, Kira considered it one of the smoothest landings she'd experienced. Mathias landed in an open field. Judging by the way he glanced around, he had no idea where they were. When Emma asked, he said somewhere in Poland.

"Poland?" Emma repeated.

"Don't worry, I'll get you back to Germany," Mathias said. "I promised Reinhardt I'd get Kira home."

"That's a big favor, Mathias," Emma said.

Mathias's heart jumped when she said his name. It was blatantly obvious that he was smitten.

"He's done bigger favors for me."

"Well, it appears we have quite the walk," Emma said, in a way to draw attention to the fact that time was not an issue.

Mathias led, flashlight in one hand and a revolver in the other. Kira struggled along, wondering if that tearing feeling was in her head or an actual tear in her stitches. Emma wasn't dressed for an incursion through the woods.

"Well, he saved my life," Mathias said curtly.

"In the war?" Emma asked.

Mathias didn't answer. Even in the darkness, Kira could see his face blush from Emma's attention. What an unfortunate quirk.

"No, I was deemed unfit for military service. I have a bad heart. Ever since I was a kid, I wanted to be a pilot. But it wasn't in the cards for me ... I ... I didn't want to live."

So many men who'd been declined for military service had killed themselves in shame.

"Reinhardt stopped you," Kira said.

"No. He made me realize I didn't want to go through with it. I could help with the war effort in other ways. Told me the men and women who worked fourteen, sixteen hours a day in factories or on farms were just as important as those fighting."

"He's right," Kira said.

The victory at Stalingrad belonged not only to the soldiers, but the nurses, operators, and countless nameless who made sure there were always new shipments of food, supplies, and ammunition available.

Emma matched Mathias's vulnerability with her own, telling him about her brother Torben. Though Mathias may not have picked up any of Reinhardt's supreme confidence, he had the same ability to listen as if there was nothing else he'd rather be listening to. They stopped often, mostly for Kira, no matter if they tried to claim otherwise. She fell asleep for twenty minutes at a time during their rests. A duration Emma and Mathias filled talking. Two hours of walking tested her limits. They came to the Oder River, the second-longest river in Poland. Mathias and Emma negotiated with an old man and his young grandson for passage north to Szczecin. The river was peaceful. Being back in nature was where she belonged, and Kira seemed to heal quicker being in it. She slept most of the way, the hot summer sun coaxing her to sleep like a soothing melody. Later, Emma shook Kira's shoulder to wake her. Mathias helped her off the boat and lumbered with the luggage in his short arms.

"Now what?" Kira asked.

"You get on a train and head east," Mathias said.

"And you two?"

"Mathias will help me get home," Emma said.

But home may not be safe. The Reich would follow her there. Kira had ruined Emma's life. And that thought crippled her more than her wound. Once at the train station, Kira and Emma sat on a bench while Mathias bought her ticket.

"If they find you, Emma, you cannot tell them the truth. I was Johanna Eisenhardt. That is all you know."

"I know."

"Please don't get hurt for my actions."

Emma nodded, then turned somber. "Home will never be home again, will it?"

Kira only listened. She'd come to that painful realization herself. No one could dull that pain. For Germans against the Reich, they couldn't root for a German victory but nor could they root for a German defeat.

"I'm going to leave Germany," Emma said.

"What about Torben?"

Emma bit her lip. "I won't give up hope. But I also must accept that I may never know."

"And where will you go?"

And for the first time, even though a German never would, Kira hoped the answer wasn't the Soviet Union. Her home. A person's life there wasn't clay to be molded into what they wanted. It was stone—set and unmalleable.

"America. Who knows, maybe you'll see me on the silver screen." She flashed a steamy stare as if she were getting headshots taken. She'd turn a lot of heads.

Kira hugged her.

"I wish I'd gotten to know more of the true Kira Kovalyova. Steal some of her strength," Emma said.

"You already have all that you need."

Mathias returned and handed the ticket to Kira. The train whistle shrieked, signaling its advance. All three rose to greet it.

"Reinhardt is lucky to have such a good friend," Kira told Mathias.

He smiled, his ears and cheeks blushing. The train doors opened and passengers unboarded. Kira let the others board first, then paused before she stepped on.

"Germany won't be safe for you. The Allies are coming. There will be no mercy. You should leave."

Kira boarded the train. Mathias and Emma waved as the train rolled forward with the *thud, thud, thud* and shrieking whistle. After the train had left the station far behind, Kira checked her wound in the bathroom. Once back in the Soviet Union, a doctor may deem otherwise, but to her, the stitches were fine. Blood stayed inside her body. There were no signs of infection, either.

Afterward, there was nothing to do but sleep and let her body work tirelessly to repair itself as she did so. But what felt like minutes later to her, the large red Soviet flag flapped in the summer breeze. Kira was back in Russia.

Big Week

The story had been spun. Minister of Propaganda Goebbels wasn't prepared to tell Germany that Von Bluthund had been assassinated in Berlin. Instead, Von Bluthund had died of a heart attack. Would they honor their unwritten contract? Or were his sons being sent to the front lines and his daughters to warm the beds of *SS* officers?

Reinhardt had kept quiet about Kira. Günter didn't ask. Plausible deniability. Klara had returned home, and for Günter, this goodbye was the hardest. Their escape from Stalingrad had been a miracle. They should have died so many times, yet somehow, they had survived. To let her go was to tempt fate. For Reinhardt, it was hard being at the Reich Chancellery. To see the Reich leadership. He contemplated what he should do. Quit? But he'd sworn an oath. If Germany lost the war, it would be subjected to more harsh years like those interwar years had been. But what if Germany won? Would it truly be a German victory? Or would it be a Nazi victory? Sadly, there was no separating them. They were forever linked now.

The summer and fall of 1943 saw more Allied victories. On 28 July, Allied bombers bombed Hamburg, killing over 40,000 people. Whatever confliction Reinhardt experienced on the ground, he didn't feel in the air. He had to protect Germany. Any enemy aircraft who made it past could drop the bomb that killed his family.

Germany needed to exert its dominance again in the East. The Battle of Kursk launched on 4 July. 3,000,000 men fought on the ground or in 8,000 tanks and 5,000 planes. 3,000 miles of trenches were dug with 500,000 anti-tank mines and 440,000 anti-personnel mines laid. A third of the German war machine was concentrated there. The Soviets had a 2:1 advantage in the air, but Reinhardt and the *Luftwaffe* had the advantage of skill, tactics, and equipment.

The sky rumbled with the hum of thousands of engines. Planes weaved through, over, and around. Bullets zipped past the lucky ones, pelted through the hulls of the unlucky. At any given moment, there was at least one plane spiraling and smoking out of control toward the ground. It didn't matter how many Reinhardt, Günter, and the other *Experten* pilots shot down. The Soviets sent plane after plane after plane into the sky, so many they looked like clouds of mayflies. When the battle ended, the Soviets had lost 2,500 planes; the Germans had lost roughly 800. History would remember it as the largest tank battle ever waged. And when it ended on 23 August 1943, it was another Soviet victory.

The year 1944 would prove to be another major turning point. For Soviet morale, the Siege of Leningrad finally ended after 872 days. Over 2,000,000 people had died of disease or starvation. The Americans and Japanese fought bloody battle after bloody battle in the Pacific. The threat of an Allied invasion in France loomed. It was a certainty—it was only a question of when and where.

Though the *Luftwaffe* had faced significant blows, it was still a mighty force. Landing men on beaches would be a slaughter if the Allies tried it now. Reinhardt knew the smart move would be to exterminate the *Luftwaffe* before an invasion. Destroy the factories that made up the backbone of Germany's aircraft industry. Factories like the one Mathias worked at. The time for Reinhardt to quit had passed. Now, he had to do what he could to defend Germany, defend those he loved.

'Big Week' was the name given to the plan to cripple the *Luftwaffe*. Allies targeted the cities of Leipzig, Brunswick, Gotha, Regensburg, Schweinfurt, Augsburg, Stuttgart, and Steyr. Reinhardt warned pilots not to be enticed to fly after Allied planes because of potential traps. The Allied fighters clung close to their bombers, greatly limiting the number of bombers they lost, but it meant the *Luftwaffe* limited their losses by not being chased. American Major Jimmy Doolittle solved the problem by bombing factories that forced the *Luftwaffe* to respond.

It made for a different feeling flying into the fight. Like knowing what your opponent had set up in chess and knowing the checkmate was inevitable. But Reinhardt would defend Germany with his life. He and Günter were ordered to defend Leipzig. He had no idea what to expect from the American pilots or their planes. How would his Messerschmitt compare?

Reinhardt and the skilled *Luftwaffe* pilots soared at the bombers, knowing the escorting fighter planes would break away. The bombers were bait. But it wasn't a worm at the end of the line, it was a shark. If they weren't destroyed, they'd unleash their bombs on Germany. The P-38 Lightnings and P-51 Mustangs flew out and engaged. Reinhardt spun his plane, avoiding the burst of fire sent his way. He returned a volley of his own, sending a plane spiraling to the ground.

He soared higher into the clouds, then dove, firing at the bomber, peppering it with enough holes that it started smoking. An engine ignited; the plane lost altitude. Reinhardt didn't have time to watch. A Mustang chased after him. No matter which way he turned, there was a new threat. German pilots expertly avoided fire, only to spin directly into another line of fire. Several Allied bombers were stopped short, but many reached their targets. Their bombs torpedoed to the ground. The explosions looked like puffs of fire. But it wasn't lost on Reinhardt that Germans had just died.

Reinhardt sped toward the bomber, pelting it with gunfire. He descended only moments before they would hit each other. Planes collided, bits of shrapnel pierced cockpits and were sucked into engines. Men bailed out of aircraft. Some were struck with errant bullets; some were inadvertently hit by planes. The fortunate made it to land or water below. Günter and Reinhardt were lethal. They eliminated five fighters and then took down a bomber.

"There's one more. He's too far away. Too protected," Günter called over the radio.

"I can't leave them ..." Reinhardt said.

He couldn't allow the bomber to drop its payload on his countrymen.

"Reinhardt ..."

Two fighter planes protected the bomber, but Reinhardt didn't care. There were innocent people on the ground. Crying children, asking their parents if they were going to die. Reinhardt steadied his breathing to clear his mind. Deep inhales, slow exhales. He thought of young Manfred Wolff and the question of whether he should be scared. Reinhardt had told him no. He had no intention of being a liar. He couldn't stay back.

He yanked on the throttle, rising into the air, up into the clouds, then ripping through them as he soared down. He fired on the first fighter plane, then spun to unleash a flurry on the bomber. Not enough to bring the behemoth down, but enough to cause alerts to blare inside. The second fighter pilot chased after him. Reinhardt spun and swerved, avoiding the machine-gun fire. The bomber grew closer and closer to its target. Reinhardt's pursuer followed his every move. A worthy opponent. There wasn't enough time to take both him and the bomber out. He had to choose: Save himself or save the innocent people below.

This was it. He'd go out the same way the Red Baron had. He'd go down in combat as Germany's greatest pilot. He could think of no better way to die than saving his beloved Germany. Reinhardt steadied his plane, flying directly at the bomber. The P-51 Mustang followed. The B-51 bomber had cannons; the P-51 was equivalently armed as Reinhardt's Messerschmitt. But if they fired, they risked hitting each other. The bomber wouldn't budge; it was on a flight path. The P-51 backed off. The bomber unleashed its cannons. Reinhardt fired, screaming as the rounds erupted all around. His instruments spun wildly; sirens wailed. Black smoke billowed out. His plane was gravely injured.

Reinhardt unleashed every round his plane had. The massive bomber shook. Internally, the bullet barrage had wreaked havoc. If it didn't go down, Reinhardt would fly his plane right into it. He was going to have to until, from the side, Günter unloaded. The bomber plummeted. Reinhardt's plane shook. The P-51 returned to finish him. Then another. And another. Even if his plane had been in perfect condition, a dogfight against these highly skilled pilots would be too much.

His engine died. The plane shuddered—its final death rattle. He was defenseless. The goal of Big Week wasn't solely a bombing campaign. It was to kill *Luftwaffe* pilots. Reinhardt was about to be among them.

The three Americans fired. Black smoke filled Reinhardt's cockpit. Suffocating him, tasting like an oil-covered blanket had been pressed over his face. He couldn't breathe, couldn't see. Unimaginable heat made it feel as if his bomber jacket would melt into his skin. His engine was on fire. Reinhardt broke the canopy glass. The black smoke vanished. Fresh air blasted his face.

He was going down and down viciously fast. Reinhardt opened the plane's flaps—doing anything he could to slow the plane as much as possible. He was over a lake. With a mighty wave, the plane crashed into the water, thrusting Reinhardt forward. His head smacked against the dashboard, knocking him unconscious. Water rushed into the plane, dragging it and its pilot down to its murky depths.

Hero of the Soviet Union

She felt lied to. Used. Manipulated. Von Bluthund's assassination had been a carefully crafted story. And because of Kira's actions, Reinhardt had possibly implicated himself in helping her escape. She had no news on Emma or Mathias. No news on Reinhardt. By the time Kira returned to Moscow, Johanna Eisenhardt was no more. Colonel Volkov greeted her with a smile. His reliance on cigarettes and vodka throughout the war showed more on his face each time she saw him. The blood vessels in his nose were ruptured and his skin had taken on a jaundiced hue. Had he known the truth about Von Bluthund? Or had he been played, too? They were all pawns in the Soviet Union. No chance to be promoted.

"You continue to delight me, Comrade," he said.

Kira forced a smile and a nod. It was all she could give him.

"Your father was a military man, yes?" he asked.

"He was."

"I know he is gone, but as a father, I know he is aware of every one of your accomplishments. As parents, we want our children to exceed us. In every way." He took a long drag of his cigarette. "Do you believe in spirits, Kira?"

Kira pondered. She wanted to. Desperately. But the pragmatist in her wouldn't allow her to. And did she truly want her parents, her sisters, to be stuck here? Amidst a world at war? Ghosts are imprisoned where they die. She did not want to believe Nousha and Lina were at that ballroom. No, she wanted to believe, needed to believe, they were somewhere better.

Colonel Volkov noted her hesitation and continued, "I do. I believe those we love stay around us, circling us. I believe your father surrounds you, that he hears the conversation we are having. So, it is my great honor to tell you that you are to be awarded the Soviet Union's highest honor. Hero of the Soviet Union."

Hero. The word had lost some of its luster. Is that what killing men made her? A hero? Kill the right man, and they give you a medal? Would her father be proud of her?

Colonel Volkov put a hand on her shoulder. Kira hadn't said a word, barely reacted. He understood, to some degree at least, that it was a lot to take in.

"Kira, I just told you you're being named a Hero of the Soviet Union." He waited for a smile, a smirk, any reaction at all.

"Colonel, did you know?" Kira asked.

His face scrunched in confusion.

"The truth about Von Bluthund. He wasn't the vile man the report stated."

Kira explained the truth she had discovered on that sidewalk in Berlin, studying his face for any signs of deception.

"I did not know, but I understand why they did it. Was it not easier to perform the task thinking he was a *Schadenfreude*?"

She accepted his answer of not knowing, but it didn't make it sit any better.

Kira would be presented with the award that night. The only thing on her agenda now was a hot bath and sleep. She was afforded both. She tried to keep her head clear as she sat in the hot water, and it worked to a degree. But the moment she lay down in bed, everything overwhelmed her. So many unanswered questions.

Her uniform was washed and pressed. It was odd that for most of her life, her hair seemed to braid itself. But she struggled to braid it now, as if the remnants of Johanna Eisenhardt and the Kira from Paris didn't want to disappear. And she didn't want them to disappear, either.

A GAZ-M1 automobile waited for her outside and drove her to the Kremlin. It was an immaculately designed building, but Kira didn't get to see it. There was no greater target to bomb in Moscow than the Kremlin. It was a fear the Soviet leadership had had ever since Hitler and the Germans betrayed the non-aggression pact. But how do you hide twenty-eight square hectares covered with buildings of various heights? The solution was to repaint all the roofs in rusty brown colors to make them appear like any other buildings. The paved cobblestones were covered in sand. Tents were then painted to look like roofs and stretched over the Kremlin gardens. The sides of buildings were covered with tents painted to look like other buildings and apartment complexes. The ingenious plan had been designed by famed architect Boris Iofan. Though Kira didn't want to see her country's history destroyed, could some of this ingenuity not be directed toward saving civilians or lifting the siege at Leningrad? Stalin valued property over people.

Kira entered the famed building alongside Colonel Volkov. Together, they traveled to Alexandrovsky Hall. It rivaled the German Reich Chancellery for opulence, so much so that the memory of her embrace with Reinhardt in the Mosaic Hall flashed in her mind. The floors were shiny, with intricate designs. Gold covered the beige walls. Soviet troops stood guard. She recognized some of the distinguished guests as the same who had been in the room when Operation Vinegar had been tasked to her.

Colonel Volkov told Kira to wait at the entrance until her name was called. He sat near the front. Stalin entered the room from a different entrance. Everybody rose to attention. Stalin removed his hat and set it on top of the podium.

"Good evening, Comrades. The mighty Soviet Union is nothing without its hardworking people. And as we have fought this great patriotic war, we have relied heavily on our brave men and women to fight with unlimited determination and resolve. Millions have answered that call. But none more so than Comrade Kovalyova. As a sniper, she has registered 296 kills. In December of '43, she was given a new mission. To assassinate German General Jürgen Wolff. She succeeded. She was once again called upon to assassinate a vile fascist capable of creating an atomic bomb. Fresh off the train, Comrade Kovalyova has returned and fulfilled that mission. Few people have swayed a war the way Comrade Kovalyova has. She is a true comrade, a valiant warrior. Comrade, *Major* Kovalyova, come forth."

Those inside turned to look at Kira as she marched to Stalin. *Major.* He had promoted her. Stalin nodded his respect. In his hand he held a gold star-shaped medal tethered to a red ribbon.

"Comrade Kovalyova, I appoint you Hero of the Soviet Union."

He draped the medal over her head. Applause broke out, echoing down from the ceiling. Kira turned to face the congregation of her nation's most powerful men. She hadn't ever fathomed this award could belong to her. She'd give it back if it meant that Ludensdorf hadn't killed her father and sisters. If the Germans had bypassed her town. She was certainly proud of what she had achieved, but to receive a medal for it? Reinhardt had shared that sentiment in Paris. If she had died and still had a family, would this medal and ribbon provide any comfort to them?

Flashbulbs flickered, breaking her contemplation. Tomorrow, her face would be all over the front pages. Her face and story used as propaganda. No doubt her face would be seen in other countries, too. Would the Nazis see her face? Recognize her? With each flashing bulb, it signified the end of her spy career. No more reasons to visit Paris or Berlin. No more chances to see Reinhardt. Not until the Soviet Union invaded Germany.

And by then, it may be too late.

The War Eagle

He struggled to open his eyes. When he did, Kira stood over him. Her emerald eyes were so striking in the light. Where was he? In a hospital bed? No. Why would Kira be here at a German hospital? She wouldn't be … which meant that he was dreaming. Reinhardt struggled to recall what he had last remembered. It came in a flash. Gunfire. The roar of engines. Black smoke.

He'd crashed into the water. This wasn't a dream. He was knocked out. If he didn't wake soon …

He gasped awake, swallowing a mouthful of water. The panic was overwhelming. He struggled to free himself and swim toward the surface. He spasmed. Death was moments away.

Not like this. Not like this.

He kicked and broke through to the surface. Reinhardt backstroked to the shore. He crawled inland, only far enough to ensure the tide wouldn't reach him. He collapsed. He was exhausted, and now that the adrenaline had subsided, he was fully aware of the pain his body was in. It ached all over. His forehead was bleeding, and a quick pat of his body showed he was bleeding someplace else, too; he was just too tired to find out where. His eyes grew heavy. The desire to sleep overwhelmed him. Reinhardt didn't fight it. He had no strength to.

When he woke next, he was in a hospital bed. His body sunk into the cot. He didn't even attempt to lift his head from his pillow. He knew he had a raging headache. The room was full of patients. Nurses attended to them; those worse off screamed for something to dull their pain. But most were like Reinhardt, lying there feeling defeated. A young nurse approached. Her chestnut-brown hair was kept in a bun and hidden under a cap.

"How are you feeling?" she asked.

"Dreadful," Reinhardt grumbled. His voice was gravelly. His throat dry.

She checked his chart, no doubt to see when he had last received pain medication. She bit her lip—apparently too recent for another dose.

"Sorry. You'll have to wait on pain medicine."

"What about water?"

"I can do that." She offered a pleasant smile and returned with a glass.

Reinhardt downed it in one long, continuous gulp. "Can I trouble you for another?"

The nurse took his glass and returned moments later with a pitcher of water. He cleared his throat.

"Where am I?" he asked.

"Berlin," the nurse answered.

After ensuring he was alright, she moved along to check on other patients. Reinhardt didn't know how long he would have to be there, but he would do everything he could to get out of there as soon as he could. He was in pain, but his injuries were nothing compared to some soldiers. With nothing else to do, he fell asleep again. Whether from the pain medicine or sheer exhaustion, he had no dreams.

He awoke rapidly. Someone had been shaking his arm. He gathered his bearings. A man stared down at him, a devious smirk curling on his lips. *Obersturmbannführer* Ludensdorf. His gray eyes looked crazy.

"Major Friedel, apologies for waking you," Ludensdorf said.

Reinhardt sat up. The motion made his head throb, but he wouldn't let Ludensdorf see him in pain.

"I have guests that requested to see you once they found out you were here. I'm afraid it would have been rude to make them wait any longer," Ludensdorf said.

He stepped aside. The family of Jürgen Wolff stepped up to Reinhardt's bedside. It'd been almost two years since Reinhardt had seen them. Manfred had grown, now all gangly limbs. Susanne was a cute young woman who still hadn't lost her crush on Reinhardt. Her cheeks blushed. She pulled her shirt tighter to showcase just how much her body had changed. And Christiania Wolff was still beautiful, but the years since her husband's death had aged her. Crow's feet had appeared around her eyes, and the wrinkles around her lips weren't from smiling, but frowning. Grief has a way of warping flesh.

"We're so glad to hear you're okay, Reinhardt," *Frau* Wolff said, rubbing his shoulder.

It was a situation Reinhardt had never expected to find himself in. He knew who had killed her husband. The person responsible for the immense pain they felt each waking day.

"Thank you. I'll be fine," Reinhardt assured. "How are you? I was so sorry to hear of your husband," he turned his gaze to Susanne and Manfred, "and your father. I did not know him well, but he treated me kindly. And this much I know, he loved you all immensely."

Frau Wolff bit her lip. Over the last two years, tears came without warning. She had had to learn how to stifle those waves in front of her children, and she did so now. They stayed in her eyes like glossy resin.

"Children, why don't you continue on?" *Frau* Wolff suggested.

Neither wanted to leave Reinhardt so quickly, but they wouldn't put up a fuss. Both were wise enough to understand the tremendous strain their mother had been under.

"That day had started off perfect ..." *Frau* Wolff recalled.

Life is dichotomous. That was the worst day of *Frau* Wolff's life. For Reinhardt, it was the best.

"The theater was so glamorous, Reinhardt!" *Frau* Wolff said.

"It was. Christmas was in the air," Reinhardt said.

"You looked so happy. Kira was stunning. Her striking green eyes, vibrant dark hair. Oh, and that red dress!"

Ludensdorf listened intently, studying Reinhardt for a reaction.

"She was. The war took us in different directions," Reinhardt said.

"True love may wander, but it finds its way home."

Reinhardt smiled and nodded. *Frau* Wolff promised to check in on him later and then continued to find her children. Ludensdorf lingered briefly.

"Rest, Major Friedel. Germany needs pilots ... and this bed," he said.

Frau Wolff had planted the memory, and Reinhardt desperately hoped he would dream of that Christmas Eve. Cruel, how the human mind has no trouble recalling traumatic events, but seldom do we get to relive in such vivid detail the greatest moments of our lives.

Reinhardt awoke the following morning, deciding it was the day he'd leave the hospital. He sat up, took a few deep breaths to test how his head and body would react to movement. He had been through much worse. In his experience, you had to keep moving. He dressed and only offered a nod to the confused nurse on staff on his way out of the hospital.

It'd been over two weeks since he had crashed into the water. His arm was in a sling; the doctor had told him he had dislocated his shoulder. A bullet had grazed his side. A bleeding wound that had gotten infected. Reinhardt had gotten more sleep in those two weeks than it felt like he had gotten during the entire war. He forced himself to walk around the city. The early March weather was fickle, and he never knew how to dress. One minute, it was spring-like; the next, another vicious round of winter. He had gotten a letter out to Günter. It only made his desire to get back in the air greater. His Messerschmitt was at the bottom of the sea. Though aware it was just a machine, the connection felt more personal. Like it had been a loyal horse. Reinhardt had gone to battle in that plane hundreds of times, and it had kept him alive. The next time he went into the air, it would be in a different plane. Maybe even a different model of the Messerschmitt.

But for now, he was a captive in his country's capital city. Flightless. No friends in the city. Kira, a world away. On 14 April, Reinhardt was notified he would finally return to combat the next day. He was about to undress and shower and call it a night. But a knock on his door put the plan on temporary hold. Reinhardt answered the door. *Obersturmbannführer* Ludensdorf, flanked by two soldiers, leaned against the door frame.

"Ah, good evening, Major Friedel," he said.

"Good evening …"

Ludensdorf took in Reinhardt's appearance—his unbuttoned uniform, untucked shirt, and unfastened belt. "Turning in already?"

"Yes."

"I envy. Of course, my duties never seem to end. No early nights for me."

"I return to the war tomorrow."

Ludensdorf smiled at the news. "Wonderful. I was beginning to wonder. But I'm afraid your night must continue like mine. There are a few questions we need answering at the Reich Chancellery."

"What questions?"

Ludensdorf made a guilty face. "I'm afraid I don't remember. General questions. All the information is on my desk. I decided to take the opportunity for a break and offer a ride to a Reich hero."

Reinhardt nodded and re-buttoned his uniform. He followed Ludensdorf, and the two soldiers followed behind him. They stepped into a black car. Ludensdorf said nothing on the drive over. Reinhardt studied his features for a clue as to what he could possibly want, but Ludensdorf's face was a blank canvas.

The car pulled alongside the Chancellery. Ludensdorf waved the guards away on their way inside. They walked through the *Ehrenhoff*. Reinhardt's eyes darted to where he had kissed Kira. They headed inside and through the long hallway. Most of the staff had gone for the night. Ludensdorf entered his office and sat at his desk. The top was strategically cluttered to make him appear busier than he was. He gestured to Reinhardt to sit.

Reinhardt politely refused. "After laying in a bed so long, I would like to stand."

"Understandable. If I had laid in a bed as long as you, I wouldn't want to sit, either."

Ludensdorf sighed, then leaned forward and looked at the contents on his desk, appearing to have forgotten why Reinhardt was here.

"Ahh!" he exclaimed when he found what he had been looking for. "*Frau* Wolff had wanted to give you something before she left. You had finally left the hospital at that point, so she entrusted it to me."

"It?" Reinhardt asked.

Ludensdorf nodded, chewing the silence like it was a delectable piece of candy. "I'm afraid I let it sit for a while. Pressing Reich business, you understand?"

Reinhardt forced a nod. Agreeing to anything Ludensdorf said was sickening.

"Do you know what she wanted to give you?" Ludensdorf asked.

He enjoyed the powerful position he was in. He in the know, Reinhardt in the dark unknown.

"I cannot fathom a guess," Reinhardt said.

Ludensdorf stared into Reinhardt's eyes before retrieving a glossy eight-by-ten-inch photograph. He slid it across the desk, forcing Reinhardt to bend forward to see it. There was no date printed on the photo, but none was necessary. Reinhardt would never forget the date. 24 December 1942. Paris, France. The Théatre du Châtelet lobby. The Christmas tree. The garland. Men and women smiling. Wolff and his wife were in the lower left-hand corner. In the center of the image were Reinhardt and Kira. He remembered there being cameras but had no idea this image had been captured. But that didn't surprise him. He had been so enamored with Kira. She was nothing short of radiant. Her left hand was raised, self-consciously checking that her hair was in place. Her shoulders were pressed back. Her emerald-green eyes were reduced to black, but not diminished. The Reinhardt in the photograph was just as enamored as the Reinhardt staring at the picture. *God, she was captivating.* Did Ludensdorf recognize her? His hand was still on the photo, unwilling to relinquish his hold on it.

"You remember this night?" Ludensdorf asked.

"I remember it well."

"The night *Oberst-Gruppenführer* Wolff was assassinated."

"Yes."

Ludensdorf released the photo but clicked his tongue and shook his head when Reinhardt went to pick it up. He searched—dramatically prolonging—for another photo. He sighed when he found it, then placed it side by side with the other photo. This photograph showed Reinhardt receiving his Knight's Cross with Oak Leaves, Swords, and Diamonds from the *Führer* as spectators applauded. Caught in the photograph were Kira and her friend Emma. She was dressed differently, but she wore the same uneasy look, had the same posture she did in the other photo. In this photo she looked less certain, more confused. Reinhardt kept his emotions hidden.

"And you remember this night?" Ludensdorf asked.

"Of course. A tremendous honor," Reinhardt said.

Ludensdorf nodded in the most unagreeing way. He tapped his finger on Kira. In this photograph, the woman was Johanna Eisenhardt. With his other hand, he tapped Kira Kovalyova.

"These are the same woman," Ludensdorf said.

Reinhardt didn't speak. He couldn't lie and say they weren't, and he wouldn't risk saying anything to give Ludensdorf any information he may not know.

He tapped the photo from Paris. "Yet, in this photo, *Frau* Wolff remembered her as Kira. A music student studying in Paris." He tapped the photo from Berlin. "Yet, I know this woman as Johanna Eisenhardt. She was a server on the night you were gifted that medal." He nodded at the Knight's Cross with Oak Leaves, Swords, and Diamonds around Reinhardt's neck. "This woman was in Paris the night *Oberst-Gruppenführer* Wolff was killed. And she was here in Berlin, the night that Randall Von Bluthund was killed."

"As was I. And I am sure there are other members of the Reich that were in Paris and Berlin. I know the woman as Johanna Eisenhardt."

"So, you are calling *Frau* Wolff a liar?"

"No, I am simply stating she is misremembering. Isn't it possible that on the day her husband was horrifically killed right in front of her, she would forget the name of a woman she had met once?"

If Ludensdorf was expecting to see some sign of nerves, he was gravely mistaken. Reinhardt was the best pilot in the *Luftwaffe*. He thrived in high-pressure situations. If hundreds of enemy planes didn't rattle him, this sadistic prick wouldn't.

"Yet, you did not correct her when she said the name at the hospital."

"I was in a plane crash. My mind was foggy."

"You know, Major Friedel," Ludensdorf continued, "I picked up a hint of an accent when Jo—no, can we call her by her true name?" He didn't wait for Reinhardt to agree. "I picked up a hint of an accent when Kira spoke. Russian." He lit a cigarette, taking quick puffs on it, then one long drag. "The shot that killed *Oberst-Gruppenführer* Wolff was an expert shot from a considerable distance. So, I found myself searching for an English, French, American, or Russian sniper with a tremendous shot. I read through many reports when I finally came across one. A report where German troops referred to a Soviet sniper as The Winter Tiger. Some reported the name of Kovalyov. But in Russian, women add an 'a' to their names. Kovalyova."

He slapped a file on the desk. "Kira Kovalyova. This file states we offered her rank and chocolate to turn sides." He slapped one more photo in front of Reinhardt. He and Kira standing closely together inside the Reich Chancellery's Dining Hall. The fourth photo was the most damning. Josef Stalin hanging a medal around her neck and declaring her a Hero of the Soviet Union. Even with how damning it was, it made Reinhardt swell with pride.

"Kira Kovalyova awarded Hero of the Soviet Union by Stalin himself. Kira Kovalyova killed *Oberst-Gruppenführer* Wolff and Randall Von Bluthund. And you, Reinhardt Friedel, aided her."

Two guards marched into the room and held Reinhardt at gunpoint.

"Do you forget, *Obersturmbannführer*, I was declared a Hero of the Reich? A recipient of the Knight's Cross with Oak Leaves, Swords, and Diamonds? How dare you slander me in such a way!"

"You helped Kovalyova escape! You are a traitor of the Reich!"

"Look at the medals that hang upon my neck and chest!"

"I have presented my findings to the *Führer* himself." Ludensdorf reached for Reinhardt's Knight's Cross with Oak Leaves, Swords, and Diamonds.

"Touch it and I will break your fucking hand!"

Ludensdorf snapped his hand away. He nodded for the men to escort Reinhardt out of his office. The walk to the courtyard seemed a mile long. Silent except for the clacking of freshly polished boots against the marble floors. The air outside was chilled, but to Reinhardt—who had survived the Soviet winter—it was nothing but refreshing.

"Where are you taking me?" Reinhardt asked.

But his question went unanswered. Across the street, where the rows of red flags hung limply, they stopped. Ludensdorf lit a cigarette. He offered one to Reinhardt. He accepted it.

"Lust is a powerful emotion, Major Friedel. I have been a victim to it myself. I like to believe you had no knowledge of these assassinations before they happened. So, I have convinced the *Führer* to spare your life."

"Why?"

Ludensdorf smirked—a way of showing respect for Reinhardt getting to the point. No embarrassing decrees of gratitude. Wise enough to know there was a catch.

Bret Kissinger

"You help us find Kovalyova. Tell us where she went, who helped her. I know you helped her escape Berlin. But you did not act alone. Give us the names. Help bring her to justice."

Reinhardt scanned the Chancellery balcony behind Ludensdorf. Two men watched. Only silhouettes lit by the lamplight in the office behind them. Joseph Goebbels and Adolf Hitler.

"So, you will help us find Kovalyova? Give us the traitors' names. Do the right thing? You fought valiantly for the Reich. Continue to do so," Ludensdorf said.

Reinhardt rubbed the cigarette between his fingers, then took a long, final drag. He tossed the cigarette to the ground and softly squished it with his boot. He stood tall and straight, shoulders pressed back.

"I never fought for the Reich. I fought for Germany. Its lakes. Its mountains. Its valleys. Its fields. I fought for my family. My friends. And I fought for Kira."

Ludensdorf flashed disappointment. "Then so be it." He flicked his cigarette. "Major Reinhardt Friedel, you have been accused and found guilty of treason. By order of the *Führer*, you have been sentenced to die for your crimes. If you have any last words, speak them now."

A sad, soft smile crept over Reinhardt's face. "My only regret is that I did not fight for Germany sooner. That I did not take a stand for the soul of Germany."

"You should know, Friedel, you will be deleted from history. Your medals. Your kills. All gone. History will never know you existed."

Reinhardt stared past Ludensdorf to the balcony, where the *Führer* cowardly watched on. Ludensdorf ordered the firing squad to aim their Karabiner 43 rifles at Reinhardt's chest. Reinhardt looked to the stars, his breathing remarkably calm given the situation. He was no longer standing in the courtyard amongst dozens and dozens of Nazi flags. He was in that supply room in Paris at the Théatre du Châtelet. Kira gazing into his eyes. Those fierce eyes that tried to mask the pain she was in. He relived the volcanic passion between them. How that striking red dress conformed to her curves. The softness of her alabaster skin. The sapid taste of her lips. Kira Kovalyova had been a dangerous drug. But even here at the end, the overdose was worth the high.

Ludensdorf screamed the command. Five simultaneous shots rang out into the silent spring night. The shell casings clanged against the stone. But Reinhardt didn't hear the shots. The memory of Kira Kovalyova stayed with Reinhardt Friedel from life to afterlife as his body folded limply to the unforgiving stone.

The Atrocity

In the winter of 1944, the Germans launched Operation Watch on the Rhine. History would know it as the Battle of the Bulge. Many considered it Germany's last-ditch effort. It failed. Kira had become hesitant to fire her weapon. Truth was tainted. Fact woven with fiction. But something happened that reiterated her desire to kill *Schadenfreudes*. A reaffirmation that she was on the right side of history. Reinhardt's morose, heartbreaking words came back to her: I'm fighting on the wrong side, Kira. History will prove it.

Kira and Red Army soldiers from the 322nd Rifle Division advanced toward the Polish city of Oświęcim on 27 January 1945. They followed railroad tracks to a red brick building that ran perpendicular to them. At the entrance was a wrought-iron gate displaying the words, *Arbeit Macht Frei*.

Work Sets You Free.

It looked as though the Germans had recently abandoned the labor camp. A fetid smell hung in the air. Kira gagged when a gust of wind blew into her face. There were rows of barracks and a fence line surrounding it all. Smoke wafted from burn piles. The Germans were gone, and it seemed any prisoners there'd been had marched out, too. But then, ahead, a skeletal shape limped toward her. A level of emaciation she'd never seen a human being in. Gaunt, gray-faced, with a shaved head, long gangly limbs, and thighs no larger than Kira's forearms. Kira's eyes widened in horror. More skeletal beings crept out of their barracks, shielding their eyes from the harsh sun. Striped pajamas hung on their frail frames like drapes. She followed other soldiers into the barracks. The smell was overpowering, as if these feeble people had already begun to decay. And as she gazed around in wide-eyed horror, many were dead. Days, weeks into decay. Vomit rose in her chest. Rats scurried on the urine and feces-covered floor, nibbling on the dead.

Kira traversed the camp, finding warehouses overflowing with possessions—suits, dresses, combs, shoes, suitcases, glasses, and jewelry. Thousands of items. Millions.

Among them, to her horror, was literal tons of human hair. Hair sheared from the skeletal slaves like sheep sent to slaughter. It was too much to process. Hundreds of thousands of people must have gone through this camp.

The Soviet medics were overwhelmed. Soldiers who'd offered food and water were crowded by a zombie-like herd. The soldiers spoke to them in Russian. Either the prisoners didn't understand, or they were too starved and thirsty to listen. Kira couldn't blame them. She asked if anyone spoke German. A girl of only sixteen called Mimi nodded. A barcode number had been tattooed onto her forearm.

"What is this place? What type of camp?" Kira asked.

"*Juden.*"

"Jewish? Are there more of you?"

Mimi raised her frail arm and pointed. Kira followed it to a dismantled building and the trees behind it.

"I don't understand," Kira said.

Had they escaped into the trees? Or were they in the building?

"They are there. But you won't find them."

Black ash fell like light snow.

"Help me understand. Where are they *now*?" Kira asked.

Mimi pointed to the black ash. Kira hurried to the building—Crematorium V. The rubble still smoldered. Kira moved bricks, trying to find clues as to what had happened. She pushed aside a large piece of concrete and gasped. A charred, black hand jutted out. The horror of understanding overwhelmed her. The black ash falling like snow was all that remained of the burned bodies of thousands.

The Soviets discovered gas chambers. Inside, fingernail scratches were carved into the walls. This was no labor camp. It was a death camp. Kira stood paralyzed, trying to process it all. Doing mental calculations of all the possessions she'd seen to figure out how many people had lost their lives here. How could human beings commit such an unfathomable evil? The Germans were meticulous record keepers. Due to the sheer volume of prisoners, they sought creative cataloging solutions from IBM. All these records were destroyed when the Germans fled.

Soviet troops continued handing out their rations until a medic rushed over and pushed the food the Soviets offered back into their chests and pockets.

"You can't give them food!" he yelled.

"Why not? They're starving," a soldier said.

"Their bodies cannot remember how to process food."

Kira and the others looked at him in subtle confusion and abject horror. Digesting food isn't something a person actively learns how to do. Not like writing or speaking. It's something innate, like breathing or your heart beating. Yet these people had been without food for so long, their bodies no longer knew how to process it. The problem arose with something called 'refeeding syndrome.' During starvation, the body's low levels of phosphate, magnesium, and potassium could result in fatal consequences when trying to process food. But the prisoners didn't understand that. They looked utterly heartbroken when the Soviets pocketed their food. They were ushered out of the camp and into the backs of medical trucks. In several languages, they screamed out the names of loved ones, begging for whoever could understand to find them. Asking where their spouses were, their parents, children, siblings, friends, and extended family. The emotional outbursts exhausted what little strength many had left and they collapsed.

Kira continued to explore the hallowed grounds before another soldier called her over. He gazed into a deep pit. There were hundreds of bodies in it, heaped on top of one another. Wide, open, unseeing eyes. Hands and legs flared about. Movement caught Kira's eye. A hand ripping through the soil of flesh. Fingers spread. Someone was still alive, left to die buried amongst hundreds of corpses. Kira was frozen. The thought of descending into the dead horrified her. But she couldn't stand idly by. She dropped her rifle and ordered those near her to help her down the steep slope. She was amongst the dead. Their bodies were cold. Some further along in decay, their slimy flesh oozing off their skeletons. Was this what Paris had been like hundreds of years ago? Only on a larger scale? So many corpses unearthed that the air went foul? She had no choice but to step on some, filling the somber air with disturbing sounds as the bodies were both crunchy and squishy underfoot. She sunk deeper and deeper until she was waist deep in the dead. The hand grasped at the air. The person was running out of oxygen. Kira grabbed the hand and heaved. But the pool of dead wouldn't give up one of their own. Fellow soldiers pushed and pulled bodies away. A face was now visible. Scared, bovine-brown eyes. Feminine features. She was free. Too weak to even show exultation. Men linked arms to lift her out. But more hands waved, and legs kicked. The muffled sounds of screaming. There were more people alive. It was like gazing at a dark lake. You knew there was life down there, but you had no idea where and how many.

But then true terror happened. The damned, so close to salvation, used every last speck of strength they possessed to break free. The result was like quicksand. The bodies underneath Kira shifted. She fell deeper. Bodies cascaded atop her. Her own screams were mirrored by the other soldiers who faced a similar fate. Errant limbs smacked her. Inanimate hands caught her clothing and dragged her further down. The sun disappeared from a corporeal eclipse. The fetid air filled her lungs until there was no air at all. Her chest constricted, the pressure so great she couldn't even kick her feet or swing her arms. The horrible horror of it was unfathomable. She was suffocating to death, buried underneath a mound of corpses, and there was nothing she could do.

Buried Alive

Her sight was gone. Sound, too. But the smell of death stung her nostrils, clung to her mouth. She could feel movement, though, as bodies were lifted and moved. A glimpse of light. Growing larger, blinding her. Hands grabbed her uniform and pulled her. Rising through the heap of bone and flesh. Gasping for air. She was free. She clawed at the ditch, trying to get out. Once out, she turned over and vomited. A waxy human substance coated her uniform, hands, and face. Kira had to consider herself fortunate, though, for when she gazed back into that god-awful pit, two of the soldiers who had tried to help hadn't been found in time. Seven prisoners had been saved from the pit. The Germans had been in such a haste to leave, they had lined up prisoners and fired, not caring if the bullets actually killed. Many prisoners had non-life-threatening injuries. Some had simply been dragged into the pit by accident when the person beside them was shot. Instead, they had died of suffocation, of being buried alive. Documents had been burned. Evidence destroyed. Auschwitz had been a place of tremendous evil and gut-wrenching heartbreak. Reinhardt had said he was fighting on the wrong side and that history would prove it. Well, history was all around Kira. Innocent people gassed and burned. The world needed to know, but she hoped Reinhardt never had to know how right his fears were. Her heart broke for these people. She also couldn't shake the claustrophobic feeling of having been buried alive. Being buried alive was a truly horrific way to die. But being buried alive by dirt differed from being buried alive by corpses. That was a whole new level of psychological terror.

Kira returned to the area called *Kanada*, where the mountains of possessions were being documented. Eyeglasses, wedding bands, coats, shoes. Every one of them had belonged to somebody. She picked a ring from the overfilled barrel. A gold band with a sapphire in it. What woman had owned this? Who had given it to her? What was their story? Two strangers from different worlds, or had they known each other since childhood? Every single ring in this barrel and in the ones beside it had its own story that deserved to be told but never would be.

The breeze was a melodic lament. Her country had lied to her about Von Bluthund. Reinhardt had proven not all Germans were *Schadenfreudes*. Yet there were plenty of them. Men who had organized and executed the systematic killing of Jews and other so-called 'non-desirables'—Gypsies, Slavs, Polish, handicapped, blacks, and homosexuals. And now, because the Americans were closing in on the Rhine and the Soviets advanced into Western Poland, the *Schadenfreudes* had no choice but to gather in Germany. Kira had her three-line and now she had resolve.

The Fall of Berlin

As the early months of 1945 turned toward spring, they carried with them the shadow of the end of the war. Seelow was thirty-five miles from Berlin and the last possible location for a defense prior to the capital city. On 16 April, 500,000 shells were fired on Seelow in the first thirty minutes of a barrage. The 150,000 Germans had expected the playbook maneuver by the Soviets and remained covered. The Germans had fought valiantly, but the overwhelming numbers disadvantage was too much to overcome. The path to Berlin had opened. Day and night, the Soviets bombarded the German capital.

It was strangely hard for Kira to watch it unfold. She had visited the city, strolled its streets, dined in its restaurants. The Reich Chancellery may have been occupied by horrible men, but it was a gorgeous building. Berlin had not been created in 1933 with Hitler and the National Socialist German Workers' Party. No, people had called Berlin home in prehistoric times. The area had been called Berlin since 1251. Millions of people had called it home. Its history would continue past the outcome of the war. The iconic Brandenburg Gate had been built between 1788 and 1791. Like the Eiffel Tower in Paris or America's Statue of Liberty, it was an icon of its country. Its image recognized by every person from the civilized world. To think that it could be destroyed in this destructive barrage pained her. If Hitler truly loved his country, his capital city, he would surrender before it was destroyed. Before his people were slaughtered. But Hitler was too busy hiding.

While Hitler cowered in a bunker underground, Germany's children had been called to serve their country. Looking through her rifle's scope, the sight of them brandishing weapons horrified Kira. How many grown men hid underground? Being a *Schadenfreude* was crime enough, but being a cowardly *Schadenfreude* was something else. Boys and girls younger than thirteen were called to fight. Her Soviet compatriots treated them like any other soldiers. They had to, for they still yielded weapons. Surviving war taxes your soul, and once pieces of it are taken, they are never reimbursed.

Kira scanned the masses from the top floor of a building, waiting for a high-profile Nazi target to emerge. Martin Bormann. Joseph Goebbels. Hermann Göring. Heinrich Himmler. Adolf Hitler. And it would not be their foreheads, hearts, or lungs she would shoot. It would be their stomachs. A singular goal to create as much pain with no chance of being saved. To watch them squirm as they died, listen to them scream.

But most of all, she scanned for Herman Ludensdorf. The first *Schadenfreude* she had been introduced to. The one who had changed her life. But none of these targets appeared.

On 1 May, news spread that a day earlier, 30 April, Adolf Hitler and his long-time girlfriend, but now newlywed wife, Eva Braun, had committed suicide inside the *Führerbunker*. It was news Kira couldn't believe. German propaganda had reached around the world. It had proclaimed a thousand-year Reich. Hitler had demanded German men give their lives for the Reich. Fight until their last breath, until the last drop of blood was exhausted from their bodies; he had allowed men at Stalingrad to die for his pride, had not even raised a weapon to fight for the ideals he preached. The ultimate coward. In Japan, disgraced leaders would disembowel themselves and were then beheaded in a practice called *Seppuku* (more commonly known as *Hara-kiri*). A practice that allowed them to regain their honor. Running a blade through your own stomach was a different suicide than taking a cyanide capsule and/or shooting yourself. Hitler had no honor to retain. The act of suicide is deemed cowardly. But Kira never thought that. Dying causes fear for everyone. But to know when your time is up because you were stopping the clock was its own form of bravery. One she couldn't believe Hitler could possibly possess.

Kira had expected the war to be over from that point, but the Germans still fought on. When she thought why, it was clear. These men, women, and children were not fighting for Hitler or Goebbels or the Reich. And at this point, they weren't even fighting for Germany; they were fighting for their own survival. Knowing the atrocities they had committed against the people of the Soviet Union, thousands of German troops fled west, hoping to surrender to the Americans.

Kira's kill tally didn't matter. It hadn't mattered to her in a long time. When she first set out, it was quantity she was after. But after meeting Reinhardt, it was quality. One *Schadenfreude* was worth more than a hundred common *Wehrmacht* soldiers. Eliminating them purified the world. Many would call the Nazis' savagery 'animalistic.' But that was not the right word. Kira had grown up hunting animals. Animals did not kill for enjoyment. They killed for survival. A tiger went for the throat to give the most-swift passing. It was only mankind that took pleasure in pain, pleasure in killing.

These *Schadenfreudes* had forfeited their right to humanity. They belonged not to the realm of man or animal. They were something else entirely. Minions of the devil.

Joseph Goebbels, his wife Magda, and their six children had stayed with Hitler and Eva in the *Führerbunker* and had also killed themselves. Not even the children were spared. Bormann was rumored to have been killed on his way out of the city. Hermann Göring had been appointed Hitler's successor, but through some backstabbing on Martin Bormann's part, Hitler removed Göring from the party. Bormann ordered Göring be executed should he return to Berlin. Instead, Göring surrendered to the Americans. Heinrich Himmler had fled. Kira's list of *Schadenfreudes* had narrowed to one.

Herman Ludensdorf.

Finally, on 8 May, Karl Dönitz, newly appointed German leader, officially surrendered.

Kira questioned every prisoner in the long winding lines of surrender. "Where is *Obersturmbannführer* Herman Ludensdorf?"

Hundreds upon hundreds of people. The German soldiers looked exhausted but relieved the fighting was over. The thought of Ludensdorf having escaped was unbearable. What type of man was he? Would he kill himself like Hitler and Goebbels did? Try to escape like Bormann? Surrender like Göring?

In the line of defeated faces, there was one she recognized. One she'd seen with Reinhardt. His handsome confidence now looked defeated. His eyes grew; he recognized her, too.

"Kira," he said.

It was Günter. If he were here, it may mean Reinhardt was somewhere in this unending line.

"Reinhardt?" she asked.

His face hung low. Sadness broke through the dirt and grime covering his features. "They killed him ... the Reich ... they knew he helped you."

The Earth either stopped spinning or changed the speed at which it did so. Her balance left her. *No.* Reinhardt couldn't die. She thought of his smile, the light in those star-blue eyes of his. Kira froze. Günter had to keep moving. She forced herself to follow.

"They looked for the girl server … Emma," Günter added.

"Did they find her?"

"No. Not that I heard."

He explained he'd been questioned by Ludensdorf. It'd been a photograph taken on Christmas Eve 1942 at the Théatre du Châtelet in Paris that had linked her with Wolff's death. The most damning piece of evidence had been the photograph of Stalin making her a Hero of the Soviet Union. The medal was nothing more than a cursed crux. Worthless.

Screams rang out from alleyways, from open windows. Screams from women. Across Berlin, across conquered Germany, Soviet men raped German women. German men were powerless to do anything but listen to their screams. And Kira was forced to accept that *Schadenfreudes* didn't exist solely in Germany. They infected every place in the world. Every gender, every race, every creed.

"Kira, my wife … Please don't let that happen to her," Günter pleaded.

He didn't ask her to help him. It was Klara he cared about. Everything about the war had blurred. It had been good versus evil, and now, that wasn't as easy as the Soviet Union versus Germany. Some of those imprisoned Germans were better men than their free Soviet counterparts. Kira wanted to save every German woman from the horror of rape. But that was impossible. History would estimate 500,000 German women had been raped by American and Soviet soldiers. Thousands of women killed themselves to prevent that fate and thousands killed themselves afterward. Many of those who survived found themselves pregnant. Potentially carrying a child that was the spitting image of the man who'd raped them. Having to decide to raise a fatherless child conceived by rape or forced to wonder which of the handful or even dozens of men who'd raped them was the father.

No, Kira couldn't help them all. But she could try to help one. Klara Mueller. She pulled Günter from the line and told the lower-ranking soldiers around that she was taking him for questioning. She kept her hand on his back, her pistol in the other hand. She led him to an alleyway. A busted water pipe trickled down; Günter drank from it while Kira searched the dead around her. A private from the Red Army had lost half his head, but his uniform was in decent shape and appeared it would fit Günter decently enough.

"Change into this," she told Günter.

Bret Kissinger

She kept a lookout as Günter stripped the soldier and then his own clothes. Once he was dressed, he followed Kira back onto the streets.

"Where is Klara?" she asked.

"Just outside the city. Staying with an aunt," he answered.

"I will help you find her."

Günter nearly sobbed his thanks. Kira commandeered a vehicle. Günter sat in the passenger seat, eating the rations of food Kira gave him. She stopped at the checkpoints and followed Günter's instructions.

"Reinhardt ..." Kira said, her eyes pleading into Günter's eyes.

His head dropped. "When we were fleeing Stalingrad, he told me you were what kept him going. He loved you, Kira. And if he were able to choose how he died, it'd be protecting you."

The pain in her chest was tremendous. Heartache is a physical pain. A shortness of breath; dizziness; your own heart beating so violently against the breastplate to flee the pain it feels. The future she had never truly believed would come to fruition, but naively had hoped for, could never be. Günter told her the Reich had deleted all Reinhardt's accomplishments. History would never know who the true greatest fighter pilot in the war was. A true hero. And a great man.

Günter pointed to a building. "That's it."

Kira pulled the jeep onto the curb. They stepped out of the jeep and hurried inside. Voices carried from everywhere. Male voices speaking Russian and other Slavic tongues. Their groans were overwhelmed by screams. Doors weren't even shut for discretion. The women who didn't scream, either had a hand or pillow pressed against their mouths, or they disappeared deeply into their minds. Soviet troops stood in line, waiting for their turns. Laughing and smiling, those next had a hand in their pants to get a head start.

Günter ran up the steps, frantic. The door to Klara's aunt's door was open. Soviet guards laughed as Klara tried to keep them at bay with a frying pan. Her aunt was face down on the kitchen floor, a pool of blood spilling out of her.

"Stop!" Kira shouted.

The men turned to look at her. To Günter's credit, he didn't run to Klara. The only way this worked was if they thought he was a Soviet. But the words that came out of the guards' mouths weren't Russian. It was an Eastern European language Kira didn't understand. But their gestures could only be taken to imply, *Fuck off.* Kira stepped in front of them. Klara looked at Günter, not knowing what to do. She held the frying pan like a baseball bat. Kira spoke in Russian, pointing at the door. Günter stood beside her, trying to stop his hands from forming fists. But if it came to it, he would defend Klara with his last breath. One of the men stared at the star-shaped medal around Kira's neck. His eyes lit up with recognition. He stood in the presence of a Hero of the Soviet Union. But it was more than just the medal he recognized. She could tell from his eyes. The way they showcased awe and fear.

"Winter Tiger?" he asked in Russian—the only words he knew.

Kira nodded. "I am."

The man nodded respectfully and then again to his two friends to head for the door. Kira closed it behind them and locked it. Günter hugged Klara, stroking her hair, asking if she was okay.

"They killed Isabella ..." she said. There was shock and disbelief and pain and sadness in her tone. Life can change so fast, it can be impossible to process.

"We have to go," Kira said.

"Go where?" Günter asked.

"I'll try to get you to a plane. Fly west as far as you can," Kira said. "Do either of you speak English?"

Klara nodded.

"Good. Klara, you'll have to look scared. This isn't your husband. It's a man who will rape you."

"Considering I'm terrified, that should be easy." She laughed to try to stop the new tears from falling.

"Do not surrender to the Soviets. You get west and surrender to the Americans. Understand?"

Günter nodded, knowing what Kira had just said was treason. The severity of that was not lost on him. And he showed his appreciation with another soft nod.

Klara knelt beside her aunt. Günter lifted her to her feet. There was nothing they could do for her now. They filed out of the apartment, Kira at the front. Kira had heard horrible sounds during the war. Sounds that instilled terror. Sounds that instilled horror. But hearing the visceral desperation of women being raped was one that broke her in a different way. And it was pain caused by her own countrymen. *Schadenfreudes* …

Kira drove out of the city. Günter clutched Klara's hand in his.

"Günter, do you know where Ludensdorf is?" Kira asked.

He shook his head, but he tried to think of anything that may help her. Klara spoke first, leaning forward from the backseat.

"That god-awful man who questioned us?" she asked Günter. "He was at the *Führerbunker* for a time. He didn't stay, though."

"How do you know this?" Kira asked, her eyes gazing at Klara in the rearview mirror.

"One of his mistresses lived in my aunt's apartment building."

Kira drove onto an airstrip. Once German, now Soviet-controlled. She led Klara and Günter through the camp. Every instinct in the two of them wanted to hold hands with one another. But they fought it. Klara looked scared, but for Günter, this wasn't the first time he had impersonated a Soviet and brazenly strolled through one of their camps. But this was less risky. The war was over. There was no need to guard an airstrip as heavily. Kira asked Günter which plane would have the most fuel. He examined them. It'd be a long-range bomber.

"We can't thank you enough," Klara said.

"Yes, you've saved our lives," Günter added.

"Reinhardt would have done the same," Kira said.

Günter helped Klara into the plane and then looked at Kira, trying to find words. Kira told him to go. He boarded the plane and started the engines. Kira stepped back. It was impossible not to picture herself and Reinhardt in the plane, flying off to embrace their future together. But that had always been a mirage. They couldn't fade into obscurity. He was a Hero of the Reich. Recipient of the fabled Knight's Cross with Oak Leaves, Swords, and Diamonds. And she was a Hero of the Soviet Union. Both were known throughout the war. The Winter Tiger and The War Eagle. The plane lifted into the air, and Kira pretended it was her and Reinhardt in it.

Justice

Soviets searched every meter to find Nazi scum. Forcing the Nazis to experience the sheer terror of hiding in attics and under floorboards, worrying that their next breath or cough would be the one to get them caught. The same terror they had forced the Jews and other so-called 'non-desirables' to endure. Tunnels were discovered. Rat lines with two primary routes: Germany to Spain, then Argentina; or Germany to Rome to Genoa, then to South America. Kira hadn't asked Volkov for any favors before, but she did now. Asking that he use his rank to help find Ludensdorf. And he came through for her.

"Herman Ludensdorf has fled into the Alps with a small contingent. Most likely trying to escape to South America."

Anger warmed her skin, but emotion nearly knocked her off her feet. The thought of Ludensdorf avoiding justice was something she couldn't fathom. She'd made a promise to kill him. If he made it to South America, he may never be seen again.

"He can't ... Colonel ... please."

Colonel Volkov put a fatherly hand on her shoulder. "I know. He won't."

It took long agonizing days before Volkov had another update. Surveillance showed there was a cabin across a pond where they believed Nazis were hiding out.

"The last of the *Schadenfreudes*," Colonel Volkov said.

But that wasn't true. It would never be true. *Schadenfreudes* had existed before the war, and they would exist after the war. It was a depressing certainty Kira had accepted. But the *Schadenfreude* who forced the rifle into her hand would be eliminated. And her part in this great and terrible war would be over.

Kira cleaned her rifle outside near the Brandenburg Gate. Citizens cleaned up rubble brick by brick. The Soviets had their own cities to rebuild. They couldn't care less about Germany's. Cleaning the rifle made her feel her father's spirit. It was the only family heirloom she had. The only tangible thing left to remember them. She had nothing to remember Reinhardt. No memento or knickknack. Only the word *Fernweh*. She had experienced it for a fleeting glimpse. Like her home, it was now gone.

Once more, Kira would have to jump out of a plane and parachute down. If it went to plan, she'd land two miles away from the cabin. From there, she'd trek the rest of the way. Four other soldiers, all competent marksmen, joined her. Kira showed them a photograph of Ludensdorf.

"He's mine. You see him, you tell me. Do not shoot him. Understood?"

The green light flashed inside the airplane. Kira leapt from the plane. Feeling the rush and surge of the wind against her face. Once all five were on the ground, they advanced into the woods, pausing when they heard movement. But it was always wildlife. Down below, across a sparkling cobalt-blue pond, was a wooden cabin. Kira laid down on the ridge and looked through her scope. The curtains were drawn.

There was no movement. No fresh footprints in the snow. Were they too late? Was Ludensdorf in South America right now with a smirk on his face? Just before failure defeated her, the front door opened. A man with black slacks and a black shirt with a white clerical collar stepped out. A Nazi shook hands with him. The priest closed the door behind him and headed toward a car. A gravel road wound through the trees. Kira aimed at the priest.

"You're going to kill a priest?" one soldier asked.

"He is helping Nazis. He deserves no mercy."

The Vatican and Red Cross aided Nazis in their escape by offering them new identities. Even with knowing the atrocities the Nazis had committed.

"But … he's a man of God."

"Then I shall introduce them."

She fired. The shot ripped through his stomach. He was in for a slow, painful death which he'd spend screaming. The soldier looked at Kira disapprovingly. She was The Winter Tiger. To hit him there was deliberate.

"What?" Kira shrugged. "God is busy. He can wait."

At least one Nazi hidden inside would come out to check. She was right. The door opened, and a man sprinted toward the priest. He never made it to him. He dropped dead halfway to him. Kira dragged the bolt, chambering another round. A face peaked through the curtain. *Bang!* The glass spiderwebbed, and the man dropped.

"They'll clamp down inside. Smoke them out," Kira ordered.

Two men readied an *Ampulomet*—an anti-tank weapon. If it could get through a tank, it would have no problem with stone and wood. They fired. It struck the cabin, and a bright flame erupted. Thick white smoke followed. The incendiary mixture was known as KS and was eighty percent phosphorus, twenty percent sulfur, and burned at around 1,000 degrees Celsius. They had hit the roof, but the heat would force the Nazis out. When your flesh started to drip like candle wax, you had no choice.

They stumbled out, coughing violently. As soon as the smoke cleared enough for the Soviets to see, they fired, killing all but Ludensdorf, who sprinted for the car. Kira steadied herself, exhaled slowly, and fired. The bullet ripped into his hip, shattering the bone. He would never walk normally again. Kira told her team to hold their fire and then advanced down to the cabin, her rifle ready. It was a long way. Fine with Kira. Let Ludensdorf suffer in agony.

Ludensdorf crawled to the car, leaving a trail of blood on the gravel. He reached a bloody hand to the door handle. A shot rang out. Ludensdorf's fingers vanished in a mist of blood. He howled. Kira switched from her father's three-line to her pistol. Ludensdorf leaned against the door, breathing heavily. His pistol was on his right side. His right hand was nothing more than a bloody stump, so he tried awkwardly to reach for his pistol with his left hand.

Kira pinned his left hand against the car with her foot, then tossed the pistol away. For Ludensdorf and his shattered hip, it may as well be an ocean away. Kira crouched in front of him.

"Do you know who I am?" she asked.

His eyes lit up. "The Winter Tiger," he said, teeth snarling.

"My real name."

"Kira … Kovalyova …"

"You created me."

His face warped in confusion, his mind searching back for recognition.

"Do you remember a ballroom in a small Russian town near Leningrad? You fled when a shooter fired from a bell tower."

416

His eyes glossed with recognition.

"I was that shooter. The two women you raped and murdered were my sisters. The old man in the house you had blown up was my father. You created me, *Schadenfreude*. And because of you, 323 Germans are dead."

His eyes showed he remembered, not because of what he had done, but because it was the closest to dying he'd gotten during the war.

Ludensdorf smiled through his snarl. "Add Friedel to the list of men you killed."

"You killed him."

"He begged for mercy. Promised to bring you to justice if I would spare him."

Kira rammed the pistol across his face. "Don't you dare slander his memory."

Blood coated Ludensdorf's teeth. Kira reached for his belt. He tried pushing her hand away. Kira used her pistol like a hammer, breaking the bony protrusion in his remaining hand. She removed his belt.

"What are you doing?" he asked. He tried to come off as defiant, but he only sounded scared.

Kira dragged him away from the car, pushing him face-first into the gravel. Stone grinded into his face. Kira wrapped the belt around his neck, pulling it taut. He gasped for breath, flailing his useless numb and broken hand toward it. Kira pressed her knee on his back and pulled the belt tighter and tighter. The same way Ludensdorf had strangled her sisters.

"Do you feel what they felt? The terror? The pain? The horror?" Kira asked.

She loosened her grip, allowing life-saving breath to trickle in through his mouth.

"But you didn't just strangle them, did you? You raped them, too."

Kira removed her Finnish knife. Showing him the gleaming silver blade. Kira dragged his pants off. Ludensdorf squirmed.

"I joined the war to kill *Schadenfreudes* like you. I never found pleasure in killing all those men. But at this moment, I confess that I am a hypocrite. For I too am a *Schadenfreude*. Killing you will give me great joy. But my joy will end with your final breath."

Kira pulled the belt taut. Veins bulged in Ludensdorf's neck and face. With her left hand, she shoved the blade into his rectum. Raping him with the sharp blade. He had

417

no ability to scream. His eyes turned red, the vessels spreading like tributaries of a river. His legs kicked. It took minutes for the final gurgle to leave his lips. Kira released the belt, letting his face smack the stones. His red eyes bulged open. She left the knife impaled. She hadn't expected some measure of instant peace to wash over her. And none came. Justice isn't peace. But it is a form of closure. Kira marched away and left Ludensdorf and the smoldering cabin behind.

Cherries

1950

The hot July sun was so different than the excruciatingly cold winter at Stalingrad. But the chill that winter had caused would never fully leave her. It stayed in her bones, aching without warning. The Wisconsin winters liked to remind her of those trying times.

Kira Kovalyova never made it out of those Austrian woods. As Kira wandered the smoldering rubble, there was one man who had not died. A bishop of the Catholic Church pleading for mercy. Kira made him forge one final document. The name to be placed on it was Kira Friedel. And the bishop helped secure transportation to the United States. Her reasons for leaving her native country were many. Mostly, no matter how large the Soviet Union was, the void of her family could never be filled. But because also the events of the war had weighed heavily on her. Stalin's willingness to forsake his people had diminished her Soviet pride. His atrocities couldn't be ignored. Kira Kovalyova would be a puppet of propaganda. Reinhardt was gone. The future they dreamed of could never be. But Reinhardt had imprinted on her soul, so in a way he was alive in her, and she'd live the life they dreamed of together. In Door County, Wisconsin, and in the quest to perfect a cherry strudel.

The people were friendly. The land was beautiful. An elderly woman taught her English during the evenings at the local school. She purchased a used double bass and rekindled the love of it she had found in Paris. She found a bluff to read. This time not a new novel, but a *Photoplay* magazine with Hollywood's newest star on its cover. The name was different, but the face was the same. The same cobalt-blue eyes and stunning blonde hair. She had retained that faint sadness in her eyes, the caliber that made you want to look after her in the same way Kira had. Emma Sanders. Inside were pictures of premieres, movie sets, and headshots. In the background of one picture at a Hollywood premiere, out of her limelight, but in front of the crazed crowd, was Mathias holding her purse.

There was another face from her past that she couldn't forget. Her loyal friend Gerasim. She hadn't known whether he had survived the war, and if he had, she didn't know if he would return to their hometown. But she wrote to him and sent the letter to his parents' address. She had signed the letter Artemis and told him to visit her. She hadn't expected a response. But one came. Gerasim had survived the war. His mother had given him Kira's letter. Gerasim had married a nurse he had charmed while he was in her care. They had wasted no time in having children. Kira's letters to Gerasim never went unanswered.

Kira had her books, she had her cherries, a bluff to read on, her double bass, and stars to gaze on. No one in the community knew about her past. The fact that she was the fearsome sniper known as The Winter Tiger. She hadn't given up on finding love, but she hadn't searched for it. That was how she had found Reinhardt. The best of things are never forced but found. Wisconsin had given her a peace, not an all-encompassing peace, but the best she could hope for. Yet, every so often, while she gazed about the setting sun warming the cherry trees, she found herself thinking about The War Eagle. His kindness. His smile. His star-blue eyes and wavy black hair. And every time, it made her smile.

About the Author

 Bret Kissinger is an author from Wisconsin. He enjoys reading, playing chess, working out, and writing. Though his writing interests vary, he enjoys writing historical fiction and bringing history alive through compelling characters and epic stories. To stay up to date on his work, join his mailing list at www.bretkissinger.com and follow him on Amazon.

If you enjoyed this book, please write a review on Amazon, Barnes & Noble, and Goodreads. I'd love to hear your thoughts on this book and my other books as well. I read them all, and I appreciate every kind word I read. Thank you!

Made in the USA
Monee, IL
27 March 2024

55840880R00249